# Derailed

A Driven World Novel

## Anjelica Grace

Published by KB Worlds LLC.
Cover Design by: Emma Nichole - Literary Graphic Design
Cover Image by: Deposit Photos
Editing by: Karen Hrdlicka - Barren Acres Editing
Proof Reading by: Kaitie Reister
Formatting by: Emma Nichole - Literary Graphic Design

Published in the United States of America

Dear Reader,

Welcome to the Driven World!

I'm so excited you've picked up this book! Derailed is a book based on the world I created in my New York Times bestselling Driven Series. While I may be finished writing this series (for now), various authors have signed on to keep them going. They will be bringing you all-new stories in the world you know while allowing you to revisit the characters you love.

This book is entirely the work of the author who wrote it. While I allowed them to use the world I created and may have assisted in some of the plotting, I took no part in the writing or editing of the story. All praise can be directed their way.

I truly hope you enjoy Derailed. If you're interested in finding more authors who have written in the KB Worlds, you can visit www.kbworlds.com.

Thank you for supporting the writers in this project and me.

Happy Reading,
K. Bromberg

*This one is dedicated to Adriana Locke—The Beckspert—A woman I admire and look up to constantly.*
*Thank you for sharing your creations and words with the world, with me.*
*On multiple occasions your stories have kept me going when life has gotten hard, they've reminded me of my purpose, and every book you release encourages me to continue chasing my own publishing dreams.*

*Thank you for your friendship and encouragement.*

*And thank you for The Castle…*

# *One*

## Liam

Sweat is pouring off me in buckets as I complete my second workout of the day. My muscles ache, my limbs are heavy, and no matter how much physical pain I'm in—no matter how hard I push my body—I can't outhurt my heart today. The thoughts are too loud. The guilt too powerful to be overcome by even the most intense workout I've probably ever done. I can't sink into an exercise-induced oblivion and shut my mind off from the world.

I wish I could.

I wish I could outrun the demons and ghosts haunting my life, my memories.

I wish I could escape this prison of despair I live in. But I can't.

I'll never be able to.

I tried my hardest to get anyone to trade shifts with me. I wanted to work today. I wanted to hide behind other people's problems when I went on calls. I wanted to save everyone else because I couldn't save him.

Nobody needed the time off though, and more than that, nobody wanted it. Everyone looked at me like I was crazy because I wanted to be at work today. I wanted the crazy calls that come with summer kickoff parties and drinking.

I wanted to lose myself in the work, the actions, staying busy.

I won't be going to any parties; I won't be going out to get drunk or celebrate. I swore off alcohol ten years ago, after it happened. After I failed to protect him. And I'll never risk letting myself go down the path of no return.

"Are you training for something?" one of the physical trainers here at the gym, a peppy small blonde with her hair in a ponytail and strands flying every which way off her head, asks me as she drops to sit on the weight bench beside mine.

"Why do you ask that?" I release the bar over my head, reracking the two hundred and twenty-five pounds before I sit up and reach for my towel, using it to wipe the sweat from my face.

"You've come in to work out twice today." She slowly drops her gaze over my damp shirt and body. "Most people only do that when they're training for something."

*Or when they're running from something.*

"Nope, I don't have work or plans today, so I thought I'd get some extra workouts in is all." She's an attractive woman, her face is bare of heavy makeup, all she has on is some shit around her eyes, and her body is an obvious ten—she'd probably be fun for the night—but I'm not in the mood for flirting and fucking today. My mood is far too dark, my thoughts too heavy, to subject anyone else to this.

2

"Oh?" She leans forward, resting her elbows on her thighs and giving me open access to take in her cleavage that's now on full display. "What do you do for work?"

"I'm a firefighter paramedic."

Her eyes shimmer—like all the women's do when they hear my job—and she leans in even closer. "You're a hero."

"I'm far from it," I answer her honestly. "I'm just a man doing his best to help people, and get a good workout in today." I hope she takes the hint here. I appreciate women who have the balls to approach and initiate, but not today. Today she's getting on my last fucking nerve.

"So humble. Do you need a spotter for your next set?" She rises and steps closer. "I'd be happy to repay you for your service."

I sigh. "I appreciate the offer, but I'm managing just fine on my own."

"Oh." The hurt and affronted look on her face tells me she didn't expect me to turn her down. "I guess I'll let you get back to it then. I'm Missy, by the way. If you change your mind. I'll be here until six."

"It's nice to meet you, Missy. Like I said, I appreciate the offer, but I'm all set today." I try to smile for her, a genuine smile, but I'm sure it looks more like a grimace from where she's standing. "Have a good afternoon and night, Missy."

Her face contorts into some weird mix of shock and frustration, but I can't be bothered with that right now. I lie back on the bench and take in a deep breath. Exhaling slowly and preparing for another set of presses that'll maybe shock my body into enough fatigue my brain will have to focus on my movements, on putting one foot in front of the other to carry me out of here and back to my house.

By the time I look back up, Missy is gone and I'm left alone with the weights in my hands, and the weight of my thoughts again.

\*\*\*\*

I managed to physically exhaust my body at the gym earlier. My arms are sore enough I can barely lift them over my head now. The physical exhaustion still wasn't enough to accomplish what I was hoping, so now I'm left trying to shake this fatigue and muscle pain before my shift in the morning, while also carrying the memories and weight of today.

I wasn't intending to punish myself like this, but it's fitting. It's good I'm acutely aware of every pain, every wince, and sharp stab of muscles spasming—it gives me some semblance of an idea what he went through—what he endured until the end.

I may not have set out to feel this way, not consciously at least, but I'm glad I do now. I deserve it. It's my penance on this day. On his day.

I walk into my kitchen and refill my water, taking in the scattered remnants of the broken picture frame with its glass still on the floor and the picture hanging out.

I shouldn't have let the anger get to me. I knew he would call today. He does it every year now. I was expecting it, but I wasn't expecting it so early, nor was I meaning to answer it this year.

Hearing my father's voice was the last thing I needed today. I can ordinarily delete the voicemail I force him to leave before I ever have to listen to what he has to say, but I was expecting another call this morning, too. It was the call I was expecting that made me answer without looking first.

I knew better.

Instead of hearing my banker's feminine, yet forceful voice, I heard his. Deep, gravelly, full of the smoke and alcohol he's poured down his throat for decades. I'm sure he's still smoking now. But I wouldn't know. I haven't talked to him in nine years, and if I have any say in the matter, I'll never speak to him again.

His apologies, his crying, the lies he had the balls to utter to me over a phone line from the California State Penitentiary set me off. The reminder of what he did, the hurt he caused, the life he took was too much.

Just like he ruined us then, his call today ruined the last piece of my little brother I have cherished for nearly a decade in a picture frame Lance himself made me help him buy. He wanted to send it to our grandmother for Mother's Day. He never got the chance to, though. She passed before the day ever got here. He loved the frame though. He was so proud of himself for saving up to buy it for Nana on his own. She was our angel on earth.

Until she wasn't.

Lance kept the frame though. He saved it for years, kept it hidden in a shoebox beneath his bed, until the right picture was taken.

It finally was. He found the perfect picture to put in the frame he once bought our grandma.

The metal letters flow in fancy cursive reading 'Family' over the space for the image. The image—lying scratched and bent over the broken frame—he chose to put in was of him and me on the day I left for basic training.

I bend down to grab the picture, careful not to cut myself on shards of glass sticking up, and hold it out to look at us. I was seventeen, barely ready to leave for something so life changing, yet I was so fucking happy to get out of our house.

I was terrified, too.

But our father swore, he looked me in the eye, knew I was serious when I made my threat, and he swore. He even followed through.

Until he didn't.

In the picture, Lance has his arm thrown around my back, his lanky body not quite to its full height yet and his limbs stretched and thin, stick out like a sore thumb. He was so fucking awkward, yet he was so fluid and the most talented football player I'd ever seen. He had such a great shot of playing ball in college one day.

Unfortunately, one day never came for him.

He never got the chance to play ball at a big school away from home. He never got to experience his first true love.

Lance never got to experience life not lived beneath a grown man's thumb, but on its own, for happiness and pleasure. He never got to experience standing up for himself or walking away for good. There are so many things he never got the chance to do, I wish I could go back and give him those.

He never got to experience true, unconditional love. I was too young and my own life was too fucked up to give it to him—though I tried my best—and our dad, well, he never had a loving or compassionate bone in his body.

Lance would be twenty-six today, six years younger than me, if he weren't frozen in time at sixteen years old, buried out in the cemetery where my grandparents were laid to rest too.

It's my fault he's there. It's my fault we aren't having a cold one and celebrating today, and I will never forgive myself for it.

He deserved better. More.

I fucked up and should have been here. I never should have run.

# Two

## Liam

Some days I get out of bed and am ready for the shift ahead. Twenty-four hours of time with my family—my firehouse family—fucking around, saving lives, and making a damn good living in a job of service.

Other days, like today, I have to force myself to crawl out of bed and every step is painful—not physically—mentally. I'm not feeling the banter, the calls, the potential sleepless night. It's a polar opposite to yesterday. While I wanted to be distracted and at work yesterday, I feel hungover and don't want to go anywhere today.

It's not an alcohol hangover. No, I was smart enough to not allow myself to reach that place last night; it's an emotional hangover. Yesterday put me through the wringer. Thoughts, memories, guilt, anger all swallowed me fucking whole.

I'm not going to call in sick though. I'm not going to shirk my responsibilities.

I made that mistake once. It was catastrophic.

I climb out of my truck, grab my bag and bunker gear from the bed in the back, slinging the heavy bag over my shoulder, and starting the walk across the parking lot toward our firehouse.

As firehouses go, ours is great. It's a big, renovated building with all the amenities, a large truck bay that houses ladder, engine, and even medic units.

The building is plaster and stone veneer, very typical of the area and surrounding neighborhood, with simple neutral colors painted over the plastered portions and a clay-colored roof. Each door to the bay is a lighter shade of the clay covering the building, and while it's a gorgeous morning already, the doors are shut. I'd like to think it's because the last twenty-four hours were calm and quiet, but it could be the exact opposite. They could be closed because the guys ending their shift need the quiet and rest until we come in to relieve them for the next shift.

Just as I get to the door, my best friend, my battle buddy, my right hand—brother from another mother— pulls into the lot, parking right beside my truck. I watch him get out and grab his gear, same as I did. He's got a pep in his step, and coffee in hand already, as he approaches me with a grin.

"You look like you're in a delightful fucking mood this morning," I growl, annoyed by the clear morning personality he has.

"And you sound like you could use a lay, or at least a gallon of coffee. Not much can be done about your looks though."

I pull open the door and hold it open for him, allowing him to pass through before me since his hands are full. I'd love nothing more than to kick him in the ass, but our lieutenant would have my ass if I caused coffee to be spilled on the pristine floors before shift even starts. "Any idea how last night went?"

Brandon shakes his head no as he walks back toward the locker room. "I'm guessing it was a clusterfuck, though. Jarret was texting me last night and said the calls coming in for PD were insane. DUIs, domestics, street racing, you name it and they saw it yesterday. I'm sure that means we got a lot of the same."

It sounds as though the calls they got yesterday were the calls I was hoping to use as a distraction—it would have been the perfect shift—Memorial Day weekend is always full of them, just like every other drinking holiday. "Great. I'm sure today will be no different then. Should be fan-fucking-tastic."

"What's your problem, Brother?" He drops his shit in front of his locker and looks at me. I know we don't have long before the rest of the guys are filling the space around us, either packing up to go home or coming in to start.

"Yesterday was shit."

"Want to talk about it?" Brandon starts to set what he needs in his locker, then drops onto the bench in front of it and looks my way.

"Lance's birthday."

I don't need to say any more than that to him. He knows. He was there with me the day I got the call, in Afghanistan of all places, that I was needed home. It didn't take long after the call came in that my leave was granted and I was on a plane back to the States.

"Shit. I'm sorry, man. You could have come to our house, you know Jess would've loved to have you, and we had more food than we needed."

"I know, I just wasn't in the mood to party or celebrate, ya know?"

He grabs his hat from his locker and adjusts it on his head; our firehouse logo emblazoned across is crisp and clean. "I do. Still, you should've come by. What did you do instead?"

"I lifted, ran, and did everything I could to drown out the day."

His lips fall into a frown and he sighs. "Next time your ass better be at my house if we aren't working."

I slam my own locker shut and give a curt nod. "We'll see. Let's get out there and start the coffee, not everyone will be so jovial they stop for their own on the way in."

"Quit whining. I have to go talk to Lieu; you handle the coffee."

Brandon walks out of the locker room and heads toward the lieutenant's office, while I head the opposite direction to the kitchen.

I start brewing our pot, an industrial-sized monstrosity full of the best damn coffee in the state. It's an easy task, and the second the coffee starts trickling out, my nose tunes in to the scent and my mood perks up. I need this today, like I need my next breath.

Hopefully, it'll pull me out of the trenches before our first call comes in and the weekend grind kicks in full force.

# *Three*

## Everleigh

I'm in dire need of a strong cup of coffee, a hot shower, and a good workout on the beach—but not in that order. I've spent more time than usual at The Castle over the past few days, welcoming new girls in and helping them adjust to the changes and rules. I need a break.

I love the girls, love playing such an active role in trying to correct the wrongs they've experienced in their young, impressionable lives, and I love the highs that come with their growth and victories. Sometimes, though, it's an awful, heartbreaking job.

It's been important for me since the incident—a dark time in my life—for me to recenter and refocus myself. It's important and crucial I show myself kindness and grace when my heart and mind are telling me enough is enough. It's time to step back and find my happy again.

I'm reaching that point right now. I'm in no way reaching rock bottom, I'm not even close to it, but I recognize the exhaustion setting in deep to my core and I know it's time I visit my happy place, do some exercising, and recognize all the good I'm surrounded by in the face of the despair I could so easily feel and carry over my shoulders like a shawl.

I pull into the drive-thru of my absolute favorite coffee house. It's not a big, corporate place, and I'm grateful for that. The turnover here is incredibly low. Each employee is kind and since I've been coming here for years, they all know me, my order, and are genuinely incredible people. They've even hired a few of my kids over the years, giving them an opportunity to prove to themselves they are so much more than the trauma and past they think defines them.

"Good morning! Welcome to Brews and Cruise, I'm Brooke, how may I help you today?"

"Hey, Brooke, it's Everleigh!" I slide my sunglasses to the top of my head and look over the menu, even though I know I will get the same thing I do before and after every shift I take.

"Oh! Hi, Everleigh! Do you want the usual today? Or do you want something else?"

"I wish I were feeling like change, but you know me. Make it the usual, extra-large today though."

"Long shift?"

"Incredibly, I haven't slept much the last day and a half." As if the mere mention of sleep is a trigger for my body, a big yawn overtakes me.

"Extra-large it is. This one's on the house today."

Every once in a while, they'll comp my drinks, but it always feels so weird. They work so hard to keep their little factory of heaven running. "You know I'm happy to pay…"

"Please pull up to the window, your order will be ready shortly." Brooke ignores me and turns into the professional avoider I know she can be. She won't respond to another word I say, so I follow her instructions and pull up to the window, reaching into my purse for some cash while I wait.

"Here you go, Everleigh." Brooke slides the window open and reaches my extra-large cup of ice-cold caramel frappuccino out to me.

"You're an angel," I praise her, reaching for my cup then passing a few bills out to her. "Take it, Brooke, it's a tip. I know you're saving for school, let me add to the jar."

She sighs, but she graces me with a wide smile. "It's too much. You've already done so much to help me, but thank you. I promise, I'll get in and then I'll make you proud."

"You're already making me proud. Just keep working hard and no matter how long it takes you; you will achieve your dreams. Just believe in yourself."

"Yes, ma'am." She pockets the cash I handed over. "Have fun at the beach. Try to get some rest later."

I want to ask how she knows I'm going to the beach, but instead, I close my mouth and smile with my lips pressed together. I know how she knows. It's our little secret, but on a particularly bad day, I took her out there, to my spot, and let her get everything she was thinking and feeling off her chest. I told her no matter what was going on, she could always visit the beach, it would be her place just as much as it was mine.

"I'll do my best. Thank you. I better get going; it looks like you have more customers back there. Have a good day. Stay out of trouble."

She giggles and nods her head. "I always do. Bye, Everleigh."

"Bye, Brooke." I pull away, waving my hand out the window until I see her disappear back into the coffee house and then pull it back in, taking control of my steering wheel with this hand so I can raise my coffee to my lips with the other.

The sound of appreciation fills my small car as I take my first big gulp. As always, it is the most delicious drink on the planet, and I can tell they added just a tad more caffeine than is their standard. It's not something they do all the time, but Brooke is usually pretty good at knowing when I need the extra pick-me-up.

I take another small drink then put the cup in my center holder, turning my music back up as I raise my hand back to the wheel and head toward the beach. "Thunderstruck" by AC/DC is blaring on my radio. I can feel the beat of the drums vibrating through my body, waking me and starting the process of my mental rejuvenation with every second that passes.

After the incident, a good friend told me sometimes it's great to have a playlist, a loud, pumping, intense playlist to play in order to get lost and build back up all at once. I listened to her. After particularly long weeks I turn on my loud, high-energy playlist and jam out.

It's my therapy.

Right along with the beach. And watching the sun set over the ocean.

\*\*\*\*

The beach today brought me clarity and a much-needed reprieve from the stress I was feeling. It brought me solitude and quiet. I was able to sort through my feelings and separate myself from them so I can do my job better.

Working for Corporate Cares is a dream job. The work is the most gratifying, difference making I could ever think of doing. I love it. There are days, though, where it's the hardest, most heartbreaking job ever too.

Working with children who have been separated from their families—due to death, neglect, abuse, or other—is bittersweet. To help them is to make the most profound difference in a child's most difficult time. To help them means they've lost everything they ever knew and they very well may be in pieces that need to be nurtured back together with the most tender, caring love and understanding.

My last shift brought in a young child, whose mother was using and abusing drugs and was selling herself to support her habit. Instead of providing nourishment, love, and parental oversight for her child, she left her home alone. At seven years old, this little girl was scouring the streets alone at night trying to find scraps of food, anything she could, to survive.

She was terrified of men, for reasons I don't know I will ever be ready to hear, and she cowered in a corner when anyone would speak loudly toward her.

I sat with her for hours upon hours, holding her, trying to get her to accept a toy or two to play with and maybe make a small breakthrough. We know her name, she will give us that much, and her mother was found and taken into custody for possession, but we weren't able to get anything else. It will take time. It will take patience. And it will take understanding and love.

At the root, my job is to love children with a sort of distant attachment, in case they leave The Castle or get placed with a new, or their original, family. Each girl who walks through the doors of our home becomes my, and the other counselors I work with, child. We foster them, help them develop and grow, we provide for them, help them, ensure they're receiving everything that is necessary to their growth and development.

We know their stories. We hold their hands through the highs and lows, and we provide them with love and support they, at times, never knew exists.

It's an amazing job.

Some cases, though, just take every last bit of fight out of me. They drain my well and that's when I need a morning to myself at the beach, just like I took today.

Yoga, coffee, and quiet time reflecting and feeling, allowing myself to breakdown so I can build myself back up stronger, were all needed.

Now, tonight, sitting in my small two-bedroom home with a glass of wine and a book in my lap, I can relax. I can breathe easier again. I am ready for my next shift and any challenge thrown my way.

I'm also ready for lunch with my mom tomorrow, and the Spanish Inquisition sure to come.

*Why aren't you dating anyone, Everleigh?*

*I told you doing this job would make you hesitant to have your own children.*

*What happened to Mack? I thought he was such a good fit for you.*

*Have you spoken to your father? How is he?*

I've been asked some variation of the same questions every time we have gotten together for lunch the past two years.

She doesn't seem to accept there are many who can't handle dating someone in my line of work. She won't accept I won't just settle for any man because they're willing. I want better for myself. I'm going to demand better than settling.

Mack wasn't a good man for me. He wasn't bad, either. He just wasn't good for me. We fought more than we got along in the end, he didn't approve of my job or the hours I put in. He wanted me to quit and find something more suitable for our dynamic: he wanted me to stay at home, give him children, and provide what he thought a woman was meant to provide. There are women out there suited for him, his lifestyle and beliefs, and there is nothing wrong with that. I'm just not that woman.

As for my dad... Well... We speak as often as we can. He's doing well and enjoying retirement in Arizona now. He was not a good husband to my mom. Not at all. He was a good dad to me my whole life though. And I love him beyond words. I just wish he would've been more loyal to my mama while they were together.

She may have ended things with him—showed me what a strong woman does when she's with a man who has hurt her and stepped out—but she still loves him. I think she always will.

These are all topics we will discuss tomorrow, again, ad nauseam.

I love her, I love our lunch dates, but they take a lot of patience and understanding—much like the kids I work with.

It's why I had to right myself at the beach today. It's why I'm drinking my wine and continuing to pamper myself tonight.

I will be ready for anything and everything tomorrow throws my way.

# *Four*

## Liam

"H ayes!" My lieutenant's voice booms through the halls of the firehouse, rousing me from a doze that would have undoubtedly led to an amazing nap.

I grumble and groan as I sit up from my bed and reach for my cap, securing it on my head before I take the journey from our bedroom to his office.

"Yeah, Lieu?" I stop in his doorway and lean against its frame, resting a shoulder against the cool metal.

"The ball is coming up." He looks from the stack of papers on his desk to me. "Were you planning on being there?"

The Firefighter's Ball is a huge event every year. It serves as a fundraiser for our firehouses and the men and women who work in them, as well as for the Fallen Firefighters Fund. "I haven't really decided yet, why?"

"I'll make the decision for you then." He smirks at me and hands a piece of paper over. "Each house has to elect one firefighter. Your relationship status and your drive to workout every single day means you're my pick for our house."

I take the paper and turn it the right way so I can read it. "You've got to be kidding? You want me to be the house's firefighter who gets auctioned off?"

"Can you think of anyone who is more suited in the house?"

He has me there. This is a task designed for a man like me. But fucking hell, that doesn't mean I have to do it. "And if I said I won't do it?"

"You'd be letting all your brothers down, and I'd imagine they'd all give you enough hell to make you regret turning down such a prestigious honor." He's doing his best to keep a straight face about his remarks, but it's near impossible.

"Prestigious my ass. We both know it's a shameful ploy to bring in more money by allowing drunk women to gawk and drop a shitload of money on us."

"You're damn right it is. But the cause is good. We are partnering with Corporate Cares this year. The ladies who work for them are ordinarily auctioned for a date, the county said we would split auction funds with them and our boys would handle it. Women can, too, for any ladies who work for the department and want to be auctioned off. But it's their choice."

"You do realize the hypocrisy in that, right?"

"Liam, quit bitching. The women of Corporate Cares are always good sports about raising money for orphaned and neglected children in their care, now we are going to step up and help raise funds for those same children and our fallen brothers and sisters. Are you really complaining about that?"

Fuck me. He knows I'd never complain about that. Everyone in the house knows how passionate I am about helping neglected and abused children.

"No, I'm not. What all do they need from me for this auction?"

"Atta-boy," Lieu says, grinning from ear to ear. "Come in and sit down, we can discuss what they need from you while you fill out the interest form."

I drop into the chair across from his on the opposite side of his desk and reach for a pen, starting to fill out the paper as he goes into great, enthusiastic detail about this year's auction and the partnership with Corporate Cares.

When I step out of the lieutenant's office thirty minutes later, Brandon is leaning against the wall with a shit-eating grin on his face. "You agreed, didn't you?"

"Did you put him up to that shit?" I walk by him, glaring him down as I pass. "That's low."

He lifts his hands up defensively and shakes his head no, chuckling. "I didn't put him up to a damn thing. I knew about the auction though, and rumor was he was going to put you up to it. When we heard the booming call for your presence, I figured that's what he was doing. It was a brave assumption, considering he could have been lecturing you over something, maybe threatening demotion, but he didn't sound pissed."

"Dude, fuck you. I don't get in trouble here."

"Except for when you do…" He joins me stride for stride, walking through the house and out into the bay. "You have a tendency to fly off the handle sometimes."

"Only when it's warranted. You can't tell me every single time I've done it I haven't been right in what I've said."

"You have. You're usually right, but Christ, Liam, you know that's not our job. You aren't paid to open your mouth."

I want to argue with him. Irritation and annoyance are prickling at me, crawling up my spine, but I really can't. "I haven't done shit in a while. We're all good."

"Thank God for that. So the auction… Are you going to do it?"

"He held orphaned and neglected children over my head, what the fuck do you think I'm going to do?"

Brandon drops his head back and laughs loudly. "Dirty. He did you dirty. Fucking brilliant. We were on the fence about getting tickets, but I think we have to go now, just to see you put on the block, meat for the taking."

"You're a sick fuck, you know that?"

He smirks at me and shrugs his shoulder. "Married life means I have to get it out when I'm here with the guys."

"That's a piss-poor excuse. One I'm sure Jess would love hearing about, too." I smirk right back at him, and wink for added measure.

"You're a prick."

"I'm smart. Jess will have fun at the ball though. She gets to appreciate much better-looking men than you and it's all for a good cause."

"You're such a dick." Brandon drops into one of the lawn chairs just inside the bay doors, looking out over the property the house backs up to. "Are you better than you were last shift?"

"Much. That day, those couple days are just…"

"I know. I remember. Everyone was wondering why you were acting like you were, I didn't tell them anything, just said you had some shit fall on your shoulders that had you stressed and on edge."

"I appreciate that, B. I don't want anyone to know what happened, it changes how people treat you, what they think of you. I don't need that."

"No, you don't. It doesn't change a damn thing about who you are or how good you are at your job. That's all anyone needs to know."

I nod my agreement and pull a second chair up next to his, dropping to sit beside him and falling into a comfortable silence.

\*\*\*\*

A shift wouldn't be good and fulfilling unless we have a big fire or call we are dispatched to. It's why we do this job, why we put our lives on the line. We want the danger, we want the flames and the accidents; we want to make a difference. Some might think it insane. Some might think it twisted. We live on the adrenaline though. The rush, the urgency, it fuels us.

I know the call we are pulling up to will be that kind of call. It's the end of shift, get us all home late, hopefully we can get everyone out alive call.

Our truck pulls up to the scene. It's chaos: a semi versus another semi and probably four or five other cars. The 405 is at a standstill in both directions. From what dispatch gathered, a semi plowed into a tanker, which careened forward into the traffic already at a standstill in front of it.

The first semi is fully engulfed and the tanker and cars in front of both of them that were impacted are going up. It won't be long before the tanker blows, and there are people pinned in their cars, trapped by crushed doors and extreme heat.

"Hayes, until we can get medics in here, you're calling the shots on med needs." Lieu starts taking in the scene, mentally evaluating where we go first. He has seconds to make a call for us, and we all have to pray the decision he makes is the correct one. It could be the difference in life and death.

The second he decides, he barks orders out and we get to work like a fine-tuned instrument. Each man knows his role, and we execute with precision and pure determination. We all want to make it home, and we want to make sure these civilians have the chance to go home again, too.

Lines are put out to try to dampen and control the flames before the tanker explodes, while rescue works to secure drivers and passengers who are trapped in their totaled cars. I'm working on the first car after the tanker. The driver is unconscious and the car is smashed-in, rear and front damage making the frame accordion and the door crumble. This will require extrication with the help of others, and heavy equipment. We have to work fast.

I call for help, watching my house and a second, which just arrived, jump into action. People shift and cover for others while they come help me. We work quickly, carefully. The flames are getting unbelievably hot around us, and the sound of the metal tanker's body crumbling and bending tells me it's only a matter of minutes now.

"We have to hurry," I shout at everyone. "Can anyone get in from the side to secure his neck? We need to get this door off."

"Coming in with the Jaws," someone shouts over my shoulder. I step aside, holding a collar in my hand, ready to get it on the driver and get him out.

We pry the door open and I slip between two men, working as fast as I can to assess the unconscious man and formulate a plan to remove him.

I bark out orders, check his vitals, and we start moving.

The crackling of the flames growing higher and hotter is like the ticking down of the clock for me.

The popping of tires sounds like gunshots, making me want to jump then duck and cover in self-preservation, as memories of my time in Afghanistan bubble up to the surface. I can't let them, though.

We aren't under attack. We are racing an enemy who doesn't give a fuck if we aren't ready yet.

"Let's pull him out. This whole fucking line is about to go," Brandon shouts over the roar of the flames and chaos of the world around us.

As a unit we pull the driver out of the car and get him clear. No sooner do we get around forty feet away than the tanker explodes. The force sends us forward, vibrating our bodies and threatening to topple us, and our patient, over. Fire erupts in every direction. The overpass above the wreck taking extreme heat and damage will have to be shut down until it can be proven structurally sound.

"Is everyone okay?" Lieu approaches us. "Is he alive?"

He nods toward the still body on our gurney. "He is, we need to get him out of here now, though. Do we have a clear path?"

"All set. Medic is waiting on the shoulder over there." He points to the waiting ambulance and I nod this time.

"We don't have time to waste. I'll ride with. They'll need all hands with him."

Lieu agrees easily. We get the patient over to the ambulance and load him up, starting transport and evaluation simultaneously.

Calls like this are everything. Saving this man will make it even better.

Like most of what I do, though, time is precious and wasting even a second could cost him his life.

\*\*\*\*

# Everleigh

Working in a home dedicated to orphaned, abused, and neglected young girls is trying at times. On the one hand, they need extra care and understanding to help them through the obstacles and traumas their lives have brought. On the other, they are still young, growing, hormonal girls who have the same thoughts, tendencies, and behaviors as any other adolescent girl, regardless of what their past is.

So when I get a call at midnight on my night off, informing me one of my girls snuck out of the house and got caught trespassing with some of her friends from school, and they had a bottle of cheap vodka with them, I'm a little peeved. Not only do I have to go to the police department to pick her up, but I also have to explain to Teddy why she was brought in and how she ran away to begin with.

It's the last thing I expected tonight, and the last thing I want to be doing, but I can't let Nichole sit there any longer.

I walk into the police station, hair piled up in a messy bun on top of my head. I must look awful. I rolled out of bed, changed into a pair of jean shorts, slipped a bra on beneath my tank top and climbed in my car. I have no makeup on, nothing to hide the exhausted bags under my eyes, or the stress and blemishes on my face.

"I'm here to pick up Nichole Malcolm," I say to the officer at the front desk. "I was called and told she was at this station."

The uniformed woman with dark, penetrating eyes looks up from her computer and takes me in. "What is your relationship to the minor?"

"I'm the lead counselor at the home she lives in. I work for Corporate Cares; we are her legal guardians through the state. My name is Everleigh Marshal." I pull my wallet from my purse and retrieve my license, handing it as well as my Corporate Cares badge over.

"Thank you," the officer says, handing back my IDs. "I'll have her brought out. There won't be any charges pressed for the trespassing or possession of alcohol. We put her and the others right across from the drunk tank so they could see people going in and out, and what could become of them if they aren't careful."

I have to swallow back the bile creeping up my throat from her words. Nichole knows, better than anyone probably, what can become of her. The exposure, while it makes sense to scare some sense in the kids, will probably have her reliving past traumas and worked up. "Thank you for letting me know. I'll just sit over there until she gets out."

The officer nods her head and lifts the phone on her desk, making the call to have Nichole brought out to me.

I walk over to the hard, plastic chairs lining the walls and drop into one, scrubbing my hands over my face. Nichole hasn't had it easy. In fact, she's had a pretty shitty go of things. She came to be with us around a year and a half ago. Her parents were both alcoholics and they died in a drunk driving accident just after her thirteenth birthday.

She had no other relatives, or anyone who was interested in taking her in, so she became a ward of the state and one of my girls.

I can't imagine what being in there has made her feel. I know from her sessions, her parents were arrested and kept in a holding cell or drunk tank multiple times. I know she was sheltered from the worries and horrors of what that could mean for them, but now, experiencing tonight, she has a very clear image of what her parents went through. The one aspect of their alcoholism she had always been sheltered from is now the final straw in a life of pain and sadness.

I look up as the door is opened and see her standing there with another officer behind her.

Her eyes are red-rimmed and swollen, and the second she sees me she crosses the room in three fast steps and throws her arms around me. "I'm so sorry, Everleigh. I'm so, so sorry." Her hold is strong, tight. I can't tell if it's her guilt, or if she's clinging to me for dear life because she's terrified.

"Miss Malcolm didn't have any belongings when we brought her in," the officer says from behind her. "There was a bit of a commotion with another individual back there. None of the kids were involved or harmed in any way, but they were witness to it." He looks apologetic, and glances at the back of Nichole's head. "Most of the other kids had alcohol in their systems, she didn't. She was just in the wrong place, with the wrong group of friends."

I nod my head and hold her tight to me. "Thank you, Officer Beady," I say, reading his name tag. "I appreciate you bringing her out and explaining. We will be having a long talk about her actions tonight later."

"I thought you might. She told me you would. When she started to have a panic attack, I pulled her out of the room with the other kids and took her into my office. We talked a little until you got here."

Gratitude fills my heart hearing he took care of her when he didn't have to. "Thank you."

He nods with a soft smile and clears his throat. "Remember what we talked about, Nichole; you don't want to hang out with the type of kids who are going to get you into trouble. You are too smart for this to happen again."

Nichole pulls back from me and wipes her eyes as she turns to face him. "I'll remember. Thank you."

"Anytime. You two be safe getting home. Nichole, I hope I don't see you here ever again. Stay out of trouble."

She nods her head and I nudge her shoulder. "Yes, sir. Thank you again."

"Thank you," I add.

We both watch Officer Beady walk back in the door he just escorted Nichole out of, and I glance down into her bloodshot eyes. "Let's get you home."

She nods and folds her arms over her chest, holding herself in a tight embrace. "I'm sorry."

"I know you are. We will talk about it tomorrow morning. For tonight, we need to get you back to The Castle, cleaned up, and to bed."

Her head bobs up and down in agreement, and we make our way out to my car, then back to the house. I'm not supposed to be here tonight, but it'll be easier to stay here and handle everything in the morning, settle the rest of the kids, if I just crash here instead of going home.

At least, that's what I tell myself as I lie down on the couch and pull the blanket over my body. It's easier than admitting I'm worried what might happen if I'm not here and Nichole or any of the other kids wake up scared or worried after tonight's commotion: discovering Nichole missing, and the disruption—when I brought her home—to the normal needed routines all these girls have grown accustomed to.

# Five

## Everleigh

I roll my neck back and forth as I unfold from the driver's seat in my car and rise, letting the hot, California sun melt down over me. I tilt my face skyward and inhale deeply, releasing it as slow as I can, then drape my purse across my body and walk toward the entrance of Corporate Cares headquarters.

I knew the couch would bring me pain last night, but it was worth it. Nichole came in to see me at four this morning. She was wide awake, feeling guilty, and she was remembering her parents a lot—watching the other adults who were paraded in and out of the station last night left an impact—and having a nightmare about what they must have experienced all the times they were taken in before the night of their accident.

I never went back to sleep after that, even as she sprawled out on the couch across from mine, and finally let sleep take her in.

I have to tell Teddy what happened, I have to mark it in her file, but I don't want to. She learned her lesson.

I pull the door open and walk into the cool, air-conditioned lobby. The contrast between the hot summer air outside and the wide-open entry I step into has my skin breaking out in goosebumps and me wishing I'd brought a jacket with me.

I step onto the elevator, pulling my phone free to scroll the local news, slipping it back into my pocket when I reach the Corporate Cares floor.

My first stop is to my office. I need to email a few teachers we keep in touch with throughout the summer for any supplemental materials or help our kiddos might need, and I need to check my calendar for any meetings I have this week.

I'm fully absorbed in an email when a gentle knock raps against my door. "Do you have a few minutes?"

I look up and grin. "You're just the man I wanted to see today, Teddy." I minimize my email and stand, holding my hand out to direct him to the chair across from me.

"You're just the counselor I wanted to see. I got an email from Sandy this morning about Nichole. What happened?"

I let out a sigh and cross my ankles under my desk, folding my hands together over it at the same time. "She snuck out with some friends she made at school. Friends who she will no longer be hanging out with. They were trespassing and were caught with alcohol."

His brows furrow, and the lines in his face wrinkle and bend with his frown. "She was drinking?"

"No, she came back with a blood alcohol of zero. She was in the wrong place with the wrong people. The cops took her in for trespassing but didn't press charges or fine her. They scared her straight though…" I match his frown with one of my own and sigh.

"What happened?"

"Being in the jail, while she waited for me to arrive, brought up a lot of emotions and feelings about her parents. She was able to see a lot of the drunk people brought in last night. She had a panic attack. One of the officers was kind enough to take her to his office once that happened and sat with her until I arrived."

"Is she okay now?" He crosses his foot over his knee.

"She is. She had a rough night, but I stayed at The Castle after I got her there. I had a feeling she would need me. She's also under my directed house arrest for the next two weeks. She can get off with good behavior after a week though."

"That seems fair." He looks at the painting hanging on my wall and smiles. "You bought that at last year's fundraiser?"

I did. It was a painting by one of our former kids. Before I moved to The Castle, I was with the boys at The House, and Andrew was incredibly talented. He worked hard in school, and he got a scholarship based solely on his artistic talents. Now he's shown in galleries all around the country, and he donated for the Corporate Cares auction last year. "I couldn't resist having Andrew's work on my wall."

Teddy smiles at that. "I almost bid on it. Do we need to worry about Nichole trying to sneak out again? Should this be put in her file?"

I shake my head quickly. "No. No, sir, not at all. She knows what she did was wrong. More so, she recognized the trouble isn't worth it and she expressed her sincere apologies and guilt for the worry she put us through."

"Okay, her house arrest and knowledge of the worry she caused is enough, for now, as a warning then."

"Thank you." I pick up a pen lying on the scratch-marred desk and twirl it between my fingers. "How is fundraiser planning going? Are you all set?"

His wrinkles and worry from before smooth into the widest grin. "Funding has been incredible ever since CD Enterprises started helping us years ago, as you know, so this coordinated effort with the fire department has been even better than I could've hoped. We have introduced some of our backers to their causes, and the community seems even more excited about the joint collaboration and events than they have in years."

"That's really great, Teddy. We plan to take the kids out for the softball game to watch the counselors take on the firefighters. Jake said he'll be taking a shift manning the grill after the game for the community picnic too."

"I'll be manning the grill, too," Teddy says, proudly. "Will you be attending the gala?"

"I will. I got coverage for my shift at the house for the night. I felt it important I be there to represent the girls, talk to sponsors, rub elbows with bigwigs." I smirk at him and wink.

Teddy laughs loudly and shakes his head. "Thank you. Your presence will be helpful, as always." He rises from his seat and starts to step toward the door, then pauses and turns toward me. "Thank you for giving me an update on Nichole. Make sure you get some rest before your next shift starts."

"I will. Have a good afternoon, Teddy."

"You too." He gives me a little wave and disappears out the door as quickly as he appeared at it earlier.

# Liam

"Why, exactly do we need to have an actual practice?" I pull the ball cap off my head and slide my fingers through the matted down mess of hair beneath it. "This is for charity, right? I'm not missing anything?"

"Would you be okay with a bunch of counselors wiping our asses next weekend?" Zac asks seriously. "Because I sure as fuck wouldn't be. We are supposed to be the best of the best."

"Relax, rookie." Brandon steps beside me and rolls his eyes. "You don't have to prove shit on the softball field, we are raising money for kids and fallen firefighters. Don't act like a dick and get too competitive."

"There is literally no such thing as being too competitive," Zac responds, sounding stunned.

I laugh and clap my gloved hand over his shoulder. "There is. And you're proving it. Go put out the bases and shit, and remind yourself this is for kids while you're doing it. Kids, Zac. Not pride."

He grumbles and walks away, leaving Brandon and I to watch him sulk off toward the equipment shed to retrieve the bases.

"We weren't that bad, right?" Brandon asks.

"When we were his age, we were fighting a fucking war, we couldn't afford to be that bad over there. But at home? Yeah, we probably were. Until you met Jess. She straightened your ass out on day one." I smirk at him, laughing loudly when he flips me the bird.

"Do you think he could handle it?"

I glance at Brandon curiously. "Handle what?"

"War. Watching people die. Having his life in danger every single day."

I ponder for a second, thinking about my childhood, teen years, and then shipping off. "I honestly don't know, but I'm glad he never had to find out. I'm glad he never will."

"I guess you're right," he concedes. "I wouldn't wish the shit we experienced over there on anyone."

"Me neither, Brother. Me neither."

I wouldn't wish anything I have experienced in my life on anyone, ever. Not my childhood, my teen years, not the war and the lives I couldn't save over there. It's a life I was thrust into as a child, and an escape I chose as an adult. I don't regret a single second of my time serving. I would do it again and lay down my life for the men and women I couldn't save in a heartbeat. But I wouldn't wish that on anyone else. I especially wouldn't wish it on a young, arrogant probationary firefighter whose idea of a bad day is having to roll the hoses and be our bitch who still has all the life—living and learning—ahead of him.

# Six

## Everleigh

"Miss Everleigh," Kristy says, tugging at my hand as we clear the parking lot and walk toward the softball field.

"Yes?" I open my hand for her, feeling her tiny four-year-old palm slip against mine and link our fingers.

"Can I have a hotdog?" She looks up at me with wide, hopeful eyes.

"Not right now," I respond, smiling down at her. "But after the game when they're ready you can have one."

She smiles wide as can be and bounces on her toes, excitement over the hotdog short-lived as she spots a playground not far from the stands. She isn't the only one, a chorus of "can wes?" and "Is it okay ifs?" ring out as the girls fixate on going to play.

"I'll take them over," Jake offers, chuckling. "I doubt they'll be able to sit through an entire game anyway."

"Thank you," I giggle, and let go of Kristy's hand. "Who is going to the park with Jake and who is coming to sit and watch the game with me?"

35

As expected, most of the younger girls want to go to the park, and Nichole, Erica, and Haylie, our three older girls, our teens, want to come watch with me.

"You three don't want to go play?" I ask, knowing exactly why they're sticking with me. I heard them in The Castle this morning talking about getting to see hot firefighters and cute boys today.

"No, everyone is playing for us, we thought we should sit and watch, support them supporting us," Erica says, with an entirely too straight face.

"Right," Haylie agrees.

Nichole dips her head toward her chest, trying to hide her smile.

"Right, it has nothing to do with attractive firefighters and cute boys," I deadpan.

Each of the girls' steps falter and their surprised expressions turn toward me.

"I heard you three talking earlier. Your secret is safe with me. I'm going to go talk to Teddy real fast, you ladies find us a good seat."

They nod in agreement and turn left toward the bleachers behind home plate when I turn right toward the dugout. "How does the team look?" I ask Teddy.

"Good. They'll be competitive, and they'll have fun playing against the firefighters. I heard they were out practicing for this all week."

"For what reason?" I chuckle. "This is a fun game, not the World Series."

"That's what I said when our lieutenant told us we had to practice," a deep, rich voice says from behind Teddy.

Teddy steps to the side and angles his body so he's open to me and our new company, who is wearing a pair of shorts adorned with the firehouse logo on one of the legs, a red firehouse team tee, and a backward cap. His eyes are hidden by his dark sunglasses, but I can tell he's giving me a once-over.

"I'm Liam Hayes," he says, holding his hand out to Teddy first, and then me.

"It's nice to meet you, Liam," Teddy says. "I'm guessing you're playing for the other side today?"

"Yes, sir, I'm the team captain."

"The one who didn't want to practice?" I quip, feeling the warmth of his hand engulf mine while we shake.

"Exactly." He smiles and moves his glasses up off his eyes, resting them on his hat. "I was told you are the head of Corporate Cares," Liam says to Teddy. "I just wanted to come introduce myself. I'll be playing today, and a part of the auction tomorrow night. I just wanted to tell you I'm proud to be teaming up with Corporate Cares and supporting both our causes this weekend."

"It's nice to meet you, too. I'm Teddy. I'm the director of Corporate Cares, and this is one of our counselors, Everleigh."

Liam gives me a breathtaking smile. "It's nice to meet you, Everleigh, and you too, Teddy."

"It's nice to meet you, too," I respond, biting back the smile that wants to break free simply from his presence in front of me. There is no denying he's an attractive man, but now is not the time nor the place to admit that, or linger on him... for too long, at least.

"Why aren't you playing?" His eyes are ocean blue with the sun shining off them, and they're holding me captive.

"I'm working this weekend." I shrug a shoulder and grin. "And I didn't think you all could handle having a woman teaching you how to play ball."

He laughs loudly, so does Teddy. "She's got a rich history in athletics. She coaches a few of our youth sports programs too," Teddy boasts proudly, grinning at me. He is the kindest, most genuine man you could meet. Once you're a part of his Corporate Cares family, you are a part of his family. Period.

"Is that so?" Liam asks, crossing his arms over his chest and smirking. "I would think if you're so good, the team wouldn't have taken no for an answer."

"They didn't have much choice. The kids come first, always. I wanted to be here and experience it with the girls, rather than play. They're the ones who we do this for. Them and the fallen firefighters, too," I add quickly.

"A woman who knows what she stands for, I appreciate that." He winks at me, "But I'm thinking it's really because you didn't want to be on the losing end of today's game. I understand and appreciate that, too."

He's teasing me. Trying to get me riled up, if I had to guess.

"I can assure you that won't be happening." I cross my own arms over my chest to match his, watching his lips tilt upward in response before he straightens his expression again.

"We'll see about that." He glances down at his watch then grins back up at me. "I should probably get back to my team, prepare to dominate today." He winks in my direction, drawing out a loud chuckle from Teddy. "I just wanted to introduce myself and thank you, both of you, for the work you're doing for these kids."

"It's our pleasure," Teddy responds. The two men shake hands again then Liam gives me another smile, and a quick appraisal, before he turns to walk back toward their dugout.

I watch him walk away, doing my best to not stare at his firm, perfect backside before he rounds the fence, crossing right in front of my girls, and know they'll be doing the same thing I would be, if I weren't here in a professional capacity.

"He was nice," Teddy says.

I turn my attention back to him and smile up at his towering figure. "He was. I appreciate what they're doing for us and the kids this year, and I'm excited we can give back to some of the heroes who have lost their lives too soon, also."

"Me too, Everleigh. Me, too." Teddy grins down at me. "I guess I should get into the dugout and support our troops. The game should be starting any minute now."

"Good luck, Coach," I say encouragingly. "Bring us home a win."

Teddy drops his head back, booming out a loud laugh. "Thank you, but try to sound more enthusiastic next time," he teases. "I'll talk to you later on. You and the girls enjoy."

He walks through the gate leading into the dugout and I turn to make my way back to my girls. Their giggles can be heard over all the chatter of families, friends, and even community members here to watch, cheer, and support the teams and our causes.

"What are you three giggling at?" I climb the bleachers up to the top row where the girls chose to sit and drop down next to Haylie.

"Nothing," they all say in unison, then erupt into another fit of giggles.

"I'm sure." I lean back against the fence and glance toward our dugout, seeing who I recognize playing for Corporate Cares, and then slide my gaze across the field at the firefighter dugout. I spot Liam immediately, and my gaze stills at his bent over form until I realize I'm staring and the girls might notice. As innocently and discreetly as I can, I slide my eyes back out toward the middle of the empty field.

"Who was the guy you and Mr. Teddy were talking to?" Erica asks.

Nichole and Haylie giggle, again, then go quiet when I turn my attention to the three of them. "He is a firefighter. I think he said his name is Liam. Why?"

"No reason," Nichole quickly answers for Erica.

"Look at that one," Haylie whispers to them, then points her finger toward another one of the firefighters on Liam's team. "What do you think?"

I look back at the girls and raise my brows, trying not to grin, but failing. "Are you three ready to admit why you wanted to watch the game with me yet?"

Instead of answering, Nichole's lips break into a giant smirk and she turns the tables on me. "Do you think he's cute?"

"Who?" I ask, not looking toward the field or their dugout at all.

"The one next to the guy you met." That makes me turn my head, and I take in the man next to Liam. He's a little shorter, but he's also a little stockier and more built. He has a sweatband over his forearm and his eyes are shaded by the bill of his cap and the glasses he's sliding over them.

"He's attractive, I guess," I admit. I try not to make it a habit of lying to the girls, and answering innocently won't hurt anyone.

"What about the one you met?" Erica asks next.

"He was too. I think they're all probably pretty attractive."

All three girls groan and mutter about how that's not true, and why can't adults just be honest that some people are hotter than others.

"Enough of that," I chastise them. "They're here to support Corporate Cares, we won't be playing hot or not with all of them. Are we clear?"

"Fine," Nichole responds.

"We're clear," Haylie adds.

"Good girls." I turn my attention back to the field, watching the players from both teams line up down the first and third base lines for the playing of the national anthem, spotting Liam right beside home plate, next to the Corporate Cares captain.

*Yes, girls, he's hot. He's very hot. Not that you three need to know I think that.*

\*\*\*\*

# Liam

"I'm old," Brandon says, wrapping his arms around Jess from behind and sagging into her body, forcing her to hold up his body weight.

"You're heavy, too," Jess says, trying to shrug him off. "And sweaty, let go of me."

Instead of letting go, he holds on tighter and buries his face in her neck, wiping his sweat-soaked forehead over her skin.

"Ew! Brandon, let go of me or you'll be sleeping on the couch, alone, tonight."

Her threat makes him retreat quicker than the enemy retreated from us in war. He throws his hands up in defense and nearly begs for forgiveness.

"You're such a pussy," I accuse, dodging Jess' arm as it flies at my chest. "Sorry, sorry. But really, the man fought in a war and he's more afraid of you and sleeping alone than he was of the terrorists."

"It's because he's a smart man," Jess answers.

"See, I'm a smart man." He glances down at his phone and groans, "A smart man who is also afraid of his mother. We should get out of here so we aren't late to the barbecue."

Jess nods in agreement. "Are you sure you don't want to come with us, Liam? You might save me from having to put up with Jarrett and his obnoxious bragging."

I chuckle and shake my head. "I'm positive. I said I'd take a turn grilling here, and the guys are going to bring a firetruck by a little later, so I'll stick around to help them show all the kids."

"Sounds good, man," Brandon answers. "Invitation stands if you want to drop by after. You know we'll be there a while."

"I do. Thanks, B. Tell your parents hey for me, and let your mom know I promise to be at the next one."

"You got it."

"We'll see you tomorrow night," Jess says, grinning. "Brandon told me you're being auctioned off; I can't wait to see it."

I groan and drop my head forward. "I'm never going to live this down, am I?"

"Nope. Not a chance in hell."

I look up at Brandon and slowly raise my favorite finger, then use it to push my sunglasses back up my nose, just in case any kids are watching. "Get out of here before I beat you with a bat. Have a good night, Jess."

"You too. Bye, Liam."

I raise my hand and give them a slight wave, then pull my phone from my pocket.

"They seemed fun," a silky, sweet voice, drawing my eyes up from the device in my hand. It's her again, the drop-dead gorgeous counselor from earlier, Ever… Everleigh.

"They are," I confirm then slip my phone back in my pocket. "I told you your team was going down. I nearly felt bad, beating you all in extra innings. Nearly."

"Such a gentleman, nearly feeling bad for beating a bunch of well-meaning, child-advocating counselors. You certainly shouldn't feel bad at all."

"Ouch," I chuckle. "You don't pull any punches, do you?"

"Nah, not with grown men."

"But you do with the kids?" I raise my brow up, questioning and curious.

"The girls get whatever version of me they need. Kid gloves, a gentle nudge, or not pulling punches, it's all situational with them." She looks over toward where a group of girls is standing, laughing at Zac and the show he's putting on for them with a few softballs being juggled in the air. "Some of them need the TLC and the soft approach."

"I can imagine the things they've gone through before they ended up with you. What you're doing is an incredible thing, truly." She hasn't taken her eyes off the girls, and I can't seem to take my eyes off her. Everleigh's face is full of soft lines and the most beautiful emerald green eyes are shining forward with pride, admiration, and a hint of sadness. It's clear how much she cares for each of the girls she is responsible for.

"Nobody can imagine that," she whispers, then shakes her head and shifts her attention back to me. "Anyway," she smiles, and I swear the force of it hitting me is nearly enough to knock me on my ass, "you played well out there today."

"Oh? Does that mean you were watching me?"

"Good Lord, no!" She lets out the softest chortle and drops her chin to her chest, but not before I see the pink creep into her cheeks.

"You can admit it, I'm good at keeping secrets."

Her chest rises and falls a little quicker than before, and she keeps shifting her body back and forth. It's subtle, barely noticeable, in fact, but she is doing it. "There aren't any secrets to keep, Liam."

She still won't look at me, but that's okay, she doesn't have to just now. "Sure there are, we all have secrets to keep. The question is, how hard are you going to try to hide yours from me?"

That gets her attention and she raises her head, narrowing her eyes. "I have no secrets you're going to be hearing now, or ever."

Her defiance and irritation are absolutely adorable, but I don't want to piss her off, so I raise my hands up in apology. "I meant no offense; I was just wondering if you were watching me during the game like I've been watching you after it?"

"I wasn't… I mean, clearly I watched the game… Wait," her eyes widen to the size of mini saucers and her lips part slightly with the tiny drop of her jaw. "You've been watching me?"

I shrug my shoulders and smirk. "That's a secret for me to know. If you'll excuse me, I have a grill I need to go man. It's been a pleasure talking to you, Everleigh. I hope we can do it again sometime."

"Oh…" She opens her mouth, then closes it; then opens it again to add, "I've enjoyed talking to you, too. Enjoy the rest of your evening."

*With thoughts of you to keep me occupied, that's a guarantee.*

"You, too, Everleigh. Be safe getting your girls back home." With that, I walk away from her and take in a deep breath of air.

I definitely did not expect to meet a beautiful, strong woman today. But I'm glad I did.

# Seven

## Liam

Monkey suit. Check.
Bunker gear. Check.
Shaved. Tanned. Smooth. Check

I never would've imagined being roped into being auctioned off would come with rules and suggestions about how I should appear tonight. Bunker gear with no shirt, smooth, tanned, and oiled chest. The goal is to drive the women wild so they want to spend the big bucks for a lunch with a hot firefighter... that's what I was told, at least.

Leave it to Lieu's wife to state it like it is. She didn't pull any punches with her description and the purpose of tonight's auction. Not that I'd want her to. Her give no fucks; straight-shooting attitude is one of my favorite things about her.

It reminds me of an intriguing counselor I met yesterday, too. I think she'd get along well with Lieu's wife. They both call it as they see it, or it seems that way at least. I can hardly claim to know anything about

Everleigh from Corporate Cares after just two short conversations, but it's a feeling I have about her.

I toss everything I'm going to need tonight into my truck and grab my wallet, phone, and sunglasses from my place, then lock up and head out.

I can't help but wonder if I'll see her again tonight. It's something I think about my whole drive to the hotel the event is being held at this year. I have no reasonable excuse why I want to see her or talk to her again, but do I need one? She's beautiful, she's clearly a good woman—I mean she works at Corporate Cares for Christ's sake—and she caught my attention in her jean shorts and tank top, with a smile that could light the world up on its own, sun be damned. Who wouldn't want to see and talk to *that* again?

I walk into the hotel after a short twenty-minute drive and the second I'm through the sliding doors leading into the bustling, air-conditioned lobby, I'm greeted by none other than Lieu's wife.

"Liam, you're here!" She's grinning from ear to ear and hurrying toward me with admirable pace. "We have a suite booked for the night for all of you to use to change in. Unless you'd rather change in your own room? Did you book one? I probably should have asked that already."

I chuckle and drop my bag on the ground, letting it land at my feet with a muted thud as I hold my arms open so I can hug her. "Hi, Kathy. I do have a room here, but I'm fine using the suite. No need to let it go to waste, right? So stop stressing your beautiful self out."

She takes a step back and grins at me. "Liam Hayes, you are always such a charmer. Get yourself checked in and then I'll take you up to the suite. A few guys from other houses are already up there. I'm sure you'll know them all though, Kevin did when I showed him the list."

46

"Thank you, gorgeous." I wink at her. "Give me a few minutes then I'm all yours."

Her grin turns sheepish and her cheeks flush. "Don't make promises you can't keep, young man. Kevin would have both our behinds if he knew I was considering your offer."

I laugh loudly and pull her in for one more hug. "I could take him. You name the day and we'll run off together."

She smacks my chest playfully and shakes her head as she steps backward. "You're too much. Go get checked in. Stop distracting me with promises of fun and naughtiness."

"Yes, ma'am. I'll be ready to go up in a few." I reach down for my bag, hoisting it up over my shoulder, and carry it over to the check-in desk, much to the receptionist's delight, if her twitterpated smile is any indication. "Hello, ma'am. I'm here for the event tonight and I'd like to check in to my room."

****

# Everleigh

"Thank you again for coming with me, Addie." I link my arm through my sister's as we walk throughout the ballroom the gala is being held in. The joint effort between the fire department and Corporate Cares looks incredible. Red, white, and black all cover the walls and tables. The centerpieces on each table either hold candles with Fallen Firefighter emblems or Corporate Cares emblems.

"Honestly, Ever, it's not a hardship being here. Hot firefighters up for bid for a good cause? Sign me up every year." She leans her head into mine and giggles. "They really went all out in here, didn't they?"

"They absolutely did. It looks amazing."

There are laminated placards on each table explaining the combined fundraisers, where all the money will be going, who will benefit, and how it will be split.

Stella, Sandy, and the crew did such an incredible job organizing and putting all of this together in coordination with the fire department team. It's so wonderful to see and be a part of.

"It does." We walk around, looking for the table with our names on it, and she points. "Look, there we are. Are you going to tell me who the hottie you couldn't quit eyeing out there is? Or am I supposed to pretend I didn't see you doing him with your X-ray vision?"

"Good God, Addie!" I shriek a little too loudly, then drop my voice to a whisper so our new audience can't hear, "I was not doing him with X-ray vision."

"You so were. I don't blame you though. He was sexy. And he was eyeing you too. So whoooo is he?"

A little part of me, perhaps the devil on my shoulder, does a little celebration with her acknowledgement he was eyeing me too. The angel, though, is chastising me telling me that is not why we're here tonight.

"Seriously, stop holding out," she prods. "Who is he?"

"His name is Liam. We met yesterday at the softball game. He's a firefighter." I take my seat and tug her down, so I can continue to speak in a hushed voice and not draw any more attention to us. "He's nice. The girls really liked him, too. All the kids did. They liked all the firefighters. Everyone was so great."

"That's amazing. Can you tell me the names of any of the other firefighters you met? Preferably the ones who did not have wedding bands." She beams at me suggestively and wiggles her brows. "Help your big sister out here."

"My God. Why did I bring you again?"

"Because you love me. Now, names. Spill. I want to be equipped when we start flirting later."

"You're too much. I honestly don't remember any of their names though. I met so many kind firefighters yesterday; they all run together. I am sure some were single though."

"You're lying." She gives me that accusatory look she mastered sometime when we were young girls, the first time she caught me sneaking into her room to play with her toys without permission.

"I am not!" I hiss in a whispered shout.

"You are, too. You do remember one name. But only one. Funny how that works, isn't it? You met a ton of amazing firefighters yesterday—your words, not mine— yet you only remember Liam. That's more telling than the obvious visual fuckfest you partook in when we arrived."

My only response, logical and mature it is not, is to glare at her and stick my tongue out. It seems a better option than to admit to her I found him as sexy as she's accusing me of finding him, and he definitely caught my attention and stood out.

"Yep, that's what I thought." She pulls her lip gloss out and applies it to her victorious grin. "I want to meet him."

"You would. But we're going to pass on that. Can we talk about something else now? Maybe about your most recent date?"

It's her turn to glare at me. "We aren't going to be speaking about that date ever. It was…" Her body tightens and her shoulders lift up to her ears as she makes a gagging sound. "Nope. We won't be going there. Let's just say I am free, and single as a Pringle, to ogle, talk, flirt, and leave with anyone I choose to tonight."

"Me, Addie. You're leaving with me."

She pouts her lips, moving her head side to side in the slightest, most contemplative action I think I've ever seen. "Nah. I'll leave with my best option. Besides... You may not want me to leave with you. There is one scorching hot man here who may be incredible at setting you ablaze then extinguishing your flames too."

"I swear on all that's holy... If you bring up his hose next, I will take you home now."

She laughs. "I didn't need to; it was clearly already on your mind. As long as you know how he will put it out, I don't need to tell you."

# *Eight*

## Liam

I'm surprised they didn't do a pre-auction auction," one of the guys from another firehouse who I don't know says, while we're all waiting behind the readymade stage to go out and parade ourselves in front of excited, loud, women—and men—to earn money for our fallen brothers and sisters, and for orphaned, in need children.

"A pre-auction auction?" I take the bottle of oil and start to smooth it over my chest.

"Yeah, auction off bottles of oil to slather us up with. They could've made a fortune." He flexes his muscles and continues rubbing himself down as the rest of the guys in here chuckle at his remark.

"You make a good point," I agree with him then finish with my own oil. "How did you end up getting to wear those and not bunker gear?"

"Kathy, the woman running all this, said I could choose. Why, didn't you get the choice too?"

I glance down at my bunker gear, dry-cleaned and as clean as can be, then shake my head. "No, I think my lieutenant's wife wanted to torture me."

This has him laughing. "Sucks to be you, dude. Hopefully you can find a sexy woman out there who will want to help clean you up tonight. Or one who might want to get down and dirty with you."

He's young, new to the job, and the same way we all were when we were his age. "Yeah, maybe." I set the bottle down, barely making it to the table beside me before dropping it because my hands are so damn slick. Lieu owes me for this.

He owes me big time.

Kathy's voice booms out from behind the curtain blocking us off from the crowd. "Ladies and gentleman, it is time! You've talked to them all already, they were all at the doors, welcoming you to this year's event and charming their ways into your hearts, now it's time to see what they were hiding beneath the suits, to see them in all their heroic glory. Without further ado, I'd love to kick off our firefighter auction and our combined Firefighters Fund gala in conjunction with Corporate Cares!"

The room erupts into loud applause and hoots and hollers from the women, and men, in the room. Loud whistles ring out with the commotion, nearly drowning out Kathy's instructions about how they will be bidding and what the winner gets.

"Time to look alive, fellas!" Lieu says, coming back to perk us all up, accompanied by the man I met yesterday, Teddy.

"Liam," Lieu says, "this is Teddy, he's the Director of Corporate Cares."

"I know, boss. I introduced myself to him yesterday. It's good to see you again, Teddy. I'd offer my hand, but

Lieu's wife made sure all of us were well oiled to enhance the bids."

Teddy's booming laugh is deep and full, and I'm sure people throughout the room can hear it. "No worries at all. Thank you for letting us grease you up and parade you around for a good cause. Some of our counselors and employees are incredibly grateful for it to be you all doing this year, rather than them."

"Happy to be of service."

"We should get back out front," Lieu says. "Kathy wants to make sure I'm out there talking you all up in the crowd."

"A little banter and ribbing to make the women laugh and us more appealing?" I ask, smirking.

"Something like that," Lieu admits. "Try to enjoy yourself out there, Liam. This really is for a good cause."

"It's for a great cause, and the kids and our staff are so grateful for your participation, I can assure you," Teddy adds.

"I know it is, that's why I'm going along with this insane dog and pony show. I'll do whatever I can to help kids, my fallen brothers and sisters, every time I'm asked to. I know the struggles and how needed support is."

They each stop to thank a few other guys on their way out; then they disappear back out into the crowd with everyone else and the auction starts, all the guys going in turn and putting on their display to the delight of the crowd.

# 'Nine

## Everleigh

There is no denying we have incredibly good-looking firefighters in our city but for as handsome as they all have been, none have come close to being as attractive as Liam yet. Even without seeing him shirtless, I know he has a fit, toned body. I stared at him during the game enough yesterday I also know the rest of his body is as well cared for as his arms. His legs had sexy definition, his calves, his powerful thighs, his ass... His arms looked damn good while he was up to bat, too. The way he would clench his fingers around the bat, flexing his biceps and triceps, his swing... his body was the perfect demonstration of finessed, controlled power.

It's all I can think of as yet another firefighter walks the makeshift runway to the shouts and catcalls of all the women here. I've bid on many of them, and I'll bid on him, too. It would not be a hardship to accompany any of these guys to lunch for a good cause, if I win. But in general, I'm just trying to drive bids up higher, in the name of charity, of course.

"And now, ladies and gentleman," the emcee's voice booms out of the speakers, "we have firefighter paramedic Liam Hayes. Liam is thirty-two and an army veteran. He served two tours overseas and when he was honorably discharged, he carried his medic career with him. Liam has been a member of the fire department for the last six years. His favorite color is red, he loves watching IndyCar, football, and most importantly, he loves serving his community and helping people."

I'm fixated on the stage as he walks out. He's in bunker gear, well he's in the pants with the suspenders draped over his bare torso, carrying his jacket over his shoulder with his helmet perched on his head.

"Holy. Fuck," Addie mutters. "He's…"

"You're not kidding…" I say back, barely whispering the words as I stare at him. His body is even better than I'd imagined, and his smile and confidence are… I don't even know if there's a word for what they are.

Liam stops at the end of the runway and strikes a pose, just as the emcee starts the bidding for a date with Liam. "We will start at two-hundred-fifty dollars," he calls out.

One sign raises, followed quickly by another upping the bid another fifty dollars. This trend continues, and continues, until the bid has easily surpassed five hundred.

"Five hundred and fifty going once, going twice, sold to the beautiful blonde at table eighteen!" The bids ending barely register in my mind before Liam's eyes scan the crowd, locking on mine before I have the chance to look away. His lips quirk up momentarily, then fall as he spins around and slowly makes his way back toward the end of the stage.

"Young lady, all of our winners, please come fill out the date card information so we can coordinate with firefighters to set up your lunch dates. With that, ladies and gents, our firefighter auction has come to an end. Dinner will be served in thirty minutes, until then you are encouraged to mingle and check out all of the items that have been donated to our silent auction, too. Remember, everything you purchase tonight will go to two fantastic causes."

I watch Liam's retreating back, donning a tattoo over his shoulder I can't make out, until he disappears behind the stage.

Why did he look so disappointed? I don't get it. Was he not happy to see me? Did I do something to offend him?

I turn to ask my sister what her thoughts are, but she's nowhere to be found. I rise to scan the crowd, but everyone is up now, talking, getting drinks, or inspecting each and every silent auction item up for grabs. I'm not sure where she ended up, but I know Addison, if she can buy something good and have the money go to a worthy cause, she'll be the first to open up her checkbook.

**\*\*\*\***

# Liam

For a brief moment, when I took in the attendees seated at table eighteen, I thought maybe Everleigh was the one to bid on me, until it dawned on me the gorgeous brunette—who I've been very intrigued by—was not the blonde the emcee stated as the winner.

I wonder if she bid on me at all. Would she have been willing to go on a date with me? Clearly not enough to pay over five hundred dollars.

I will gladly have lunch with whomever the lovely lady is, willing to donate so much money for such incredible causes, but I will do so with a hint of disappointment she isn't the other woman seated at table eighteen.

This is all I can think about as I make my way from the ballroom to my own hotel room. I need to shower, get the oil off my body, and change out of this heavy gear and into my monkey suit. Maybe that would've made her bid higher. I've heard women can't resist a man in a well-fitted suit.

It's hard to tell, though.

Maybe she isn't as interested in me as I am her. The way she was looking me over with her friend when they arrived, I would've sworn she was in the same boat as me, but maybe she's just incredibly polite.

I'm only going to allow myself to wonder about her while I finish washing my hair and getting ready, then when I get back downstairs, I'm going to be the perfect ambassador for our firehouse, for our cause, and for all the families of fallen firefighters, as well as orphaned and in need children.

With a fresh, oil-free body, perfectly tailored monkey suit, and cologne that drives all the women wild, I walk back into the ballroom, ready for whatever the night may bring.

"Damn, Brother," Brandon nearly shouts from probably twenty feet away, "you actually look like you're worth that hefty price tag!"

Jess smacks his arm and smiles wide when I walk over to them. "First of all, fuck you. I was worth it before I cleaned up. Second of all, it's probably best they didn't auction you off, they'd have had to pay the bidders for you."

"Screw you." Brandon laughs, and Jess shakes her head.

"Are you two enjoying yourself?" I glance around, looking for a waiter or waitress walking by so I can get a drink.

"It's been a lot of fun. Did you see who bid on you?" Jess beams at me, and I shake my head no.

"Did you see who bid on me? I have no idea."

"Nah, we tried to get a look, but we weren't close enough to that table." Brandon lifts his beer to his mouth. "You got a room for the night?"

"Yeah, when the words oil and body were used together, I knew I'd want to shower after the auction. Just easier to do it here, rather than driving home."

"So we could take your room key and—"

"Brandon! Don't you dare finish that thought," Jess scolds, rolling her eyes. "We will not be using Liam's room for that, or anything else tonight. Do you hear me?"

I'm fighting back my laugh by biting the inside of my cheek. I love watching my best friend get scolded by his wife. It's priceless. Especially since he was the man who had to do countless pushups and run God only knows how many miles for not listening when we were in boot camp.

"Yes, ma'am," he says as sweetly as he can. "I was just thinking that my wife is the sexiest woman in here, and I would love nothing more than to get her out of the dress she has on, show her my appreciation." The man has game; I'll give him that.

"Oh, baby…" Jess coos. "You're already out of the doghouse. We can leave early tonight. After dinner, if you want."

"We could leave before dinner and I'll make you my meal," Brandon offers, and Jess's knees literally go weak.

"You two are way too disgustingly cute for me. I'm going to go find a drink without alcohol and see if I can figure out who bid on me. If I don't see you before your hormones drive you out of here, be safe getting home."

Brandon clasps my shoulder, grinning like a jackass who knows he just got himself out of trouble, and Jess barely tears her eyes away from him. "Enjoy yourself tonight, Liam. Really. Have fun, talk to some girls."

She always worries about me. She wants me to settle down with someone good, but I'm not worried about it at all.

"I'll do my best. You two enjoy the night too."

"We will, believe me." Brandon slips his arm around Jess and kisses her temple. "Catch ya tomorrow, bright and early."

"I'll bring the coffee."

They walk off, fingers linked, and leave me to go get that water I want, and look at all of the silent auction items.

There are so many great things up for grabs; we should raise a ton of money. There are spa days, sunset cruises, Disneyland tickets, vineyard tours, getaway weekends, and pit passes for the Firestone Grand Prix of Monterey offered by CD Enterprises.

Holy shit.

I almost would've missed them, tucked in between so many other things. They are the one item I will be bidding on... The chance to go into the pit area and see the team in action would be incredible.

"I heard you like IndyCar during your walk of glory." Her voice hits me like a freight train, and I have to consciously work to not respond as such.

"So you were paying attention?"

"It was kind of hard not to with you up on the stage, shirtless, oiled up, and dressed in your gear. Everyone in the room was captivated."

*And yet you didn't bid on me.*

I turn my head toward her and smile. "So what you're saying is I was irresistible?"

Her laugh is loud and sweet, and her face lights up. "Definitely what I'm saying." She steps closer and takes a look at the items up for auction. "I saw this when I was looking earlier." She points to the VIP passes. "Are you going to bid?"

"I was thinking about it. Think I should?" I look to her for her answer, and her head bobs up and down.

"I would. I mean, if you love it enough to list it in your catwalk bio, you may as well put your money where your mouth is." She leans in for the pen, her soft arm brushing against mine, and writes my first name down. "There, now you have to bid, you can't scratch your name out, that would seem weird."

She straightens out and smirks at me, holding out the pen. I take it from her, chuckling, and lean over the form, putting my bid amount in. "You're pretty persuasive."

"More like demanding, I think," she admits rather cutely. "Sorry if I overstepped, but the way you were looking at that thing, I felt like you needed the push."

"And you were the one who had to give it to me?"

She rests her hand on her hip and quirks her head. "Nobody else was here to do it. And now that we're old friends after our two whole interactions, it was my duty. Wasn't it?"

After I drop the pen, I turn to face her straight on and give her an amused grin. "Oh, absolutely. You would have been a terrible person had you let me walk away without following my dream here."

"See, that's what I thought!" She starts to giggle a little. "Seriously though, I'm sorry if I put you on the spot, it wasn't cool of me."

I step a little closer to her so someone else can look over the auction items on the table beside me. The new closeness allows me to smell the distinct scent of perfume and feel the heat radiating from her body. "You didn't. I was going to bid on it. I would absolutely love to have the opportunity to hang out in the pits at the races and see how they do things. The fact it's an offer from CD Enterprise makes it even better."

"So you're a fan of Colton Donavan?" I must do a miserable job hiding my astonishment she knows Colton Donavan or any of the racers, because she emits a chuckle and a snort, then shakes her head. "Really? You think women don't know racers?"

"I know women do, I guess I'm just surprised you do. Are you an IndyCar fan?" She's surprising me beyond words tonight, and this new little revelation makes me want to get to know even more about her.

"I don't watch it religiously, no. In fact, I don't watch it much at all, however, his wife—and he—made Corporate Cares the well-known organization it is. His wife is a counselor here, too. She interviewed and trained me."

"Holy fuck. You know Colton Donavan?" I can't believe what I'm hearing. I've heard rumors about the good things he does, I know he partners with foundations every year, but I never looked into his personal life.

"No, I know Rylee Donavan. I've seen him around a time or two, though. He's a big part of the boys' lives at The House."

"Wow. I'm not the type to get jealous over something like that ordinarily, but I am now. You have met him though, right?"

She lets out a little chirp of a laugh and nods. "Once, in passing, honestly. I think we maybe exchanged a few words. He was really nice though."

"Fuck, that's cool."

"I guess it is. He just seemed like any normal guy to me. I only know he races because, well, it's hard not to."

She shrugs her shoulder as though what she's saying is no big deal, and I don't get it.

"He's not just any normal guy," I correct, smirking. "He's Colton Fucking Donavan. I would give almost anything to meet him."

"Hmmm." Her face transforms from amused to intrigued. "I guess I'll have to keep that in mind. I have to go; my sister is here tonight and I'm afraid she's going to get herself into trouble if I don't intervene in whatever she's doing."

The last thing I want is for her to go, but I can't exactly say that. I'd come across as some creepy, overbearing dude. We hardly know each other; it would be crazy. But… "Could I get your number, take you out for a coffee sometime?"

Her eyes rise in surprise, and her mouth forms an O. "Don't you already have one date in your book from tonight?"

"Huh? No, I haven't asked anyone out."

"No, the auction. You have a date with someone who paid good money, wouldn't it be rude to leave here with another woman's number, too?"

I shake my head no; my heart is beating a little too quickly in my chest for my liking. I don't know if she's about to turn me down, or if I can accept it without feeling embarrassed and crushed. "One is a date for charity, I don't think I'll even get her number. I don't even know who it is. I'm asking you for yours because I want to hear more about your work."

"And Colton Donavan?" she teases.

"Him, too." I give her my best smile and shift my hands down, sliding them in my pockets. "So what do you say? We can exchange work stories over a cup sometime. I promise I won't bite, or bring harm."

"Don't make promises I might not want you to keep." She gives me a mischievous grin and pulls out her phone.

"Give me your number and I'll text you before I leave. I will agree to coffee and conversation, but only coffee and conversation."

"I'll take whatever I can get." I rattle off my number to her, feeling my own little victorious pump of happiness surging through my body when my phone vibrates in my pocket, proving she did as she promised and texted me her number to have, too.

# *Ten*

## Everleigh

Steel blue eyes brightened even more by a crisp, pressed cobalt blue shirt framed by a jet-black, perfectly fitted suit filled my every dream last night. His voice, gravelly and confident, gave me goosebumps and chills even as I slept. His hands were sure and skilled, and he left me wanting for nothing… until I woke up—chest heaving, mind racing, body needing—to realize it was all just a dream.

The auction was a blast, being there with Addie, even better. Seeing him, oiled up and donning nothing but his bunker pants and suspenders was something I'll never forget. But after, when he was cleaned up and dressed in a tailored suit and confidence… That's an image I think I will cling to and store in my memory to treasure forever.

I took a walk on the wild side, owned my actions and attraction to him, and gave him my number. I'm nearly too old for the 'date 'em, screw 'em, leave 'em game,' but as Addie so eloquently reminded me last night, I may be getting older, it doesn't mean I'm getting less single by sitting on my ass and not doing anything about it.

I highly doubt coffee will turn into anything more, but it's a step out of my comfort zone and into the realm of possibilities.

"Why are you up so early?" Addie half-asks, half-moans as she groggily drags herself into my kitchen and up to the coffee maker.

"Because I didn't have one too many to drink at the hotel bar last night, unlike someone else in the room this morning."

"When fun counselors and hot firefighters invite you to the bar after the event to drink, you go with them, Ever. That's the whole point I was making last night. If you don't want to be single the rest of your life, you kind of have to put yourself out there."

I slide the creamer across the counter to her and point to the cabinet over her head. "Cups are up there, you already found the pods, so by all means, help yourself."

"Thanks, but I already was. Stop trying to change the topic though." She puts the pod in the coffee maker and presses the buttons to get the cup brewing; then turns to face me with her arms crossed over her chest. "You won't ever find love if all you do is work and come home."

"Did I, or did I not go to the bar with you last night?"

"You did," she concedes, "but you also turned down an insanely sexy firefighter, who was more than into you. Why did you blow him off like that?"

"He just wasn't my type." I shrug my shoulder and take a too large sip of coffee, the scalding liquid burning my lips and the roof of my mouth as it passes through them. "Holy…. Fuck! Ow!" I'm trying not to swallow the scorching liquid, swishing the coffee back and forth, talking around my mouthful.

"Good Lord, did you really just burn your mouth so you could avoid this conversation?" She shakes her head in frustration. "I don't know what to do with you. At all."

I flip her the bird and shake my head in obvious disagreement, but instead of reacting she starts putting her own coffee together, paying me no more attention.

I could tell her I turned down one firefighter's number because I already gave mine to another, but I don't want to. I want to keep our little talk last night; his cuteness over the pit passes to myself. I want to have coffee with him and learn more before I start spouting to my sister, and therefore everyone else in our lives, about the incredibly sexy blue-eyed man I was having dreams about last night.

"You aren't wrong, ya know?" I give her instead, drawing her surprised attention back to me.

"Say that again." Her tone is a mix between shock and arrogance, and it causes me to roll my eyes far back into my head.

"Don't be a bitch. You heard me."

She clasps her coffee between her hands and presses her lips together momentarily, making a show of not being a bitch, before she says, "What was I right about?"

"I didn't say you were right, I just said you weren't wrong."

"Semantics, Little Sister. Now, spill."

I take another smaller, more cautious drink of my coffee and set the mug down on the counter. "I do need to put myself out there more, and I will. I promise. He really just wasn't it for me. His arrogance was condescending and rude, not charming and attractive. He made it incredibly clear all he cared about was my body, too. He was a dick. That's why I didn't give him my number at the bar."

"That's fair enough," she responds quietly. "I didn't know he was that type, or I would have taken him by the balls and yanked him away from you."

The image is vivid in my mind, and I know she would absolutely do it to protect me, and it makes me giggle and cross the small kitchen to hug her. "Thank you. I'll listen, I promise, just give me time."

Her mug makes a gentle click as the ceramic hits my granite counter, then her arms wrap tightly around me. "You have all the time in the world. You'll find the right guy eventually, until then, have some fun and enjoy the rides when they come." She follows her own words up with a laugh, and I catch on to her meaning.

"Oh my God, Addison Marshal! Do not… I don't need to hear that. Go away." I step back from her, mortified and making a disgusted face, which only makes her laugh.

"You do need that. Trust me. Butttttt, I'll do my best to respect you and your boundaries. For now."

"So big of you," I murmur. "Thanks."

"I try, Little Sister. I try. Now, if you'll excuse me, I'm going to use your shower, get ready, and then head out to work."

"It's Sunday," I remind her, taking a seat at the counter. "Why are you working?"

"You aren't the only one who is passionate about their job. I have a new client right now, a huge one, so it looks good if I'm working over the weekend and completing things early."

"Kiss ass." I smirk.

"You think I didn't see you with Teddy last night? Boss's pet." She grins, tossing her soft insult back my way.

"He could give me the keys to everything I've ever dreamed of, so… I'll gladly be the boss's pet." I cup my coffee between my hands and eye her over the faint puffs of steam coming up.

"You do good work, if he's smart, he'll give you the position. The promotion should be yours, kissing ass or not."

"I'm keeping my fingers and toes crossed. I want it so bad," I admit.

"You'll get it, honey. Believe me. I saw how he, and everyone, was so invested in your words, your thoughts, plans, and actions last night. You've got the promotion in the bag. And then, then we'll work on you bagging a guy, too."

\*\*\*\*

# Liam

"She wants to do lunch that soon?" I ask incredulously, coordinating the winning bid date I owe from the auction last night. It's as though the winner thinks I don't have a life or anything remotely resembling one, being so specific that our date has to be tomorrow as soon as my shift ends. I listen to the reason the winner gave for why things have to move so quickly and roll my eyes. Some obnoxious, rich, thinks the world revolves around her would win and demand I drop everything for the only time she can meet.

Brandon is leaning against the truck with his arms crossed over his chest and a shit-eating grin spread across his arrogant, irritating face. He knows what the call is, and he clearly finds amusement in my irritation.

"Yes, I will be there with bells on after my shift ends tomorrow." I end the call as quickly as I can and stare him down, hoping looks suddenly can kill. "I don't want to hear it, so walk away now."

"Quit bitching, saddle up, and fulfill your obligations with a better mood than you have now, or you'll make us all look like fucking assholes." I swear on all that's holy he's doing his best to get me more pissed off, and true to his very knowledgeable form, he's achieving his goal.

"Go fuck yourself, Brandon. I don't want to hear your bull today. We both know whoever bid on me is going to be a stuck-up, prissy bitch who thinks the world revolves around her."

"Dude, what the fuck is your problem? Really. You agreed, you put on the show last night, now you're acting like this lunch date is the worst thing to have ever happened to you. What gives?"

"Nothing. It's all just such a fucking joke. Everything is right now."

"Care to elaborate what everything is? I suspect it has something to do with the cactus lodged firmly up your ass right now."

"I got a letter in the mail from my father yesterday, apparently, he didn't think I'd answer on Lance's birthday. So it was a double whammy from him…"

"Fuck. I'm sorry, Brother. But that doesn't give you right to take it out on people working to do something good, something you willingly agreed to be a part of."

He's right, I know he's right, but I can't help it. I wish I could move on—forget my past—forget all about him. "I know it doesn't, but he laid it on so thick, I can't get that shit out of my head. It's making me see everything through a haze of anger, regret, and hatred."

Brandon tips his chin to his chest and his lips form a tight, thick line. I know he's thinking, that he's going to have something to say to me, so I wait him out and take a seat on the back step of the ambulance next to the fire truck. "You can't let him get to you. You know, every single year, he's going to call around the same time. It's his way of maintaining some level of contact and control. Stop giving it to him. Because instead of taking it out on the man you should be, you take that shit out on everyone else. I know why. I get it. Others, though, Liam… they have no idea what crawled up your ass, so all they see is a giant prick who could potentially make us all look bad."

"You're right. I should call her back and apologize, see if I can do or take anything. Maybe get a name so I at least know who I'm looking for."

"You're smarter than you look," he chides and pushes off the truck. "I'll leave you to your groveli—"

Brandon is cut off by the call ringing out over the speakers. We have a pool accident to go to. Sounds like one adolescent male, unconscious, with a potential head or neck injury. Just as quickly as the call comes in, the rest of the guys on the truck, and our paramedics filter out of the house and into the truck and ambulance.

Our minds shift from personal to professional as though a switch were flipped, and the only focus now is on getting as much information from dispatch as we can on our way to the scene. While we may not all be needed, in the end we take enough for any worst-case scenario and adjust accordingly once we arrive. As the medic on our truck, I know my services will likely be needed along with the EMTs on the ambulance, especially if there are any open wounds or life support measures needed.

"I hate these calls," Terrence says over our headphones, to the agreement of all of us. Kids and teens are the worst, lives too young to be lost, the unknown of what we may see.

"Information isn't clear, it may not be as bad as it could be," I offer, pulling a pair of gloves on as we turn onto the block the call is located on. "Fingers crossed it's a simple, easily recovered from accident that brought more of a scare than anything else."

We pull up to the single story, ranch-style house and a frantic father meets us at the front door. "It's my son. He's out back. He's unconscious and he hit his head on the wall."

"The wall? I thought it was a swimming accident?" I clarify, following him through his home out to his backyard.

"Yes, yes he did. It was the pool ledge. I'm sorry. I'm… just help him. Please." He shows us where his son is lying, motionless on the ground, while his mom is bent over his body and a group of other boys stands back, eyes wide in fear and shock.

"Do you all know what happened?" I ask, kneeling beside his body and starting a check on his vitals. Anyone can answer, but I need to know what we're dealing with, so I raise my head and survey each of them, hoping someone will come forward.

"We were getting bored," one boy says, stepping forward. "He said we could jump off his roof into the pool. He was showing us what to do."

"So he jumped off the roof? Did he hit the water first or did he hit the ledge?" I can feel he has a pulse, it's weak, but stable and his breathing is shallow.

"He sort of cannonballed into the water, but his body tilted back and he hit his head and neck on the wall. He sank to the bottom of the pool after and never came back up. We got him to the surface as fast as we could." The kid looks terrified, but at least he's being honest. "I even did CPR."

The other two paramedics on our shift, Dalton and Lyn, join me around the boy's body, and they start administering aid. His IV goes in, they secure his neck with a collar and two lateral support straps to stabilize his head.

71

"We need to get him to the hospital immediately," Lyn says, holding the fluid bag up for me to take. "Help us get him up, guys."

Brandon, Mack, and I work quickly with Dalton and Lyn to roll the kid and get him on a board, then we all carefully and gently move him onto the gurney.

"Mom, Dad, one of you can ride along," I inform them.

"I'll go," his mom says, rising from the ground, tears spilling from her eyes, and voice shaky and full of emotion. "My husband will follow behind."

"You can ride up front with me, ma'am," Dalton says, following the dad as he leads us out the side gate so we can get their son to the hospital.

We load the kid into the ambulance and I jump in with Lyn to help her get him hooked up to the EKG machine and grab another quick set of vitals for her. "You're good for transport."

She nods her head and I hop out, closing the double doors and leaning out so Dalton can see and hear me. "You're good to go, man."

He holds a thumb out the window and the ambulance lights flash on as they pull away. "That doesn't look too good," Brandon says, stepping up beside me as the sirens roar to life when the ambulance hits the end of the block and gets to a busy street.

"No, not at all." I look at him and shake my head. "It's not good."

The boy's dad ushers all the other kids out from the back. "I have to follow my wife and son; their parents are all on their way…" he barely gets out.

"Will your parents be here fast?" Brandon asks.

"We're all going to go home together," one of the boys offers. "My mom will be here in five."

I nod my head at Brandon and he answers, "We will stay here until she arrives. Dad, you go be with your family. They're going to need you."

The dad thanks us and quickly locks his house up, then jogs down the drive to his car, hopping in and leaving in a hurry, rushing off to be with his family.

I turn my attention to the boys still here, taking each of them in. "Are you boys okay?"

They all nod and mumble they are, but I know they're shaken. Seeing a friend hurt, witnessing the color drain from their friend's face, his body lying nearly lifeless, isn't something you're okay with.

"He has a long road ahead of him," I admit honestly. "He's going to need your friendship now more than ever, but you all need to make sure you know it's okay if you aren't okay right now. What you saw today isn't something you can ever be prepared for. It's okay to want to talk about it with others, and it's okay if you are scared. Do you hear me?"

They all nod again, and one kid in particular locks eyes with me. "Is he going to die?"

"I hope not," I answer honestly again. "I can't make you any promises, and I won't. It's not fair to you all. He was breathing on his own still when they left though, and for right now, that is a good sign. Okay?"

"Okay," the same boy answers. "Thank you for helping him, for staying calm. His parents were freaking out."

"Seeing someone you love hurt like that is hard. You boys did the right thing getting him out of the pool though. If you hadn't, we would be having a different conversation. So you should be proud of your quick actions."

"We didn't want him to drown." The other boys shake their heads, and a red SUV pulls up, stopping in front of the neighbor's house.

"Oh my God, TJ, what happened?" the woman asks, as she gets out and rushes to us.

The boy who's been talking to me clears his throat. "It was so bad, Mom. Mitch jumped off his roof and he hit his head and neck on the ledge. He was barely breathing."

"Are you boys okay?" she asks, shifting instantly into calm and protective mom mode as soon as she hears the tone and break in her son's voice.

"We're worried about him," TJ responds, then looks to me.

His mom does the same and I clear my throat. "Mitch is on his way to the hospital with his parents. His injuries seemed pretty serious. I can't tell you what will happen, but you're going to want to inform the other boys' parents, and maybe reach out. Their family will need all the support they can get in the coming days and weeks."

"I will. I've already spoken to the moms of the boys here. We are going to head to the hospital and their parents will meet us there."

"Wonderful, they took him to Peace River General."

"Thank you." The mom nods her head and ushers the boys, still in their trunks with damp tee shirts on, to her car so they can be on their way.

"I hope they get good news..." I glance at Brandon and nod my head in agreement with him.

"Let's get back to the house, I need to decompress after that call."

We get back into the truck and make it halfway to the house before we are dispatched to another emergency. This time a home on fire, one person or pet, still possibly trapped inside.

We reroute and head toward the location of the house, and I confirm the address before saying to the guys, "Buckle up, fellas. I think we are in for a long, busy shift today."

# Eleven

## Everleigh

My sister has never been more demanding than she was today. She incessantly texted, called, snapped, and possibly even sent carrier pigeons to make sure I showed up here to meet her at exactly eleven o'clock. Never mind the fact I was supposed to be taking a yoga class today. Never mind the fact I was looking forward to a quiet morning getting ready for another twenty-four-hour shift at The Castle.

I walk through the doors into the bustling café and look all around for her. She's not at the counter, she's not at a table, she isn't out on the patio, Addie is nowhere to be seen, and my annoyance with her is climbing to Swiss Alps proportions.

I step to the side of the door and lean back against the wall, tucking myself into a little cranny so I'm out of the way of others who are coming, going, and actually meeting their friends, family, or dates here. Five minutes late turns to ten, and by the fifteen-minute mark, I'm pulling out my phone to call her. I hit speed dial two and wait, impatiently tapping my foot for her to answer.

"Yes?" she answers, voice too chipper, as though she hasn't a care in the world.

"Where the heck are you?" I hiss out, trying to keep my voice low enough to not draw attention to myself. "You made a huge deal over me being on time today and you aren't even here."

"Oh, yeah, about that—"

"About that? Addison!" I screech, drawing curious eyes, then turn my back and whisper this time, "why did you make me change all my plans this morning to meet you here when you aren't even coming?"

"Well," she basically sings, "you're meeting someone else. A blind date, if you will."

Red. That's all I can see. Flaming hot red.

"Excuse me? You set me up? On a blind date? And you didn't bother to tell me or even ask if it was okay?"

"It's not exactly blind," she says. "You know him. I just did you a teeny favor is all.

"What does that even mean, Addison?" In order to avoid more curious, watchy, judgy eyes, I step back around my little barrier and toward the door. I'm so distracted by my inconsiderate, annoying big sister I'm not watching where I'm going and I run into someone. "Oh my God, I'm so sorr—"

I look up at the person I ran into and nearly swallow my own tongue. Instead of doing the one thing I probably should, I hiss into my phone at my sister, "Addison Marshal, what did you do?"

"You couldn't take your eyes off him. I did you a favor, I saw how you two looked at each other when we got there Saturday night and I bid on him for you. Best money I ever spent too. Now stop being pissed at me and go enjoy your date. Love you. Bye."

She hangs up immediately and I'm left standing right in front of Liam, stunned, mouth hanging wide open, looking up into his amused, vivid eyes.

"Everleigh?" he questions, smiling down at me. "You seem like you're in a hurry, are you working today?"

"Nope, I was supposed to be meeting someone here, she bailed on me. How about you? Do you not work today?"

He shakes his head and lifts his hand to my elbow, gently guiding me back to the same corner I was standing in while l thought I was meeting Addison. His touch feels hot and sharp, as though his fingers are little sparklers igniting my skin. "I just got off a long, long shift. I'm meeting someone here, too." He clears his throat. "It's my auction date. I have no idea what she looks like, though. I only know her name is Leigh, and she has long, apparently brown hair now. Do you recognize anyone from the event?"

*God dammit, Addison. I'm going to kill you. Kill. You,* I vow to her silently, hoping she hears me with some weird, creepy telepathic power siblings sometimes have.

"I... No, we are the only two here from the gala. In fact," I pause and take a deep breath, preparing to spill the truth to him, feeling nerves and embarrassment overtaking me, "it seems my sister was your bidder."

"What do you mean?" His brows furrow, and deep ridges form in his forehead from his confusion.

"My sister told me I was meeting her here this morning. I was just on the phone with her when I ran into you. Apparently, she thought it was her duty to bid on a coffee date with you then pull the ol' bait and switch on me... And you. She was supposed to be who you met. Instead, she gave you one of my nicknames. And my hair color."

He still looks confused as he reaches up and rubs his neck. Now that the amusement has faded from his face, I can see how exhausted he looks, and it makes me feel even worse for Addie's stunt.

"So your sister bid on me, not so she could have a date with me, but so she could set us up? Am I getting that right?"

I nod my head and frown a little. "I'm really sorry. I don't know what came over her, but she had no right to put you, or me, on the spot like this."

"I'm not mad," he says, giving me another smile that threatens to knock me off my feet. "I'm surprised though. And a little slow on the uptake today. I didn't sleep more than an hour and a half last night."

"I'm so sorry. She was so headstrong and determined; she didn't stop to think about you, your plans, or even your life. You should go home and get some rest."

He glances around the café and asks quietly, "Have you been here before?"

"A time or two," I respond, glancing around. "They have good breakfast, pastries, and strong coffee."

His tired gaze shifts back to me and he tilts his head. "Do you have somewhere you'd rather be, or do you want to have a bite with me?"

"Seriously?"

He chuckles deep and low. "I did ask you for a coffee date on Saturday night. This isn't exactly how I imagined it going, but since we're both here…"

"I will totally accept a rain check, given the insane circumstances my sister has put us in. Go home and sleep. Really, I won't be offended. Plus, it'll give me time to go and kill her before my shift starts this afternoon."

His thumb grazes over my elbow before he pulls his hand away, and the sensation of losing that heat and pressure from his skin on mine is immediate, and unpleasant. "Let's grab a table and some food, and I can add fuel to your sister fire." He smirks, and this time, the twitch of his lips and the glow in his eyes are full and powerful.

"Dear God. Do I even want to know?" I shake my head, heart racing, thoughts of what Addison may have done making my hands clam up in anxious worry.

"It wasn't awful. Hindsight being what it is, now I'm glad she was so demanding."

"No, she wasn't."

"She was… apparently it runs in your family." His hand finds the small of my back this time as he leads me toward the hostess stand. "Once we get a table, I'll fill you in on every little detail of my call with the auction coordinator."

Somehow, I have a feeling I'm not going to like what he has to say, and I'm sure I'll be leaving here needing to call and yell at my sister.

But…

As far as secret, unplanned blind dates go...

Addison actually knocked it out of the park with this one.

# Liam

Never, in my wildest dreams, would I have imagined when I walked in at eleven this morning I would still be sitting here, in a café I've never been to before, talking to my date three hours later. I would've laughed if anyone had said today would be anything more than a contrived date for charity. Yet, it's been so much more than that.

The one woman I wanted to spend time with from Saturday night is the woman I've spent my whole afternoon with. I didn't even need our first cups of coffee to get my energy back up. Being here with Everleigh has done that all on its own. She's so full of life, humor, and smarts I could sit here talking to her for another three hours, if she could.

"So your day yesterday was long?" she has tried to segue to my work a few times, but I've tried to avoid it, mostly because I had no idea what to even say to her.

A phone call a few minutes ago changed that, though. Lieu called me to tell me the kid from yesterday morning pulled through his surgery today. He's going to survive, and there doesn't seem to be any permanent damage to his cord. "Yeah. It started with a teenaged kid who thought it was smart to jump off the roof of his house into their backyard swimming pool. Things only got worse from there."

Her eyes widen and she shakes her head. "This is why I am so glad to work at The Castle. Not that the older girls are much better, but they at least try not to pull off stupid stunts. They just sneak out and get caught trespassing where they shouldn't be." She rolls her eyes, but the fondness in her voice tells me no matter how frustrating the girls can be, she wouldn't change a single thing.

"The Castle?" I ask first then add slightly concerned, "Sneaking out? With a boy?"

"No, with friends she shouldn't have been with. We call it The Castle because we try to treat the girls like princesses when they come to us. They've experienced so much bad; they should get the chance to feel the way so many girls in normal homes do."

"I really love that," I admit, smiling. Kids who experience anything that would land them at The Castle deserve to feel special, like princesses, for a change.

Everleigh takes a drink of the water she switched to about an hour ago then asks, "What happened to the boy who jumped?"

"That's what my call was about, actually. My lieutenant was letting me know the kid pulled through his surgery this morning and they think he'll make a full recovery with time and rehab. He broke his neck and has a pretty serious concussion, but his spinal cord is okay, swelling has gone down since yesterday, and he was awake and talking."

"Wow. That's amazing. How did he do so much damage? Did he not land in the pool?"

"He did. He apparently cannonballed right into the pool, but his body tilted and he was so close to the ledge of the pool that when he hit water, his head and neck angled just enough he also hit the edge of the pool. His friends said he lost consciousness immediately. They saved his life. They got him out of the pool, and from what I've heard, one of the boys did CPR until the water came up."

"He was a hero." She smiles gently. "Kids do amazing things, stupid things too, but we don't give so many of them enough credit."

"I agree, there are some incredible kids out there." I can't help but think about him, how amazing and kind he was, how strong and brave... I have to shake the memories flooding my mind before she notices, but one look at her face tells me she knows I'm thinking of someone specifically.

"I get to work with them a lot," she says cautiously, "how about you?"

"Not as much as I'd like. I saw a ton while I was serving overseas. And I come across some great kids, like the ones from my shift yesterday, at times, too."

Her lips quirk up, and she has the most genuine expression of happiness and appreciation on her face. "I don't know if it's proper to say, but thank you for your service."

I take a moment to inhale then grin back to her. "Thank you for that. I never know how to respond to people saying it; I didn't back when I wore the uniform every day, either. But I appreciate your support."

"I always try to show it. I considered joining, back when I was in high school." She shrugs a shoulder and lifts her bottle to her mouth, taking a small drink.

"Why didn't you?"

"I was a chickenshit." She giggles, and I laugh loudly. "Not joining doesn't make you a chickenshit…"

"No, I know it doesn't. But I chose not to because I was afraid I'd actually see combat in some way and…"

She doesn't need to finish. It's a reality I know all too well. It's a reality so many of us know all too well. "I understand. I think what you're doing now is equally as important. Children like those you care for need strong, brave, and beautiful advocates like you."

The apples of her cheeks shine pink, and her eyes avert mine, focusing on the table and her hands instead. "I'm not brave."

I reach across the table carefully; slowly enough I don't scare her, and place my finger beneath her chin, tilting her head up so she's forced to see me. "You are. You're all of that. And more. Anyone who can save kids is a hero, Everleigh. You don't need a uniform, gun, or combat experience to fall into the category. Trust me."

"Thank you." She blinks a couple times and breathes in deep, then releases it with a nervous laugh. "I'm not used to so many compliments."

"Surely you're joking. Men, hell, other women and kids, too, must compliment you all the time."

She shakes her head, and I pull my finger back. "No? They're crazy. But men see you; they believe it and think it. I promise."

"I don't date often," she admits. "My time is dedicated to the kids, to working toward my promotion."

"You don't date often, meaning you don't hear how incredibly gorgeous you are enough?"

"I don't hear it at all." Her blush spreads farther down her face, into her neck, and she pulls her lip between her teeth.

"Well then, let me be the one to set you straight. You, Everleigh Marshal, are a beautiful, brave, and strong woman. And even if it isn't said, I'm not the only one who sees it."

"You aren't so bad, yourself, Liam," she says, clearly uncomfortable with the praise and trying to shift the focus back to me.

"Why, thank you." I act like I'm popping my nonexistent collar and readjust my sunglasses on the back of my head. "I try damn hard. I call this my just off shift chic look. I'm glad it's working for me."

She laughs at that and some of the uncomfortable embarrassment fades from her expression. "It definitely is." Her eyes slowly pass over me from head, to mid torso where the rest of my body is hidden by the table between us.

She's not doing much to hide her appraisal, but I don't mind. I would call it an honor to have a woman like her eyeing me, so who am I to call her out.

Her eyes climb back up my body and meet mine, and I can't help the satisfied smirk she's greeted with. "Can I ask you something?"

She nods her head wordlessly.

"Would you agree to go out with me again? I know you have to get to work soon, but I've really enjoyed talking to you."

"Do you mean a coffee date? Or… Like… A date date?"

*Definitely the latter.*

"You decide. I'd love to take you on a real date, but I won't push you into anything you aren't comfortable with."

She ponders, folding one hand over the other on the table, drawing that lip back between her teeth again. It's probably not a good sign, her taking so long, but I can't bring myself to speak up either. I'm afraid if I break the silence before she's ready, it'll persuade her to say no. But maybe, if I show my patience, she'll agree.

"Yes." It's all she says, but the second I take in the expression on her face, the wide grin and the happiness shining in her eyes, I know she's agreeing because she wants to, not because she feels forced.

"Are you sure?"

Her brow raises and she responds, "Are you trying to get me to reconsider?"

"What? No, not at all. Why?"

"Why are you asking if I'm sure?" she challenges.

"Well…" I think about that and have no good reason, so I shrug and continue, "I have no idea. I guess I just didn't want you to feel forced."

"I don't feel forced, Liam. I'd be happy to go on a real date with you. I may even dress up, not act so surprised to see you next time."

"At least we will both go into it with an open, happy mind. No surprises waiting for us."

She nods. "Exactly. I might tell my sister today was awful though. Just at first. It's been a lot of fun, but I still can't believe she set me… us… up. The brat."

My laugh is loud and vibrates up my chest. "Older sibling's prerogative."

"You speak like you have experience…"

"I do. I would have done the same thing to my younger brother." It's hard to say out loud, to admit what I know she's going to ask next.

"Would have?" she asks softly, quietly.

84

"Yeah. My brother died ten years ago."

To her credit, Everleigh doesn't give me that pitiful look I'm so used to getting... not right away at least. Instead she takes the information in, digests it; then looks at me with the sorrow that comes from a genuinely good, empathetic person. "I'm so sorry. I didn't... I wouldn't have said anything had I known."

"It's okay. I don't talk about him often, but he was amazing, brave. I was in Afghanistan when he died. So it's hard knowing I wasn't here for him."

"I can't even imagine." She reaches across the table and lays her hand over mine. "I'm sorry for your loss. And if you ever want to talk about him, I'd love to hear. But with my job, I know how hard it can be reliving and discussing those memories, so I will leave it up to you. *If*, or when, you ever want to talk about him, I'll be here to listen."

"I appreciate that." I look down at her hand, and she gives mine a gentle squeeze before pulling it back. "I should let you get to work. It's already pushing two now, you said your shift starts at four?"

"Today, yes. Usually I start around six, but I'm covering for another counselor for a few hours."

"That's nice of you." Her hand is no longer covering mine, but I can still feel the heated imprint of it over my skin.

"I love being there with the girls, so it's no bother." She starts piling our cup and plates up for our waitress to grab.

"I can handle these." I reach forward and busy myself with our pile of utensils, using the few moments to breathe and get past thoughts of my brother before returning my focus to her.

"I really enjoyed this," she says, slinging her purse over her head and across her body.

"Me, too." I push her chair in and let her walk in front of me toward the door. Instinctually I lower my hand to her back, guiding her and claiming her as with me to keep anyone from invading her space as we walk through the still bustling café.

Once we get outside, she steps to the left of the door and out of the way of incoming and outgoing traffic. The sun is bright and shining right in her eyes, causing her to shade herself with her hand until I step in front of her and block the sun with my body. "When would be the best time to go on our date?"

"I swear this isn't a gentle blowoff, but can I look at my schedule and see what nights I have free?"

"Yes, those are acceptable terms," I joke, "but only if you promise to let me pick you up for it."

"You drive a hard bargain."

"I'm a gentleman, I believe in door-to-door service." I smile down at her and the hitch in her breath is beyond evident with us being this close.

"I will agree to your terms, too." She steps closer and slowly opens herself up to me, offering an unexpected hug.

I step in and hug her back, careful not to squeeze too hard, or make it anything more than a friendly gesture, then step back. "I will text you later, see if we can find a night that works with both our schedules."

"I look forward to it," she responds, sounding honest and a little excited. "Thank you for today. It was the best, most unexpected blind date I've ever been on."

"Me, too. Drive safe going to work. Tell those girls no sneaking out tonight."

She giggles and nods. "I will. Go home and get some sleep, Liam. I'll text you later."

I watch her walk to her car, get in, and fiddle with her phone and belt before she eventually pulls away. For a day that started out shitty, full of exhaustion, irritation, and dread, today has turned into one of the best I've had in an incredibly long time.

# *Twelve*

## Everleigh

It's been nearly two weeks since our blind date at the coffee shop, and Liam and I haven't both had the same night off yet. If he's got a shift, I have a night off. If he has a night off, I've got a shift. Or, my favorite case, we both end up working or picking up extra shifts and our plans get derailed due to our jobs, and our obligations.

It's frustrating and exhausting.

Yet, there's something about the closeness we have achieved just talking and texting over the last two weeks that makes all the changes of plans, all the missed opportunities, worth it. With how attractive I find him, and knowing exactly what's waiting for me beneath his clothes—at least from his chest to his waist—I'm not sure I could deny my physical need for him if we had been together in person. Add a little bit of liquid courage to the equation, and I'd say the likelihood that I jump and climb him like a tree would be high.

Now, though, I actually know the man he is. Two weeks of nonstop texting, snapping, and phone calls have added a level of friendship I've never had with any other man I've ever been interested in before. It's nowhere near those connections before, during, or after any of our relationships.

We've covered all the menial topics that usually serve as first date small talk. We've also gotten into the fun stuff—the real interests and dreams—and the somewhat dirty stuff.

He's a brown-haired, blue-eyed former soldier who loves sparkling water and caffeinated sparkling water, who has the sweet tooth of all sweet teeth for Skittles and Jolly Ranchers, does not drink—ever—and loves nights out with friends at clubs, amusement venues and parks, or at sporting events. He hates school, but is planning on working toward a bachelor's degree in a field he could best utilize in his work.

I know he loves IndyCar, Colton Donavan is his favorite racer, and he was a pretty good football player in high school.

I know he believes in putting children first, protecting them at all costs, and having better programs in place to identify and help children in need, and children who may be in bad family situations who need a way out. It's why he did so much volunteering for the events this year. From the softball game, to the barbecue, even allowing himself to be auctioned off, it is a cause he fully believes in and supports. It helped, too, that it was split with fallen firefighters. He said he hasn't lost anyone here yet, but the bond they have as firefighters is the same type of bond he had with his fellow soldiers, and he's lost a few of them.

Liam Hayes is probably the best, kindest, most humorous, sexy man I've ever met and gotten to know. He's also the most mysterious. For everything I do know about him, there's an edge, and a deeper layer I haven't even come close to reaching yet, that I know is there and hidden from me. I can't push him, we haven't even gone out again yet, and we aren't together, though I think we are heading that way, and I have zero right to pry.

Just like he has no right to question some of the aspects of my life I have yet to share with him. I sense his are darker, more serious—he did serve in Afghanistan—but mine are still a part of me I don't know if I can trust him with yet. Mine will make me cautious with men, with letting them in, and with allowing them to get close to my girls.

"Hey, Everleigh," Haylie says, sticking her head into the kitchen at our palace. "Do you have a minute?"

I pull my hands out of the sink, and turn the faucet off, drying them on the cloth hanging from the oven handle. "Sure I do. What's on your mind?"

We walk over to the large dining table together and sit down in our normal seats. For as long as she has been here, Haylie has always taken the seat right beside mine. While we never assigned seats, most of the girls have always occupied their own spot, unspoken dibs around the table, and it's just where we all naturally return to now.

"How old were you when you had your first boyfriend?"

Her question throws me off, because it's the last thing I expected her to say, but I'm glad she feels comfortable enough to ask me. "I was sixteen."

She draws little invisible hearts over the tabletop and takes a few moments before she continues, "Was that a rule your parents set for you? Or was that the first time you noticed a guy?"

Her fidgeting and inability to look me in the eye is a good indication this has more to do with her own interest in a boy, rather than wanting to get to know me and my past, but I'll be open with her if it establishes further trust we can have between us. "It was a little of both. My dad really didn't want me, or my sister, dating. But she had already sort of blazed a trail for me since she was older, so he was laxer about me going out. But I didn't meet any guys I was really interested in until I was sixteen."

"Oh," she says in a low voice.

"Is there a reason you're asking?" I haven't had to get into these talks with my girls here, yet, and I want to approach and handle this with a gentleness and understanding that doesn't make her withdraw and hide from me or any of our counselors.

"Um, no, not really…" She doesn't sound all that convincing, and I know her well enough to be aware she doesn't do anything without reason.

"You sure about that? You can talk to me about anything. We may not always agree on everything, but I promise I will always listen with an open mind and caring heart."

She finally lifts her head, allowing me the first opportunity of this conversation to see the hesitation and worry on her face. "Would it be wrong for me to like a boy?"

"No, honey. It isn't wrong of you to like a boy."

"What if I, um, kind of wanted to do something with him?" She drops her hands into her lap and starts picking at her nail bed. It's a nervous habit for her. Her therapist told me she does it because the pain that comes from picking masks the stress she's feeling.

"Don't pick." I reach over and cover her hands with mine. "I'd want to know about him. Who he is, how old, where you met him."

"Does that mean I can go?"

"No, it means I want to make an informed decision, and I want to make sure you are safe. You just turned fifteen, and you are the most mature young woman I know, but I can't let you go out with anyone who I don't know or feel one-hundred-percent comfortable with."

"His name is Ty. He goes to my school, but we were hanging out at the pool the other day, when Josie took us. I think he might like me, too, and he asked if we could get ice cream sometime this summer, maybe go to the mall or a movie."

There is a slight tilt to her lips when she talks about him, and the glimmer in her eyes tells me she is really interested. "I'll tell you what. Invite him over here or to one of our outings when I'm working, and let me meet him and get to know him a little here, then we can discuss you going on a date with him. Okay?"

Her face falters a little, but to her credit, and a testament to her maturity, Haylie nods her head. "Okay. Promise me you won't decide for sure until after you've met him and given him a chance?"

"I promise, Haylie. I'm not saying no, not right now, I just want to meet him. Your safety, all you girls' safety, is my top priority. Does he know you live here?"

"He does. He knows a little bit of my story, but not all of it. Not yet. I'm being careful." She smiles knowingly at me. "Just like you always teach us."

"Good girl. I promise I will give him a chance before making any decisions."

"Thank you." She pushes out of her chair and starts to walk out of the kitchen.

"Hey, Haylie?" I call to her.

"Yeah?"

"I'm really proud of you for coming to me with this. I know it must've been hard and a little scary, but you were such a brave, mature young woman for doing it. That is something I will take into consideration when I decide about your date, too."

This earns me one of her million-megawatt grins that you can't help but return, then she bounces off down the hall toward the bedrooms.

*Lord help me. I am not ready for this.*

My phone vibrates in my pocket and I pull it out, answering with glee. "Hey, Hot Stuff."

His chuckle fills the line and I can almost feel the deep vibration in my own chest. "So that one's sticking, huh?"

"Well, you do work at a firehouse…" I state, very obviously.

"Babe, if you want to call me Hot Stuff, I'm perfectly fine with it." His term of endearment fills me with a warmth I never knew the word babe could. "Nothing has come up yet, right?"

"Nope." I check the spaghetti sauce with the meatballs and sausage simmering on the stove. "Josie will be here to take over at six, I brought my clothes to change into here. Nichole and Haylie are looking forward to helping me get ready for our date."

"Does that mean I should expect one of those teen trends when it comes to your makeup?"

I know he's teasing, but I can't help but think he might not like it if I did have a lot on. "I'm not sure what it would be. Are you not a fan?"

"I'm a fan. I love a beautiful woman who is made-up, or dressed-down and barefaced. I was just trying to imagine what two teenage girls might do."

His words cause a wave of calm to drown out the apprehension building in me. "Nichole is a makeup fanatic. She watches tutorials constantly. She'll make me look amazing."

"You don't need her to make you look amazing, Everleigh. You are already incredible, all on your own. I'm looking forward to seeing what she adds, though."

His words, the sincerity and seriousness in the tone of his voice, cause the riotous flutter of butterflies in my stomach. It may be a line; it may be a part of his game—if he has a game—but I love the things he says to me.

He's got this ease about him, a genuineness that makes me feel all sorts of things.

"I'm just looking forward to finally being able to see you tonight," I admit. "I love how much talking we've done, and I enjoyed coffee and pastries, but I'm really excited for what dinner and..."

"Nope, no hints," he says, amused at my attempt to get his plan out of him again.

"Ugh, so frustrating. What if I didn't bring the appropriate clothes for your secretive plan?"

"Whatever you wear will be perfect. I need to take a shower and get ready. I'll pick you up from your place at six thirty tonight. If that still works?"

"Six thirty it is. I'll see you later."

"Later, Everleigh." He hangs up almost instantly and I set the phone down on the counter, bracing myself with my hands against it and trying not to squeal in delight.

I might have an inkling as to what Haylie is feeling right now with her Ty, because honestly, I'm pretty sure I'm feeling the exact same thing with Liam.

\*\*\*\*

# Liam

Stunning. That's the only word I can think of that comes anywhere close to describing how Everleigh looks tonight. Her eyes are an even brighter, more vivid green than the first three times I saw her. Nichole did a damn fine job making the few colors around Everleigh's eyes neutral and understated, yet incredibly powerful and mesmerizing at the same time.

I've been staring into them across the table for the last hour, and I've yet to tire of it. She's held me captive with vivid smiles and loud, full laughs that make her emerald greens look like a color straight out of heaven's pearly gates.

"Okay, dinner is over. Do I get to know our plans for the rest of the night yet?" She moves a loose, curled strand of hair behind her ear and looks at me expectantly.

"I'm still undecided. I may tell you after we leave here though. Or maybe I'll wait until we get there and you can find out then."

"You are the world's most frustrating man," she huffs out, shaking her head. "I'm already out with you, you can't scare me off now. You're my ride."

It's my turn to laugh and draw the attention of other patrons here. "You think I'm afraid you're gonna bail when you find out what it is?"

She nods her head and takes another sip of her drink.

"I didn't plan anything that would scare you. I figured slow and easy was best for our first time."

Everleigh gasps around her straw and inhales quickly, triggering a round of strangling and coughing.

I rise and pat her on her back, taking the drink from her hand and setting it down on the table for her. "Are you okay?"

She nods and coughs for a few more seconds. "Yes, thank you." She coughs again and carefully rubs at her teared-up eyes. "You caught me off guard."

"How did I do that?" I didn't intend the innuendo to fall out so perfectly, and I didn't even catch it at first, but the second her eyes bulged and she started sputtering around her straw I realized what I said.

"You just… Your words…" She hides her face behind her hands and laughs nervously.

I can see the color starting to flush her cheeks around her fingers, and her neck is pinker than normal.

"My words, yes, I realize the… double entendre… I inadvertently used. I'm sorry."

She shakes her head back and forth and grins at me. "It's okay. I just wasn't expecting it. I know you mean our date, though. You aren't going to take me into a burning building and expect me to put it out or anything."

"Had I known it was an option, I probably would've considered it." I wink at her and sign the check when the waiter brings it and my card back out to me.

"Oh, it's not. At least, I don't think it is. I'm not sure how I would feel about fire and smoke. I'd be up for anything else though."

"Anything?" I ask, with a playful grin meant just for her on my face.

"Oh God. Can I take it back? Do I get a do-over?" She hides her face and laughs again, and it's the most angelic, euphoric sound I've ever heard.

"Nope, no do-overs. You're stuck with your answer. I'm going to capitalize on anything tonight, babe. You walked right into it."

She moans behind her hands; it's a sound that lodges itself into the forefront of my mind and sends a signal straight down my body to wake up and go on high alert. "But I didn't mean *anything*. Just… anything. Do you know what I mean?"

"No, I do not. I have absolutely no idea." I rise from my seat and hold a hand out to her. "Shall we get to doing anything and everything we want together?"

"Within reason, yes." She slides her hand into mine and I close my large, calloused fingers over her dainty, smooth ones.

"Fair enough."

We walk out of the restaurant and she tries to hang a left, heading back in the direction of my car, but I stop her and gently tug her to follow me going right.

"We aren't going back to my car yet."

"We aren't?" She looks back down the street toward the parking lot, and then at me. "Is this the part where you drag me off to a secluded place and have your way with me, then leave me for dead in an abandoned building?"

Her question has me coming to a stop and turning to face her, mouth agape, eyes wide in shock.

"Oh shit," she murmurs. "I said that out loud, didn't I?"

My head bounces up and down in affirmation, but I can't quite bring myself to close my dropped jaw.

"I'm so sorry. My imagination gets the best of me sometimes, and you seem too good to be true, so you have to be a serial killer." She shrugs a shoulder as if what she just said is the most normal thing on the planet.

"Do you frequently wonder if your dates are serial killers? Or is it just me?"

"It's not a you thing," she says, squeezing my hand within hers. For such tiny, fragile hands, she does have a strong grip. "It's me. I trust you, Liam."

"If that changes at any point, you can say no more."

"I'm in it for the long haul," she reassures me. "I really didn't mean to imply you pose a danger to me. I was trying to be funny. Clearly it fell flat."

"Next time, make sure your funny doesn't sound like kidnapping and murder," I respond on an exhale. "I'd feel less like a creeper."

"Yes, of course," she says more sheepishly this time, "it won't happen again."

"I think it will," I admit, pulling her closer to my side so we can walk with my arm around her shoulder. "You speak without fear and your mind works that way. Next time, though, I'll know to expect it not as an insult, but as another piece to the Everleigh puzzle."

Her hand slips around my lower back. "Next time? You mean me calling you a serial killer didn't scare you off?"

"Not yet. If you turn into a psycho at our next stop, though, I think the tides could turn and not in the right way."

"Smart thinking," she credits me. "I swear though, I trust you. It's really weird how much I trust you, in fact." She glances up at me while we're walking down the street with her lip tugged between her teeth again.

"Why's that?" I hold her tighter, closer, keeping her pressed into my side. I like having her here, at my side, in my arm, smiling up at me like I hung the moon, the stars, and everything else in the sky.

"Our conversations, your openness. I just have a good feeling when I'm with you. I don't have a better reason than that."

I halt us in the middle of the sidewalk and look down into her eyes, lowering my forehead to hers, and whispering, "You don't need one. I'll prove you right."

She doesn't pull away or back in even the slightest bit. Instead, she presses her head harder to mine and closes her eyes. "I believe you," she murmurs.

"If I leaned in to kiss you," I ask, angling my head slowly so our lips start to align, "would you stop me?"

Her breath is warm against my lips as the word spills past her, "No."

Her hand glides from my lower back, around my side, stopping on my midriff and flattening out over my abs, as our lips connect.

It's a gentle, tentative exploration of lips and comfort. Her fingers graze and grasp at me, my hand drops to her hip, holding her in place, and our mouths taste and move in the perfect, easy way. We could be the only two on the planet right now, not just two people blocking the sidewalk as they start to make out.

With some regret, remorse, and irritation I break away from her and take a deep breath. "We're going to a beach concert. No shoes, good music, dancing and talking beneath the moon and stars with the sound of the water licking and lapping at the shore."

"Liam…" she breathes out. "That sounds incredible."

"I hope it is."

"I'm sure it is," she says, wiping carefully at her lips then slipping her fingers back into my grasp. "Why a beach concert?"

"Because I heard you when you said the water calms you… I want you calm and at ease with me. I want you to know I hear you, and I respect you."

# *Thirteen*

## Everleigh

I f our first date was the perfect—yet unexpected—date, date two tonight is a rare occasion when the sequel is even better than the first. I got lost in conversation with him so easily at the café, but sitting here in the sand, on a quiet patch of beach we have all to ourselves, I'm finding it hard to focus on just the words this time, because the mere presence of him, strong and confident, careful and deliberate, is driving me crazy in the absolute best way possible.

He's so relaxed out here. He ran back to his truck and brought out a big enough blanket for both of us to sit on after we danced through the concert, he even carried my shoes for me so I could walk barefoot in the sand and feel the cool, grainy texture of it beneath my feet and between my toes.

"I don't come out here often," he breaks the silence between us, leaning back on his elbows with his legs outstretched and crossed at his ankles. "But I have to admit, this is pretty nice. I see why you love it."

"You really don't come out here much?" I can't imagine not visiting the beach as often as possible. It's my safe haven, my place of serenity.

"I don't. I'm not sure why, I loved it when I was a kid, but now, I'd usually rather have a relaxing night and a fire at home."

"Firebug?" I grin at him.

"Me?" He hangs his head back, looking up at the sky.

"Yeah, you. I've heard firefighters are firebugs. They like playing with the flames and starting them as much as they like putting them out."

His laugh is rich, full, and loud, and I know it's a sound nobody else could ever replicate. It's also a sound I'd love to hear over and over again. "No, I'm not really a firebug. I mean, yeah, I like a good bonfire or firepit, but I don't have the itch to watch things burn. Firefighting isn't my bread and butter at work, either."

"You prefer the medical aspect," I confirm, recalling one of our previous conversations. "Saving lives and making a difference is your favorite part of the job."

"Exactly." He shifts off his elbows and lies back flat on the blanket, tucking one arm beneath his head, and moving the other down to his side, between us, where I feel his fingers searching for mine before they clasp together.

I turn my palm up to his and adjust the grasp of our hands, then lie back beside him. "I like that your priority is helping people. We haven't talked much about your time in the military, or about your family; are those off-limits?"

His deep, heavy exhale tells me they are before he even manages to say anything, but I stay silent, wondering how he will answer.

"Yes and no. I don't like talking about family because talking about my brother is incredibly hard for me. I have very fond memories of our bond growing up though. As for the military, I'll talk about it. So often people don't want to know, they don't care, or they just don't know what to say so we all leave it be."

I know his brother passed, but I have no idea how or why. I'm sure he's lost others, too, because he was over in a war zone where anything could and probably did happen. "No family, got it. You said Brandon served with you. Is that where you two met?"

"Mhmm," he answers, brushing his thumb along my hand slowly. "He was a Colorado boy who ended up in basic with me. He was the only guy I didn't find irritating off the bat. We just got each other."

"He irritates you now, though," I point out and turn my head toward his, grinning.

"Ain't that the truth." Liam turns his head toward mine and has the cutest little smirk I have ever seen. "Now he's my brother. He irritates me, but he understands and knows me better than any other person on this planet. He's seen me through the worst days of my life, and made sure I came out of them still alive, mostly whole, and out of jail."

"Exactly what a sibling should be."

His reaction is immediate. His eyes go dark, his lips flatten into a tight line, and his body tenses beside me.

"I'm sorry, Liam," I roll onto my side. "I didn't mean to upset you. Not at all."

His hand is still in mine, and my anxiety has me lifting his up so I can wrap both hands around it, careful not to lose my balance on my side and fall into him. "I should've chosen my words more carefully."

Liam curls his arm in, pulling me to fall into him so I'm landing on his chest, and then his arm slips beneath me and wraps around my body. "No, I'm sorry. I was just thinking about my little brother..." His hand stops on my hip and his fingers splayed take up a good chunk of my ass.

"How can I make it up to you?" I lick my lips and smile at him, wanting to lighten the mood, and feeling incredibly drawn to him—I have the urge to soothe and distract—wanting to get closer.

"I could suggest an idea or two," he whispers, breath hitching when I lay my hand over his chest, "but I think you have an idea or two of your own already…"

I nod my head and lean in closer. "You asked last time. This time, it's my turn…"

He angles his face down, leaning in just enough that I don't have to go far before I'm caressing his lips with my own. They're shockingly soft, and full, and he uses them quite proficiently to tease and tempt me to deepen this connection.

One suck and tug of my lower lip turns into me swiping his with my tongue, seeking access as though it is the password to open his sealed lips.

I dip past his parted lips the second they open and brush my tongue over his, drawing out a deep, appreciative groan from the back of his throat. His mouth tastes of peppermint disks and lemonade, and his tongue twists and tangles with mine urgently, as though he won't survive if the kiss ends too soon.

He uses our position—his arm around my hip—to roll us with effortless ease as he presses me to my back, his body now hovering over mine, as he takes control of the kiss.

I'm not sure how long it lasts before his mouth breaks away from mine, then blazes a warm, tender trail along my jaw to my neck where he buries his face in, kissing the sensitive skin there and inhaling.

"You are intoxicating, Everleigh." He nuzzles into my neck then nibbles playfully. His breath is warm against me, sending a shiver along my spine and causing goosebumps to erupt over my arms from his proximity and words.

"You're not so bad yourself," I whisper, moving my fingers up the contours of his back. His body is heavy over me, but it's the kind of weight that calms and soothes, like he's a weighted blanket designed solely for me, my comfort, my calm.

He kisses back up my jaw then presses his lips to mine in a quick, chaste peck. "I could do that all night, but I brought you out here to watch the sunset together, and if we keep going, we'll miss it."

"We can't have that," I sigh out, then slide my fingers down his triceps and the back of his forearm, looking up at him with what I'm sure is a crazy, stupid giddy smile.

His head moves side to side slowly, and he beams down at me. "That won't be the last time I kiss you, just so you know."

"I'm glad." I lift my head quickly and kiss him with a smack. "Look, I already proved you right."

He chortles and pushes himself up to his knees, where he is towering over me. "From this angle, you look insanely sexy." His eyes rake over my body, over my disheveled dress and my messy, windblown hair fanned out over the blanket and beach beneath me. I can't look very good, I know how the beach and wind wreak havoc, yet in his eyes right this second, I see me as he does— sexy and content—all because of him.

I don't know how to respond though, so I do what comes most naturally. The heat from my discomfort crawls up my cheeks and I turn my head to the side, taking in the stretch of empty beach to the right of us.

"Don't hide from me, babe. You have nothing to be ashamed of." He holds his hand out and when I place mine in his, he pulls me to sit. "I haven't gotten anywhere near enough of you, yet."

I'm not sure what he means by that, until he moves so he's behind me, then he sits with his legs stretched out and wide, leaving a space between them for me.

Derailed

"That looks like the most inviting seat I've ever been offered." I comb my fingers through my hair quickly then shuffle backward until my back meets his front. I fit so perfectly against him it's like he was made just for me.

Once I'm settled, I feel the gentle touch of his hand carefully moving my hair off my shoulder, then being draped around the back so it all hangs over the other side. With that, he has perfect access to my shoulder and neck, and the warm stubble of his five o'clock shadow brushes over my skin, settling in the crook between my neck and shoulder.

"The sunset is beautiful," he murmurs, "but it doesn't hold a candle to the woman I'm here with tonight."

In lieu of a verbal response, I snuggle back closer to him and move my hands over his thick, powerful thighs covered by his long, khaki shorts. I give him a gentle squeeze and exhale contently. "Thank you for bringing me here tonight. I'm glad I get to share it with you."

\*\*\*\*

# Liam

The sun's reflection as it sank lower and lower over the ocean, the purple hue, and orangish red glow of the sun dancing across the deep blue ocean, the sound of the tide rolling in, and waves crashing against the pier not far away from where we were snuggled up set the perfect scene for the single most romantic and exhilarating date of my life.

I didn't need a bar, a bowling alley, or an amusement park. I didn't need an action-packed movie or a comedy to keep us upbeat and laughing for two hours. I didn't need a single thing other than her leaning back against me, body warm and small, fitting so perfectly with my own it was like she was literally made to be a part of me.

I needed nothing more than our hushed conversation, the flirtatious touches, or the memory of not one, but countless earth-shattering kisses from the moment we sat, to the moment we landed right where we are now, at her front door.

Her cheeks are rosy and windburned, her hair is a windblown mess, and she looks incredible. The porch light is casting a soft glow over her face, and her green eyes are bright and gleaming at me. "Did you want to come in for a drink?"

"I don't drink." I slide my hands around her lower back.

"I know," she says, wrapping her arms around my torso. "I have sparkling water, in many flavors. I thought I'd try it after you told me how much you love it."

Fucking hell, this woman is incredible. She's kind and intelligent, funny, quick on her toes, and thoughtful. And someone who I would love to spend even more time with… Tonight and as often as I can until whatever this is fizzles out or grows stronger. "I'd love to come in for a drink. Thank you."

She lets go of me to raise her purse and fishes her keys out of it, opening the door to her small, quaint one-story home. When we step inside, I'm met immediately with a fresh, citrusy, watery spring smell that reminds me of days off exploring with my brother when we were kids. It's pleasant, a little stronger than subtle, and not overpowering at all.

She flicks a light on, allowing me to take in every inch of her living room with its neutral-colored couch and chairs—which all look fluffy, soft, and large—that complement the light wood flooring, bright white walls, and artwork and pictures hung all over. The kitchen is visible with its spacious layout and marbled counters, and her refrigerator seems far too big for such a small, perfect woman.

"Make yourself at home," she says, looking around. "It's not a lot, but it's all mine."

"It's great," I respond, stepping over to look at a black-and-white photo hanging on the wall. "Who's this?"

"My sister. The one you were supposed to have the first date with."

I hear her footsteps coming up behind me, so I wait until she's by my side to speak again, "No offense to your sister, but I'm glad she set us up instead."

"Are you saying she isn't attractive?" Her voice is loud, clipped, angry.

"Shit, Everleigh, no, that's not it at all," I turn to her, already continuing on, "it's just that I really like—" When I take in the shit-eating grin spread over her face, I let out a relieved sigh. "You little shit. You're going to pay for that…"

Her eyes widen and her head starts shaking. "I am not."

"Oh, yes, you are." I turn on her fully, lifting my hands and smiling sardonically. "You better run while you can, Miss Marshal. I will show no mercy to the woman who thinks she can give me a heart attack like that."

She jumps backward—at the same time I lunge forward—and squeals. "No, no. You wouldn't. Don't you dare."

I start wiggling my fingers and moving toward her as she retreats, using the couch and coffee table to distance us. "You aren't going to be able to escape me."

She swallows hard, and her eyes scan every possible escape. While she looks, I track and see no matter where she tries to go, I will easily be able to cover and stop her.

"Try to get away, I dare you," I goad, feigning going right to force her left. She bites, and starts to creep to my left as I'm shifted onto my right foot. It's exactly what I wanted though, as I push off the balls of my foot and converge on her before she has any idea what is happening. She tries in vain to run away, but she can't. I easily wrap her up in my arms, using my fingers to tickle and torture her, careful to dodge the violent shakes from her loud laughs as she tosses her head back. My fingers don't stop their attack, not when she starts wiggling back against me, not when I know she feels my arousal as acutely as I do.

I don't give up until she calls out between loud cackles, "Uncle! Uncle! I give. You win."

The second the words fall from her lips, I stop my ticklish torture and wrap her even tighter, holding us both upright while we laugh together.

"Oh my God," she breathes out heavily. "I can't believe you actually did that."

The amusement and lightness in her voice makes me smile like a fool. I can't believe I did, either. I don't regret it though. For the first time in all my adult life I felt like a kid again for a few brief minutes, and I owe it all to her. "You were asking for it."

"No, sir." She giggles a little more and lays her arms over mine, leaning back against me. "You were the one who basically called my sister an ugly duckling."

"I did no such thing." I kiss the back of her head; the remnants of the ocean mist making her hair smell stronger of salt and shampoo. "I just said I'm grateful you were the one I met. I'll stand by that until the day I die, too."

She turns in my arms and her expressive eyes twinkle up at me. "I'm glad she set us up, too."

Everleigh pushes up on her toes and steals another kiss, as though we've been together for an eternity, and not just on two dates.

"Careful," I warn her. "I want to respect this being our first real date, and keep things light and easy. If you keep kissing me like that, wiggling against me…"

"Sorry," she giggles then steps back from my embrace. "Why don't I get us some drinks so we can talk a while longer?"

"That sounds like a great plan to me."

"Perfect, I'll be right back, then." She strides past me and into the kitchen, allowing me a moment of privacy to readjust and hide further proof of how much I like her. "What flavor do you want?" she calls from behind the refrigerator door.

"Surprise me!"

"Okay then," she calls back out, "make yourself at home."

I step up to another picture and immediately recognize a few of the girls from her castle. They all have their arms wrapped around Everleigh, and the happiness and love between them is apparent in the gleeful looks on all their faces.

None of it surprises me, though. We've been on two dates, and we've spoken daily for two weeks, and in that time, I've learned when it comes to Everleigh, she is so much more than meets the eye.

Everleigh Marshal is the type of woman who loves hard, fights harder for those she loves, and gives everyone else in her life her all.

Everleigh Marshal is the once in a lifetime catch any man, woman, or child in the world would be more than lucky to have in their corner.

I just hope I can keep her in mine for a while.

# Fourteen

## Liam

W hat is that stupid, shit-eating grin on your ugly mug about?" Brandon asks, dropping down onto the couch beside me. We're on another shift together, and the fucker knows I had a date last night, so he's fishing.

"Not a damn thing." I raise my eyes, challenging him to question me again, and he bellows out an irritating laugh.

"Clearly you didn't get laid, so... why the hell do you look like you did?" He flips his hat backward on his head and leans forward, bracing his arms on his legs, turning his head just enough to give me an annoying side-eye.

"Does Jess have you on the couch or something? Why the hell do you care so much about whether I'm getting screwed? Unless you aren't. Do you need to live vicariously through me? Has your sex life with your wife dried up already?"

"I will beat the shit out of you," he threatens, and I double down on my grin.

"I'd really like to see you try," I taunt, knowing I've hit my mark and gotten under his skin as much as he was trying to get under mine. It really pays off working with your best friend, and having lived with him both in barracks and in the middle of a war zone. He can't pull shit on me without me being able to return the favor.

"Jess and I are absofuckinglutely great, thank you. This has nothing to do with me getting laid, and everything to do with you not. What happened last night that has you smiling like a well-fucked man, when the attitude and tone you have is that of a man yanking his own chain?"

"Christ, you're a fucker. No, I didn't fuck Everleigh last night. I didn't want to. Me, Bro. Not her. I made the decision early on the night wasn't going to end that way."

"Why the hell would you do that?"

"She's too good to be the love 'em and leave 'em type." I shrug. "We had a great night. Dinner, trip to the beach, drinks at her place after…"

"Yet you didn't get freaky?" His eyes are wide enough I'm afraid they may actually pop out of his head.

I shake my head and roll my own eyes. "Contrary to what you clearly believe, I am not a horn dog. I can control myself, especially when it comes to an incredible, respectable woman."

"Who are you and what have you done with the real Liam?"

"You're looking at him. Listen, there are women who you hang with because they are the fuck buddy type. I can think of a few women at the gym I could have gone there with. The offers were there. Everleigh is not that type of woman though. I actually like that about her. She's different. She's better than that."

"Someone cut your dick off and replaced it with a pussy. I'm certain of it. Do you hear what you're saying? You're the man who swore he'd never settle enough to really date. You're the one who vowed not to go down the relationship and marriage hole with the kids and a white picket fence waiting for you on the other side." He's reminding me of the words I've sworn over and over. I could never, ever subject a kid to the shit I experienced. And I refuse to be the type of man who causes any harm to a child. It's easier to avoid it all than risk taking the chance. But fuck me, little Everleighs and mini-mes running around would be quite the sight.

*No. Shut that down now, Liam. Do not go there.*

"Slow the fuck down, B." I reach over and grab my piping hot cup of coffee from the end table beside the couch we are occupying, and take a slow, careful drink, clearing my head of my own runaway thoughts. "We aren't talking marriage and kids. We are talking a possible girlfriend, consistent dates, and company. We are talking sex on the regular with one person and plenty of condoms."

"That's what we all say, man. Just know when you step into the world of commitment, you lose control of things. Decisions fall on both of you, and before you know it, that shit turns into shared bathroom space, then exchanging keys." He pauses to make a face and shiver in disgust in an overexaggerated fashion. "Then she's overtaken your whole fucking home. Half the shit in your closet will be her clothes, your bathroom will have all that girly shit that will send you running, and then talks go from where should we go on our next date to, if we start planning and saving now, we can buy our dream house for our twenty kids to grow up in within five years." He stands and starts pacing in front of our flat-screen TV. His words, his reaction, and the fact he looks like he's seen a ghost has me thinking we aren't talking about me and Everleigh anymore.

"Whoa. That was a large leap from dating steadily to twenty kids. We will address the number later. What the hell is going on with you, though?"

He stops in the middle of the floor and looks at me with his hands on his hips and the most serious expression I have ever seen Brandon have in all the years we have known each other. "Jess is pregnant."

"Fuckin' A man! Congratulations!" I push up off the couch and go to congratulate him when he shakes his head.

"No, dude. I'm not done yet. She's pregnant with twins…" He looks up at me and all the color is drained from his face. "One fucking kid is scary enough. Now I have two little ones on the way and I don't know what the fuck I'm going to do. Our house was meant for a family of three, Liam. Three fucking people. In roughly seven months, we will have four people."

He starts to pace back and forth again, and I watch him with a smile plastered on my face. "You were the one who always boasted you would never shoot blanks, and you'd always hit your target. It was the same in Afghanistan, too. You were too strong, too determined to be any other way. Sounds like your dick has the same mentality."

Brandon stops pacing long enough to glare me down. "Not funny. You heard what I said, right? We are having twins. Two babies. Two constantly crying, shit-making machines."

This time I have to laugh. He is really freaking out and I love it. If Jess knocked him down a peg or two, these babies have knocked him off and put him on his ass. "I heard you. You aren't going to be raising them alone, jackass. Jess will show you how it's done."

"She'll have to do it all alone. Remember the house I told you to be prepared for? Yeah, she told me last night we need to start saving so we can move. We have to fucking move already, Liam. And the kids haven't even been born yet. But she says the four of us will outgrow our home too fast. There isn't enough room for two adults and two energetic toddlers. We need something bigger, with a yard. And more bedrooms."

At this rate, I think he may actually start to hyperventilate soon. It's hilarious, and I'm also worried he may have a coronary on top of it, leaving his wife and two children way too early. "Calm the fuck dow—"

Before I can finish the tones start going off, with dispatch sending us out to a possible domestic with an injured woman, child in the house, and a potentially dangerous situation.

Brandon and I both stop instantly and our focus and drives shift. Forgotten are his worries about his incoming twins, a new house, and being scared shitless of fatherhood. Forgotten is my relationship with Everleigh.

Instead, we are both solely thinking about the situation we may be walking into. Domestic is something I don't take lightly. None of us do. But Brandon knows there is an added layer for me. These types of calls are personal, and they send me into overdrive.

Without another word, we move perfectly. We head out toward the trucks and ambulance, and we get the equipment we need so we can get to the call as soon as possible.

Today, I'm on the ambulance. As the senior medic on the fire truck, when one of our other paramedics is out, I shift over and work the medical calls while someone else covers me on the truck. It's easier than bringing a brand-new paramedic on shift, and it allows us to keep things as fluid as possible.

When calls come in, we move on autopilot, preparing physically with little to no thought. Mentally, we all go through different things.

I climb into the passenger seat of the ambulance and give the go-ahead that I'm ready to leave. During the drive from the firehouse is when memories replay in my head for calls like this. Fists landing, words slicing and dicing, the smell of alcohol and hatred permeating the air are as vivid and strong as they were back then. The punches land, the words cut just as powerfully as they did fifteen, twenty years ago.

We pull up to the house and the second I'm out of the truck, my mind shifts again. No longer is the little boy or teenager occupying my subconscious. Now it's the man who vowed to make a difference, to save as many lives as he can.

Given the circumstances of the call, we aren't cleared to go in until the cops have the situation under control. They walk the wife-beating piece of shit out of the house, past us in cuffs. There is a special place in hell for the man, and the second our eyes lock; I do everything I can to convey that thought to him. Lieu walks over to the officer on scene and gets the rundown, then gives us the thumbs-up. We grab our kits and head into the house.

It's a scene you can never fully prepare yourself for, no matter how many times you see it or experience it.

We walk into the home and find a woman, beaten and unconscious, lying on the floor. The trauma she experienced is clear before we even get to her, kneeling beside her to check her vitals. Not long after Derek—my partner for the day—and I step in, Brandon and the guys from the truck follow behind us.

"Fuck," I hear Brandon mutter.

I nod my head and continue to work on the woman, until one of the cops calls for our attention. "Can one of you come check on this little girl?" he asks.

115

My head immediately shoots up and I scan the room. Sure enough, there is a terrified little girl rocking back and forth, tears streaming silently down her cheeks. She looks like she's in shock.

"I've got it," I say to no one in particular, yet to everyone in the room. I rise and pull my gloves off then approach her slowly. She shrinks back into the couch, eyes darting between the cop and me. I recognize the look on her face.

I recognize the terror and the worry in her expression, and I slow my steps down. "Hi there," I say in the calmest, softest voice I can manage. "I'm Liam." I don't want to approach her too quickly. She's in shock and she probably doesn't trust any of us right now. "Can I come talk to you? I promise I won't hurt you. I just want to talk."

She nods her head the slightest bit, and watches me with pinpoint focus. The closer I get to her, the slower I move, and as soon as I'm able, I drop down to her level, crouching and inching forward on the balls of my feet so we are eye to eye, and she knows I'm not coming at her in an aggressive, dangerous way.

"Hi, Little One," I nearly coo. "Can I talk to you and make sure you are okay?"

She doesn't speak, not that I expected her to, so I tug at the button on my lower leg pocket and slide my hand down into it, reaching for one thing in particular. It is full of necessary things like tape, gloves, random stickers, and the one thing I need most right now.

I pull out a small, blue bottle of mini bubbles. They're my secret weapon with young, scared kids. "I love bubbles," I tell her, then untwist the cap and pull the handle out, blowing a wave of small bubbles up in the air.

I glance her way and she's looking up at the bubbles with an incredibly small smile and her body looks tense.

Just this small sign of encouragement from her has me blowing another round, this time at her eye level. "Quick, try to pop them before they hit the floor."

The little girl follows my directions and reaches forward carefully, poking at the bubbles with her tiny, extended finger. She pops a few and then looks toward me again, full attention on the bubbles in my hand.

"Would you like to try blowing them?" I ask.

She nods her head and I hand her the little bottle.

"Hayes," my lieutenant addresses me, causing me to look back over my shoulder at him.

"Yeah, Lieu?"

"Is she okay?" He starts to walk our way and I shake my head, warning him against it.

"I think so. She hasn't let me get a good look yet, but I think we are becoming fast friends over my bubbles, so she may settle enough."

He nods his head and watches over her mom. "We need to roll; Mom needs care fast."

I turn back to the little girl, and she lowers the bubbles to look at me. "Do you think you can tell me your name?" I ask her, slowly putting a fresh pair of gloves on.

She whispers so quietly I'm straining to hear her, but in the sweetest, softest voice she informs me, "I'm Sky."

"Hi, Sky. Do you remember my name is Liam?" I smile again when she confirms remembering my name, and point to the bubbles. "Do you like those?"

She nods her head.

"I do too. Do you think we can blow these in my ambulance?" I scoot a little closer to her and carefully look over her small body, checking for visible bruises or lacerations while she blows another round of bubbles out.

"Okay," she agrees, just as quietly.

"Is it okay if I carry you out there?" I wait patiently for her answer before reaching for her, but as soon as she nods her head, I lift her into my arms and make sure I'm holding her in a way I can shield her from all evidence of the trauma her mom suffered.

I cross the room, successfully navigating around evidence the cops need untouched, and carry her out to my ambulance. Her mom is being loaded into the additional ambulance that showed up on scene, allowing me to load Sky in the back of mine. I get her down on the gurney and encourage her to blow more bubbles. "I'm going to buckle you in so you can't get hurt while we go for a ride," I tell her, making sure she understands before pulling the strap over her small frame.

Once she is secured, I let Derek know we are ready to pull out and follow her mom to the hospital. Doctors are going to want to get a good look at Sky. I didn't notice anything of concern on first glance, but it's too soon to tell if there are any other marks I can't see.

By the time we arrive at the hospital ten minutes later, Sky has opened up to me, but the second the back doors open, and nurses and doctors appear, along with a cop, she withdraws again, pulling her legs tight to her body, posture stiff and terror written across her face again.

"Hey, Little One," I say softly, "don't worry. These guys are all my friends. Can they help you and play with your bubbles too?"

Sky looks from me to them then shakes her head no.

"Okay. Can I carry you inside?" I glance at everyone else, watching as each of them takes a step back so she doesn't feel trapped or vulnerable.

"Okay," she whispers.

I slowly unstrap her and hold out my arms. "Ready for a bouncy ride into the big, fun hospital?" No part of a hospital is fun, but with bubbles and hopefully a couple toys, we can keep her less fearful.

She nods her head and I lift her up, careful not to bump either of our heads while I step out and follow a nurse back to a private room.

"Hey, Sky?" I ask when I set her on her bed. "Can I put this little red light on your finger so we can make sure your heart is strong and loud?"

She looks scared at first, so I grab an extra pulse ox strip and slip it over my finger. "Look up there, you can see my heart first."

She looks up and watches the lines move, and the numbers register. The nurse watches silently too, waiting for Sky to agree.

After watching for a few seconds, Sky holds her finger up just like I am, allowing the nurse to slip the small sticky strip over her index finger.

"You did so good. Do you want to keep blowing your bubbles?" I ask.

Sky nods her head and holds out the bottle for me to open. Once I do, I hand it back to her and explain to the nurse that Sky and I like blowing bubbles.

The nurse says she does too, and asks if she can play, but Sky shakes her off and scoots closer to the edge of the bed, closer to me.

"She's comfortable with you," the nurse says, watching Sky closely. "Has she spoken to you yet?"

I nod my affirmation and her expression turns pensive. "They're probably going to want you to stay with her until social workers can come in, same with cops. You've established a rapport, and it's important. I'll have one of our docs call your boss; let him know we need you. Is that okay?"

I glance down at Sky, who is sitting as close to me and the edge of the bed as she can, then look at the nurse. "I'm good with that. We'll keep playing with our bubbles."

"I'll go let the doc know, give him a heads-up about this little cutie pie." She walks out of the room and I pull a chair over so I can sit down beside Sky.

"Can you scoot into the middle of the bed for me?" I ask, smiling. "I don't want you to fall and get an owie."

She takes my direction, scooting away from the edge then blows bubbles at me. I start trying to pop them and catch them, being as upbeat and silly as I can, trying to make her laugh. This girl has had one of the most traumatic days anyone can go through, but to be her age and go through it is unspeakably awful. If I can help her in any way, I will. Even if I have to stay here all night.

\*\*\*\*

# Everleigh

One of the worst parts of my job is when I'm called and asked to go to a hospital because a child is in need of our services, and their parents are unable to care for them. I'm not sure what the circumstances are tonight, but I do know there is a young girl, six years old, who is sitting in the emergency room and needs to be placed for tonight and the foreseeable future. There is no indication of family yet, and there is no need for her to be held over in the hospital.

I glance at my watch, seeing it's already eight o'clock; then I clip my Corporate Cares badge into place as I approach the check-in desk.

A young girl, likely a CNA or an MA is sitting there, clicking away at the computer. "Please take a clipboard, fill out the information, then bring it back, I'll get you checked in then," she repeats, nearly robotically.

"Actually," I correct her, "I'm here from Corporate Cares. I was called in for a child placement. I just need to be buzzed in."

The girl looks up and sees my badge then she nods quickly. "I'm so sorry, you can go right on in."

"It's okay," I say, cutting her slack because I'm sure she would rather not be spending her Friday night working the admit desk in the emergency department. When the door buzzes, I step forward quickly and pull it open before it can relock, then I walk in to the familiar hospital.

I've come here too many times in my career already, and I have experienced this for family, sick and hurt, enough in the course of my life it's not foreign to me at all.

I approach the nurses' desk and clear my throat, "Hello, I'm Everleigh Marshal, I'm from Corporate Cares. Your social worker called me in for a young girl, Sky Adams. Can you direct me to her room and let your social worker know I'm here?"

The nurse looks up and smiles. "Absolutely. Sky is in room ten. She's quiet, but has opened up as long as her new friend is in the room with her."

"Okay, thank you."

I go to walk away, but another nurse chimes in quietly, "He's quite the friend. He's been here since they brought the little girl and her mom in this afternoon. She won't let him leave. We've all fought over who can go in to check on them because he's quite the looker, and watching him with her is…"

"Everything," the first nurse supplies. "They're adorable together. Don't be surprised if she doesn't trust you right away though."

"Noted," I say, smiling. "Thank you, ladies." This time I do walk away, chuckling to myself. I can only imagine what the man looks like to have the nurses so twitterpated, I just hope he has a good personality and is helpful to go along with his supposed good looks.

When I get to room ten, I pull out my own magical tool I use with scared kids from my purse, then knock on the door and push it open. "Is this Sky's room? I hear she is such a fun little girl, and she might like bubbles."

Before I fully walk through the door, I blow some big bubbles so they fill the room before I do.

"Look at that," the distinctly familiar male voice says, a hint of amusement lacing his words, "more bubbles! And they're even bigger than ours."

A small, delicate giggle follows his exclamation, and I step in blowing even more bubbles. As soon as I look up and across the small room, my steps falter and the bubbles stop mid blow. "Liam?"

"Everleigh?" He looks as stunned as I am, and for the briefest moment, I forget I'm walking into a hospital room to take custody of a scared little girl. Instead, all I see is him. His smiling face, his relaxed posture in the chair he's seated in beside the little girl's bed. His uniform.

He's clean-shaven with it on, too, and his hair is neatly done with gel and whatever other product he uses to keep it in place.

He is sexy as sin in that uniform. And under any other circumstance, I might attack him, claim his lips, and every other part of him I could before I let him go.

I can't do that though. I have to focus. So I clear my head then shift my smile from him to the tiny, brown-haired little girl sitting in the giant hospital bed beside him. "Hi! I'm Everleigh. Are you Sky?"

She looks from me, to Liam, and doesn't give me another glance until he nods his head.

With his encouragement, she turns back to me and nods hesitantly.

"It's so nice to meet you," I tell her. "It looks like you and Liam were already blowing bubbles in here. Do you think I could blow more of mine with you too?"

Sky agrees silently again, and I approach slowly, blowing my own big bubbles. I could stay on the side of the bed opposite Liam, but I don't want her feeling surrounded, and I wouldn't mind feeling some of his confidence right now. Maybe we can present a united front and a friendship, which will allow Sky and I to bond quicker.

Liam smiles up at me the second I step beside him, and I return one of my own. "Sky, this is my really good friend, Everleigh," he says, winking at me and then turning his attention back to her. "Do you think she could sit with us for a while and get to know you like I have?"

Sky ponders and then says quietly, "Okay." She glances at my bigger bottle of bubbles, then at her small one. "Can I play with your bubbles?"

Her talking to me to ask for bubbles is huge, and I hand them over without hesitation. "Liam's are too small, huh?"

"Hey!" he says in mock offense. "My bubbles are not too small. They're fun-sized."

"Is that what you tell all the ladies?" I mutter very, very quietly beneath my breath.

This makes Liam laugh, and Sky looks between us, cracking a small grin of her own as a result of his loud, surprising laugh. "Oh, Everleigh…" He shakes his head and smirks at me. "Sky, do you think you can tell Everleigh how old you are and what your favorite color is? I think you might both like the same one."

Sky's eyes widen in delight.

"My favorite color is purple," I tell her first, knowing hers must be the same because Liam and I just talked about colors the other day.

"Me too!" she says excitedly. "Then blue. Blue is my next favorite, just like Liam. Right?"

"That's right, Little One," he agrees.

"Blue is fun," I agree, "but I think my second favorite is probably green."

Sky's nose crinkles and she makes a disgusted face. "No way," she says so animatedly I would almost think she's a teen and not a young girl. "Green is not cool."

Liam laughs, and I grin wide. This is the kind of interaction and response I want with kids. If she is warmed up to me, it gives us some of a foundation when I get her to The Castle and introduce her to the girls and our other counselors.

"How old are you, Sky?" I know her age, but it helps if she can answer the simple, mundane questions honestly and without fear.

"I'm six," she informs me.

"Wow! You're such a big girl." I lean forward on the bed. "Do you think you could keep blowing bubbles and show me and Liam how big and brave you are while we step outside the door to talk really fast?"

She goes still and looks at both of us. I can see the panic starting, but Liam speaks right up, "You can do it, Little One. We will be right outside that door, and we'll leave it open so you can see us and we can hear you. Okay?"

The man is a godsend, because Sky agrees hesitantly.

I walk out of the room and hear him pushing out of his chair and following behind me. As soon as we are through the door, I step far enough away Sky can't hear us, but staying close enough keep his word. "You were on the call today?" I ask, confirming the obvious.

"I was." He exhales a long, deep sigh. "It was bad. Her mom is… I can't believe she's still alive, Ev. Sky had to have seen it all."

I drop my head and shake it sadly. "I hate these cases. I've had a few and they never get easier. Did her dad do it?"

"Yeah," Liam answers, then slips his finger beneath my chin and raises my head slowly so I'm forced to look into his eyes. "I'm glad you're here tonight."

His finger is warm beneath my chin, and his smile has the butterflies rioting in my stomach again. Those damn flutters are impossible to ignore.

"I'm glad you're here, too; I'm glad you were there for her today." I step closer to him, and reach out just enough to graze my hand down his shirt. I'd give almost anything to fall into him right now, find calm and comfort in his arms, and get lost in his kisses again; I can't do any of that, though. I have work to do here.

"Will you take her back to The Castle tonight?" He apparently doesn't have the same personal versus professional boundaries, because he slides his whole hand along my jaw and cradles my face in his palm tenderly.

It sends the best kind of chills down my spine instantly.

"Yeah, they don't need to hold her over. No sign of abuse or neglect, she's healthy…"

"I'm glad she'll be with you, but you weren't supposed to be working tonight." The concern in his voice is nice; it feels good knowing he cares.

"It's okay. For her, any kids like her, I'll take an extra night of working if it means getting them to safety."

"You're a good woman, Everleigh Marshal." He draws me in closer and kisses my forehead. "She may need to talk to cops again," he whispers into my hairline. "They're tracking down family now, if they can."

I nod against his lips and whisper. "Thank you."

"For?"

"Being here for Sky. Being here right now for me. Being incredibly sexy when you're interacting with kids…"

He chuckles, and the sound vibrates against my head. "My pleasure. We should get back in there for her." He steps back, but not before he plants a chaste kiss on my lips. "Do you need to know anything else about Sky or anything from today?"

"Does she have any clothes from her house or anything personal with her?"

"Shit." He moves his hand up and rubs the back his head. "She doesn't have anything."

"That's okay. I'll take her for a happy meal and we will pick up a few essentials; pajamas, toothbrush, maybe a blanket and pillowcase of her choosing. She'll be set for the night."

He pulls out his wallet, "I don't have much cash, but you can take it all."

I put my hand over his and shake my head. "We have the funds for all of this, Liam. It's what we do. Don't worry."

He nods and slides the wallet back into his pocket. "Okay."

"I should go in and say goodbye to her, tell her what's going to happen tonight and that she gets to have a fun sleepover at The Castle with you, and all the other princesses. I'll save the part about being jealous, though." His lips spread, and his eyes shine mischievously.

"Soon," I tell him, laughing, then pushing forward quickly to kiss him. "Go tell our friend she can trust me and get out of here. I may not be able to stop myself from searching for another kiss if you don't."

"That's not going to convince me to leave," he answers huskily, eyes hooding over with intense desire.

"Go, Liam." I chuckle and step back so he can't touch me. "I'll take good care of Sky tonight."

"Fine, fine. I'll check on both of you tomorrow, okay?"

I nod my head. "I'll text you later."

"Thank you." He walks into Sky's room and starts to explain what's going to happen the rest of the night while I watch from the doorway.

He can't really be this good? Right? Like there has to be something wrong with him because nobody is as perfect as he seems. They can't be.

# *Fifteen*

## Liam

My shift is nearly over, not that I really needed to come back last night. Lieu called in a replacement when I was asked to stay at the hospital, so we've had an extra body here for the remainder of the shift.

It's been good having the extra hands, though. We've had some shit calls where extra bodies were helpful overnight.

I haven't slept more than an hour and a half, and going home to crawl into bed sounds incredible. First, though, I need to check on my girl and Sky.

I pull my phone from my pocket, double-checking the time, then sending her a text.

**Me: Morning, Babe. How did last night go?**

Little dots pop up on the screen almost immediately, surprising me. I figured she'd see it soon, but I didn't expect her to read it right away, much less reply this quickly.

**Everleigh: Hey, Hot Stuff. The night went well. Sky had a bad dream, but we settled her down pretty**

easily. She's getting ready to meet some of the girls right now.

**Me: Are they pretty good with meeting new girls?**

**Everleigh: They are. They all know when a new girl arrives it's because she's had a rough life, just like them. Our older girls are really great about leading by example and taking the new kids under their wings, too. They'll make sure Sky fits in, feels like another princess, and knows she belongs, no matter how long she's here.**

Her words reassure me, and I realize how truly grateful I am for a place like her castle, and for a company like Corporate Cares. I only wish they had existed many years ago. Maybe things would be different now.

**Me: Good. I'm glad. I'd like to drop by and check on her, see you, too. Would that be okay?**

**Everleigh: Yes, that's fine. I'd like to see you, too.**

**Me: I'll be leaving the firehouse in about an hour or so, unless we get a call. Then I'll head over.**

**Everleigh: Sounds good. Be safe.**

**Me: Always. See you later.**

When it's clear she isn't going to reply again, I set my phone down and head into our kitchen to refill my coffee. The anticipation and jolt of adrenaline knowing I'll be seeing her again gives me a burst of energy I feel immediately. I know the adrenaline will be short lived, though, so I pour another twenty ounces of coffee into my mug and twist the lid on it. Hopefully we don't get any more calls this shift; I want to get out of here as soon as I can.

Thankfully, the last hour of work goes by without a call or incident, and I'm able to climb in my truck and head toward Everleigh and the Corporate Cares house she works in. I have my music blaring, all loud songs with heavy bass and upbeat lyrics. It helps fend off the exhaustion, and with the air-conditioning blasting at full strength; I know I'll be good to go for a few hours, at least, of leisurely activity. If I get into something more active, I could probably last the whole day without a nap.

When I pull up to The Castle, I really take it in. It's not huge, but it's certainly big enough to host eight to ten girls and two counselors. I know the kids double and triple up in rooms with the use of bunk beds as well as singles in most of the rooms. And I know thanks to the fundraising efforts they've used every year; they were able to build this home from scratch to the specifications they needed.

It's nice. It's a pale yellow color, with white trim, a big porch hosting a swing and a few chairs. The front yard is gated and decently sized, and there are flowerbeds along the front of the porch on each side of the sidewalk. It may not be a real castle, but I can see where a scared child might feel like it's one.

I walk up the two porch steps and stop at the front door, knocking a quick four taps then stepping back. I can hear voices and laughs inside, and a bit of a commotion before two older girls answer the door together. Their grins are wide and they both have that look. The awed, young crush look.

"Hello, ladies," I say, smiling their way. "I'm Liam."

"Oh, we know," the first says. "Everleigh told us you were on your way. I helped her with her makeup for your date."

"So you must be Haylie, then," I respond, enjoying the shocked look on her face. "If I had to guess, that makes you…" I think for a moment, trying to recall the older girls' names. "Nichole?"

The second girl's eyes go just as wide as Haylie's, and she nods. "Wow."

"I got your names right?"

130

"You got both their names right," Everleigh says from behind them as she walks up. "Forgive them, cats clearly have their tongues."

I chuckle and both girls' mouths snap shut.

"It's nice to meet you both," I say, holding my hand out.

Haylie takes my hand first. "It's nice to meet you, too."

Nichole is next, and she states, "It's really nice to meet you. Like, really nice."

"Nichole…" Everleigh warns with an amused tone. "Why don't you girls go help the younger few with the dishes, and then sit them down and get them started on worksheets?"

Both girls look back at Everleigh, then at me, before they both agree and walk away.

"I think they like you," Everleigh says the second they're out of earshot.

"I think you might be right," I agree. "They seem like good girls."

"They are. They have good taste, too." Everleigh's eyes scan over my body and stop at my face. "You look tired."

"I didn't sleep last night; we had a lot of calls."

"You should go home and nap, then," she chastises, stepping back to let me in. "You could've called us later."

"No, I wanted to see you."

"Just me?" she challenges.

"And Sky. But definitely you." I stop in front of her just inside the doorway and peer down at her. "I haven't been able to stop thinking about kissing you since I left the hospital last night…"

Her breath hitches, and she glances toward the living room and kitchen area, I presume. "If you make it fast…"

"I can do fast, for now…" I step closer and duck my head down, kissing her. It's meant to be quick and light, but the second our lips meet it becomes more. We are careful not to get carried away, but it's a deep enough kiss it fuels my desire for more, and takes everything I have to stop and break away from her.

"Wow," she whispers.

"My thoughts exactly." I press a kiss to her forehead then step back. "How's Sky?"

"She's doing well," Everleigh answers, then shuts the door. "Come in and I'll introduce you to the rest of the girls, and you can see Sky."

I follow her into the main living area of the house and take it all in. The space is open and bright, there are two wraparound couches, a recliner, beanbags and toys, and more Disney Princesses and dresses than I've ever seen. Just beyond the living room is a dining room with a large table that's long enough to accommodate at least six or eight people. The kitchen is big and the appliances shiny and new. It's an incredible space and doesn't feel like I would have expected a group home to. At all.

"Wow, this place is incredible."

"It's a home, we want it to feel like one for the girls. It's their home." She turns around to face me with pride and accomplishment etched in her features, and in a lower voice adds, "They deserve that."

"I couldn't agree more," I respond just as quietly, taking one more look around. "It's probably a thousand times better than what they had with their first homes. Kids like them need the love, support, and security this place gives. That you and your other counselors give."

"Liam!" a tiny, sweet voice shouts from across the kitchen.

"Sky!" I exclaim, just as excitedly.

She runs across the kitchen and the open space right to me, with a chorus of people telling her no running in the house. I squat down just in time to catch her and give her a hug.

"How's Mommy?" she asks. "Where's Daddy?"

I let go of her and make sure she's steady on her feet as she steps back. "I'm not sure how your mommy is, Little One. I haven't been to the hospital today."

"Oh." Her face falls. "Okay."

"We'll see if we can call and get an update in a while, okay?" Everleigh responds. "Liam wanted to come see us before he goes home to sleep though."

Sky's frown inches up just the slightest to give me a small smile. "You came to see me?"

"I did," I answer. "I wanted to see you, and Everleigh."

"Are you her boyfriend?" One of the girls in the kitchen asks, and when I look up, I see it was Haylie.

"Hay—" Everleigh starts to chastise.

"I think I am," I answer over Everleigh. "Rather, it feels like I am. And I like her a lot."

All the girls in the kitchen start ooing and awing, and Sky prances back over to join them all.

The other counselor in the kitchen is watching us with a smirk. I stand from where I was squatted down for Sky and find Everleigh stunned, a nearly unreadable expression on her face.

\*\*\*\*

# Everleigh

Girlfriend.

Am I his girlfriend? Is he my boyfriend? Am I ready for a label? Do I want one? Isn't it too soon?

All of these thoughts flood my mind and render me speechless. We've been talking for like two and a half weeks now, constantly.

We've gone on one real date.

Is that enough to warrant a label? Isn't it still in the casual dating timeframe?

Liam stands to his full, tall height in front of me and searches my eyes, then whispers, "Stop overthinking, we can talk about us later."

I nod my head and try to focus back on our audience in the kitchen. All of the girls are watching us with the most elated grins on their faces.

"Everleigh finally has a boyfriend," Nichole chirps.

"My makeup skills really *are* good," Haylie adds, giving Nichole a high five.

Liam chuckles at their responses, then winks at me. It's a wink nobody else can see, one meant to calm my frazzled nerves… I think.

"Girls, are those dishes done yet?" I'm not sure what else to say, but I want the focus off of Liam and me, and back on just about anything else.

"Just about," they answer together.

"Finish those then make sure you all get your worksheets done." I glance past Liam's large form and give them the look.

"Do we have to?" Kenzie asks. She's one of our younger girls. At only ten, she's incredibly smart, she's experienced far too much, and she's the most stubborn of the bunch. "It's summertime. We shouldn't have homework during the summer."

"It's not homework, it's practice. You know that. It's one sheet, you will breeze through it then you can play all day." My entire focus is on her, but I can see the mirth on Liam's face in my periphery.

Kenzie sighs in the most dramatic fashion. "Fine."

"Ten going on sixteen," I mutter to him.

"I don't know how you parent this many kids at once, but you might be my hero," he praises in a low, muted voice.

His words aren't anything special on the surface, but their meaning and implication strike a chord in my heart. I work hard to be the best I can be for these girls. Sometimes they need a mom, a disciplinarian. Other times they need a friend, a confidante, and someone they don't feel is trying to be superior to them.

"Thank you."

"My pleasure, babe," he answers.

Again, the words aren't anything special, but they lodge themselves in my chest, while simultaneously reminding me we need to have a conversation. "Let's go out front and talk," I suggest.

He agrees wordlessly and we walk back toward the front door, leaving the loud bustling and energetic house and stepping out onto the silent, warm porch. I lead him over to the swing and drop down, waiting for him to do the same.

He sits and the swing shifts under his weight, then slowly starts to go back and forth, his strong, lean leg pushing us gently. "That may have been a bit presumptuous," he starts, before I can even say a thing. "And I know me saying it doesn't make it true, hell you may not even feel that way. But in a room full of young girls, it made more sense to stick to the simplest answer than to try to explain the ins and outs of our dynamic."

"I… You… Slow down, Liam." I glance at him; trying my best to give him the same type of look I'd give one of the girls after they word vomited an excuse before I can even tell them I'm not mad.

"Sorry." He smiles sheepishly, and it instantly makes him look younger, hints of his youth and what he may have looked like springing free with his expression.

"It's okay. All of it. I was stunned. Nothing like being put on the spot, but I put that on the girls, too." With him rocking us, I lift my legs and cross them in front of me on the swing seat. "When you call me that, what does it mean to you?"

"It means I can kiss you whenever the hell I want, without it being weird or whatever. And it means as long as this is happening between us, there will be no other women. It's a simple title that implies monogamy and trust for me. That's all."

He makes sense, and where he could have claimed some weird possession or uncomfortable ownership of me, he's made it about what it means for him and how he behaves with me and without me.

"Those are pretty good guidelines."

"We're grown-ass adults, Everleigh. Calling you my girlfriend is a couple steps above calling you my friend, and still a long way away from a commitment for life."

"Does that mean you don't want a commitment for life?" I ask, partially teasing, and partially trying to make him squirm.

"Ha. No, it doesn't mean anything. It just means we've been talking and dating just long enough for me to know I see you as more than a friend, and I enjoy our time together too much for you to only be my fuck buddy."

I look back to make sure there are no girls trying to eavesdrop from the front windows then laugh. "That would imply we were…"

"Yeah, so see, it was the best word to use given the circumstances."

"That's sound logic. I follow it. And while it may mean some ribbing from the girls, I think I like the idea of knowing you're as interested in where this may go as I am. Plus, it probably sets a better example for my girls than casually dating or fuck buddies might."

"Always looking out for the girls…"

"I always will. I'm honest with them, to the most appropriate extent possible, so they know they can always be honest with me. Having a boyfriend who is an amazing man and a firefighter is probably the best example I could set." I scoot a little closer to him on the swing and rest my hand over his muscular thigh. "No making out in front of them, or being overly affectionate. Not while we are here and I'm working at least."

He nods his head and covers my hand with his own. "I had no intention of being a horn dog in front of your girls. I respect the need for boundaries and restraint. I promise."

"Thank you." I spread my fingers out beneath his so he can fit his between mine. "You really should go home and get some sleep. I'll be here until tomorrow morning; I have a twenty-four-hour shift this time."

He rests his head back on the hard edge of the swing and hums, "You're probably right. I could sleep right here."

I give his fingers a little squeeze between my own. "Go, I don't want you to wreck on your way home because you passed out. Text me later."

"Yes, ma'am." He slows the swing to a stop and pushes himself up to stand. "Have a good day, don't let them give you too much crap."

I giggle. "I'll try. But with teenage girls, who knows what they'll have to say about our little declaration."

"Remind them any teasing they give you; you are allowed to return. It should work. It always did for me at least." His words bring a slight shift in his appearance. Sadness and regret quickly blend in with his exhaustion before it's all I see again.

"That's a good idea. Go home, Hot Stuff."

He steps in and presses a kiss to my forehead. "Have a good day and night. I'll talk to you later."

As he's walking away, I raise my hand to my head and touch just beneath the spot his lips were just pressed into me. He's so comfortable showing affection, being kind and gentle. I'm not sure what made him that way, we haven't spoken enough about our upbringing, but I'm grateful to whoever taught him to be soft. I know some see it as a sign of weakness. I don't though. It makes him an even better man to me. He's a magician with his lips, he can be hard and thorough, but the sweet moments, the forehead kisses and unexpected touches make him strong, kind, and incredible.

# Sixteen

## Liam

"Hayes!" Lieu calls out from across the field, signaling for me to join him. I excuse myself from the group of people I've been talking to and make my way over to him.

"Yeah?" When I get to where he's standing, roughly twenty yards from the parking lot, I stop and cross my arms over my chest. "What's up?"

"I just got word," he starts. My heart instantly lodges itself in my throat. Those are words that never precede good news. In fact, in all my experience and life, those words usually come right before a death notification. Potential casualties cross my mind in a storm of fear.

*Brandon and Jess.*

*Everleigh.*

*The boy we saved from the pool a few weeks ago.*

*Sky's mom.*

"Who died, Lieu? Give it to me straight."

His face contorts into sunburned confusion. "What do you mean who died? Nobody died."

"You should really work on your delivery then." I shake my head and exhale deeply. "Christ, I thought for sure you were about to tell me you got word of something happening to Brandon and Jess, or Everleigh. They're all on their way here…"

"Shit, I'm sorry. No, not at all. I just got word the mom from our call last week, the one who was beaten badly by her husband?"

"Sky's mom, yeah, I know her."

"Right, well, she's regained consciousness. She's still not completely out of the woods. They need to see where she's at with potential brain damage or whatnot, but she's awake."

A lightness fills my chest, and I know Sky needs to know immediately.

"The nurse called the firehouse," Lieu continues, "Captain O'Keefe knew that was our call, he wanted to pass it on. He knew we were all together today for my birthday."

"Thanks for letting me know. I'll have to tell Everleigh."

"She's Teddy's girl, right?" he asks.

"No, sir. She's my girl, she works for Teddy, though."

His roar of laughter is heard across the park. "Down boy. Fuck. I didn't mean Teddy's girl as in… Neverfuckingmind. Calm your ass down. You don't need to piss on her or anything, we all know she's yours."

"Oh, are we talking about Everleigh?" Brandon asks from behind me, making me jump in surprise.

"Put a fucking bell on next time," I shout. "Fuck. Where the hell did you come from?"

"The parking lot, dipshit. That is how we get into this little shindig."

Lieu steps to the side, opening up room for Brandon and Jess in our conversation.

"Hi, Liam," Jess says, snickering.

"Yeah, hi, Liam," Brandon mimics, trying to make his voice as light and high as hers.

"Hey, Jess. Go fuck yourself, Brandon." I glance over their heads toward the parking lot, spotting Everleigh's car pulling in.

"So touchy. You all must've been talking about Everleigh," Brandon tries to provoke me, wearing a smug expression.

"We were," Lieu confirms. "I was just telling Liam the woman from the call last week is conscious..." He doesn't use names or more descriptions, not wanting to violate privacy in front of Jess.

Brandon glances at me, asking the question as to whether it's Sky's mom, silently. We've talked about her, about Sky, and Everleigh enough in the past week for him to know.

"That's great news," Brandon responds then adds for Jess' sake, "the woman was pretty bad off, it was touch and go, but it sounds as though she's making progress."

"That's really great," Jess says sincerely. "Is Everleigh coming today, Liam? I'd love to meet her."

"She is," I answer, watching Everleigh step from her car with a phone held to her ear. "In fact, she's here now."

Jess and Brandon both turn their attention to the parking lot, following my eyes until they see her too.

"Wow, she's beautiful," Jess says. "Good job, Liam."

Brandon slides his hand around Jess' hip and agrees, "He did do good. Our boy is finally growing up and becoming a man."

Even I have to laugh at this. "Fuck off, B."

Lieu, Brandon, and Jess all talk among themselves while I step away to walk across the lot and meet Everleigh. She's ending her call just as I get to her, and the joyous look on her face tells me she probably knows about Sky's mom, too.

"Hey, babe," I say, greeting her with a kiss. "You look happy."

"Sky's mom regained consciousness. Sky can't see her yet, and they still have a lot of tests to run, but it's a step in the right direction."

"I heard," I tell her, taking her hand as we start to cross the street. "My lieutenant just told me. In fact, he's a part of your welcoming committee. I think he wants to meet you as much as Brandon and Jess."

"It's his birthday, right?" she asks.

"Yep. Old bastard is forty today."

Everleigh laughs and elbows me in the side. "That is not old. Don't be mean."

"I'm just being honest."

She doesn't say any more as we get closer to our three-person welcoming crew, choosing instead to stay silent until introductions are made.

"Well," I say, "here she is, everyone. You can all officially quit gawking or acting like she's a ghost." The last comment was directed at Brandon, because the asshole kept saying she couldn't really exist. Nobody who could get me to be monogamous could really exist.

Brandon's eyes reveal his amusement at my remark, but it's Jess who steps forward with her hand extended, and speaks first, "Hi, I'm Jess. Don't mind the guys, they're children. It's so nice to meet you though."

Everleigh slips her hand from mine and reaches out to shake Jess's. "Hi," she chuckles, "I'm Everleigh."

She and Jess shake and then Jess takes a step back and slides her hand around Brandon's back. "This is my husband, Brandon. He seems like an asshole sometimes, but he's a giant teddy bear."

I appreciate Jess so much right now. She's doing the best she can to put Everleigh at ease and be an ally. It's not always easy coming into these functions. We are a tight group, and most of us don't think twice about slinging insults or jabs at each other. We have a bond that makes it okay. To an outsider, though, it can be a lot.

"I've actually heard a lot about you," Everleigh says, holding her hand out to Brandon. "I'm Everleigh."

Brandon takes her hand and gives her a polite smile, before snarling at me, "You can't believe anything he has said. He gets his panties in a bunch because I'm the stronger, better-looking man."

Lieu guffaws and shakes his head. "Jess is right, they're children. I'm their lieutenant, Kevin. You can call me that, Kev, or Lieu. You'll probably hear all three today."

"It's so nice to meet you, Lieu," Everleigh says, "and happy birthday! This is for you." She reaches into her purse and pulls out a card. "I wasn't sure what you liked, so hopefully it's okay."

"You didn't have to bring me anything," he answers, taking the card. "Your being here, and keeping our boy happy is plenty good enough."

Everleigh smiles up at me then back at Lieu. "I was taught it's not nice to show up at someone's event without a token of gratitude or a gift."

"Well, thank you." Lieu seems speechless, and appreciative. "I'm going to let you four talk, if I don't get back to my party, the missus might actually have my balls and effectively end my life."

We all laugh, and Lieu walks away.

"It really is so nice to meet you," Jess says. "Liam has told us a lot about you, but I'd love to sit down and have a soda or something, and a chat, just us girls. The guys will get loud and rambunctious soon, and it'll be nice having more estrogen to connect with."

"I'd love that," Everleigh agrees.

We all stand around and talk a little before we join everyone else for Lieu's party. Everleigh and Jess have hit it off like old friends, and everyone seems to adore Everleigh already.

I don't think this introduction to my world, my family, could've gone any better for her.

**\*\*\*\***

# Everleigh

"Today was so much fun," I say as I step out of my car and walk into his garage to meet Liam at his driver's side door. We went from Lieu's party at the park, over to Brandon and Jess's for dinner and a game, and now we're back at his place.

I had no idea what to expect coming into today. I knew I'd be surrounded by a bunch of alpha firefighters, I figured there would be a lot of ribbing and probably a good bit of crass and hard talk, but I didn't expect it to feel like any normal family gathering. The single guys, like Zac, were loud and comical, the married guys were kept in check by their wives—yet still found a way to slip the crass man talk in—and the kids were close to literally every adult there. Liam has mentioned on more than one occasion the men and women who work in the firehouse are like his brothers and sisters, but I always thought it was just a figure of speech. It's not, though.

They are family. They're a family who welcomed me in with zero hesitation. They made me feel at home and very at ease from the get-go.

"I'm glad you enjoyed yourself," he yawns out. "They all adored you. Jess was so happy to have a partner in crime tonight, too. She's always stuck alone with me and

B, and you saw how we can get. You were the perfect partner for her, too."

"She was a lot of fun. They both were. Really, everyone was."

Liam takes my hand and leads me into his house through the garage. We step in to a small entryway and his laundry room, which to my surprise, holds a top-of-the-line, heavy-duty washer and dryer set. The space is filled with the typical laundry room and mudroom attire, but over the washer and dryer are where his uniform is hanging.

"You don't keep those in your closet?" I point to the uniform.

"Nah, usually here. It's more convenient to grab and go. I keep my turnouts in here, too, when I bring them home to wash."

"Turnouts?" I cock my head and try to figure out what the heck he is talking about.

"Bunker gear. We call them both, the name is interchangeable."

"Got it." I pull open the frontloading washer door and peek in. I'm being nosy, but I'm curious if he has clothes in it, or if he stays on top of laundry.

"Looking for something?" he asks, sliding his hand up and down my spine.

I suck in a quick breath caused by the unexpected, but incredible contact. "Just seeing if you're on top of laundry."

"Always." He walks his fingers back down my spine and along my waist, curling them around my hip. "Come on, I'll show you around so you can snoop more."

Gratefully he doesn't remove his hand when I stand up and close the washer. In fact, I think he is keeping me closer now, even though he just gave me carte blanche to snoop in his house.

"This is the living room," he says, leading me into the wide-open room. "I just renovated last year." He uncurls his fingers from around my hip and lets me walk freely. The room is larger than mine, but not much. His floors are wood throughout too, but they're a darker wood framed by bright white walls, a giant television, and dark leather furniture. The couch looks so soft and comfortable; I can't wait to use it.

"It looks amazing, Liam," I admit with a bit of awe. "I didn't take you as the neat and tidy type at home."

"What type did you take me as? Slovenly?"

"No, not slovenly," I answer quickly; trying to dig myself out of the little hole I just dug myself into. "I just didn't think it would be immaculately clean. Unless you knew I'd be over tonight?"

This has him looking at me lasciviously, his eyes bright and dancing with mirth. "Not a plan, if it were, I'd have invited you here from the start."

"Oh?"

"Yeah, then you could have ridden with me all day, we would have already had the tour out of the way, and I could already be doing what I want with you, instead of playing gracious host."

If his increasingly more suggestive touches and looks through the afternoon were any indication, I think I can guess what he would rather be doing. I would rather be doing it, too. He's been the perfect, teasing gentleman all day.

Small touches in sensitive areas have driven me wilder and wilder. Looks that suggested he was picturing me under him, over him, and every other way he could have me, all while naked.

And kisses.

My God.

The kisses. Even the chaste, public friendly ones have had my toes curling and body clenching in unfettered need.

The man is the God of Kisses. Statues should be erected in his honor, and an official title should be given to him. His mouth should be worshipped and praised and granted holy status.

"You make such a gracious host, though," I quip, shooting him an amused grin, which he instantly smolders at. If he's trying to come across as angry, he's not. The stern, irritated look I think he was shooting for is nowhere near that, it's sexy, and powerful. "Butttt… You can finish the tour later."

"You're enjoying this, aren't you?" he asks, stepping into my bubble. "You like teasing me."

With every step closer he takes; I match in playful retreat. "What if I do?"

"If you do, I think you need to be taught a lesson." He keeps prowling toward me, and I keep stepping backward, until I reach a solid surface—the wall—behind me, hindering me from backing away any more. His victorious, predatorial smile has my heart racing, pulse thumping in my throat like a giant drum.

"Whatever you're planning, I should warn you, I won't go down without a fight." He keeps advancing on me and stretches his arms out, caging me in between him and the wall.

"I'm looking forward to it," he taunts. "You really shouldn't tease a man who has worked really damn hard all day to be the perfect, polite gentleman. Not when even the tiniest little thing could set him off and break the restraints that have kept him bound all day."

His words have my thighs clenching, and my mouth watering. I'm not afraid of him, I know for a fact this, what he's insinuating, the restraints I've broken are all sexual. I'm ready for whatever he has to offer. I want the gentle touches from earlier to be reformed into hard and demanding, controlling, insistent paws of desire. "I'm not afraid of you," I state boldly, in challenge.

"You really shouldn't have said that." He steps in closer, body nearly pressed against mine, and whispers into my ear, "You're going to get it now."

"Bring it—"

He moves with scary quickness, pulling his hands away from the wall on either side of my head and dropping them to my body, assaulting me with tickles to every single place on my body I'm most susceptible to them. It's like he knows, somehow, exactly where to direct his attack to render me helpless. My laughs are strong and loud, and the force of them, and his incessant torment has me ready to double over. I can't though. I can't let him win.

I could try to dodge him and duck around, make a run for it to the safety of the couch, or the kitchen counter, but I don't think I'd be fast enough to escape him before he catches me. I could give up, cry uncle. Or... my mind races, trying to think of any alternative that will allow me to fight back... I could tickle him!

While he masterfully moves his fingers over my ribs, up my sides, tickling me to hysterics, I push at his chest, catching him off guard enough he has to slow his attack to keep his balance. With the slight distraction, it's my turn to pounce. I push him back harder, and harder, using what little spatial awareness I have of my new environment to know there is a couch not far behind him.

"You do have fight in you," he laughs out, starting to tickle me again. Every time I shove him back, he lets me. Yes, lets. I know if he were really fighting me, I wouldn't be able to budge him. But he's letting me.

Shove... retreat... shove... retreat... shove...

He drops onto his couch, laughing and pulling me down with him, over him. He uses my mistake to his

148

advantage and holds me tight to him while he tickles more. This time it's not just my sides he attacks.

He finds the ticklish spot on the back of my legs, his teases and threats of more he's whispering into my ears with his warm, intentional breaths has tingles spreading throughout my body. I have to move, to try to avoid the onslaught of feelings his fingers are drawing out of me. But my wiggles of avoidance are only adding to the intense feelings I have.

Not only does he have my body writhing and wound tight but my motions have brought out his noticeable desire. The harder he grows beneath me as I wiggle, the more I want.

"Jesus…" he hisses, stopping his ticklish torment to move his hands down over my ass. He squeezes and grips, pulling me up his body so my core is now perfectly aligned with his arousal. "You. Win."

"Mmmm," I hum, intentionally rolling my hips over him for both our sakes. "I love winning."

Gone is the playful glint in his eyes. In its place, untamed passion.

He slowly, deliberately slides his fingers from the safety of the denim covering me down to the soft, sensitive skin of my legs. His fingers dance slowly, purposely from the back of my legs in toward my inner thighs. If everywhere else is ticklish and causes my body to respond in a variety of ways, the territory his fingers have now charted are a direct path to my pleasure. It doesn't tickle, but it arouses and delights me.

"Told you I'd put up a fight," I gloat. "What do I get for winning?"

"Whatever the fuck you want." He maneuvers his hands higher, forcing my jean shorts up as far as he can, and slips his fingers under, using their strong, dexterous length to his advantage and teasing them over my panty line.

149

"Kiss me," I demand.

He obliges, raising his head up from the arm of the couch and capturing my lips with his. They move against mine, tongue tracing my lips, but he pulls back before I can give in. He nips at the plump, tender flesh of my lower lip before he sucks it into his mouth. It's nowhere near enough, but I think he knows that. He's reclaiming victory for himself by turning my winnings against me.

"More..." I take over the kiss impatiently, sealing my mouth over his and using my position on top of him to my advantage. Where he was slow to go deeper, I dive right in, tongue first, commandeering his mouth to use as my own personal altar.

Liam doesn't fight me, or try to regain control. He takes his cues from me, parting his lips to allow me the opportunity to tickle and taste.

The deep, long vibration of his groan when I tickle my tongue over the roof of his mouth drives me wild. As I claim his mouth, tasting and teasing him, before he returns the same enthusiasm joining our mouths in the most sensual dance of my life, his hands claim me. They move without hesitation over my body, beneath my shirt, expertly releasing the clasp of my bra without the slightest hitch.

With how we are lying, the intensity of our soul-searing kiss, he can't do any more than that. But he doesn't need to. He's nearly as proficient with his fingers as he is his mouth, and the touches he does grant me are lethal. Tickles and tender traces along my sides and spine, in conjunction with the way his mouth is now owning mine, are like blow after blow to my own restraint.

"Stop. Wiggling," he growls, then puts my hips in a viselike grip between his hands. "You don't get to get off dry-humping me. Not for our first time together."

I didn't realize I was still moving against him, grinding down over his erection like an inexperienced, horny young girl, but now that I'm stilled, the ache between my legs is pulsing and in need of soothing.

"Then do something about it," I mewl wantonly, needing more than anything to feel him there, using me for his own pleasure as he gives me mine.

# Seventeen

## Liam

She's perfect in every fucking way imaginable. And if she doesn't stop grinding against me like she has been, I'm going to blow my load in my pants and not make it to the finale of our little bout. The desire in her demand to do something about her need is nearly enough to snap all my resolve to make this last.

My body is screaming, raging for release. My cock is painfully hard; it needs attention, it needs to be relieved and released of the desire that's been building all day.

"Sit up," I instruct her, waiting for her to shift up onto her knees before I reposition myself and sit up. I've never been more aware of how small my couch is, but I plan on taking full advantage of the limited room we have to keep her as close as possible. "Actually, stand up real fast."

She gives me an irritated look that makes me chuckle. "This is the opposite of you doing something about it," she whines.

It shouldn't, but her whine gives me a sense of pride and power like I've never felt before, knowing I've driven her so crazy that stopping us long enough to get her and me naked so I can fuck her into tomorrow pisses her off. "I can't do anything with our clothes on," I point out, scooting to the end of the couch the minute she stands, so she's standing between my spread legs.

"Oh," she says, followed by an even sexier, "ohhhhh," when I pop the button on her shorts and lean forward to move my mouth over the soft, smooth skin once covered by thick denim. Her hands move into my hair and grip it tightly between her fingers as I lay kiss after kiss over her freshly exposed skin and panties.

I tug the jeans down completely and let them fall to the floor. She's standing in front of me now in only her panties and flip-flops, with her tank top and loose bra coving the rest of her. "I didn't say it earlier, but you look so fucking sexy today." I slide my hands up and down her bare legs, then lean forward to kiss them.

"Thank you," she sighs out. Her grip loosens in my hair momentarily and I glance up to see her tugging up the hem of her tank top, then pulling it off her head.

"Fuck. Me," I mutter, as the tank goes flying then she wiggles out of her bra, letting it fall into my lap. Her tits are phenomenal. They're not huge, but there's enough to fill each of my hands, and the nipples, perky and pebbling in all their pretty pink glory are mouthwateringly appealing.

"Is that a request, or a command?" She draws her finger down the space between her breasts, capturing my full attention as she moves it lower and lower, past her belly button and to her blue panties.

"Yes," I rasp out, watching her slip her finger into the waistband, then push the material down her hips. She wiggles back and forth seductively, causing the material to drop the rest of the way, leaving her naked and exposed in front of me. "You're perfect," I praise then pull my own shirt off in one practiced, perfected move.

"You have a tattoo," she exhales in observation when I bend forward to pepper kisses over her pelvic area. Her dainty fingers move over the back of my shoulder, tracing the ink stained into my skin. I don't want her focusing on it too much, it would put a damper on the mood we've established, so I do what any logical, sex-craved man would do. I drop my head lower, her alluring scent guiding me to the uncharted territory I'm ready to claim as my own.

"Mhmm," I hum against her skin, nuzzling into her, planting kiss after kiss in a descending line from her waist and along her pubis. Given our position, I can't go any lower with my mouth, but I'm just as good with my hands.

It's a fact she finds out and reacts to instantly.

The moment my thumb grazes over her slick labia and up to her clit, she expels a deep, guttural groan. "Mmmooore," she manages to get out as I circle over her clit. She grinds down on to my hand with her head dropped back, throat extended in the most perfect, enticing line ever. Her unbridled response fuels me, causing the inferno of desire inside me to rage out of control.

I rub and tease her into one climax, watching in awe as she falls apart over my hand, before I pull one hand back and make quick work of the button and zipper on my shorts. I raise my hips just enough to push the damn shorts and my underwear down, making sure I grab the condom in my back pocket before they fall to my feet.

Her eyes hooded, yet nowhere near sated, fall to my cock as I stroke and cover myself. I take hold of her hips and guide her to straddle me on the couch. With my back against the couch, legs planted on the floor, I'm in prime position to help her ride me to oblivion.

\*\*\*\*

# Everleigh

I feel as though I'm his to claim, to play with, to do as he wants with me, and based on the way he just directed my first orgasm—like my body was his own orchestra to drive toward a loud, stunning climax—I will let him do as he wants, without hesitation.

In my haze of ecstasy, I barely had time to take him in, admire his body, before he was covering himself and guiding me over him, with my knees braced outside his strong, powerful hips, and my hands on the back of the couch on either side of his head.

He's murmuring something right now, but I can't focus on a single thing beyond the crown of his cock sliding through my lips, glancing over my clit, revving me up to get me moving at full speed toward the finish line again.

Nothing but the indescribable sensation of his mouth closing over my breast while his large, thick head nudges past my tight opening, squeezing around him, and stinging at the unfamiliar intrusion of a man's presence there again resonates with me. The house could go up in flames around us right now, and as long as I got to enjoy every blissful moment of our first time together, I wouldn't even care.

"Christ," he utters, before he circles his tongue over my nipple then grazes his teeth over in a deliciously painful tease. "So tight."

His fingers dig into my hips and pull me down on to him as he thrusts up, filling me completely. The bite of the unexpected ache gives way to total pleasure as he grinds me down against him, ensuring my clit rubs over his body, providing me body tingling pleasure.

"Oh Godddd…" I bring my hands from the couch to his shoulders and dig my fingers in, using him as leverage to rise back up, then letting him bring me back down again. We work together in unison, giving, taking, thrusting, and bouncing, bodies slapping together in a cacophony of pleasure and need while we both rush closer and closer to release.

His hand moves between us, cradling and rubbing exactly where I need to set me off, and I dip my head to his neck, finding his movements get more wild, animalistic with every suck and swipe of my tongue over his pulse.

"I can't…" I groan into his skin. "So. Close." I'm panting already, and my body is wound so tight when he sets me free, I'll spiral out of control and get lost in a heavenly oblivion I never want to return from.

"Let go," he grunts, pulling back and exposing me to his wild, bright blue eyes while he watches the result of his handiwork.

With a final powerful thrust up, he shatters my control, and I unravel over him like I've never done before. My body arches and tightens from my toes, all the way up, spasming around him and craving his release as though it needs it to function.

"Fuck, Evvvvv," he moans out, as his eyes roll back and he reaches his climax with me. His body is suspended off the couch from his final thrust, and his muscles are taut and flexed beneath me while he unleashes every built-up ounce of pleasure inside me.

Our bodies fall back to the couch together, spent and heaving beneath the weight of our exhausted breaths.

"Holy shit," he breathes out, wrapping his arms around my body and pulling me into his chest where he can bury his face in the junction between my shoulder and neck.

"Mhmm," I agree, wrapping my arms around his neck and threading my fingers into his mussed hair.

His lips flutter over my damp skin, kissing me lightly. "Stay here tonight," he says, the words sounding hopeful and like a question against me.

I absolutely want to stay. I want more time with him, and I want to take my time exploring every hard ridge of his earned muscles. "Does that mean you aren't done with me yet?"

He shakes his head no against me. "I haven't finished being a gracious host, yet. I still need to show you my bedroom. Maybe even my shower."

I can feel the smile on his lips against my shoulder, and I just laugh. "Well I can't say no to my gracious host. It would be rude of me to not see every room in your house, if that's what you want."

He nods then adds, "I'd be happy to show you all your favorite rooms twice, too."

"I'll stay," I say, tugging on his hair so he has to look up at me. "I'd like to start in your kitchen though. That counter looks really nice."

He leans in and kisses me, murmuring into my mouth, "Your wish is my pleasure to fulfill."

# Eighteen

## Liam

Everleigh is sleeping soundly beside me with her body folded back into mine, fitting so perfectly against me it's like we were made for each other. Her head is tucked under my chin, and still damp from the shower we took together.

I gave her the grand tour in the kitchen, my bathroom, and then right here in my bed before exhaustion overtook us both and we fell asleep clinging to each other, bodies tangled and legs entwined. I slept for a while, but she started whimpering in her sleep and it woke me. She didn't do it for long, especially after I held on to her a little tighter and whispered my reassurance she was okay, but I haven't been able to go back to sleep yet.

While she sleeps, I'm memorizing as much about her right now as I can. The tiny freckles spattered over her shoulder, the birthmark on the back of her neck, the smell of my shampoo in her hair. All of it is being stored in my memory as one of the best nights I've ever had.

Everything about her has my undivided attention. Her fingers squeeze over mine tightly, warming them further, and she grumbles something beneath her breath.

I can't tell if she's waking up, or if she's dreaming again, so I brush my lips over her shoulders, hoping to either soothe her or let her know I'm awake too.

"Why aren't you sleeping?" she asks, voice heavy with sleepiness. "Did I wake you?"

"No," I fib a little. "I thought I heard something and then I just couldn't go back to sleep. I was too busy taking you in."

She releases my hand and turns her head back, allowing me the chance to kiss her lips. "What do you mean?"

"Well, with the dim light of the moon cast over your body, I could see these freckles," I drop my head and kiss along them, "and this birthmark." I kiss it, too, then nuzzle in. "I was able to take in the curve of your hip, to feel how perfectly you fit against me, and to watch you sleep making soft noises coming from the dreams you were clearly having."

She buries her head in my pillows and groans. "I wasn't making noises, no way."

"Way," I chuckle. "What were you dreaming about?" I kiss her shoulder again.

"I don't remember, really. It was weird, though." She turns her head back up then slowly rolls over so she's on her back, head rested on my arm, looking up at me.

"You don't remember? Or you aren't ready to tell me?" I question, feathering my fingers over her collarbone.

"I don't remember."

"Okay." I lower my head and kiss her lips. "You look beautiful like this."

159

"Like what?" She reaches up and cradles my face in her small hand, brushing her thumb over my lip like it's the most natural thing in the world.

"Half asleep, wholly fucked, with wild hair, no makeup, in my bed." I nip at her finger playfully then kiss it.

"Oh, like that," she snickers. "Your tattoo. I saw it the night you were auctioned off, but couldn't make it out. What is it?"

I drop my head briefly. Talking about the tattoo means talking about Lance, and talking about Lance stirs a lot of shit up in my mind.

"It's a memorial for my brother, and a nod to my time in the Army," I answer honestly, warily.

"Can I look at it?" she asks.

I sigh and nod my head, "You can. But I don't like talking about it…"

"Oh, you don't have to show me then." She frowns, and I feel like shit instantly.

"You can look at it." I pull my arm from beneath her head carefully and roll onto my stomach so she can take a look at the design over the back of my shoulder. "I need to get it touched up." Maybe if I give a little, she won't press for anymore.

I feel the bed shift, so I turn my head so I can see her. She kneels beside me, pulling the sheet up to cover her then grazes her fingers delicately over the design. "This is amazing," she says in awe. "Even in the relative darkness I can make out every detail. It's so intricate."

"The guy who did it for me did a great job," I agree. "Took quite a few hours to complete, but I've never regretted a single second, or bite of pain."

"So it did hurt?" she asks, curiously. "I've considered tattoos before, but I don't think I have the guts for one."

"It smarted, but it wasn't awful. It wasn't any worse than other pains I've experienced," I let slip, then add quickly, "Ya know, in basic, war, and being a dumb-ass kid."

She giggles right before I feel her lips over my shoulder. "Did you do stupid stuff when you were younger?"

She replaces her lips with her hand again then starts rubbing my back slowly. Her fingers are like magic over me, calming and relaxing me instantly. "I've done dumb shit most of my life," I admit. "I got in my fair share of trouble at school, at home, even in the military."

"Really?" she sounds surprised.

"Yeah, I'm a hothead sometimes. But I've learned to control myself a little better lately. B helps. He usually sees when I'm about to spiral and he reins me in."

"I never would've guessed." She straddles my back and both hands dig into my shoulders, massaging the tense muscles.

"You're going to knock me the fuck out if you keep doing that," I yawn out, reaching back to rub her legs.

"That's the goal, Hot Stuff." She works her thumbs into the little knots always present and dissolves them expertly.

"I'd rather stay awake and have more fun with you, though "

"I'll still be here when the sun comes up." She bends down and presses her lips to the back of my head. "Sleep, my new favorite troublemaker. I have more poking and prodding to do when you wake."

"I know something I'd like to poke and prod again," I murmur, as my eyes get heavy and start to close on their own accord.

She giggles again, the sound angelic and pure, and I know I want to hear it over and over, as much as I can, before our time together is up.

\*\*\*\*

# Everleigh

I should go back to sleep; I have a busy day tomorrow before my shift starts and I know I won't get much rest when I'm with the girls. I'm not ready to give tonight up yet though, not now that I'm awake again. Not now that Liam is asleep beneath me—literally—while I straddle his back and hips. Without a sheet or us in the middle of some form of physical activity, I can really take in his tattoo, his back, each freckle and scar that mars his skin. Through some of our conversations, he has mentioned some of the physical wear and tear he withstood being in the military. He may have only been a medic, but he saw combat, he experienced bombs and threat to his life; he felt things I could never imagine.

I'm guessing that's where some of the little scars come from, but there are a few that look unique, shaped specifically, unlike any of the others. I'm not sure what they're from, or where he got them, but I wish I knew. I carefully slide my fingers over the slightly raised skin, wishing I could bend and kiss each mark away, erase him ever seeing or experiencing any of it.

From his scars, I take in every marking of his tattoo. From the blue ribbon wrapped around a rifle, to the overturned helmet at the base of a red cross, each object is clear and precise. It's a beautiful tattoo. Just beneath the cross is the memorial for his brother. Inscribed beautifully in dark ink is *L. Hayes 1994-2010*.

His brother was so young, he had so much life to live still. I can't even imagine the hurt Liam felt losing him, much less how he felt being away when it happened. He hasn't shared it outright, but I know he was serving from

2009 through 2013 before he joined the fire department. If I were to lose my sister, I think it would kill me. I couldn't survive without my other half, my best friend, the one person I still go to for advice, comfort, security, and help to this day. He lost that.

Thinking of my and Addie's bond has me clutching my chest, feeling an ache deep inside for Liam's loss.

Beyond the scars and tattoo, Liam's back is sculpted perfection. Just like every other part of him, the definition, each smooth plane that climbs into a pronounced ridge of muscle along his shoulders and traps. I can't even imagine how much working out it would take to reach this level of physique, but I know it has to be a lot.

He's perfection, sleeping, gorgeous perfection. The turn my life has taken in the past three weeks is nearing a one-eighty right now, and my mom will be all too thrilled to hear about him during our next lunch. After our last, when she nagged and questioned like I knew she would, I told her it was time she stops until I offer information. We left on rocky ground with her looking immensely disappointed and hurt I would ever even think to tell her to stop meddling.

I have to shake the thought from my mind as it starts to take off down a shadowed, tumultuous alley full of memories from dark nights listening to her bringing a new man home, hoping he would be the one she could convince to stay and fill my dad's shoes after he was gone. It's full of tears, drinks, and one attempt to end it all I will never forget, no matter how hard I try. We don't discuss it ever now, though. We act as though it never happened. It was an accident, something she never meant to happen.

That's what she swears to this day.

She was strong enough to walk away, to show me and Addie she deserved more than what Dad did, but for as strong as she was then; she gave up on herself after.

It's those days, not knowing what would happen to my mom, what would happen to us, being angry at my dad that brought me to the career I have. I found a community center after school that introduced me to an incredible counselor. Her name was Pepper, and while she may have only been there a few months, her mark on my life has lasted every day since.

My mom is so much better now. Stronger, standing proudly on her own two feet, my hero who I love unconditionally, but it's not without its bumps.

"Lie down," Liam murmurs beneath me, causing me to jump in horror at the unexpectedness of his voice.

"Oh my God!" I shriek, throwing my hand to my chest and rocking over his body. "You were sleeping."

"Was, until my masseuse quit touching me and decided to use me as a bench and nothing else." His sleepy, husky voice sends a shiver down my spine.

"I'm sorry I woke you," I murmur, bending to kiss between his shoulder blades.

"It's okay," he rasps out into his arm, "come lie with me. You need sleep too." He holds his arm out and I scoot off of him, stretching my body out beside him now instead.

His eyes peek open and he gives me the cutest, sleepiest smile I've ever seen. "You okay?"

I nod and scoot in closer, letting him reposition until I'm tucked beneath his arm and we are cuddled together, face-to-face. "I'm perfect now."

"Good." He presses his lips to mine briefly, then to my forehead. "Sleep, babe. We'll have plenty of time to talk and play in the morning."

# Nineteen

## Everleigh

Y ou're telling me you've never watched any of the *Lord of the Rings* movies?" Liam asks incredulously, as he plops down on my couch with popcorn and one of his waters. "What is wrong with you?"

"Um, I'm not a nerd?" I grab a piece of popcorn and toss it at his face. "I never would've taken you for the type to watch them. Seriously."

"They're cinematic masterpieces." He's talking about them with such conviction, I nearly feel guilty for avoiding them like the plague my whole adult life, nearly. Who cares about the mythical creatures in these forever-long movies? Nerds. That's who.

Apparently, my boyfriend is one of them.

"They're all over three hours, Liam. That isn't a cinematic masterpiece. It's the script for a nap. One you will catch me taking after the first… ten minutes. If you're lucky."

.

"If I'm lucky?" He munches down on a handful of popcorn and kicks his legs up, perfectly comfortable and at ease in my home.

"Yes, if you're lucky I'll make it ten minutes. Really, it could be as quick as sixty seconds." I go to reach for more popcorn, but he holds the bowl out of my reach.

"You could try to go longer; I know you have the stamina. I've seen you last hours before." He smirks, and wraps his free arm around me when I try to lunge over his body to snag the popped goodness from him. "Now, now. Ask nicely and maybe I'll give you some."

"Liam," I warn.

"Everleigh," he counters, eyes glinting with mischief and playfulness. "Sit and watch thirty minutes, just thirty, and then we can turn it off if you still aren't enjoying it. But I promise you, it's so good."

I glare at him, sticking out my tongue.

He clucks his at me and shakes his head. "I wouldn't want that thing in my mouth, either," he quips, without skipping a single beat.

"Bullshit." I lean in, whispering in his ear, "You love when it's in your mouth, on your body, stroking your—"

He lets out a low, feral groan just as my doorbell rings loudly, preventing me from finishing my thought.

"Who the heck is that?" I whine. "And why are they bothering us?"

"Be happy we were interrupted, I was about to show you what happens when you tease me like that," he threatens in vain.

Before he can even see it coming, I lean in and lick up his face, then hop off the couch laughing while he makes noises of mock disgust and wipes his wet face off. "You deserved that," I chirp, heading to my door.

"Paybacks are a bitch. Just remember that, babe." He sets the popcorn down on the table and fires up the movie as I'm opening the door.

"Holy shit!" I shriek. "What are you doing here, Mom?"

"Is that any way to welcome me?" she questions, looking me over. "Everleigh, why are you in those clothes? Shouldn't you be ready, presentable? What if your new boyfriend comes by? You know men have certain… standards."

I hang my head and sigh. "Mom…"

"I'm just saying," she says in defense of herself. "You can dress and act however you want after you've reeled them in for good, but while you're still trying to catch the man of your dreams, you should put some effort into looking like the beautiful thirty-year-old woman I know you are."

"Mom…" I say again, louder this time.

"Everleigh, do not interrupt—"

Her mouth snaps shut, and I don't have to turn around to know she is seeing the man who stands at just around six feet tall walking up behind me, dressed similarly to me in a pair of shorts, a tee, and his signature backward cap.

She looks from Liam, back to me, and whispers hurriedly, "Why didn't you tell me he was here?"

"You wouldn't let me," I whisper back, rolling my eyes. I clear my throat and take a step back, opening myself up to both of them. "Mom, this is Liam. Liam, this is my nosy, opinionated mother, Jane."

Liam approaches with a warm smile and extends his hand. "It's very nice to meet you, Jane."

She sputters and reaches back, letting his big, strong hand fully engulf her much smaller, aged one. "It's so nice to meet you, too, Liam. My daughter, well, my other daughter told me about you. She said you were quite handsome, but I never imagined…"

*Thanks a lot, Addie.*

"I was going to tell you all about him at lunch next week, Mom. I've been busy. Work, a new relationship, you know how it goes."

"You were avoiding me, Everleigh. Don't try to convince me otherwise."

I let out a deep sigh. "Would you like to come in and have a drink with us?"

Mom's eyes light up and she steps inside my cool, air-conditioned home. "I would love that. I need to know all about the man who has finally gotten your attention."

Shoot. Me. Now.

"I'd love to talk, Jane. I'll just go turn our movie off really quick, babe. Then I'll join you two in the kitchen?" he asks, sounding more than a little unsure of things.

"That'll be perfect. Do you want anything fresh to drink, or do you have your water still?"

"Everleigh, don't offer the man water."

"It's okay, ma'am. It's what I prefer," he says, smirking at the astonished look on my face. He glances at my mom over my shoulder, then leans in and whispers, "You won't look good in prison orange. And I'm not sure they'd give us conjugal visits."

My face of seriousness and armor cracks with the laugh I emit, and he grins proudly.

"There it is," he says. "I'll be right there."

While Liam steps over to turn the movie off, I follow my mom into my kitchen, where she takes a seat at the island counter. "I don't like having to hear about your life from your sister," she lectures me. "He seems like a good man."

"Mom, you literally just met him…"

"And? Am I incapable of recognizing a good man when I meet one?"

I could answer in so many ways, but none would be fair to her, or to what she went through with my dad, so I step forward and hug her, answering, "You're right. He is a good man. He's a firefighter."

"Addie told me," she confirms, releasing me from our embrace. "That's a very noble profession."

"I agree. Even better, he accepts the work I do. And the hours I keep."

"Well, that's good," she agrees. "Though I still think you need to find a job with less hours, and in a safer field."

"Her job seems pretty safe to me, ma'am," Liam answers for me, padding into the kitchen. There's something so sexy about the fact he doesn't feel the need to alter his laid-back appearance even one bit for my mom.

"The children she works with, they could be dangerous, or come from dangerous homes," my mom justifies.

"While it's true the girls might come from dangerous homes before they move into the house with Everleigh, they aren't dangerous girls. And the love she shows them, love I know she gets from you, saves them. It's a love they need to survive. To thrive. What Everleigh does is the work of an angel, ma'am. Her quitting would be a travesty."

My mom is rendered speechless, and frankly, so am I. I know he is an advocate for Corporate Cares. He wouldn't have volunteered so much of his time this year if he didn't believe in our cause, as well as theirs. But I have never heard him speak so passionately about anything.

Hearing him defend me, The Castle, my girls, it stops my heart and brings tears to my eyes.

"Everleigh is exactly what the girls need. She's exactly what I need: work, girls, comfy clothes, and smart-ass attitude all included." He winks at me as he finishes, then focuses on my mom.

"Oh my," she expels as her first words. "I've never looked at Everleigh's job in such a way, but... maybe I should have. For a man to be as passionate as you are about it, and my daughter..." My mom looks at me, her eyes softening and her lips turning up into a proud half smile. "Maybe I should hear you out more often, rather than focusing on the hours."

"I'd love to share more," I agree, fighting back the burn of the tears threatening to form. I look at Liam, heart going from being frozen in stunned gratefulness to speeding up as though it's the timer on a bomb indicating the last few moments before detonation, "Thank you," I mouth.

He steps forward and kisses my forehead before he takes a seat next to my mom, giving her his undivided attention, and using the unexpected opportunity of her visit to get to know her.

\*\*\*\*

# Liam

"You know, your mom is a riot." I pull my shirt over my head and fall back onto the bed, grinning over at Everleigh as she gets ready for bed, too. "She seems sad, though."

Everleigh finishes adjusting her clothes and kneels on the bed, bending over me to kiss my lips. "She has her moments. Mom's had a rough go since my dad cheated."

Her words shock me. I never, in a million years, would've expected her to say that. Not that I have a good reason to think anything, but still, it's something you don't expect. "I had no idea."

She leans back on her bent knees, resting her ass on her heels and feet, shrugging. "We don't advertise it, obviously. It happened a long time ago. She left him when she found out. She told us a strong woman makes her own decisions, values her worth."

"Sounds like the kind of woman I'd want to be with, strong, independent." I reach out and rest my hand on her leg. "I feel like there's more to this, though."

"There is. Mom may have left Dad, but she never quit loving him. For a while, too, she would go out and look for someone new, hoping some other guy would steal her heart and dull the ache of my dad's betrayal. She paraded new men in and out of my and Addie's life constantly. When nobody could fill the shoes my mom apparently forgot to send off with my dad, she got really depressed. In truth, I think she was depressed all along. Anyway…" She pauses and takes a fortifying breath, the kind that causes her whole body to move with the inhale, and the exhale. "Anyway, after a while it all got to be too much for her. She was so strong walking away from my dad, but then her mind betrayed her and she tried to end her own life."

"Oh shit, babe…" I sit up and pull her into my arms. "I'm so sorry." I can't imagine what she went through, to see a parent break that way; it would be awful. Its own helpless hell.

"It's okay," she says, curling into me. "She overcame with help, and she's the strongest woman I've ever met. But she's a walking contradiction at times. She'll be the first to tell you to walk away if a man isn't treating you right, or if he's cheating. She's also the first to tell me

171

and my sister we need to find good men, and we need to do our best to keep them."

I chuckle into the crown of her head. "Sounds complicated."

"You have no idea. The woman drives me insane, yet I love her beyond words."

"As you should," I murmur, nuzzling into her hair. "Hopefully my presence here today will calm her a little."

This draws out an unexpected booming laugh from her. "Oh no, now her focus will shift. Instead of telling me I need to find a man, she will insist on advising me on how to keep you, while also prodding for grandbabies before I'm too old."

"Christ," I chuckle. "That sounds fun."

She turns her head up against my chest and kisses beneath my jaw. "You have no idea. She was smitten with you. That will be a point in my favor; though, she may encourage me to attack you every chance I get, for obvious reasons."

"Reasons like I'm the most handsome, incredible man, with the greatest body ever, you should be appreciating and worshipping every second of the day?" I smirk at her and raise my arms to flex and pose.

She laughs out a snort and shakes her head, "You are too much. No, that's not why." Everleigh uses her hand to put the image of her with a round, pregnant belly into context as she acts like she's rubbing one.

"Ah, so she doesn't think you should be climbing me like a tree as much as possible just to get off and have fun. Got it. That's really disappointing."

Everleigh rolls her eyes and smacks my chest. "I seem to do that anyway; I don't need my mom's encouragement. How about you? What are your parents like?"

"My mom passed when we were younger, it was sudden and unexpected. She left for work one day and instead of her being the one at the door that night, it was the sheriff, letting us know Mom had been in a fatal accident. My dad, he's a dick. We don't speak anymore."

"Do you want to tell me—"

I slip my hand around her dainty neck and draw her into me, sealing my mouth over hers in an attempt to stop this conversation in its tracks. The last thing I want to do right now is talk about my fucked-up life and family. I avoid it on a good day, and today is beyond good, it's great. I'm not going to ruin what we've had with my sob story. No way, no how.

"Liam," she protests then moans as I tug her lip between my teeth. "I want to know about you."

"Later," I respond, kissing down her jaw, "right now I think we need to explore you climbing me like a tree and worshipping my body again."

She lets out a playful huff, "Fine. Twist my arm why don't you…"

*Crisis. Averted.*

We won't get anywhere near talking about my dad, Lance, my childhood, or my hatred for everything but my brother.

By the time I finish with her tonight, Everleigh will be spent, in need of sleep, and sore enough she'll remember every second of our time together with every step she takes while she's at work tomorrow.

So will I.

I'm the master of avoidance and losing myself in the physical activities that shut my mind off. This time, though, the exhaustion and exertion will be framed by desire, lust, and passion spurred on by the sexiest woman I have ever had the pleasure of getting to know.

# Twenty

## Everleigh

Kristy," I call out across the backyard of the house. "Your ice cream is melting. You better come finish it."

I watch her run from the swing set, laughing and twirling every few steps along the way. She met a family today, one she really liked. I'm hopeful they adored her just as much; she deserves a stable home to grow and thrive in with a family who can give her the world and love her.

Every girl here deserves that. They all deserve the princess treatment. Sadly, not all of them will get it. That's why we do everything we can to provide them with everything they need. It's why I can't help but love each girl who comes through our door as though they were my own flesh and blood.

"Can I have more when I'm done?" she asks when she reaches me.

"No, ma'am, you may not," I answer, correcting her grammar and smiling. "Dinner is in a couple of hours and you don't need any more sugar.

She sits down with an exaggerated huff then takes a big, melty bite of her chocolate and vanilla swirl ice cream. "Everleigh, will they be my new mommy and daddy?"

Her question stills me, and causes my heart to sink. I don't know the answer. I can't get her hopes up and I can't lie, but I don't want to hurt her or break her heart, either. "I don't know, sweetie. They might be. They would be so lucky to call you theirs. You're such a smart, sweet, adorable little girl. But even if they don't, there's always the chance of another better family to come along."

"Okay," she says. I know it isn't what she wants to hear. She just wants a family who will love her, same as any other child in the world.

"Hi, Everleigh. Hi, Kristy," Sky says, walking out of the house with her own bowl of ice cream.

"Hi, Sky," Kristy answers, waving her spoon like a wild child, flinging ice cream across the deck.

"Watch it, missy!" I chastise playfully, wiping my face. "Hi, Miss Sky. What kind of ice cream do you have?"

"Chocolate," she answers proudly and plops down into the seat beside me.

"Is it good?"

She takes a big bite, and nods with wide, happy eyes and a chocolaty smile.

"Wanna play with me?" Kristy asks, scooting back from the table, and her still unfinished bowl.

Sky nods her head and gets ready to rise.

"Nuh uh," I say quickly. "Finish your ice creams then you can play. But I don't want them out here, melting and getting yucky. It's wasteful."

"Okay," they both agree, then dive back into their treats.

With them both occupied by ice cream and the idea of playing together after, I rise from the table and go inside, pulling the blinds up on the door so I can see out and watch them while Jake and I work on dinner.

"How are things going with the firefighter?" Jake asks, as I walk into the kitchen too.

I give him a curious look as I'm washing my hands. "Who said I was with a firefighter?"

"The girls," he admits, chuckling. "They're loud when they gossip. Haylie also couldn't quit talking about getting to do your makeup, it meant a lot to her."

"She did a great job. How'd you know it was more than a couple dates, though?"

"Your mood." He starts to sauté the vegetables while I start cutting up the chicken. "I don't mean that like you're always in a bad mood, you just seem lighter right now."

"I don't know if that's a result of Liam, or the promotion I'm still up for, my mom being off my back about a relationship for the time being, or it's just things going well with the girls. Maybe it's all of it?"

"Or maybe it's the new beau. Don't discredit the power of a strong relationship to go home to."

"I don't go home to him." I start tossing all of the chicken into a big serving bowl.

"Maybe not every night, but I know you aren't spending all your time alone," Jake answers in a low, excited whisper.

"We can't all have the man of our dreams," I remind him, shaking my head in exasperation. "You got lucky, found that one of a kind love."

"No, honey, he found me." Jake winks and turns back toward the stove, whistling the latest country hit I'm sure he can't get out of his head.

Jake is lucky. He and his husband met, fell hard, fast, and haven't looked back. They've been married for years now, and seeing them together is a terrifying combination of goals and utter disgust. No two people have ever seemed so genuinely perfect for each other, it's sometimes hard to swallow how insanely happy they are.

Jake couldn't deserve it any more, though. He is such an incredible, kind, outgoing man who would give anyone the shirt off his back if it meant being of assistance to them. His husband has the patience of a saint, putting up with our job, too. They were made for each other.

"Whatever, you found each other. Not all of us are that lucky." I start on the rice next, minding my own business until the doorbell rings.

Jake turns the heat down and points from the stove to me, then takes off out of the kitchen to answer the door, calling back, "If you step out of your own way for a change, you might be surprised how lucky you get."

\*\*\*\*

# Liam

A tall, lanky man with thick, black glasses is the last thing I expect to see once the door is opened to me. I had pictured Everleigh, but maybe one of the older girls, or maybe even Sky if she saw me. I did not expect any man to open the door though.

He slides his eyes over my body and grins. "How can I help you?"

"Uh, I'm looking for Everleigh." I clear my throat and shift uncomfortably from foot to foot.

"Speak of the Devil," he hisses out, laughing. "You're the new boyfriend, I presume?"

His acknowledgement of our relationship loosens me up a bit, and I nod in agreement. "Guilty as charged. I'm Liam."

"I'm Jake," he responds jovially, holding a hand out to me. "It's nice to meet you."

"You, too. I thought Josie was working with Everleigh tonight?" I step inside and let Jake close the door, staying out of his way so he can walk into the living room and I can follow.

"She was supposed to be. I'm not allowed to stay overnight, naturally. The poor thing has a bad tooth and required a root canal this morning, though, so I'm covering for her until nine or so, then I'll head home while Everleigh takes the night shift. Josie's not feeling up to a night with the girls. She needs rest."

"Ouch," I say sympathetically. I'm glad to hear he doesn't stay the night, though. He seems like a great guy, but I know some of the girls they've had have struggled around men for various reasons, and it wouldn't seem right to put them in that situation

"Jake, who was at the—" Everleigh steps out and comes to a stop when she sees me. "Liam, what are you doing here?"

"I wanted to see you. I'm trading shifts in a couple of days, so we won't have the same time off for a few. I thought dropping by now might be my last chance until after the weekend at least."

Her face droops into a frown. "I understand. We were just making dinner, want to come sit at the counter?"

"We don't bite," Jake adds, grinning wide.

"He's lying," she jokes. "We might even have enough for you to join us."

"That sounds great," I agree, sitting at one of the stools up at their counter. "How's Sky?"

Jake glances toward Everleigh, and Everleigh sighs. "I shouldn't be telling you this, but since you were on the scene, I don't suppose it's anything you couldn't find out on your own. Her dad is out on bond. He showed up at the hospital today."

"Say that again?"

"I'm afraid it's true. He hasn't come by here, the police showed him out and reminded him of the restraining order against him, the rules about him not going back to their home, near the hospital, here, but we were warned he could show up, just in case." Jake shakes his own head and does something at the stove I can't see.

White-hot rage is filling every vein in my body, burning hotter and hotter by the second. "Does she know?"

Everleigh nods. "She was supposed to get to go visit her mom today, we had to postpone."

"Christ," I mutter. "Is she okay?"

"Seems to be," Jake answers first, turning toward me with his hands full of a giant pan. "She's eating ice cream out back with Kristy right now."

"She is, then they were going to play until dinner," Everleigh adds. "You can go out and see her if you want. She's asked about you a few times."

"Are you sure?" I ask, not wanting to cross any lines or risk getting Everleigh in trouble.

"Positive," she confirms. "We'll let you both know when dinner is done."

"Thanks." I walk out the back door to see two girls swinging across the yard. One is Sky; the other must be Kristy.

I saunter over to them, catching Sky's attention first. She pumps her legs forward, back, forward, back propelling herself higher and higher on the swing, then laughs freely. "Hi, Liam!"

"Hey, Little One," I respond, loving the carefree joy on her face. "You must be Kristy," I add to her friend.

She nods her head and slows on her swing. "Who are you?"

"I'm Sky's and Everleigh's friend, Liam."

"He plays with bubbles," Sky adds, proud and excited. "Did you bring any today?"

"Sorry, I'm fresh out. I'll buy more later though, then I'll bring you some."

Sky's eyes light up with the promise of bubbles and she looks at Kristy, glaring her down as though the one look can chase the girl away.

She does it for no more than twenty seconds before her swing buddy is hopping off and running across the yard, going inside.

"She could've stayed out here." I shouldn't encourage Sky to be antisocial; she needs friends and support. But a small part of me is proud of how strong she's gotten.

"Nope." Sky doesn't say anything else while she swings back and forth, waiting until she jumps off and lands with a thump, followed by a fist thrown victoriously in the air.

"Wanna talk?" I ask, as she sits back down on the swing. "I heard you were supposed to see your mom today."

"I couldn't."

All it takes is those two words for my heart to start hurting for her, for the loss of the man who should have protected her at all costs. "Do you know why?" I ask.

"My daddy," she whispers, nudging herself side to side slowly on the swing.

"What about your daddy?" I don't want to put any thoughts into her head, but it's important to get a sense of who this man is to her.

"He was visiting. I can't see him."

"Does that upset you?" I ask her carefully.

"No. I miss Mommy." She looks up at me with sad, droopy eyes.

"I'm sorry, Sky. Do you miss your daddy?"

She shakes her head no, and another knife digs into my chest. Children shouldn't ever have to endure this in their life. It is so not fair.

"I'm sorry."

Sky shrugs and changes the topics, pointing out the giant yellow butterfly on the slide instead.

"You know," I start carefully, slowly, not even sure where the words are coming from. "My dad wasn't very nice, either."

She looks at me curiously. "He wasn't?"

I shake my head no and squat down on the grass beside her swing. "Not at all."

She hears the words and silently accepts them, then starts to swing again. No child should bear the weight she has had to; I know it. But I want her to know she's not alone.

I understand.

I'm here for her.

# Twenty-One

## Liam

"Having a girlfriend has made you a new man," Brandon says, checking the air levels on his tank. "We've all noticed it. Jess has even commented."

I roll my eyes and set my own air tank down on the compressor, ignoring him momentarily while the loud air refilling my tank drowns out everything else he might be saying. A quick glance up allows me to see him laughing. But if I don't pay any attention, I can take a few moments to think on his words.

Everleigh has been a positive change in my life. I feel more in control, happier, lighter. She is kind and smart, funny, and perfect. She makes me want to be better. Not that I was bad before her, but I want to focus on the positive, enjoy life more now.

"She's a special person," I admit, pulling my tank off the compressor and setting it down. "She makes me happy." Telling him that isn't a huge proclamation or anything, even though he's smirking as though I just told him she's the woman of my dreams and I'm going to ask her to marry me.

I won't be. Not anytime soon, at least.

"She is. We both really liked her. Since she's used to working with kids every day, she's great at handling your attitude and childish behaviors."

"Fuck off," I laugh out, taking his tank from his hands. "Say anything else and I'll clock you with this."

"You wouldn't. Your ass would miss me too much if you killed me, or if you tried to kill me and landed yourself in prison."

"Ain't that the sad fuckin' truth." I fill his tank with air and give it back to him. "Do you know what Lieu told me this morning?"

Brandon shakes his head and secures his tank in its harness. "What?"

"I'm on the fast track for lieutenant. They want someone with med experience to fill the position on some shifts, due to bad judgment calls happening in some stations around the state, not taking medical repercussions into consideration."

"Shit, man!" He claps a hand against my shoulder, "That's great. Congratulations!"

"Thanks." I nod. "Lieu said my change in demeanor on calls, my focus as of late, made him throw my hat in for talks. There may be some shifts I step in as an acting lieutenant to get a feel for it, show whether I have the chops."

"You will," Brandon assures me. "You were made for shit like this. I know. I've seen you thrive in the most high-pressure situations a man can be put in. Bullets flying, roadsides detonating, you owned that shit and led us when nobody else was willing to…"

We don't talk about that day much. Our commander was injured, unable to lead us, and we were in a shitstorm with a couple hundred men whose single mission was to kill as many of us as possible. It was one of the worst days we endured over there. None of us were prepared. All of us feared we would never make it back home.

I stepped up when shit hit the fan and found a way to focus, lead, and fight, when my mind and heart were practically begging me to retreat and get the hell out of Dodge, with or without our men, so I could keep my own life.

I couldn't have done it, though. I could never in a million years leave my men, my brothers… Not again. Never again.

"I do what I think is right," I finally respond to him, shrugging a shoulder. "Any one of you would've done it had I not stepped up first."

"That's bullshit, man. We all signed up to fight. We all knew the risks, the potential costs. That day though, none of us were ready. Yet you found a way to be. That's the decision of a natural born leader, Liam."

My body physically rejects his words, his praise. I'm not a natural born leader. If I were, things would be so different today. They aren't though, because I'm not. I acted out of self-preservation. It wasn't heroic; it wasn't inborn ability. It was selfish.

I didn't want to die.

"Whatever, it's done, in the past. No point arguing when we will never know the truth."

"You stubborn fucking ass. I know the truth; we all knew it. If you don't want to admit it, fine. But the rest of us know. We will always know, Liam. Live with it."

*Live with it.*

The phrase of my life. There is so much I live with. Good and bad, past and present, inconsequential and significant, I live with it all.

It wraps around me like a noose, threatening to suffocate me day in and day out.

Except when Everleigh is near. Her positive, caring, outgoing attitude loosens the rope and lets me breathe again.

"We should double sometime," I change the topic, looking at Brandon expectantly. "I'd like Everleigh and Jess to get to know each other better, maybe we can make a habit of it eventually."

"That sounds good to me, man," he agrees.

"It sounds good to me, too," the most unmistakable, majestic voice says. Brandon and I both turn around and there she is, Everleigh in all her beautiful, confident glory, standing just inside the raised garage door.

"Hey, Everleigh," Brandon says first, while I stand smiling like a fool at her.

"Hey, Brandon," she replies, walking in. "I didn't expect you to make it so easy to find you here."

"What are you doing here?" I ask, still stunned.

"I think what our man here meant to say was, 'Hey, Everleigh, thanks for coming by. I'm happy to see you. You look beautiful. What a surprise.' Take any one of those as your pick."

Everleigh laughs and shakes her head, and I raise the one-fingered salute in his direction. "Hey, babe," I amend, realizing as annoying as he is, he was right.

"Hi, Hot Stuff," she giggles, stopping in front of us. She's wearing a skirt and dressy top, with light but stunning makeup adorning her eyes and cheeks, and a hint of color on her lips. "I was on my way into the office and had a few minutes to spare. I wanted to come see you in your element for a change."

"His element would actually be a jungle, or an asylum, but I can see where you might think this would be it," Brandon jabs at me.

"Brandon…" I warn in a low, threatening tone.

He drops his head back laughing hysterically. "You're so damn easy to get going. I'll leave you two to it. Make sure you come in and say hey to the rest of the guys, though, Everleigh."

"I will," she agrees happily. "We'll be in shortly."

Brandon salutes and walks away, disappearing into the firehouse with a whistle.

"You look incredible." I step closer and slide my hands over her hips, bending to kiss her. "Something special going on?"

She kisses me back then wipes some of the lipstick that transferred off my lips. "I have a meeting with a social worker this afternoon, and authorities, to discuss one of the girls."

"Is it Sky?" I ask immediately. "What's going on?"

"I can't share that information. I'm sorry. It's against the rules, a violation of privacy, something I could lose my job over. I promise you, though, that no matter what girl it is, I will advocate and fight for them always."

She kisses me softly again.

I want to argue with her, I want to fight the point, say I'm a firefighter, I understand privacy and laws, but I won't share anything. I can't do that to her though. I know she is up for a big promotion at Corporate Cares, and I would never do anything to jeopardize that for her.

"I understand. Will you do me a favor, though?"

"What's that?"

"If anything happens with Sky, will you at least let me know in as few, and legal words as you can? I don't want to be blindsided. We've formed a bond, too, and I don't want her to think I abandoned her."

"I swear, Liam, Sky will always know you are on her side. I won't let her forget."

\*\*\*\*

# Everleigh

I know what he wants from me, I know why he wants it, but I can't tell him. I can't share I'm meeting with her social worker today, that we are discussing her mom, the status of relatives in the area, her dad's bail hearing, and what steps we take next. I am bound by law, by obligation to work, and by my duty to Sky and every girl in our house to protect them, their information, and to advocate for them in an unbiased and trustworthy manner.

Before he can call me on not answering him directly, I try to change topics, "Can I put in a request for you to wear your uniform while you're off duty? You look very sexy in it."

"You're changing topics," he states correctly, "but I'll go with it... for now. I might be convinced to wear it more, if the right incentives are given."

I place my hand on his chest and step as close as I can, grinning up into his beautiful blue eyes. "What sort of incentive are you looking for?"

"The kind that makes wearing, and unwearing, my uniform worth it."

"Unwearing?" I can't help but laugh. "You seriously just made the word up. You know it's not real, right?"

"Who cares?" he quips. "Give me enough incentive and I'll wear whatever the hell you want me to, then I'll take it off slowly, just for you."

"My own striptease?" I push up on my toes, letting my heels rise minutely off the ground, and kiss his jaw.

"Would you enjoy that?" His hands slide from my hips to my ass, and link over it.

187

"Duhhh." I roll my eyes at the absurdity of his question. "You stripping would be the highlight of my year.

"And the lowlight of ours," one of the guys stepping out of the main house says. "We basically have to beg the man to keep his shit on now that he's been auctioned off."

Liam takes his hand off my ass and lets me reposition myself so I'm standing with my back to his front, where his hands are able to rest on my hips possessively. "Bullshit. I keep my clothes on here. Zac is the one who's always stripping."

All the guys laugh as they file out into the big, open garage area.

"We heard there was a beautiful woman in here who needed rescuing," Lieu says, filing out after all his men. "He isn't holding you against your will, is he? Because I'd take him."

I giggle and shake my head no. "Hey, Lieu. Hey, guys."

I know most of them already from Lieu's birthday party last week, but I didn't get a chance to talk to or introduce myself to all of them.

"Hi, Everleigh," Lieu responds with a chipper tone. "Brandon told us you were out here."

"And you all had to come see her?" Liam questions. I can't see his face, but I can hear the amusement in his tone. "Interesting."

Zac, the probationary firefighter here at the house, crosses his arms over his chest in a display of misguided machismo. "Dude, of course we did. She's se—"

Brandon quickly smacks Zac upside the head while another one of the guys literally covers his mouth.

"She's gorgeous," Brandon covers for Zac. "Better looking than all these ugly mugs for sure. Plus, she gives you shit regularly and you don't fight back, we like seeing it."

"You would." Liam's thumbs rub slow circles over my hips and his body relaxes. The second all the guys came out, he went rigid, protective, and defensive. But I'm not sure why.

"Guilty as charged," Brandon agrees, winking at me, letting me know he's trying to rile Liam up because they're best friends and he can.

"How are you all doing?" I ask, taking in all the men dressed in the same uniform, all physically fit and wearing their hair in all different styles. Some even wear a hat instead of styled hair.

"Can't complain," one of the guys I didn't get a chance to meet yet, says. "You work at Corporate Cares, right?"

I nod my head slowly. "I do."

"That's really cool. My brother and sister-in-law adopted a little boy who was staying in one of the houses your company runs. Our whole family appreciates all you do there."

Hearing him share this makes my heart swell with pride. "That's really amazing. I'm so glad hear the little boy, and your family, got a happy ending. We hope that's what happens for each and every one of our kids."

"We want that, too. It's why we were so big on donating and helping with the fundraising efforts this year. It was personal to us on all fronts."

"Well, on behalf of Corporate Cares, thank you." I smile at him and am ready to step away from Liam to introduce myself to this kind man when a loud tone fills the space around us. Not long after the unexpected, startling noise starts, a voice replaces it, making each of the men in the room jump to action.

They all start moving in unison, grabbing gear, slipping pants and boots on.

"I have to go, babe," Liam says, turning me in his arms. "We have a big fire to go to. Be safe driving to work. I'll call you later."

"Okay," I agree, "be careful. Let me know when you're back and safe."

Just as I press up to kiss him, he dips down to kiss me, and we meet in a hurried embrace of lips and arms before he pulls back with one final kiss to my forehead.

"I mean it, Liam. Be careful…"

He nods once and winks as he rushes to step out of his shoes and into his boots, then pulls his pants up over his hips. I've never seen anything like this before, and for every ounce of pride I have for him, all of them, I can't help the tense, constriction in my chest.

It's one thing to know they have a dangerous job. It's another thing completely to hear the call, hear what they're walking into, then watch your man walk away from you and right into the fire.

# Twenty-Two

## Liam

S he seemed worried," Brandon's voice rings out over the headset we all have on inside the truck as we race to the call.

"Wasn't Jess the first time she experienced a tone and seeing all of us react like we did?"

"She was. Still is. I'm just saying, there's no faking the look of worry, admiration, love on her face. She needs you okay, just like all the rest of us have families who need us okay. It's not just you now, Brother."

Love? Nope, no way. It's a preposterous thought, one that has me a little more aware I need to do things by the book, be safe, and get me and my guys out so I can get back to her.

"Noted." I pull on my gloves and adjust my coat, securing it the way it needs to be to keep me safe in the flames.

"He's right. There's no denying how much she cares about you," Lieu adds from the front. "It may not be as serious as love yet, but she's who will be waiting for you to come home now. Enjoy the feeling, but don't take it for granted." Once he lays his words of wisdom on me, he goes quiet again, silently directing the truck around another when we pull up to a blazing apartment complex.

"This shit is bad," I shout out, ripping my headset off and jumping out of the truck. "How many buildings are affected?"

"Two," Lieu informs us. "We have word of victims still inside. Rescue, get your asses in there, find them and get them out before this place is a loss."

We all move into purposeful action instantly. With multiple ambulances here, my focus today will be on the fire. Brandon and I mask up and grab a hose. "You got lead?" he asks.

I nod my head and we both move toward the apartments, heat radiating as soon as we're close enough, with the fire blazing and roaring intensely.

We move as a unit, dousing what we can as we climb the stairs from the ground level, up. It appears the fire started higher, but it's spreading quick, and the breeze is making it easy for the flames to jump from structure to structure, wall to wall.

"It's fucking hot," Brandon screams. "This thing is going to go off. I can feel it."

I don't say anything to him, but I think he's right. There's a feeling you get, a near sixth sense when you've been working as long as we have, that warns you. It's like the internal alarms in your subconscious ring loud enough to make you consciously aware this isn't right.

We have a job to do though.

We pound on doors, clear apartments, work methodically to make sure there are no residents still inside who may not make it out otherwise.

We climb floor to floor, walking into hotter, more stifling flames with each level. My mind is racing, listening to communications from the ground coming over the radios, listening to the fire destroy the building around us, listening for innocent cries for help.

"Station Eighteen, Station Eighteen," Lieu's voice echoes in our radios. "All truck and rescue teams need to pull out. The fire is too hot, too dangerous. Get out now."

Brandon and I look at each other, reading each other's minds, even though our masks hide our expressions. We have to start working down, or we won't make it out.

An explosion shakes the ground, causing wood and rubble from the building to start collapsing as we run down the steps. We went in at a structurally safe location; we had crews all around going into worse spots with the most risk of injured civilians. While we couldn't find anyone, there is a good chance others could.

The roar of the fire, the cracking of wood, the sound of air breathing more and more life into the flames threatening our lives give rise to a symphony of danger and death. We are descending the second flight of steps, halfway to the ground, when above the chaos of the beast we're fighting, the one call you never want to hear as a firefighter shouts out over the air, "Mayday! Mayday, Mayday, Mayday!"

Brandon's steps falter, I skid to a stop before plowing into him from behind, and we listen as the incident commander responds, asking for confirmation of the mayday. His confirmation is met with heart stopping silence.

Our pace is quickened by the prospect of one of our own being trapped, injured, in need.

The commander asks again for a mayday, when a broken, strangled voice calls back, "Mayday! Truck eighteen. Second level sweep, building one. Trapped, injured... mask lost."

Truck eighteen.

Our truck.

One of ours.

The commander starts giving instructions, first to our man injured and trapped, instructing him to activate his PASS alarm and shine his flashlight up if he can.

We need to clear the building; it's a loss. But not before we get him out. We have to fight. We can't leave him.

Everyone switches to a new channel, leaving the original to keep in communication. Brandon and I aren't in building one, so we need to get out and assist on the ground in whatever way we can.

I have a sinking feeling in my gut, though.

This is bad. It's really bad. I just don't know who it will be, or if we'll get them out in time.

Seconds feel like hours, and minutes like days while Brandon and I safely clear and exit the apartment building, heading to our truck, looking for any and every man we work with to be there, trying to identify who it is.

The scene is mayhem.

Residents of the apartments are littered around us, some being tended to, others wrapped in blankets on this sweltering afternoon due to shock. Firefighters are clearing the building, ripping their masks off, searching for news of our injured man. None of that even addresses the destruction of the property we were trying to save around the team of men trying to rescue their injured brother.

There is nothing any of us can do now as we stand and wait, watching for any sign of them coming out.

I'm not sure how long it takes, but as the building burns hotter, a crew of men carry the limp body of our fallen brother out. From here I can see he sustained massive injury, likely smoke inhalation, potentially severe burns.

As a medic, too, I rip off my mask and rush forward to assist in getting him on a board and stretcher, ready to aid our paramedics and get him transported to the hospital.

There were a few of our men I couldn't find, though, so before I can help save him, I need to know who it is.

****

# Everleigh

The meeting went better than I could've hoped with the social worker and detective today in reference to Sky, her mom, and the case against her father. The detective is hopeful Sky's dad won't get out of all this without time, but he can't make any promises. Her dad only has minor offenses on his record, mostly traffic related, and beyond the abuse to his wife, poses no risk to society.

Since she's failed to report any other incidents, never filed any charges, this occasion seems isolated, too. We have proof from Sky he's harmed her mother before, but the judge can only slightly weigh the words of a young, traumatized girl.

The detective assured me Sky would be protected, and when the time comes for her mom to be released from the hospital, they will help relocate them to a safe house, somewhere they'll be protected until the trial is over.

Given the circumstances, I couldn't be any more pleased, and that's exactly what I plan on telling Teddy as I watch him cross the floor toward my office.

Just as I'm about to speak when he reaches my door, the look on his face silences me. He's pale, with worry etched in every feature on his face.

It scares me.

"Teddy, what's going on?" I rise instinctively, expecting him to tell me something has happened to one of the kids or one of my girls.

"Do you have the radio on or anything in here?"

I shake my head no, fear creeping from my heart outward, saturating every vessel in me, weighing me down, and starting to suffocate me. "What's going on?"

"Is Liam working today?"

Liam?

My heart stops, literally stops in my chest when his name is mentioned. I'm not sure if he sees it or not, but I think I'm nodding my head in a mechanical response.

"There's been a fire, it's bad. A firefighter was injured and is being taken to the hospital now."

"Teddy," I somehow manage to whisper around the huge lump in my throat. "Is it Liam? Do you know?"

He shakes his head no.

"Which hospital?"

"I'm not... They don't broadcast that on television. If I had to guess, General... The fire was only a few blocks from it."

"I have to go." I move on autopilot, grabbing my purse, my keys, my phone. I want to call him; I want him to answer and tell me he's okay. But if he was at the fire, he won't have his phone, whether he was injured or not.

"I don't think I'll be at The Castle tonight."

"I'll make sure it's covered," he says, then takes my keys from me as I try to pass by him. "Let me drive you. I don't want you wrecking in your hurry or fear to get to him."

I nod silently and follow him out to his car. He doesn't waste any time maneuvering the streets and getting me to the hospital. In fact, I think he may have violated a few laws in the process, but I couldn't be certain.

All I am certain of is I'm terrified Liam could be injured. I'm scared to death the amazing man who may just capture my heart might be in pain, or worse…

It's been a little shy of four weeks since we started to talk, but in that time, I've grown so attached to him. He's become my best friend, the person I look most forward to talking to every day. He's even the first person I call when my day is shit and I need a comforting voice.

It's too soon to love him, but if we get the chance to keep seeing each other, learning about each other, I think I could love him eventually.

That thought threatens to halt me in my tracks, but the fear of losing him outweighs its magnitude and I push forward, dodging news crews outside the hospital, and walking through a sea of smoke-covered firefighters. They all look at me, pain and worry the only emotion visible on any of their faces.

So far I have seen nobody from Liam's house. It makes me hopeful, maybe he isn't even here. I can pull my phone out, text him or call him, and he'll answer or reply as soon as possible.

That hope drains from every pore of my body once I slip past the next group of men, though. Lieu, Brandon, a couple of the guys I don't know, are sitting in chairs or pacing in the heart of the waiting room.

If all of the other men here look worried, Liam's crew looks distraught, broken. I scan each of their faces, but he is nowhere to be seen.

"Oh, oh my God." I raise my hand to my mouth, covering it and swallowing down the bile crawling up my throat.

Brandon must have heard me, because he pushes out of his chair and rushes over. "Everleigh? What are you doing here? How did you find out?"

"Where is he?"

197

"He's back there with them." He nods toward the doors closing us all out. "They're doing everything they can."

I choke back a sob and look into his eyes. "Will he be okay?"

"It's not Liam," Lieu says, stepping up beside Brandon, clearing his throat and blinking back tears. "Liam is fine. Physically at least."

I look from him, to Brandon, and back. "Liam is okay?"

"Yes, Liam is okay," Lieu answers again.

"He is helping the docs. Trying to help save—"

Just as he starts to tell me who Liam is trying to save, the automatic doors open, and Liam walks out. His head hanging, soot is covering his face, and I can't be sure, but it looks like he has blood on his hands.

The waiting room goes silent when everyone else notices him too, and Lieu, Brandon, and I step forward.

Liam lifts his head up, locking eyes with me first, showing me the misery and despair he's feeling before he looks at Brandon, then Lieu. "He's gone. Zac is gone. There was nothing they could do."

# Twenty-Three

## Everleigh

He hasn't spoken a word since breaking the news to all of us. He's sat quietly in a waiting room chair, with his head hanging, resting between his hands, but he has not given me, or anyone, any indication what he's thinking or feeling.

Lieu told me the chaplain and one of their chiefs would make notification to Zac's family. His next of kin is his parents, so they will be informed and brought to the hospital to say their final goodbyes. That's why we're all still here. That's what we are waiting for.

I've never experienced a death in this manner, but the brotherhood and bond they all share is palpable. Each person here has been profoundly impacted by the loss of one of their own, and as his brothers, they will remain here, holding vigil and being strong, so when Zac's parents arrive, they won't be alone.

It's special. It's incredible.

It's also so sad.

I'm sitting on Liam's right side, and while I'd love to take his hand, to take some of the grief or pain as my own, I know I can't. I can simply be here. Brandon let Jess know what is going on, and from what I've heard, she is on her way down, too.

I guess she had met and spent time with Zac's parents at a firehouse function not long ago, and they all got along and hit it off.

I'm not surprised, really. Everyone who meets Jess likes her; if Zac's parents are even half as outgoing and fun as he was, everyone would easily like them, too.

"Can I get you anything?" Lieu asks, walking up to us and stopping in front of me. "Any of you?"

Where I'm on Liam's right, Brandon dropped down to Liam's left. His posture is nearly identical to Liam's, but he raises his head and answers solemnly, "I don't want anything, Lieu. But thanks."

I look to Liam, then back at Lieu and shake my head. "I think we will pass for now, too. Thank you for asking, though."

"I feel like I have to do something," he admits quietly. "I hate standing here and waiting. Our chief will let us know when they arrive, but until then, there's absolutely nothing I can do."

"I understand. Is there anything I can get you?" I offer. "I feel like I'm just taking up space that should be meant for you all, your family. I'd be happy to go and get anything for anyone. It's the least I can do."

Lieu's eyes soften and he gives me the kindest smile. "You belong here, and we're okay. Plus, I think you're needed more than you know right now." His eyes shift to Liam and he frowns.

I don't know what happened today. I don't know why Liam was back with Zac and nobody else was when I got here. I don't know why he seems to be taking the blame for all of this, because it feels like he is, but I couldn't even begin to guess where he got the idea.

"I'm not going anywhere." We both know I'm saying it for Liam, not for Lieu. He may not be responding to much, but I know he can hear everything we are saying.

Sure enough, after Lieu walks away, Liam lowers one hand from his face and laces his fingers through mine. It's the simplest act imaginable, but the force of his touch, the strength of his grip is all I need to know he doesn't want me going anywhere.

I lean into him and kiss his shoulder, then whisper, "Do you want me to get you anything?"

He shakes his head no, but keeps quiet.

We sit in silence for five or ten minutes before Jess walks in and goes right to her husband. Brandon is up and out of his seat in an instant, wrapping his arms around her in an act of need, love, and support. I'm not a part of the hug, just watching, Brandon looks like a lost little boy, clinging to Jess for dear life while she supports them both. She is taking everything on her shoulders right now, she's being the strength he needs and the pillar of support he can lean on through the rest of time.

I'd love to be that for Liam right now. I want him to trust me so much he can let it all go, give everything else over to me. I can bear the weight of his world right now. I want to if it means he will be comforted.

When Brandon and Jess let go of each other, Brandon moves back to his seat and Jess steps over to us, bending to give me a hug of greeting and of solidarity, then she squats down in front of Liam. She must know he won't look up, because she ducks forward and looks up at him, making sure she finds his eyes before she speaks softly, "Do not go there, Liam. You aren't responsible. Don't take blame on your shoulders."

I can't decide if she knows something I don't about today, or if she just knows my boyfriend so well she realizes he will internalize this and take the blame no matter what, but a pang of jealousy ping-pongs in my chest and bounces around between my ribs and heart. I should know these things. I should know what to say and how to handle him.

I should know he's going to take on the blame and carry it as his burden.

I should know, but I don't. It took his best friend's wife arriving to tell me what I should have already figured out... Liam is taking responsibility for Zac's death, and he's drowning in guilt and grief right now.

Jess and I exchange glances as she rises, and she mouths incredibly slowly, so I understand every word she's forming, "He always blames himself. He'll need you."

I nod just as silently and then kiss his shoulder again.

My heart is breaking for him. My heart is breaking and there's nothing I can do right now except sit here and hold his hand.

\*\*\*\*

# Liam

I should have been with him. We should have paired up and cleared the building together. I should have reminded him to leave an escape route no matter where he searched.

He's too damn young to be gone. Why did it have to be him, a kid with his whole life ahead of him to fuck up, grow up, find a family, realize there's more to life than sex, games, and work? Just like when I was in the military, I know the world has lost another person who made it better while it's left me here, a failure to everyone I should be able to protect. Why do I get to keep living my life when I have yet to be there for the ones I should be protecting most?

It's just not fair.

It's like a sick, cosmic joke at this point.

So is the fact I have an amazing woman sitting beside me, holding my hand, showing me she meant what she said to Lieu... she isn't going anywhere.

Every few minutes she kisses my shoulder, or she rubs her thumb over mine. It doesn't matter my fingers still have remnants of blood. It doesn't matter I smell like a chimney that's been burning for days. It doesn't matter that I failed yet another person.

Everleigh isn't going anywhere.

How do I deserve such an angel in this life? I will never know, but I'm grateful for her. She could do better, but for the time being, she's set on being with me and I'll hold on tight for as long as I can.

I'll keep her hand in mine all night.

I'll accept her care and support.

I'll cherish her blind faith in me, until she realizes the broken failure of a man I am and lets me go.

\*\*\*\*

It's been three and a half hours now. Three and a half hours since I witnessed the line filling the monitor; heard the sound indicating asystole. It won't be long before Zac's parents come out, having said goodbye to their only child.

When they've left, the hospital will prepare him for transfer and we will escort him in heroic fashion from here to the mortuary. I, along with multiple other brothers and sisters in red, will sign up for sentry duty, standing watch and holding vigil for Zac until the day he is laid to rest.

I experienced my fair share of military funerals, processions, and send-offs, but this is the first time a brother from our firehouse has been lost, and it feels so surreal.

"What happens next?" Everleigh whispers.

"After his parents have had their time with him, we will escort him to the mortuary. By now, local law enforcement, other firefighters, and volunteers will have been notified, and he will be escorted as a hero should be."

She nods her head and takes in everything. "What do we do?"

"We?"

"Significant others, spouses, girlfriends." She shrugs a shoulder and looks around the room. Many of the wives have arrived, our family is tight-knit and we all want to be together.

"You should follow us. You can stick with Jess, too, and I can take you back to work for your car later."

"I'll do that." Everleigh looks to Jess.

"That sounds good. We will follow Lieu's wife's lead. She's like the station mom." Jess forces a smile and shakes her head sadly. "She's going to take this hard too, when the days settle and she's not being a shoulder for his parents. She adored Zac. He flirted with her even more than Liam."

Her words crack a smile on my face. She's right. Zac had no problem flirting with anyone and everyone who gave him the chance. He could swoon all the women right off their feet without even trying.

"Do you know if she ever got her striptease?" Brandon asks.

"What?" Everleigh exclaims in humorous shock. "A striptease?"

Brandon and I laugh, and I explain, "We were at a pool party, and he was loading up on oil, not sunscreen, and she offered to help…"

"He let her, of course," Brandon continues on, "and it turned into a huge joke when Lieu walked out. He couldn't believe she was oiling up Zac."

"Still can't," Lieu interrupts, smirking, glancing in Kathy's direction where she's talking to a few of the guys. "I told him if he ever dared to try stripping for my wife, I'd bounce him from the program so fast he wouldn't know what hit him."

Lieu's response makes us all laugh, and for just a moment, we find the happy before reality stabs us all in the heart again.

"He was a good kid," Lieu says.

"He was a good fireman," I add.

"He was good all the way around," Brandon confirms. "This fucking sucks."

It does. All of it. There is nothing about today I will hold on to or see as anything but a shitty fucking situation that never should have happened.

The doors open to the long hallway where they led Zac's family, and his mom and dad step out. His mom is crying; his dad is stone-faced and pale, holding his mom up and bearing the weight of the world for both of them.

They shouldn't be going through this. They shouldn't be getting ready to bury their only child.

We all feel it, know it, as the room mutes and every man and woman here rises and forms a line, honoring their son and their loss as they exit with the chaplain and their own department liaison flanking them.

Zac's dad was on the job years ago, so when they get to Lieu, he stops and says in a tortured, broken voice, "Please don't leave him alone. Not yet. He deserves everything."

On the last word, his dad's voice cracks and gives way to a stifled sob.

"He won't be alone, sir," Lieu says, remaining stoic and strong, even when this has to be hurting him, too. "You have our promise. Zac will always have a brother with him."

His dad nods, and they're escorted out of the hospital to a waiting car that will take them home, so they can try to understand how their lives just got flipped and upended so suddenly.

We all stand in line until they've cleared the building, and then a quiet exhale, silent tears, hurt, guilt, and wonderment why him and not any of us hits.

We break away into small groups, everyone talking quietly in whispered words we'd all deny saying if we were ever asked.

A doctor walks out and clears his throat, getting a few people to go silent. "Firefighter Zac Ralston will be ready for transport shortly. If a procession is planned, now would be the time for everyone to prepare."

Lieu steps up to talk to the doctor then shakes his hand as they finish. Lieu turns to all of us, addressing every man and woman who has shown up all at once, "You heard him. We will be taking Zac to the funeral home momentarily. Sentry sign-ups will be online; anyone who wants time will get it. Today wasn't easy for any of us, and the days ahead will be just as hard. Some may feel guilt, wonder why Zac, wish they could've done more, and will feel angry. It's all normal, but the department will have extra counseling available, use it if you need, there is no shame. We will all get back to work, back to putting our own lives on the line again before we might be ready. Use today as a reminder to stay vigilant, always stay with your partner, and give thanks at the end of every shift you get to go home. We continue on now for Zac, as we've continued on for every other fallen firefighter. Go home, be with your families, mourn how you need. Zac lived as a fun, humorous, brave hero; he died the same way. We will continue on for him."

Everyone says in a loud, agreement, "For Zac." Lieu gives a strong nod then Kathy walks up and takes his hand, supporting her husband, showing a united front for each and every one of us.

Everleigh wipes at her eyes, and I turn to her. "What's going on, babe?"

She shakes her head and looks up at me, "For a moment, I thought it was you. I was terrified, Liam. Beyond terrified."

"Why would you…" Before I finish, I remember she was standing here when I came out, when I made the announcement. She couldn't find me.

"Brandon and Lieu told me, but from the second Teddy told me about the news, until the moment you walked through those doors… I thought I had lost you."

"It's not my time," I whisper, and pull her into my chest. Despite the stench of my clothes, the day of work, and hospital pacing, she lets me. "Thank you for being here. Thank you for… for caring."

She wraps her arms around me, rubbing my back and listening to my heart beat. "I wasn't ready for us to be over. You're not allowed to die on me, I have plans, Liam."

*So do I, babe. So do I.*

207

# Twenty-Four

## Everleigh

The procession out of the hospital was one of the most tragically beautiful things I have ever witnessed or been a part of. First responders from all over the state gathered to escort Zac, their lights lit up the darkening sky, their occupants showing solidarity and compassion to the men and women who knew and loved Zac most.

Once the procession ended, Jess drove me to their firehouse, then Liam and I stopped off at Corporate Cares for my car before we came back to his place. He's quiet again. Jess told me in the car Liam takes on a lot of responsibility for others, whether it's his job to or not. They haven't dealt with a death in house like Zac's, but she said Brandon has shared some of their military experiences with her, I need to be ready for Liam to become obsessed with being better, being stronger, more in control.

She also warned me he may turn into himself, go down a dark hole. She said she couldn't tell me why, but he has already been on the verge lately. I pulled him out, but this might be enough to push him right back in.

I'm terrified he will fall into the hole.

I'm terrified I won't be able to stop him.

I'm terrified if he does, I won't know how to get him out.

He's still wearing his uniform. It's the same one he had on when I stopped by the firehouse, which feels like an eternity ago and not sixteen hours ago.

He's still just as sexy, but I can see the brokenness. It's like the uniform, remnants of the call, of Zac's final moments, are covering him right along with the uniform, weighing him down further. Soot, dirt, and I don't even know what else smudges and covers his neck, face, and arms in patches, and all I can think about is stripping him of all of it, taking the weight of the reminder off him. Washing the day away so he's bared, so we can get through Zac's death together and he isn't cloaked in it.

"Come with me," I whisper once he's kicked his shoes off in the laundry room. I take his hand and he follows me wordlessly.

I've spent enough time here, off and on, since we started seeing each other that I know exactly where I'm going, even in the shadowy, darkened rooms.

I lead him through the house, into his bedroom and past his king-sized bed, pulling him into the master bathroom with me. I close the door behind us, switch on the light then reach into his shower, turning the water on.

"Everleigh, what… I don't need this. I'll shower soon. You don't have to—"

I turn and face him, pressing a finger to his lips to silence him mid-sentence. "Let me take care of you. Please."

He nods his head, and I smile warmly. As the shower slowly heats, and the room begins filling with steam, I start to undress him. I start with his shirt, inching it slowly up his torso, allowing him to help me when it's high enough I can no longer reach.

I lean in and press kisses to his chest, over his heart, and slide my fingers down his defined abdomen. I work the pants he's wearing open and loose, pushing them down his hips, guiding him to step out of them once they hit the floor.

I bend in front of him, rubbing my fingers over his legs, massaging them carefully, then lifting each foot one at a time to pull his socks off.

The entire time I'm undressing him, Liam is watching me. He tracks my every move, eyes exhausted but alert, as he complies with every whispered direction and touch of his body.

When all he's left with are his underwear, I reach in to check the temperature of the water, unsure what's too hot for him, but assuming given his profession, he can probably handle the sauna level of heat I'm used to.

I let the water heat my hands then I dry them in the hand towel, leaving them warm so when I slip my fingers into the waistband of his navy blue boxer briefs, my fingers aren't frozen.

Any other day, this act would be so sexual. I'd probably tease him, stroke him, try to drive him mad, but today, I don't want to do any of that. I want to take care of him. Plain and simple.

I look up into his eyes as I push the cotton fabric down his hips and let it drop to the floor. "Get in the shower, I'll be right behind you."

Part of me expects him to argue, to make this sexual and playful. Part of me is sad he doesn't, too. I'm not sad for me, I'm sad because the complacency, the exhaustion, pain, and torment written all over his face, that's evident in his every move, is palpable. I'm sad because even doing this for him might not be enough to ease the ache or the hurt, and that's what I want for him most right now.

After Liam steps into the shower, hissing at first, then dropping his head down to let the water run over his body, I make quick work of my clothes. I pull my top off without bothering to be careful not to snag it on anything. I shimmy out of my skirt and underwear without second thought. I quickly take my fitness tracker and watch off, laying them on his counter before I step into the shower behind him and pull its door closed behind me.

"I don't know what to say to make this better," I whisper, wrapping my hands around him from behind and hugging him as tightly as I can. "But I'm here for you."

He doesn't answer right away, but his hands slip down and land over my arms. He links his fingers with mine and pulls me tighter into his body, making it so my front is flush with his back with not a single millimeter between us.

I kiss between his shoulder blades and hold as tightly as he needs. I hold him as his head drops forward, as his body starts to shake with the silent tears I realize he is crying. I hold him through the soft sobs that wrack his whole being like a powerful force of nature, showing him no mercy.

Now isn't the time for words. Now is the time for Liam to feel all he is going to feel, and for me to be his own force, his shelter, his support bracing him against the emotions ripping through his body.

We stand here, just like this, him letting it all out, me holding him as tightly as possible, for minutes. As his sobs start to give way into hiccups, and those fade into stillness, his grip on my hands loosens. His fingers start grazing over my arms slowly, and then he turns in my embrace.

When we come face-to-face again, I find a miniscule look of peace where despair was lodged before the shower started.

"Thank you," he whispers then backs up so the water rains down on me, too. Once we're both below the hot, steady stream, he pulls me into him again, my chest pressed against him, feet touching, bodies slick from water. "Thank you."

I kiss his chest again, then tilt my head back and lift up on my toes, sliding easily along his torso so I can kiss his chin and jaw. "Don't. I want to do this. Let me."

He dips his own head, nodding slightly and kissing my lips. "I'm yours..."

The words hold so much meaning in them. The implication evident in his eyes, the words literal as he releases his hold on me, allowing me the space to do as I will.

Once I'm free from his embrace, I look around the shower, grabbing his bodywash and the loofah he has, lathering it so I can wash him.

"Arms first," I whisper, starting first with his right side, carefully scrubbing all evidence of the day, the fire, what happened, from his body. Then I move onto his left arm, doing the same. Once each arm is clean, I gently scrub over each hand, along his nail beds, working as much of the debris, residue, and everything else filling the spaces around and beneath off.

From his arms I move on to his chest and stomach, rubbing over them, keeping my eyes trained on his as I scrub lower, moving past his belly button down his rectus abdominis, along the tops of his thighs.

His eyes widen, more despair seeping away, being replaced by desire this time, and he sucks in a breath, but he remains speechless. Even more than that, he remains motionless and allows me to care for him.

I know I need to get his legs, too. But right now, kneeling in front of him is something I fear would take us into a territory I'm not aiming for, so I step back and say with quiet dominance, "Turn around."

His lips show signs of twitching up with that, then he follows directions and turns. With his back to me, I can take in his body; focus on any sign of bruises or injury. I still have no idea what today's fire did to him physically. I don't know if he was with Zac, or if he was somewhere else. I have no idea, so I need to take this time where he's completely at my mercy, and on full display, to make sure I haven't missed anything.

There is nothing new on his back, so I scrub over it with the same determination and softness as I did the rest of his body, moving slower over his tattoo, the memory of his brother. When I finish washing, I lean forward to kiss over the scars I've seen multiple times. I'm not tall enough to kiss over his tribute to his brother, his service.

Instead, I trace my finger over it lightly. "You're all clean. Hand me your shampoo, please."

Instead of reaching for the location of his shampoo, he spins around again. The second he's facing me, I can't help but notice the effect my care has had on him.

"I know this wasn't about anything more... You're taking care of me... But please, Everleigh, just let me find peace in you."

I nod my head and step close enough I can feel his erection thickening between us against my stomach. "I'm yours."

"Thank you," he mutters, before his lips crash against mine.

Where my touch was soft, gentle; his is frantic, needy. We both move with purpose, but where I was trying to settle him, he's trying to get lost in me.

\*\*\*\*

# Liam

I need her now like I need oxygen. In fact, in here with her is the first time I've been able to breathe all day, so maybe she is my oxygen. The only way I can continue to breathe, to survive, is to take from her.

Her touch is the softest, most delicate match I've ever had ignite me. Each pass of the loofah, each kiss, each time our eyes lock, the flames continue to ignite deep in my soul.

I know comparing her touch to a match and fire is ironic, given it was a fire that brought us here to begin with, but it's the only way I can explain what she does to me.

Everleigh is the match to the tinder that's my body and soul; our chemistry is the oxygen that allows our flame to burn hotter once it's lit.

I slide my hand along her jaw and around to the back of her head, threading my fingers into her wet hair and using the grip I have to bend her neck, exposing the throbbing carotid. I can feel its power as I nip over it then kiss along the artery.

Everleigh moans quietly, but the sound is magnified by the tile walls of my shower, and I kiss again.

Her hand moves over my body, along my flexed abs, over my hips, and then she's stroking me. Her fingers are velvety soft and insistent as she closes them around my cock and slides them up and down my shaft from root to tip.

"Chriiist," I murmur, then lower my lips to hers, kissing her with a desperation and need like I've never felt before.

She gives me control of the kiss; her mouth is mine for the taking. She swallows every moan her fingers elicit. She lets me taste and tickle, then takes her turn returning the same delicate dance between our tongues.

I'm so hard, so on edge. I need this to settle the demons fighting their way to the surface. I need to give her this so she knows I'm with her. I'm still here.

"Liam," she pants out and pulls away. "This is about you. Not me."

"Being with you is helping me." I cradle her angled, dainty jaw in my hand and brush my thumb over her lips.

"I want to take care of you tonight. In every way..." As soon as the words are out, she begins to kneel in front of me. She picks up the loofah she dropped sometime while we were kissing, and she starts to wash the backs of my legs as she swipes her tongue along the underside of my cock.

Pleasure sizzles up my spine, and I have to slap a hand out against the wall to brace myself for her next assault on my control, and my heart.

She raises her eyes up, meeting mine as she takes me into her mouth and swirls her tongue over my sensitive, swollen tip as though it were a sucker.

"Evvverleigh..." I reach down and move a strand of wet hair off her face, watching as she takes me deeper into her mouth.

Her teeth sheath my throbbing dick, and the loofah scrapes up my legs and over my ass, before dipping down, brushing between my thighs and along my perineum to the underside of my scrotum. The sensations she's giving me have my body tensing and tingling.

She's watching me close, using my reactions to spur her on. The only thing that would make this better would be if she were getting off too. I know she wants this about me, but I can't let her go without. "Spread your knees, touch yourself too…"

I know this might mean losing the insanely erotic touch of the loofah, but watching her pleasure herself will be even better.

She does as I say, dropping the loofa, pulling her hand from my body, and guiding it down her own. Her fingers dip between the valley of her breasts, slide down the line of her stomach, and go lower and lower, until she's touching herself.

She starts to circle herself and moans against me, sending earth-shattering vibrations along the length of my shaft, causing the pleasure forming in the base of my spine to grow larger.

I want to drop my head back and close my eyes, feel every sensation without warning, but I don't want to miss a second of her fingers fucking her expertly.

"That's it, baby," I rasp out. "Imagine those are my fingers between your legs. Imagine me rubbing over your swollen little clit, while I dip my fingers into your tight pussy, getting you ready for my cock."

Her eyes roll into the back of her head as her fingers do what I described, disappearing inside her body, forcing a deep, powerful groan to reverberate over me.

"Fuck your fingers, Ev, use them to get yourself off while you blow me…" I can feel the change in her instantly. Her motions are getting quicker, more demanding. She moves over my cock with gusto, taking me as deep as she can before sliding back, sucking and dragging her tongue along my shaft, flicking over my frenulum as she reaches the tip, and driving me absolutely fucking crazy with need.

"That's it. Keep going. Let me see you fall apart over your own hand. The second you do, I'm done for. Is that what you want?"

She nods her head and fucks herself harder until her mouth starts to move slower over me while she reaches her release. She looks absolutely fucking incredible with her hair wet, eyes closed, makeup smudged from the shower, from gagging on my dick sliding down the back of her throat, as she comes with a body shaking moan.

Once she's able, she takes me deeper again, humming with the aftershocks and tiny flicks of her fingers over her still pulsing body, then adds her slick, juice-soaked fingers into the mix, massaging my balls, tickling the overly sensitive skin just beneath me, until my release is on the precipice of shattering me.

With a flick of her tongue. A deliberate stroke of her finger. My body tenses and I erupt into a flash of uncontrollable heat until I explode in her mouth, jet after jet of my release filling her until every ounce is out and the blaze inside me is extinguished.

"Holy… Shit…" I close my eyes, still bracing myself on the wall, chest heaving, water pouring down my body.

I open my eyes and look down on her, met with the most beautiful proud, green eyes I've ever seen. She slowly pulls her mouth off me, licking up any remaining release as she does, then stands.

I step closer, dipping down to kiss her, tasting myself still on her lips. The emotion of the day, the moment, catches up to me and I rest my forehead against hers. She just let me use her, without any regard for herself or her own needs, so I could feel something other than deep, dark despair. "Everleigh…" I whisper.

"I'm yours, Liam. All night. I'm not going anywhere." She reaches up and cradles me this time; her small hand is framing the right side of my face, her thumb brushing over my cheekbone.

She is selfless. Stronger than I deserve. Too damn good for me.

# *Twenty-Five*

## Everleigh

I walk into Brews and Cruise and pull my sunglasses off, allowing my vision to adjust from the bright sunny outside, to the dimmed, more neutral interior of the coffee shop.

"Hey, Everleigh," Brooke chirps out, waving from behind the counter. "Are you having your usual today?"

"Probably, I'm waiting for my sister before I order, though." I walk up to the counter so we can speak without shouting across the shop. "How are you doing?"

Brooke lights up and beams at me. "I got into college!"

"Brooke! Oh my God. I'm so proud of you, congratulations!" I reach over the counter and pull her into a hug. "Where at? When do you start? Tell me everything."

"Let me take a break, I'll come sit with you for a few while you wait so I can share. It's only fair, after all, I wouldn't be here if it weren't for you."

Her words mean everything to me. They aren't true, she's here because she worked incredibly hard for it; I only supported, encouraged, and loved her through the rough times so she wouldn't give up on herself after she came to the house. "You got you here, Brooke. Not me. I'll grab us a table."

She prances back into the storage area and I grab us a table, then take a seat.

Brooke comes back out with two cake pops, a wide grin, and joins me, sitting across from my spot at our table. "You did get me here," she says, going back to that again. "I never in a million years would have put in the work, believed in myself, known I could overcome my childhood, and everything that happened had you not made me believe it. Had you not believed in me first. I owe everything to you, Everleigh."

"Honey," I reach out to take her hand and shake my head, "you are too kind. You're an amazing young woman who always had this ability. The only reason I could believe in you and encourage you is because you let me. You. Let. Me. So it's still all your doing."

She refutes my words with the movement of her head, wiping tears away before they can fall. "Say whatever you want, I know the truth. I brought you a cake pop, too."

"Your favorite," I answer, taking mine from her, trying not to get choked up by the memory of the first time we ever had these together. "Maybe we should thank these for your success."

She laughs and agrees. "They were our go-to for every serious talk and deep conversation. I thought it fitting we celebrate with them today."

"I think it is, too. Now, tell me everything."

Brooke starts her story, sharing she'll be going to school in Nevada, she's getting grant and scholarship money, and Brews and Cruise are going to help her find work out there for weekends part time, too. She shares all about the application process, the essay she wrote explaining her childhood, the role of Corporate Cares, our bond.

I couldn't be prouder if I tried right now.

She is the prime example of why I do this job, why I dedicate more than forty hours a week to young girls like her. She is thriving, overcoming every obstacle her life has ever thrown at her, and it's possible because we provided her a loving home.

There is no work I'd rather do.

It's why I'm fighting so hard for my promotion. A higher position within the company means I have a say in ideas, planning, implementing programs and activities to help other young girls and young women in our care— just like Brooke was—to become so much more than society would have ever given them credit for.

Addison joins us halfway through Brooke's story, so she takes a seat beside me and listens, just as proud of Brooke as I am. Before Addie started her own work in law, she spent countless days at The Castle with me, volunteering with Corporate Cares at activities, getting to know my girls. She and Brooke were around together, and she is just as invested in Brooke's success.

"If you decide to get into law," Addie says, "you let me know. You know I'm in your corner. I'll do what I can to help you, too."

"I know you will, Ad," Brooke says affectionately, "thank you. I should get back to work and leave you two to talk, I'll make your regulars now." She winks at my sister then takes our cake pop trash and walks away.

"Your regular?" I ask, confused. Addie doesn't live close enough for this to be her everyday go-to.

"Do you think I wasn't going to check in on her too?" she asks me, as if thinking anything else would be insane. "I love that kid as much as you do. She could be my little sister. You may have had a more maternal role in her life, we had a different bond."

"Wow. I didn't… Thank you for loving my girls just as fiercely as me."

"How could I not?" Again, her question is posed as though it's the most obvious, ridiculous thing to insinuate at all. "Now, let's get to the real reason we're here today. Tell me all about your hot firefighter. It's been damn near a month now, and you don't spill any beans."

"A woman doesn't share the private stuff."

"My ass. A woman recognizes her sister is single, and allows her sister to live vicariously through her. I'm assuming you have…"

"Good Lord, Addie!" I shake my head, smirking. "Yes, plenty of times. I'm not a child, and we both have needs stemmed in our biological makeup. We can't fight science."

She laughs loudly. "Not at all. That would be wrong. Are things going well?"

"They seem to be. He's special, different than other guys. He supports me and our work at The Castle passionately. He understands when I have to stay the night there, or when I cancel a date on short notice because there's an emergency. If he's missing our time together, he will drop by. The girls love that." I roll my eyes, but grin widely.

"I'm sure they do. Liam is not hard to look at."

"Nope, not to look at…" I give her a suggestive, you know what I mean look, and she gasps.

"Ever, you better start sharing now. You can't say something like that and leave me hanging."

"I'm not leaving you hanging," I argue, "just letting you use your imagination."

She denies this and then thanks Brooke for our drinks when Brooke brings them out, waiting until Brooke is gone again to say, "So are we talking thick and hard, long and hard? Are we talking his thing at all? Or is it his body? I mean, the night of the auction, he definitely looked like he works out."

"Yes, yes, yes, and yes. It's all of it. The sex is mind-blowing, but he's so much more than that. Our chemistry is off the charts, though, Addie. Seriously, it's explosive and amazing. But his work ethic is incredible; he takes such good care of himself physically. I have zero complaints in the body department."

"You lucky bitch. To think, I could've been the one to meet him…" she teases, but we both know she never would've done that. Liam and I had a chemistry even before our first date. "You say you have no complaints physically, but what about in other areas?"

"He's an amazing man, honestly. He's selfless, he's caring, he's there for everyone."

"But…" she interrupts.

"But he takes the weight of the world on his shoulders and instead of unloading when he can, he keeps piling on. The firefighter who died, Zac Ralston?"

"So sad, I know who he is, I read all about him in the paper."

"Yeah, he was an amazing guy, too. He worked with Liam, same shift, same firehouse, they were both at the call that killed Zac."

"Oh my God, Ev… is Liam okay?"

"Physically, he's fine. But he's taking losing Zac exceptionally hard. The funeral is in a few days, and I'm hoping it brings him some closure, but he's been different since the day of the fire."

"Different how? Grieving is normal, you know that."

"It feels like more than grieving, Addie. He feels like a ticking time bomb. He's wound so tight all the time; he's easily irritated. It's like he can't be still at all, otherwise, he loses his mind. The agitation is there always. I can pull him out, comfort him at times, but not always. He's sinking into this deep hole; I can feel it. His best friend's wife even warned me it could happen."

"Did she explain why? Is it more than Zac dying? Is it because he hasn't faced death like this before?"

"His little brother died, he was in the army and saw men and women die over there. He's experienced death. I've tried talking to him, but he changes the topic, he brushes it off like it's all nothing."

"Maybe he just needs time?"

"I hope so. I've spent every night I'm not working at his place. I rarely go to mine. Which is insane, right? Like it's been a month, yet I feel like I'm basically living with him."

"Whoa." She takes a drink of her coffee, then mulls over the words she has before she starts, "You know I think falling in love fast, the notion someone is your soul mate or meant just for you, is insane."

I nod my head; she's pounded those beliefs in my mind since she had her heart broken in college.

"Well, maybe it does apply to some people."

I release the straw from my mouth and look at her like she's grown a third head. "Do you want to run that by me again? Explain yourself?"

She chuckles a little. "Listen, Ever, I'm not saying I think you and Liam are destined for a life spent together necessarily, but I am saying if you feel a pull, a connection you can't necessarily explain, but that you feel, that you are following, then see what happens. You've changed since you met him."

"I have not." I'm immediately defensive about the notion that any man could change me, but I've started to feel different, too. It's scary, though. So it's easier to argue than to admit maybe there is something more to us than the typical relationship.

"You have. In a good way, though. You are happier, you seem more confident. It's like being with him has allowed you to see in yourself what we all already saw in you. You seem stronger and, Little Sister, you were already the strongest woman I've ever met; yet there's also this intangible change, something I can't quite pinpoint, but I feel it. It's radiating off you and making me feel better, stronger, happier just being around you. It's like you're glowing now."

"I'm glowing?"

Her eyes go wide, and she nearly spits out her coffee. "Everleigh, you better not be pregnant!"

"Whoa, hold your horses! I'm not pregnant. I have the tender boobs and the cramps to prove it."

"Those are signs of pregnancy, too!" she shrieks.

"They are, but the other part of this week is a definite sign I'm not pregnant. I started yesterday."

She visibly relaxes with my words then she looks at me curiously. "Wait, did you think you could be?"

"No, I didn't. We are safe, and I'm on the pill."

"Okay, good."

I roll my eyes. "Weren't you just saying maybe he is different, maybe you were wrong about two people being meant for each other? If he and I are, wouldn't a baby be a good thing?"

"In about two years, yes, absolutely. Just because I think you and Liam might be different doesn't mean I want you diving headfirst into a lifelong commitment he may not stick around to fulfill..." She shivers as though the mere thought of me being pregnant is terrifying to her.

"I'm not pregnant and I have zero plans to be anytime soon. I promise."

"Good." She takes a small sip again then says around her straw, "Do you think Liam's change since Zac's death could be bad for your relationship?"

I shrug my shoulder and frown a little. "I don't know. I'm not going anywhere, but I'm afraid he may push me away. There's something deeper; I can feel it. I can tell by how he shuts down some conversations about his family, his past… He tries to push me away before I get too close."

"Oh, Everleigh," she sighs out, "he would be an idiot if he pushed you away. Liam doesn't seem like an idiot to me, so have faith in him. You'll get him out of this before it's too late."

\*\*\*\*

# Liam

"Do you and Everleigh want to come over for dinner tomorrow night?" Brandon asks, while he cleans trash out of the fire truck. We're in the middle of a shift that's been pretty quiet so far. It's not something any of us will speak out loud, though.

The second we do we will bring chaos.

"I'll ask her." I'm looking through all the compartments on the truck, making sure everything is in place, in stock, and ready for the next call we may need to use it at.

"Don't sound so enthused."

I look up at him, finding him watching me. "Don't start." I have no patience for his shit today.

"Start what? Are you having trouble in paradise already?"

"We're fine."

"Says the man who sounds like someone just shoved bamboo beneath his nails. What's wrong?" He sits down on the step and grabs his empty bottle of water so he can screw with the lid.

"Nothing, B. Christ, I'm just not in the mood for shit right now."

His brows rise up into his hairline. "Something must be fucking wrong. The man who was whistling "Zip-A-Dee-Doo-Dah" out his ass two weeks ago is long gone. She started to change you, lighten you up after your dad's call, your brother's birthday... Now you're back to this dark, brooding asshole. So what's going on with you two?"

"Nothing. Everleigh and I are great. Just drop it."

It has nothing to do with her. She's literally keeping me from drowning right now, but he doesn't need to know that, nobody does.

"No. I'm not going to just drop it."

"Brandon," I warn in a quiet, hard tone I hope he heeds. "There's nothing fucking wrong. Not with me. Not with me and Everleigh. Now get back to your fucking job." It's an order, one I'm using to my advantage as our acting lieutenant today.

"Fuck you, Lieutenant." He rises from the step of the truck and tosses his water bottle across the few yard gap between us and the trash where it lands inside with a thud. "I've been your best friend for years, Liam. I know there's a fucking problem. But hell if I'm going to let you treat me like a subordinate piece of shit because you're pulling the same thing you always do. Fuck that. And fuck you."

I watch him as he walks back into the firehouse, leaving me alone to stew in my own thoughts. If I could shake them free from my mind, I might care I was just a complete dick to my best friend, but as it stands, I don't give two fucks. He can go pout for as long as he wants to.

With him gone and off my back, I focus on the work at hand, thinking about Zac. About Lance. About the day each of them died, how they were so different, yet so similar.

The common thread from both was my inability to be there when they needed me. I failed Lance. I failed Zac.

Broken promises in both instances where I let two lives who looked up to me and counted on me down.

*Lance.*

*Zac.*

*Broken.*

*Bruised.*

*Bloody.*

The cycle repeats over and over in my mind until it's broken by the sound of a tone, alerting us to a call. The rest of the guys filter out, taking their places, getting ready, and so do I.

I move on autopilot, dressing, climbing in the truck, listening to dispatch relay all the vital information we need on the way.

One truck, one ambulance dispatched to a baseball field for a tournament. It's the same field we held the charity game at.

Where Zac hit the game winner.

It's not a far drive from our firehouse, and when we arrive, there's a team parent flagging us down, leading us to the injured kid once we're parked.

Our medics on shift grab their bags and we all make our way over. There's a group of coaches and parents huddled around second base on the field.

They're surrounding a little boy, probably ten or eleven years old, who is lying on the ground sobbing, and scared.

"It hurts," he whimpers out, as our medics kneel and start assessing him.

It's clear immediately his leg is broken, and based on the angle of it, he will probably need surgery to repair the damage. "What happened?" I ask the coach, who rises and stands beside me to give our team room.

"He was stealing second," the coach starts, talking in a lower voice so the boy doesn't hear, but I do and our paramedics do. "The catcher threw down and he slid to beat the throw. His leg jammed into the bag and the second baseman came down right on top of it, foot first. You could hear the snap across the field."

"Ouch," I mutter, "how long has he been down?"

"Probably fifteen minutes. As soon as I got out here, I knew it was bad. We called you all immediately then."

"Good. That's good." I bend down, asking the little boy, "What's your name, buddy?"

He looks up at me, blinking and trying to breathe through the pain and tears. "Andy."

"It's nice to meet you, Andy. We are going to give you some medicine for the pain, okay? Then we are going to get you to a hospital."

"Hey, Hayes," one of our paramedics says to me, "We need to talk, boss."

He and I step away, then he starts, "His leg is broken, clearly, but his pulse is weak in the foot, and getting weaker. He's going to need immediate surgery, at a level one center. With traffic, bypassing local…"

"You're thinking an air evac?"

"I don't think we have any other options. Call the hospital and be sure?" he asks.

"I will." I pull my phone out and put in a call to Peace River General, speaking with an ER doc about the particulars. "I'll put the call in now, thanks, Doc."

I glance down at Derek, who is placing an IV in Andy's arm, and nod then I call radio dispatch. "We are going to need a flight crew out here. Patient is an eleven-year-old boy in need of an ortho surgeon and immediate response for a likely tib-fib fracture causing diminished blood flow to the foot. Peace Gen's ER doc agreed the best course of treatment is a level one children's hospital. Due to traffic, air is quickest."

Dispatch responds instantly, "We are sending out a crew, ETA is fifteen minutes."

"We'll have him ready." I let go of my radio and bend to talk to Andy, and his parents. "Hey, buddy, your leg is hurt pretty bad, and we want to make it better as fast as we can, so we are having a helicopter brought out to take you to a bigger hospital. You get to ride in it with your mom or your dad, and they will take care of you."

His dad looks worried when he asks, "Are you sure it's necessary?"

"We are, sir," I respond, "Andy needs care the closest hospital can't offer. He'll be in great hands, though."

"Okay." His dad nods then starts rubbing his son's head, comforting him like a good dad should. Andy's parents wipe at his tears, hold his hands, try to distract and support him, and I love seeing it. I'm glad there are parents out there like them, who love unconditionally.

"Excuse me," a man shouts from the dugout area as he steps onto the field, crossing it in a hurry. He's wearing a polo with a team name and colors that don't match either team from the current game. "We have next game. When will you be getting this kid off the field so this game can finish? We are ready to play and some of our parents and players have to leave by a certain time."

"What did you say?" I ask, grating my molars together as I turn to face him, standing at my full height with my arms crossed over my chest.

"When can you get this kid off the field so we can get going with games again?" He slides his glasses up onto his forehead, matching my posture, thinking he's going to intimidate me.

229

"Who the fuck do you think you are?" I ask. "Do you see this little boy is in excruciating pain with a clearly broken bone?"

He glances down at Andy, then back at me. "I do, and I'm so sorry for him, but it shouldn't take this long to get him off the field, right? There are other teams here waiting for it to open back up."

"Hayes," Brandon says, stepping up beside me in a silent warning. "This man clearly doesn't know this little boy requires a helicopter evacuation, and no matter how fast we can get him off the diamond, it still can't be used so that our helicopter can land in the outfield."

"Your what?" the man shrieks. "I demand tournament officials come out and sort this out. This is unacceptable. We paid good money to be here."

"Listen here, you entitled, arrogant piece of shit," I seethe, stepping right into his space, standing toe-to-toe with him. "This little boy is going to need emergency surgery if we want to save his Goddamn foot. So you can shove your entitled, whining head up your ass and let us do our job."

"Shit," Brandon mutters, just as the man steps into me, trying to rise up over me, putting his face in mine.

"Get the fuck out of my face."

"How the fuck are you going to make me, pretty boy?" he asks.

I laugh sardonically, not even bothering with another word as I shove him backward with all my might, sending him flying back and landing on his ass. Once he's on the ground I rush him, bending over him so he doesn't try to get up. "Try me again, you piece of shit. See what I do. Get your ass off this field and let us do our job."

Before he can respond, Brandon and a couple of the coaches around the boy are pulling me back and away from him.

Blood is throbbing throughout every artery and vein in my body, causing the pulsing sound to be loud and apparent in my own ears.

"Liam, control yourself," Brandon is whispering in my ear. His arms are around my torso; the coaches are all putting themselves between me and the asshole on the ground.

"I'll have your ass for that, pretty boy!" the man screams.

"Do not engage again," Brandon bites out. "Walk the fuck away, clear the outfield, and keep your fucking mouth shut."

I do as he suggests, heading out toward the outfield, making sure there's room and nothing on the ground that can be kicked up from the propellers and turned into hazardous material that could injure any of us.

Within fifteen minutes, the helicopter arrives, we get Andy and his father into it, and they take off while his mom makes the drive to meet them at Children's Hospital.

Nobody speaks to me as we drive back to the firehouse.

Everyone keeps their distance the rest of our shift.

Even Brandon avoids me after he pulls me aside to scold me in private, and reminds me this could very well cost me any chance at making lieutenant for real.

*Just fucking great.*

# Twenty-Six

## Everleigh

Yesterday was another first for me. Zac's funeral was sad, it was moving; it was a reminder how quickly life can change, end.

I loved getting to hear stories about him from his family, from childhood friends, and from firefighters who knew him. It was a true celebration of his life and testament to the wonderful man he was. Liam was a pallbearer, so I mostly stayed with Jess again. She introduced me to so many people, but some seemed a little hesitant to really talk when they heard I'm Liam's girlfriend.

It seemed weird, even knowing he's suspended right now.

He made a mistake. He knows it, he's apologized, and he's even being punished accordingly, but for people to act like he's a bad apple right now is comical. I know he's a good man, he's a great firefighter, and by all accounts, the guy he put on his backside deserved it.

He won't make the mistake again.

Nobody was hurt.

Brandon even raked him over the coals, took him to task over letting the guys down, putting them in a bad position to betray their brother because his actions warranted it, and while they love him, they couldn't stand by and be okay with what he did. They couldn't keep quiet about it.

He's beaten himself up enough since his suspension started without judgmental women snubbing their noses at him.

"Hey, Hot Stuff?" I walk up behind where he's seated on his couch and scratch my fingers into his scalp. "What do you want for dinner?"

"You pick, I'll eat whatever. I'm not all that hungry, really." He keeps playing his videogame, barely giving me the time of day. It's been like this a lot.

"Okay. Pizza it is."

"Great." He keeps flying his thumbs over the controller, tuning me out as quickly as the next zombie appears on his screen.

I sigh and walk away, grabbing my phone to order when it starts to ring.

Corporate Cares pops up on my screen, so I scrap my pizza ordering plan and answer immediately. "This is Everleigh," I say, not sure who might be calling, or what's going on. "Hi, Josie, are all the girls okay?"

She's at The Castle tonight and my immediate thought is something's wrong with one of my girls. We stopped in to check on them all earlier, making sure Sky was okay after her dad's release on bond.

She was none the wiser about any of it. Her focus is on the fact her mom will hopefully be released from the hospital next week sometime.

She's healing well, we've secured a safe home for them where the address will be private and only Corporate Cares, the social worker, and legal representatives will know how to find them.

My question gets Liam's attention, and the killing pauses on the screen while he shifts his body to watch me.

"What's wrong with Kristy?" Liam's body relaxes, but his gaze stays serious, following my every step as I pace back and forth in his kitchen.

"She's sick? Does she have a fever?" I stop walking immediately and look up at him. "I'm on my way now, I'll take her in, you keep the other girls away, we don't know what's wrong or if she's contagious. I'll be there as fast as I can."

I end the call and look up at him. "She's got a one hundred-and-two-degree temperature. She's having a hard time keeping liquids and solids down, and they can't get anything to break, even with medicine and popsicles. Everything they try comes back up."

"I'll grab my hat and wallet," he says, tossing his controller onto the coffee table and turning off the TV. "I'll meet you in the car."

"Liam, you don't have to."

"I want to…" His tone leaves no room for argument as he walks back to his room where I know his wallet and hat are both on the dresser.

I grab my own purse off the kitchen table and head out to the car, not waiting long before he's walking out of the house, ready to leave with me.

\*\*\*\*

# Liam

It's been a long night by the time we walk back into my house at three in the morning. Kristy has a stomach virus, and there is a good chance every girl in the house will get it at some point. Everleigh and the rest of the counselors are all hopeful they won't, though.

Once we got Kristy back to The Castle after the hospital, I helped them start to sanitize the whole house. We put Kristy in her own room, and the older girls agreed to share rooms with anyone they needed to, hoping to keep anyone else who might get sick quarantined.

We bleached tables, sanitized laundry, sprayed down every surface in the house we could. The toys were all soaked in bleach, and anything disposable was thrown away.

Hopefully nobody gets it.

But they could be in for a long few days if it starts to spread.

"Thank you for tonight," Everleigh says, as she steps out of my bathroom wearing one of my shirts and a pair of sleep shorts. "You were incredible with Kristy. Then taking control at The Castle, helping us clean and sanitize, disinfect everything... we couldn't have done it without you. I couldn't have done it without you."

"It was my pleasure, babe." I pull my shirt off and step out of my shorts, crawling into bed in only my underwear.

"It was nice having you back again," she says carefully, then crawls beneath the covers beside me.

"What do you mean?"

"You've been so distant, so... I don't know how to describe it. Tonight you were the same way you were a few weeks ago, before..."

"Before?" I push, even though I know what she's going to say.

"Before Zac passed."

*There it is, the thing everyone keeps going back to.*

Ten years ago, it was Lance.

Now, it's Zac.

*Why can't people just leave it be?*

"I've been fine, Everleigh," I say, irritated. "We haven't been together long enough for you to have an opinion, or anything to base this unfounded concern off of."

"Excuse me?" She sits up and glares at me. "You asked me to stay, Liam. You needed me. Remember? Do you think I haven't worried all this was happening too damn fast, seeing as we've been together for all of a month?" She rises out of bed and walks across the room, pulling her bra out of her overnight bag.

"What are you doing?"

"I'm going home. If you inviting me into your bed, your life, spending nearly every day either together or talking for the last month doesn't give me the right to be concerned, I don't want or need to be here." Her voice is strong, but her eyes betray her stoic attitude. The hurt is evident. The betrayal is written deep in her soul, and I can see directly to it through the emerald green orbs fighting back tears.

*It's do or die, Liam. Shut the fuck up and let her walk out, or give her something.*

The inner voice in my head is loud and taunting. It's right, though. I either share something, or I risk losing her, and whatever we have and are building together.

"Stop," I sigh, then rise from the bed and pad over to her. I take the bra from her hand and drop it back on her bag, then lead her onto the bed. She tries to pull away, resisting my attempts at changing her mind and keeping her here, so I say the one thing I know will stop her, and make her stay, "Zac's death hit me hard."

I can't tell her the whole truth, not without opening up a can of worms I have zero intention of opening, but I can share half-truths. I can be moderately honest so she maybe has some idea where I'm coming from.

# Twenty-Seven

## Everleigh

*Zac's death hit me hard.*

That's probably the only thing he could have said that would make me sit back down on the bed and listen, rather than walk out and not look back tonight.

"You have five minutes," I say stubbornly, making sure he knows I'm in no way excusing his dickish behavior by stating what's been obvious to everyone around him since it happened.

"I'll take it." He grabs my hand and starts playing with it, using it as a distraction of sorts. Long, silent seconds pass, making me think he's not going to actually say anything, when he exhales out a deep sigh. "I should have been partnered with him. I usually am. He was a probationary firefighter; he needed guidance still. But we were paired off differently on the call." He stops talking, and I glance his way, seeing him staring off vacantly.

I don't want to stop his story, or force it out any quicker, so I wait him out, flipping my hand for him so he can thread his fingers though mine.

"Brandon and I were together in the second building. The smoke was thick, the fire had jumped; you could tell everything was going to go. We know now the apartments weren't up to code, so it explains a lot. We were all ordered to evacuate, it was too hot, too dangerous. B and I were finished clearing our building, up on the top floor when the evac came in, so we hauled ass, worked our way back down every flight of steps. And then it came…"

He shakes his head and blinks a few times, looking away. "Zac's mayday. We didn't know it was Zac at first, but based on the info he was able to get out, we knew he was from our station and he didn't have air. We knew he was in building one, too."

He looks at me again with tears pooling in his eyes, and it takes everything I have not to reach up and wipe them away. I want to; I know, though, that sometimes an action like that can interrupt the flow of a story. Working with kids who experience traumas, I've learned it's often best to just let them get it out, tears and all.

"By the time we got out, I was trying to figure out which of our guys was missing, but a few were, a couple went in search of Zac. When they brought him out…" Liam shakes his head and dashes away at his own tears. "It was so bad, Ev. His mask broke when a floor collapsed on him. He was separated from his partner minutes earlier, they were splitting up to clear the floor, and it collapsed on him…"

This time I do reach out, wiping away at his tears, then taking his hand. "Keep going."

"He was in agony, he had a few burns, internal injuries, smoke inhalation. I did everything I knew how to, stuff from my time in Afghanistan, procedures I've seen done here; we exhausted our every option. The docs in the ER were surprised he was still fighting when we got there. He coded not long after we got him through but they brought him back, for a few minutes. His face, Ev, it looked like he'd gone ten rounds with a heavyweight champ. When they cut his gear off—" Liam chokes up again, and holds back a sob. "His body was already covered in bruises. It didn't matter what I did, what I said, I couldn't stop it from happening. I should have stopped it. I should have been there. My own wishes didn't matter."

With his final words he hangs his head, crying and burying his face in his hands. Zac's death isn't his fault; even he knows that. He said it himself. Yet he blames himself, he thinks he should have been there.

I rub his back and drape my body around him to the best of my abilities, trying to hold and console him.

He may be double me in size, but I don't care. Not tonight. My big, strong boyfriend is letting me in, he's trusting me with his heart, and I will protect it with my everything.

"You couldn't have done anything, baby," I coo, talking into the warmth of his neck. "You didn't choose to separate, you didn't leave him, Liam. You were both doing your jobs. You were doing what you had to." He shakes his head, disagreeing with my every word silently, even as he leans more into me, as he lets me hold him and love on him.

"I could have done everything differently. I should have saved him." He turns into me this time, wrapping himself around me in a way that forces me onto my back on his bed, where his body can cover mine, and I can hold him. His head rests on my chest, his arms bar me in between each other, and he nuzzles in close. "His death is on me."

"It isn't," I say as a quiet, reassuring chant, starting to scratch my nails gently into his hair, holding him to me, trying to give him what he needs to survive the night of guilt swallowing him whole.

\*\*\*\*

# Liam

I fell asleep in her arms last night; the steady, confident beat of her heart beneath my head was my own personal lullaby. She accepted my apology. She understood my pain, the watered-down, half-honest version of it I shared with her.

I could never tell her what his lifeless body truly looked like, or reminded me of. The bruises on him were eerily similar to the images of bruises I saw ten years ago.

They would have been the same age. Instead, they're both gone, far too young; with far too much life left they should've lived.

I will never stop blaming myself.

I will never not feel guilt.

I might feel just a little better today, though. All because of Everleigh. She's still sound asleep on my pillows with her hair fanned out in a wild mess, her blankets wrapped and tangled around her are evidence of the restless chaos the night brought.

"You're staring at me," she whispers loudly, into the pillow she's now burying her face into.

"You're gorgeous," I respond, lying back down and rolling to face her. "You can come out, I'll protect you from the sun."

She slowly turns her head, as though she doesn't trust me, and squints her eyes at me. "What time is it?"

"It's early still. I couldn't sleep anymore."

"Monster," she groans. "Off days mean no getting up before at least eight."

"You can go back to sleep. I'll make you breakfast, as an olive branch and apology for last night."

She shakes her head. "You don't need to do that. Just stay in bed with me. You'll go back to sleep."

I lean in and kiss her forehead. "No, I won't. Trust me. I think I have some bacon, eggs, maybe even some pancake batter in there. How does that sound?"

"Too good to be true. You can cook?" She seems skeptical, even with her face half-hidden.

"I'm a firefighter. While we do have a ton of people cook for us and bring us shit, we all have to take our turn in the kitchen, too. Most of us can cook at least a little, and pancakes are easy."

"Do you have chocolate chips?" she whispers.

"I might. Do you want them inside the pancakes if I do?"

She nods her head over the soft, blue case covering my pillow. The smile on her face and look in her eyes remind me more of a little girl than a strong, beautiful woman. "Yes, please."

"Coming right up." I kiss her lips, ignoring her potential morning breath protests, then slip from bed and head to my kitchen.

I have everything I need, including the chocolate chips, to make us a great breakfast, and hopefully it'll be a good start to making up for last night, everything I said, everything I did.

She doesn't need the weight of my shit on her shoulders. She already has enough loving all her girls.

# Twenty-Eight

## Liam

"I never knew a suspension could mean I'd have so much fun during my time off," I say, chuckling, as I lift Sky up on my shoulders.

Having the day off, I was able to come and act as an additional chaperone with Everleigh and Jake at the zoo.

"It's not a vacation, Liam," Everleigh groans, and rolls her eyes. "You're being punished for what you did, not rewarded." She holds out hand sanitizer for everyone to put their hands beneath while she applies it generously to each of them.

"Yet, here I am, at the zoo with a bunch of the most amazing girls and women in the world. And Jake." I smile at her and wink. "I don't feel like I'm being punished. I feel like I'm being encouraged to get through my down mood with the best, most amazing therapy a man could ever be given."

"He's good," Jake praises from the ground where he's knelt, tying Kristy's shoes. The family who visited her decided now is not the right time for them to adopt, so we wanted to bring her, all our girls, out for a day of forgetting and fun.

"He's the type we should be looking for as adults, right?" Nichole asks, smirking.

Everleigh glares at each of us, muttering how she doesn't know why she even tries, and we all laugh.

"You try because you love us," Haylie reminds her. "Isn't that what you always say?"

Our suddenly silly ribbing shifts to a subtly more serious conversation.

"Yes, Hay, I do say that. If you love someone, you always try for them. That's why I'll always try for you girls. No matter what."

"And you're trying for Liam, too? Cutting him slack, right? Because that's what you do," Nichole adds.

Jake freezes, I am stock-still, and Everleigh looks as though her heart has jumped somewhere up past her throat, cutting off air and all potential of formulating an easy response.

"Liam knows I'm here for him. It's a little different," she tries to explain, "but I have his back too."

I know what she means. It's too soon to be tossing around that word, those emotions, even as all we've been through in our short time tells me I could easily venture down that road with her.

"It's not all that different. You said if you loved someone you try, you defend them, stand by them, love them through it. No matter what kind of love it is. Right?" Haylie asks, reminding Everleigh of their conversation.

Ev is a smart woman, and I know if she was telling the girls that, it was for a great reason. It stands to reason she'd focus her support on her love for them, but their talk is somehow coming back to bite us on the ass.

"Yes, I did say that." Everleigh's eyes flash to mine momentarily, causing me to stop and question what she's about to say.

"So you love Liam, right?"

Everleigh looks to Jake, who shrugs his shoulders and takes a step back, easily rendering him out of this conversation and without a say.

When he steps back dodging, she looks at me, and all I can do is smirk.

Anger and annoyance flicker in her eyes before she's back to compassionate and understanding with the girls. "There are so many different types of love in the world," she qualifies, before continuing, "so yes, I think I might love Liam as a good friend, a good man, and a great firefighter, even if he's suspended."

"Oooo," the girls all say in unison. Even some of the younger girls, Gracie, Kenzie, Cassandra, Kristy, and Sky join in.

"Everleigh and Liam, sitting in a tree," Nichole starts. Then Haylie continues, "K-I-S-S-I-N-G…"

"First comes love—" they both say together, right before Everleigh raises both hands and covers both girls' mouths.

"Finish that song and neither of you gets ice cream." She looks at them both seriously, and they nod their heads with wide, stunned eyes.

"Don't worry, girls," I whisper, "I'll make sure you get ice cream. No matter what."

This has them both giggling and giving me conspiratorial thumbs-up.

"What animal should we go see next?" I ask to the group, watching Everleigh carefully, looking away as quickly as I can when she shifts so I'm in her view.

We've made it to kissing, all that's left is the part the girls were just getting to… Love.

"Monkeys!" Kristy and Sky both shout.

"We don't need to go anywhere to see those," I tell them, bending forward so Sky starts to topple off me. "We already have two of our own!"

Sky screams in delight and fear, then laughs hysterically.

Everleigh screams in fear, "Liam, do not drop her!" Then she slaps her hand over her chest, eyes wide, when I catch Sky in my arms at a weird angle so she's hanging upside down. "You're going to be the death of me," she says in horror.

"Never, babe." I wink at her and right Sky, setting her down on the ground. "You can walk a while, you little monkey."

"Okay, Liam!" She bounces ahead of us a few feet then she stops dead in her tracks.

"Sky?" Everleigh asks.

All of us look around at each other then her, confused why the sudden stop and change in her expression.

"I think I see my daddy," she whispers, looking straight ahead.

"There's no way, Little One," I step up beside her, looking forward in the same direction. "He's not allowed to be around you, remember? He can't hurt you or your mommy again." I say the words I'm supposed to, but the hair on the back of my neck is standing on end, and I glance out around us. I've only seen the fucker once, but someone staring at us should be easy enough to identify. He's not, though. But somehow, I know, I just know she's right. He's here, watching, and if I could find him, I would make him pay for every last bit of his crimes.

"Liam's right," Everleigh says, squatting down to her level. "Your daddy can't come around you, and we won't let anything happen to you ever. I promise."

Sky nods her head and then looks up at me, "Hold my hand." She thrusts her tiny hand upward, and I take it in mine immediately. She looks terrified; it's a look I recognize. It's a fear I know. I've been in her position before; afraid of the one man you should trust most in the world.

I bend down, whispering in her ear, "Do you remember the story I told you?"

She nods her head. "Yes."

Everleigh looks between us, clueless, silently questioning what we're talking about.

I ignore her. There is no need to share everything between me and Sky. "I promise you, you're safe. Remember everything?"

She nods again.

"Do you trust me?"

Sky nods again and then turns into me, hugging my legs tight. She squeezes for a few seconds then pulls back and looks at Everleigh. "Liam has superpowers."

"Does he?" Everleigh looks stunned and smiles, but it doesn't quite reach her eyes. I can tell she's concerned and confused.

"Yep. He'll save me."

Everleigh smiles wide at her then looks up at me. "That I believe."

****

# Everleigh

"What story did you tell Sky?" I try asking him again. I've brought it up multiple times today, ever since they had their little talk at the zoo, but neither one of them will share anything. Sky is keeping the story to herself because she super pinky promised Liam she wouldn't tell anyone, even me.

Liam just changes the subject anytime I bring it up.

"It was nothing, really," he says this time, as he grills our steaks for dinner. "Just an experience I had with a bully growing up. I told her I understood what being afraid was like, because I was once too."

His answer is plausible. It even sounds sincere, but I can't help but wonder if he's still hiding something from me. If that were the case, why wouldn't he have told me earlier? There is nothing wrong with sharing something like that with her. "Ohhh," I draw out, "okay. Well thank you for sharing something that would make her more comfortable."

"It's my pleasure. You know I adore Sky, she will always hold a special place in my heart. I don't want her to be afraid of anything. Especially not her dad or any other person."

"I don't, either." I set the table, putting out the salad and our drinks, making sure our napkins and silverware are in place. "Her mom will be released soon, then Sky will be leaving us."

He stills at the grill, goes completely silent, and only moves again when the steak sizzles in front of him.

"Liam?" I step out of the house and up to the grill. "You did know Sky wouldn't be staying with us forever, right?"

He sighs and nods slowly. "Logically, yes. Her mom wasn't unfit; she was abused. I was just getting used to having the Little One in my life. I really like her. We've bonded." He closes the lid on the grill, then turns to me. "Do they have a safe place to go?"

"They'll be set up in a safe home, yes." I lean my hip against the table beside his grill. "We won't have anything to do with that. I'm not sure if she'll testify against her husband, either."

"Excuse me?" Anger sears across his every feature, and he shakes his head. "Unacceptable. If she doesn't, you all have to find a way to keep Sky."

"Liam," I say, stepping closer and rubbing his arms, trying to cajole him into calmness, "we can't do that. Legally Sky has to return to her mom. The DA, social workers, everyone will do their best to encourage her to testify. But none of us can force her."

"If she doesn't, he will hurt her again. He may very well turn on Sky, too. Do you want that?" His voice is loud, mad, forceful. I know he isn't really thinking I want for Sky's mom to stay silent, or that I want to even consider Sky being hurt. But the words sting nonetheless.

"I can't do anything except be here for Sky now, Liam. Don't act like I don't care about her and want the best. I've been doing this for years. I've had girls come and go, family taking them in, perfect strangers adopting them to give them new homes. I've had some girls go home to return even more broken later, and others live under our roof until they age out. I have seen and experienced it all, Liam. Don't you dare think I don't care. Don't you dare insinuate I don't want the best for Sky, or any other girl I love like my own when they walk in our doors!" I'm shaking by the time I finish, my throat hurts from screaming at him, and based on the stunned look on his face, he's just as surprised by my outburst as me.

"Babe... I didn't mean, I know you care. I know you love them, all of them. I know you love Sky as much as I do. But you don't know..."

"I don't know what, Liam?" I cross my arms, hoping to still the tremor in my hands by tucking them into my body.

"Nothing, it doesn't matter. I've just experienced so many calls with abusive parents, I've seen the homes, the

249

injuries," he rushes out. "I can't bear to think of Sky being one of them."

"She won't be. I believe her mom will protect her, Liam. She loves Sky so much. I see it when I take Sky to visit." I hope he believes me, most importantly, I hope I'm right. I think her mom would do anything to protect Sky, but after a beating like the last she took, her husband will hold all the power. He almost killed her. I'm not going to bring that fear up now, though. I'm just getting Liam out of his Zac caused slump. He's still quick to trigger.

"I hope so," he says quietly. "I can't lose another one. I won't."

He puts so many people's lives on his shoulder; it's amazing he can stand upright. I don't want him doing it with Sky. He doesn't need to. She isn't his responsibility. Most of all, I don't want him transferring any of that fear or disdain to her, even by accident, because he thinks it's his job to be her savior.

"You won't lose anyone, Liam." I step up and push forward on my toes, kissing his lips. "You're an amazing man, who will make the most incredible dad one day. I hope you know that."

"Where did that come from?" he asks, smiling against my lips then kissing me again.

"What?"

"Me, being a dad…" He wraps his arms around me, the huge, cheesy grin staying firmly in place, Sky and her mom all but forgotten for now, I hope.

"Well, I see you with Sky. From the first day, until now, the way you are with the older girls. You are forceful when you need to be, but even the moments you have to be sterner, it's always laced with a caring tone. You can comfort with the absolute best, trust me, it's my job to know that. And… while I haven't seen you with a baby, I bet seeing a tiny human who absolutely does require your protection, folded and held in your big arms, framed by your strong body, would be the sexiest sight on the planet."

"You've put a lot of thought into this," he murmurs, resting his forehead against mine.

"When I'm with someone, it's not with the intention of a few good months and then walking. I'd like to think I'm at an age where if it's right, it could be right for life." I shrug my shoulders. "Does that make sense?"

"Yeah, it does." He angles his head to kiss me again, and he nips at my lip playfully. "There will be no little Liams running around anytime soon," he says so matter-of-factly I'm surprised. "I love practicing for the day I might be ready for that though. I'd love to show you more of my moves after dinner to prove it, too."

"Is that so?" I close my hands around his shirt and pull him in. "You're going to have to show me something really great to impress me. Are you up for the challenge?"

"When it comes to you, I'm always up for it. Always."

# Twenty-Nine

## Liam

I avoided the conversation I have never had with anyone other than Brandon last night. I managed to deflect, turn, and maneuver myself away from talking about how I know what Sky is going through, and maybe, just maybe, I did it without Everleigh noticing when I froze briefly, or when I backtracked and tried to swerve right over the fact I almost shared too much.

I hate lying to her, but Lance's story isn't for anyone to hear. My failure isn't something I want put out there, or judged, especially not by a woman I've become absolutely crazy about.

"Hey, Hot Stuff?" she asks, interrupting my thoughts.

"I didn't hear you get out of the shower," I admit then look her over. "Damn, I was hoping you'd appear in nothing but a towel."

"I probably would have, but I have to head over to get Sky. She has a visit with her mom today, and we should be getting discharge plans for her."

"Already?" I'm surprised to hear this. I know we were talking about it last night, but I was hoping for a few more weeks, to make sure she's truly healed and strong enough for Sky.

"She can finish recovering at home. She's insisting on not being away from her little girl any longer than she has to be. Teddy let me know this morning over voicemail."

"Can I go with you?"

She pauses, face contorting into something I don't like to see. "I don't know…"

"Listen, I was there that day. I just want to meet her in person, let her know how amazing she is, and how well Sky has done."

"You can't bring up any of the shit you were saying last night." Her words are like a slap in the face, but I try not to let them get to me.

"I'm entitled to my opinion," I remind her.

"Yes, you are, and you can share it with me anytime. You can't, however, share with my girls, or their families. For one, you shouldn't even be coming with me, so for another, it could cost me my job."

"I will keep my opinions to myself."

*Unless she says something outrageous.*

"That's all I'm asking," she says. "I need to finish putting on my makeup, then we can go."

"You don't need the makeup, babe." I grin at her. "You look beautiful just as you are."

"Way to try to smooth things over." She rolls her eyes and walks back to my room, and my bathroom.

I love having her here. It seems so unconventional, but she's made the riotous thoughts go away, so I keep insisting she stay.

It's for that reason I'll try even harder to keep my thoughts to myself today. I don't know if I could handle a night alone with myself right now. Especially not one where she isn't at least talking to me.

While Everleigh finishes getting ready, I change into a pair of khaki shorts and a black polo then walk into my bathroom to do my hair.

"Whatcha doin?" she asks, watching me in the mirror.

"Getting ready." I stare into the mirror, our eyes locking in the glass, then smirk. "Is that okay?"

"Of course," she sighs, with her tongue poking out to swipe over her lip. "You were already ready, though. You've left the house in shorts, your hat, countless times."

"True, but we are going to the hospital. I've grown attached to this woman's child, and the hospital staff is used to seeing me more professional looking."

I don't know if I've ever stepped foot in the hospital wearing anything other than a uniform or department paraphernalia. If I'm going to be there today, I still want to look my best.

"Okay." She shrugs her shoulder and applies some of her light pink glossy lip stuff before she smacks them together. "I'm ready. Are you?"

I turn to face her, arms stretched wide, hair done and gelled perfectly in place, grinning. "You tell me."

She steps up and rakes her nails down my thick shirt. "If we weren't on a time crunch, I'd make you all messy and unkempt."

"Later," I chuckle and lower my arms, wrapping them around her. "You can make me as unkempt as you want later."

"At my place?" she asks, raising a brow. "I have to get some work done, and it's easier using my home office. Plus, I kind of miss my bed…"

"You aren't kicking me to the curb?"

"I'm saying you can either stay here tonight, so you have everything you need for your shift, or you can pack a bag and come to my place. But I need to go home."

It's odd she's saying this now, when I was just thinking about her leaving a while ago. But if she's not making it mandatory that we spend the night apart, I think I will be okay.

"I'll stay at your place."

Her face expresses the shock she keeps to herself, for her. I doubt she's ever been so attached to someone with such a new relationship before, but fuck if I can stand the thought of being alone tonight.

"Well then pack a bag, Hot Stuff."

I do as I'm told, loving how bossy she can be when she wants to, and pack my bag. Call me a pussy. Call me insane. Call me what you want, right now, I need Everleigh too damn much to not be around her.

****

# Everleigh

"There's your mama's room," I point out to Sky, letting her little hand go so she can skip ahead of us and inside to visit her mom. She disappears inside the room, and her laughs and elation echo out. "She needed to see her. They need to be back together." I glance at Liam, then reach down to give his hand a quick squeeze before I let it go again.

I know he is adamant about Sky's mom testifying, pressing charges, making sure Sky is safe. I get his feelings. I agree with him. But my top concern is Sky's safety; if that means not pressing charges for her mom, I will respect it. It isn't my call to make.

"I know she does," he agrees. "I just hope nothing happens to her."

"Have faith," I whisper when we are just outside the door, "that's what you have to do in my job sometimes. Just have faith." I wink up at him and then walk into the hospital room.

Her mom looks so much better now. The bruising is healing incredibly fast, the cuts are all in various forms of scabs and scars now. It's been a couple weeks, and so far everything seems to be progressing even better than doctors thought it might the first time I was here.

"Hi, Everleigh," her mom says. "How are you today?"

"I'm doing great, thank you, Monica. How are you feeling?"

"Stronger and better every day," she answers with a smile. "Thank you for bringing my baby by. I'm hopeful I'll be able to get out of here soon, then we can be together for good."

Sky squeals in delight and wraps her arms around her mom's neck in a tight embrace. I watch for any signs of discomfort, not catching a single thing. It's a good indication she will be released very soon.

"Who might this be?" Monica asks, looking at Liam.

"Mommy, this is Liam. He's my friend. He lets me play with bubbles."

Familiarity burns in Monica's eyes. "I heard about you," she says quietly. "You were there?"

Liam steps forward, nodding his head. "Yes, ma'am. I'm a firefighter paramedic. I was the one who helped Sky that day…"

Monica is an incredibly strong woman, stronger than anyone I've ever met, maybe. But I see the tremor in her hand as she pats Sky's back. I see the waver in her expression, the battle between appreciation and embarrassment. "Thank you," she says, steeling herself

256

against any other emotion but strength. "I heard how you cared for my daughter. I am grateful she had you."

"It was my pleasure," he answers. "It's good to see you doing so well."

Monica nods her head, forcing a smile to her face when Sky pulls back. "When can I stay with you?"

"Soon, baby. So soon." Monica boops Sky's little nose. "The nurses left some coloring books in here for me, but I think there's one for you too, will you color me a picture while I talk to Miss Everleigh and Mr. Liam?"

Sky nods and carefully scoots off the bed, moving over to the little basket on the chair full of coloring books and crayons.

Monica makes sure Sky is completely occupied with the books then signals for us to move closer. "I'll be going home in two days," she whispers quietly. "The social worker has secured a safe place for us, and she swears he won't be able to find me or Sky there."

I nod and smile warmly. "Good, that's really good. Do you need anything from me?"

"It won't be a problem when he's in prison, either," Liam adds. He's smiling softly, and even sounds mostly encouraging, but there's something in his tone, an assumption and a guilt he's trying to convey to Monica.

"If he ends up there, you're right," Monica agrees. "Everleigh, could you put me in contact with a counselor or therapist you trust for her? I want her to know she has plenty of people to talk to."

"I'd be happy to." I look at Liam, and he's seething over Monica's blowoff about her husband going to prison. "We can give you and Sky time to visit for a while, if you want?" I ask, loud enough for Sky to hear.

Sky's head pops up from her coloring book and she grins so wide I'm surprised it doesn't split her face in two. "Pleeeease, Mommy!"

We all laugh at that, and Monica nods. "We would love some time together."

I nod and grab Liam's hand, basically dragging him out of her room behind me. "Do not go there, Liam Hayes. I told you, I shouldn't have even brought you today, do not try to guilt that woman—who has been through hell—into anything."

"I'm not," he whisper-shouts. "I'm just reminding her that's where he'll end up if she just tells what he did. Because he will, Ev. He will go to prison where he belongs."

"It isn't that easy, Liam. She needs support, encouragement, she needs to not feel alone if she chooses to make that decision, because if he gets off and she betrays him in that manner, she thinks, maybe even knows, he will kill her."

His expression changes from anger to pure rage, and something dark passes in his eyes quickly. If I weren't staring right at him, I would've missed it.

"I won't let that happen," he grates out, then turns and walks away.

# Thirty

## Liam

Sleeping in Everleigh's bed last night was different. The bed is smaller than mine, the room is smaller, too, but she felt distant. I'm sure my reaction at the hospital yesterday put her off.

Her words did something to me, though. Monica being killed, Sky potentially being killed, it took me back.

Back to the day I got the news.

Back to the day I decided to leave.

Back to being helpless and a failure.

I won't let that happen again.

"Hey, boys," I shout out, loving being back at work. "Let's go for a ride. There's a beautiful woman I owe an apology to."

Brandon walks out and raises an eyebrow. "Your mood swings are damn near impossible to keep track of."

I shrug a shoulder. "I fucked up with Everleigh yesterday, she's at the Corporate Cares offices today, I just want to stop in and apologize. Take her a peace offering."

"Jesus," Brandon murmurs and shakes his head. "You're pussy-whipped. I hope you know that. So you can keep any comments you ever make about me and Jess to yourself now."

"Whatever," I chuckle. "I really like her, Brother, I just don't want to lose her over anything stupid."

"What did you do? And how are you making it up to her?"

"I said shit I shouldn't have. I have her favorite chocolates in my truck, and a stuffed bear I thought she would love."

Brandon makes the sound and motion of a whip being cracked. "You all heard Romeo, get your shit together. We're going for a ride."

I toss my shit in the fire truck and then jog out to my pickup real fast, grabbing the candy and bear for Everleigh. As the engine rolls out, I climb up inside it, giving Terence the address of the Corporate Cares offices so we can get there.

Once I'm settled in my seat, I put the headphones on, then pull my phone out and send her a text.

**Me: Hey, babe. We're swinging by, I have something for you. Meet you when we get there in a bit.**

**Everleigh: Okay, I'll head down to meet you as soon as I'm off the phone.**

It's a relatively quick trip, all things considered.

When we pull up, I hop out of the truck, grateful for being in the engine so we can use the fire lane. "I'll be back in a few. My radio will be on."

"Pussy. Whipped," Brandon gives me shit, making all the guys laugh. "Hurry up, if we get a call, you have thirty seconds to get your ass down here."

"Fuck you. I know how to do my job, I won't be late." I flip him the bird then walk into the building, opting for the stairs instead of the elevators.

The only way my plan will work is if there isn't a run-in too early. I pull out my phone and text Everleigh again...

**Me: I'm here. See you in a couple.**

I know she's going to hop on the elevator and come down, and while she's doing that, I need to haul ass up to her office.

She doesn't reply, not that she needs to, and I know everything will work out. I jog up the stairs, taking them two at a time, feeling the burn deep in my quads from the hard pounding on the cement steps.

I look through the door window on the Corporate Cares floor and scan each area I can to make sure Everleigh isn't there.

When I'm sure she isn't, I step onto the floor and out of the stairwell, making a beeline for her office.

Thank God.

She isn't in here, which means I have maybe two or three minutes to do what I came to do before she's back up here.

I put the bear and chocolates down on her desk, setting them up to be the first thing she sees when she comes back in, then I move around to sit in her seat in front of the computer.

I need to do this fast. Hopefully I can find what I need.

I get to work, and before I have time to cover my tracks, she's walking back in.

"Liam?" she asks, then stops short when she sees the bear and candy. "Oh my God."

While she's looking at them, I make a few clicks then stand and hold my arms out. "Surprise!" I say, grinning wide.

"I thought I was supposed to meet you downstairs?"

"I wanted you to think that," I inform her. "I wanted to surprise you, make a show of apologizing for being such an asshole yesterday. I knew you were upset last night, and I wanted to make it right."

"So you bought me a bear and my favorite candy?" She lifts the bear up and snuggles it into her chest. "You get good boyfriend points for this, even if I did have to go all the way downstairs just to have Brandon tell me you came up here."

"I'm sorry, babe." I walk around her desk toward her and take the bear, tossing it into one of the chairs off to the side of her desk, then slide my hand along her jaw and kiss her deeply, breaking just long enough to add, "For the walk and my attitude."

She lets out an appreciative moan when my tongue glances over hers and she reaches up, wrapping her fingers around my wrist to keep my hand still. "You're forgiven."

I should feel guilty for doing this, for lying to her. But it's for a good cause. It's only if I really need it.

"Where is everyone?" I murmur against her lips, trying not to think about what else I'm doing, and realizing there were very few people in the office as I walked through.

"Colton and Rylee Donavan brought their new car to show off. Teddy wanted to see it."

"They're here, now?" I ask, kissing her more. Somewhere in the back of my mind, I know I should be thrilled to hear this. He is my favorite driver and athlete, after all.

"In the parking garage," she pants out, as I slide my lips from hers, down her throat.

"Why aren't you down there?" I tug her earlobe gently then kiss back along her jaw. Just kissing her has me growing hard, and the prospect of having to move quickly or get caught has me aching to fuck her.

"Already went. Want to go meet him?" she asks, as her hands start working my pants open, giving me instant relief for my growing, straining cock. "We can stop."

"Fuuuuck," I hiss. Then she slips her hand inside my pants and underwear, gripping me in her hot, delicate fingers. "Don't you dare stop. I'll meet him another day."

"Good answer," she yelps out in shocked delight when I lift her and set her on the edge of her desk. "Close my door."

I reach back and shove her door closed, foregoing the lock in my hurry to get back to her. With the small, cotton dress she has on, it won't take much work to have her bare and ready for me.

She doesn't take long shoving my pants down my hips and ass, either. "We have to hurry, Liam…"

"I know." I reach beneath her dress and slide my fingers over the silky-smooth panties she has on, feeling the damp center immediately. "Christ, babe… How are you already this ready?"

"You. Uniform. Groveling. Gifts. Maybe getting caught."

"Dirty, dirty girl," I praise, moving her panties to the side now so I can tease and toy with her while she strokes me.

"Condom?" she asks, as her eyes roll back into her head when I stroke my thumb over her clit, then circle it with a little extra pressure.

"Fuck," I hiss… "I don't have one."

"I'm covered, but there's always a chance…"

"You, this, totally worth it…"

She nods in delirious agreement as I pinch and tease her more, then pulls me closer, wrapping her legs around my hips, guiding my cock to her pussy.

I move my hand from the apex of her thighs and close it over hers, so we are guiding me inside her together.

"Jeeesus," I croak out as she takes me in, wrapping me in the hot, tight confines of her body.

"Hurry," she whispers in encouragement as we hear voices starting to come back into the office.

I tug her even closer to the edge of her desk and guide her back so she has to put her hands down to support herself on the desk.

I start moving with slow, deep, intentional thrusts then add my finger back into the mix. Her body shudders beneath me and her head hangs back, exposing the line of her neck and the deep V of her dress that ends just before her arched, protruding breasts. She's breathtaking like this.

I pick up speed, rutting into her harder, faster, each voice outside indicating more danger, a higher chance of someone walking in on us.

The moan she emits comes right before the people just outside her door go silent, causing her to cover her own mouth to stifle any other noise. But instead of looking fearful of being caught, I see the delight, the thrill at the idea.

My good, child counseling, beautiful girlfriend gets off on the idea of being caught. It's such a fucking turn-on it kicks me into overdrive. I need to feel her, I want to test her, push her. See how far I can push her to stay silent before she snaps and detonates around me.

The talking outside starts again, as though the noise was nothing, and it gets louder as people pass by her door.

Her body is so close, it's humming; her muscles are fluttering around me with every deep glance of my cock inside her.

Then we hear Teddy. "Let me just ask Everleigh," he says.

Her eyes go wide briefly, until I finish my thrust, then they roll back in her head. She's there; one more is all it will take for both of us.

We are at a point of no return now.

Teddy could walk in this second and I'd have to finish fucking my girl.

I withdraw quickly, then slam forward again, rolling her clit between my thumb and forefinger with a biting pressure I know is sure to make her combust.

And she does.

She arches farther back, her fingers go white over her mouth as she catches the long, deep moan before it can pass through her lips, and her body trembles beneath me.

The viselike spasm of her orgasm clamps down around me and just like her, I'm biting back my own shouts, feeling myself release deep inside her with quick, long jets of pleasure and built-up need emptying within the sacred confines of her body.

Teddy's laugh seeps from beneath the door, but the volume tells me he's still not here yet, so I wrap an arm around Everleigh's waist, help her sit up completely, then I reach down for her purse.

I know she always has a few things inside for the kids.

I pull out her small body spray, then let it spritz in the air around us so we can hopefully replace the smell of sex surrounding us. Then I pull out the pack of wet wipes she keeps in there. I tug out a few wipes and then pull out of her, using the wipes to clean her up and myself, then we both right our clothing in a hurry.

I stay between her legs and kiss her. "Wow." I kiss her again, just as the door opens.

"Ever—" Teddy's voice carries across the room. "Oh! I uh, Liam…" Teddy clears his throat.

I take a step back, knowing both our clothes are righted, and making sure the kiss I was caught laying on her would be enough to make her blush like she is.

"Hey, Teddy," I say, stepping back and winking at Everleigh conspiratorially, "sorry, I came by to grovel and beg for forgiveness, and I got carried away."

Teddy laughs, and Everleigh hides her face behind her hands. "I'm so sorry, Teddy," she says, her voice about a hundred decibels too high. "I know how unprofessional this looks..."

Teddy holds up a hand, shaking his head, "Say no more. We've all gotten caught kissing our significant others in places we probably shouldn't have been before. Don't make this a habit though."

"No, sir," she and I both say together, bringing on a fit of laughter from all of us.

"Everleigh," Teddy says, "Do you have Kristy's files handy? Rylee is asking for them."

Everleigh nods. "Yes, yes I do." She's still squeaking, but she sounds more composed now. "Is Rylee here? I thought she and Colton were leaving."

"They are, right after she looks over the file. She caught something in one of the boys' files and wants to see if Kristy's has the same note. They're in her office."

"Colton is with her?" Everleigh grins wide, looking from me to Teddy.

"Yep," Teddy answers. "Did you want to take her the file?"

Everleigh nods. "I'd be happy to. Liam, would you like to meet Rylee Donavan and her husband?"

*Play it cool, Hayes.*

"Yeah, that'd be great. I'm a big fan of his."

Teddy chuckles. "Aren't we all? You have a good afternoon, Liam. Thanks for taking the file for me, Everleigh."

After he walks away, Everleigh steps up to me and presses a kiss to my jaw. "Let's go meet your hero, Hot Stuff."

\*\*\*\*

# Everleigh

I can feel the excitement and nervousness rolling off of Liam in waves right now. It may be the most adorable, amazing thing I've ever seen from him.

My always cool, usually calm and collected, badass firefighter is nervous and excited to meet Colton Donavan.

His palm is even a little sweaty in my hand. I love it.

It's like he's a little boy again, getting to meet this superstar who he's idolized forever.

"Knock knock," I say, tapping on Rylee's office door. "Teddy said you were looking for something in Kristy's file?"

Rylee looks up from her desk with a wide grin. "Hey, Everleigh. I am, I noticed some similarities in a few of the boys' files from their social worker and I wanted to see if the girls that person has worked with have the same things."

"I haven't looked closely for inconsistencies," I admit, "but they could exist in here. I'd love to go over them quickly with you."

"Do we have a few minutes, Colton?" Rylee asks, looking over to where Colton Donavan, racer extraordinaire, hero to my boyfriend, is sitting, scrolling through something on his phone.

He looks up, smiling at Rylee like she hung the moon. "We have as long as you need." Colton looks from Rylee, to me, and Liam—who is gripping my hand so tightly

I'm afraid I'm losing circulation—and gives us a polite, smile of acknowledgement.

"I won't keep you too long," I promise, then add, "Rylee, Mr. Donavan, this is Liam. He's with me, and he's one of the firefighters who took part in the auction and softball game this year."

Colton rises from the soft, plush chair he was occupying and extends his hand, "Call me Colton. Nice to meet you, Liam. Thanks for helping Corporate Cares, and for your service."

Liam drops my hand and stands taller, but I can feel the nervousness coming off him in silent steady waves, "It's great meeting you," he says, taking Colton's offered hand. "I'm a huge fan."

Colton has a subtle smirk mixed in with his smile, and Rylee grins wide watching them. "It's nice to meet you, Liam," she adds, amusement lacing her tone. Then she looks at me and whispers, "Should we work while the guys talk? I'm sure they'd both rather we not bore them with legal details."

"That's fine with me," I agree easily.

Rylee says in a sweeter, lighter voice I know all too well, because I tend to use it on Liam, "Hey, Ace, why don't you take Liam down to see the car? He seems like the type who would appreciate it."

"I don't want to put you out," Liam says.

"It's no trouble at all, right?" Rylee asks Colton, and he agrees. "We won't be long, but we do have some legal stuff to discuss and it would probably be best we not have an audience." Rylee winks at me, because they could just as easily stay in here and not have a clue what we're discussing.

I smile back at her, mouthing, "Thank you." I turn to Liam and grin wide at him. "I think some of the guys from the firehouse who are still waiting for you might want to see it too. Right?"

Liam grins at me and nods. "I'm sure they would. If you wouldn't mind, Colton?" he asks.

"Have them meet us in the garage." Colton leans over Rylee's desk and gives her a kiss then he and Liam walk out of her office.

"Thank you," I say again. "He's a huge fan. He tried bidding on the day at the races, but he lost out. I think this is probably a thousand times better for him, though."

"I understand." Rylee points to the seat across from hers and I take it. "Colton will show the guys the car, they'll all lighten up and we will sort out these notes. Are you and Liam a new thing?"

I nod my head. "Very new. We've been together for roughly a month."

She smiles softly, her violet eyes reflecting an understanding and knowledge in them. "He's nice. If you want, I can see what I can do for you as far as the race goes? I have some pull with the boss."

I laugh loudly and nod. "I bet you do. I would really appreciate that, thank you."

We get to work on searching and discussing the files, and Rylee points out all she can that I'd never taken into consideration. My promotion would put me in a relatively similar position in the company as her, only on the girls' side of operations, so just like I did when she hired and trained me, I absorb her every word like a sponge. There is nobody better to learn from than the woman who has made Corporate Cares what it is today with her drive and love for the kids.

# Thirty-One

## Liam

"I still can't believe I got to meet Colton Donavan." I drag my eyes up her naked, gorgeous body to Everleigh's smiling eyes. She's sprawled lazily in her bed, and I'm resting on my side and elbow, facing her from the foot of the bed. "He was nothing like I expected."

"Is that good, or bad?" She bends her leg back a little and taps her toes over my bicep.

"Good, it was good, he was so laid-back, easy to talk to. I felt like we were old friends, not like he was some superstar."

"I think he looks at most of the people associated with Corporate Cares that way," she says, as though it's no big deal. "Rylee is a big part of the company, and Colton is as invested in it and the boys she works with as she is."

"I get that," I say, reaching my free hand for her foot and pinching her big toe carefully between my fingers. "I feel that way about your girls. I know how important they are to you, and I know they come from shitty circumstances that required them to end up in your home."

"They did," she agrees. "You're very attuned to their struggles, Hot Stuff." It's an innocent enough statement, but I can't let her dive deeper into it, so instead of answering, I do the most natural thing there is, I smother her in kisses, licks, teases, and earth-shattering sex, again, to keep her from prying any more or getting any closer to things I don't want to share with her, or anyone.

By the time we're finished, she's in a sex-induced stupor and her eyes are heavy with sleep and exhaustion.

"I could get used to coming home to this after a night at The Castle with the girls," she says in a half-asleep tone. "Sex, snuggles, and sleep. S-cubed." She giggles at her own little creation and then rolls into my chest, nuzzling in. "Thank you."

I kiss the top of her head and chuckle. "For the orgasms, or the pillow?"

"Mhmmmm," she answers, before her breathing evens out over my skin, and her body relaxes completely into mine, indicating she's given in to the sleep part of her S-cubed.

I've waited two days, had guilt nearly suffocating me every time Everleigh has brought up work, the girls, Sky, but nothing has come from it. She has no idea, and I plan on keeping it that way.

She can't get into trouble for something she didn't do.

While she sleeps on me, finds comfort and ease with me, I know I'll do anything in my power to protect her at all costs, too. From me. From the world. From anything and everything.

# Thirty-Two

## Everleigh

A re you ready to go, Sky?" I ask, bending down to her height and smiling, readjusting the tiara we got her to remember us with, then grabbing her bag for her.

"Yep!" She's so ready, and so excited to get to be back with her mom today. Monica was discharged from the hospital early this morning, and the social worker and crew got her set up at home, helped get groceries and everything she and Sky will need.

They're all set and ready. It's hard letting Sky go. She's made such an impact on my heart, my soul. She's probably the biggest catalyst for my and Liam's relationship, too. I can't help but look back at the first time I met her, when he was sitting in the hospital room, blowing bubbles, making her laugh, and comforting her in his strong, silly, amazing way.

It shouldn't have happened. I still question whether it's real, or possible, but I think I've fallen in love with him.

In all honesty, though, I think he stole a piece of my heart when I saw him with Sky that day and it wasn't long before he started chipping away, piece by piece, until he owned most of it.

That's something for me to evaluate at a later time. Right now, my focus has to be on this little girl, getting her back to her mama, and not letting it hurt too bad when I have to say goodbye for now.

I know where she'll be living.

I know I can see her again, and I likely will.

I have to keep my distance after I take her to the justice center, though. The handoff to the social worker will happen there, and then they'll securely take her to her mom, making sure her dad can't follow.

It's all being done with as much care as possible. He poses a risk to them both, and as long as Monica is set on pressing charges, seeing him go to jail for his crimes, their identity will be hidden from him for their safety.

"I can't take you to your mommy, I have to take you to my friend, Robin, but then she will take you to your mom. Okay?"

Sky nods slowly. I'm sure she doesn't completely understand, but she will. By the time she's home and in Monica's arms, Sky won't even remember how she got there. All that will matter then is being with her mom again.

I give her a big hug. "I will always be here for you. You'll always be a princess welcome in our castle, just like every other girl here. If you ever need anything at all, you can call me, or you can have your mommy call. She has my number."

Sky hugs me back just as tightly and nods. "I love you."

"Oh, sweet girl, I love you too. I'm so happy you get to be with your mom again." I pull back, smiling and kiss her on the top of her head. "Let's get out of here."

She grins wide and nods. All of the other girls have already said their goodbyes. Losing Sky will be hardest on Kristy. They came in not too far apart from each other, and they are the closest in age. My older girls will help her, though.

I rise, carrying Sky's bag, and open the door, letting out a little gasp when I do. Outside, with the big, shiny red truck, in his uniform with his arms crossed, sunglasses over his eyes, looking sexy as hell, is Liam and his guys.

The second Sky sees him, she bolts out the door, shouting, "Liam!"

His badass firefighter look shifts into the softest, happiest look of love I've ever seen and he steps forward and bends his knee, catching her when she launches herself at him.

I was wrong. This will be hardest on Liam. He has gotten so attached to Sky, he loves her fiercely already, and now she's going to be gone from his life.

I'll have to worry about that later, though. I can only handle so many things in one day. Today, Sky has to come first.

Tomorrow, when we are both off work, I can focus on him again.

"Hey, Little One," he says, standing with her in his arms. "Look at that tiara! You are the cutest princess ever. That's why I wanted to come say goodbye to you, and I thought I'd bring my big fire truck and some of my friends."

Sky's eyes light up and she wraps her arms around his neck, squeezing him in the tightest hug. She's gotten just as attached to him as he has her. I'll have to make sure to let Robin know about him, make sure her mom has his contact information, too.

All of the guys walk over to meet Sky, talk to her, and then Liam lets her see the fire truck. I glance down at my watch and then pull out my phone and text Robin to let her know we will be a few minutes late.

I give Liam, Sky, and the guys a couple more minutes then I step up. "Sky, we have to go so you can see your mommy."

She looks from me to Liam, and he forces a wide smile for her. I can see it doesn't reach his eyes though. I don't know if he's ever gotten to say goodbye to someone he loves before. Zac, Lance, other men and women in his life have been lost unexpectedly. This time he's getting closure, with hopes of seeing her again, but it's probably his first true goodbye... that's hard on anyone, no matter the age.

****

# Liam

Sky is standing in the fire truck and holding the big headphones we all wear to stay in communication during our drives and on calls.

"Hold on one second, Little One. Put the headphones back on real fast."

She does as I ask and puts them back on, then I pull out my phone and take a picture of her. It's the only picture I have, the only I will ever take, but it's a picture I will cherish for the rest of my life. "Thank you."

Sky takes the headphones off and Brandon helps her put them away, giving me a moment to turn to Everleigh. "I hope it's okay I took that?"

She nods. "Of course, Hot Stuff. I think it's great you did. Will you send it to me?"

"Gladly," I agree, smiling at her, then stepping up to the truck. "Okay, Little One, let's get you out of this truck so you can go see your mom." I hold my arms open to her and she walks right into them, letting me lift her from the truck, then letting me hold her. I don't care if she's six, or if she's technically too old, I need this right now. I need to have this last conversation with her, too.

"Do you remember my story?" I whisper to her.

"Yes," she whispers back. "Your daddy was like mine."

I nod. "If you ever need anything, you can always call me. If anything bad ever happens, do you remember the number you call?"

She nods her head and whispers again, "9-1-1."

"'Atta girl. They will always answer and send help." I pull a laminated card out of my back pocket. "Keep this. It has my number and Everleigh's. You can share it with your mommy too."

Sky takes the card and holds it tight to her chest, then leans in close to my ear, cupping her tiny hand around her mouth so she can whisper as quietly as possibly, "Daddy can't hurt me?"

I shake my head then whisper in her ear, "No. I promise. I won't let your dad hurt you. I'll protect you."

Sky hugs me tight again and kisses my cheek, then lays her head on my shoulder while I walk her over to the Corporate Cares van so I can set her in her booster seat.

"Be good, Little One." I set her down in her seat and help buckle her in. "Oh! I have one last present for you; let me go get it from the truck real fast. I stand and turn, nearly running Everleigh over. "I have one thing to give her, then you can go. I'll be fast."

The look on her face is one of sadness mixed with pride, worry, and love. "We'll wait right here."

I reach down and squeeze her hand, then walk toward the truck, seeing Brandon standing there holding the stuffed firefighter bear I had made for Sky at that bear-building place in the mall.

"Here you go, Brother." He holds the bear out to me. He knows how important being here was, he told Lieu, too. Apparently, everyone at the house has been walking on eggshells with me since Zac's death, and they know how passionate I am about Sky, her case. Brandon knows why, and my past, too. He understands everything I'm thinking and feeling right now.

"Thank you." I take the bear from him and give him a nod, the type that conveys my appreciation, the type a brother understands without words. I walk back over to the van where Everleigh and Sky are waiting, then bend back in, pulling the bear from my back. "This is for you. He will always keep you safe."

"A bear!" She takes the bear and squeezes it tight, hugging it around the neck. "He looks like you."

"He's a firefighter, just like me. If you ever miss me, you can hug him and I'll feel it. I gave him my special powers."

"Safe powers?" she asks, concern filling her young, too innocent to have to worry features.

"Safe powers. Fire Bear will keep you safe, just like I would."

"Thank you," she says softly.

"You're welcome, Little One." I go to stand, then think better of it and kiss her forehead first, instead. "I love you, Sky. I promise nobody will ever hurt you."

"Love you too." She nuzzles into Fire Bear's head and smiles wide.

That's my cue. I can feel my heart breaking, the knowledge I may never see this special little girl again nearly too much to bear.

When I stand, Everleigh is close, with her hand on my back, rubbing soft circles. "I'll make sure to check on her, give you updates as often as I can," she whispers.

"Thank you." I turn to face her, trying not to let the feelings show. "Her mom's still pressing charges? There's no way her dad can find them?"

"As far as I know, yes. Their location is safe. Nobody knows where they'll be except a small handful of us, and none of us will ever share." She rests her hand on my chest, over my heart and whispers, "She'll be okay, baby. I promise."

I nod and step closer, kissing her forehead, her nose, then her lips, letting it linger momentarily. There is nothing sexual about it; I just need her strength right now. "Thank you."

"Do you think you could show the other kids your truck? They're all sad about Sky, too."

"Brandon is already at the door having them come out." I nod in the direction of the front door where Brandon is lifting Kristy into his arms, and then leading all the girls out to the truck. "We'll do right by them, babe. Always."

"You are an amazing man, Liam." She presses her lips to my heart and kisses over my shirt. "I lo—I lucked out getting to meet you at the softball game."

"I'm the lucky one," I respond then kiss her again. "Be safe driving. I'll text you tonight."

"Stay safe at work." She drags her hand across my chest then lets it fall away as she walks around the van and gets in. I take a step back and watch as she and Sky pull away.

*God, please don't let anything happen to either of them. It would kill me.*

# Thirty-Three

## Everleigh

Thank you both so much for having us over tonight." I set my napkin down on the table; then look out over the deck at Brandon and Jess' toward their pool. "I don't think I've ever eaten so much in my life. I'm stuffed."

"We are so happy you two could make it tonight," Jess says, rubbing her hand over her belly. "This will probably be one of our last get-togethers here. We think we found the perfect forever home." She looks so happy as she says it. Liam spilled the beans that Jess is expecting twins; it was his way of explaining why I shouldn't bring wine tonight. They have everything. At least, it appears they do.

It's everything I want one day. The forever home, kids, a man who looks at me like Brandon is looking at Jess now. The love, the happiness, their future: it's all so bright.

"When B said he was grilling, we couldn't turn him down," Liam answers. "He said you would show us pictures of the new house tonight. He didn't want to spoil it for you."

"Oh my God! Yes!" Jess gets up and moves quickly into their house, then returns with her tablet. "This will be better than the phone, larger screen."

"I'm so excited," I say, scooting my seat a little closer to the seat she's in between Liam and me now. "Is it far from here?"

"No, not at all. It's only about fifteen minutes away, but it's a little closer to the firehouse, it's close to a really great school, and there are a few parks nearby. It's the perfect home."

"That's really great, Jess," Liam says, genuinely happy for his best friends. He puts his arm over the back of her chair and leans in on her other side to look at the pictures.

Their new home is gorgeous. It's recently built in a new development, it's spacious, has a pool in the backyard, the floors are all wooden and polished. The marble countertops and stained cabinets are stunning. Everything is amazing, and it's big enough for them to grow into, even after the twins.

"Wow, this is beautiful. When can you move in?"

Jess hands Liam the tablet so he can go back through the images and talk to Brandon. "Within the month. It's all ready, they need to do a final walk-through, but then it's ours. I'm so excited. Since I'm not too far along yet, I can help and not be a giant lump of a whale sitting and watching."

I giggle. "You won't be a whale. You're beautiful, you're glowing, and even with twins, that won't change."

"You're too kind." She glances at the guys, then back to me. "How's he doing? Brandon told me about the little girl going home a few days ago. He said it hit Liam hard."

I nod then murmur beneath my breath, "He's okay. He's been struggling since Zac's death. Losing Sky was just another thing on top of it all. He seems edgy, distracted a lot, anytime I bring up work, he freezes. He thinks I don't notice it, but I do. I don't want to push him though."

Jess exhales. "I'm not surprised. Liam has gone through more than anyone should ever have to. It's not my place to say more, but I'm so glad he has you, Everleigh. Don't let him push you away. Okay?"

"I have no plans to," I assure her, "I'm in this for the lon—"

My phone rings loudly, interrupting me. Everyone goes quiet at the table, and I pull it out, answering immediately when I see Teddy's number. "Hello?"

"Everleigh, good, I reached you."

"Always, Teddy. What's going on?" His tone tells me this is business; so I stand and excuse myself from the table, then walk into Brandon and Jess's silent house so we can speak in privacy.

"I just got a call from Robin, Sky Boughton's social worker."

"Is she okay?" I ask, glancing out toward the patio to make sure nobody can hear us.

"She is right now, yes. Her dad is pushing for visitation and custody of his daughter. The social worker and attorneys need to speak with you tomorrow, get your statement about your time with Sky, anything she may have shared. Our advocacy should keep him from the rights, but you know judges don't like severing ties for any amount of time unless it is completely necessary."

"In this case, it is. I'll be in the office as early as I can be tomorrow to make sure all my files, all my notes, everything are as accurate as possible."

"Thank you."

"I'd do anything to keep any of our girls safe," I remind him. "You might want to bring Liam in at some point, or tell Robin about him. He and Sky are incredibly close. She may have told him things she didn't tell me. He was the first point of contact the day her mom was hurt, too."

"Bring him with you tomorrow, if you can. Or we can set up an appointment if he has work."

"I'll talk to him tonight. Thank you for letting me know, Teddy."

"You're welcome, Kid. Try to enjoy the rest of your night, we'll build a united front and advocate for Sky in the morning."

"I'll try. You have a good night too. Bye."

"Bye, Everleigh."

We end the call and I put my hand on the counter in their kitchen, letting my head hang. This isn't what Sky needs. It's not what Monica needs.

*It's not what Liam needs.*

I know I have to tell him. He may be able to help Sky, same as the rest of us, but I know this is going to upset him. He's so volatile still. Losing Zac is such a fresh, open wound. Sky going back with her mom only added to it. This new development with her dad will undoubtedly be salt in the gaping wound he already has.

"Is everything okay with the girls?" he asks from behind me, making me jump out of my shoes.

I whip around to face him, clutching my phone to my chest and breathing hard. "Where did you come from?"

He chuckles and hitches his thumb over his shoulder. "The patio. The only time you take calls like that is when it's The Castle, or Teddy. Are the girls okay?"

I nod my head yes, while saying loudly, "Things could be better."

"Babe," he says, approaching me. "The act of nodding, while simultaneously telling me they aren't good are contradictory. What's going on?"

"Let's go back outside," I offer. Brandon was on the scene too, so he may be able to put things into perspective. If I'm honest, I hope if I tell Liam with Brandon around, Brandon can calm him down if he flies off the handle. "I can tell Brandon and Jess, too. They might want to hear anyway."

He looks at me, concerned. "Oookay…"

I walk out of the kitchen, taking his hand in mine as I pass him, then lead him out onto the patio. "I'm sorry, I had to take that. It was my boss. Anytime anyone from work calls, it could be about the girls, I have to answer."

"We understand," Jess says, moving over into Brandon's lap. "Is everything okay? Do you have to leave?"

"Answering that is, complex. We don't have to go, but I'd like to share what the call was about with you all." I look at Brandon, hoping he somehow puts what I'm trying to convey to him silently now together with what I'm about to say, the need I have for him to help Liam if he needs it.

"We're all ears," Brandon says, looking back at me, confused.

"Why don't you sit, Hot Stuff? I think we all may need it for this one." I wait for Liam to sit then I scoot my chair closer to his and take his hand.

"What's going on, babe?" He laces his fingers through mine then lifts our hands up to kiss over my knuckles. It's such a small gesture, but it puts me a little more at ease. I love how he's trying to be strong for me already, but I feel awful what I'm going to say is going to hit him hard.

"Teddy just got word I need to give a statement tomorrow…" I pause, and look him in the eyes before I continue, "Sky's dad is petitioning for visitation and some form of custody of her."

All color drains from Liam's face, and his grip around my hand tightens, before he realizes how hard he's squeezing and lets my hand go. He starts shaking his head back and forth.

"Fuck," I hear Brandon mutter across the table. I sort of see Jess sliding from his lap out the corner of my eye, but I'm more focused on Liam right now.

"No fucking way!" he rises shouting. "Over my dead body will he go anywhere near that little girl. It's fucking impossible. We can't let it happen. I won't let it happen."

"Baby," I stand with him, reaching for his arm until he shrugs me away. "We are all going to do what we can to protect Sky and keep that from happening. Teddy wants you to talk to Robin, the social worker, too. He wants you to tell her anything Sky has told you about her dad."

Liam keeps clenching and unclenching his fist as he paces the patio, back and forth. "I'll do whatever is necessary," he says, mostly to himself, I think. "When do I need to talk to her social worker?"

"Teddy said you could set up an appointment. Or you can come with me tomorrow."

"Tomorrow, yeah. That works." He keeps pacing back and forth.

I look from Liam to Brandon, where he's watching Liam come unraveled. "Brother," Brandon says, standing up, giving me the 'I've got this look' I'd hoped he'd give. "Why don't you stop for a minute? We can talk this out, make a plan. You know I'll help in any way I can. Any of the guys at the call that day will, too. We can speak to her mom's injuries, the condition in the house, how Sky was so terrified. We will help you protect her."

Liam's steps slow momentarily, but the red-hot rage present on his face scares me. I've never seen him like this. "I'll kill him before he can lay a hand on her," Liam says.

Jess puts her hand over her mouth, and tears bubble in her eyes. I don't think she's ever seen him this way, either.

"That won't be necessary, Brother," Brandon says, stepping closer to Liam. He's moving cautiously, as though he's approaching a caged, wounded animal. "Why don't you and I go for a drive, talk a little?"

Liam's eyes are wild, angry. The usually cobalt blue is dark and dangerous now, more akin to navy blue. There is a storm brewing in them with the potential to destroy everything. I can't let that happen.

"I think that might be a good idea," I whisper, stepping closer, into Liam's path, forcing him to stop when he walks back in my direction.

He tries to walk around me, but I reach out and take hold of both his arms, feeling the tension with every flex in his biceps. He's not doing it to show off or to be funny. He's so mad, so tense, the force of each ball of his fists radiates up his arms, tensing his forearms, biceps, everything. "Liam…" I try to keep my voice strong, yet soft and soothing. Seeing him like this is nearly enough to break me.

"Everleigh… I can't…" He tries to release some of the tension in his body for my sake. "I think I should go for a ride with Brandon. I don't want to take this out on you tonight, but I'm mad. I'm so fucking mad."

"I understand." I slide my hands around back, rubbing over his triceps too. "Please be careful tonight. I'll go back to my place, but if you want to come by, if you need me…"

He lifts his hand up to my neck and pulls me close, kissing my forehead hard. "Thank you. I'll meet you at your office in the morning. We have to protect Sky."

He takes a step away from me and turns on his heel, walking into their house and toward the front door.

I look at Brandon, trying not to cry. "Keep him safe tonight?"

"I would go to hell and back for that man, Everleigh. In fact, I have a time or two. I've got him. Jess can take you home."

"Thank you." It's all I can say. It's all there is to say right now.

"Always." Brandon kisses Jess goodbye then follows after Liam, grabbing his wallet and keys on his way out the door.

"Will he be okay?" I ask, not risking looking at Jess while I try to fight back my own surge of emotions.

"He will," she reassures, stepping closer and putting her hand on my shoulder, "Brandon will make sure of it."

# Liam

We've been driving for hours, and now we're on the way to the beach. I should let Brandon get home to Jess; he has a shift tomorrow. Technically, I do too. But I've already gotten the first six hours of my shift covered so I can take care of business in the morning.

We pull into an empty parking lot at one of the piers, and I get out, walking away from Brandon and his truck toward the beach and ocean.

He follows behind me, and the sound of his truck locking and alarm engaging rings out in the silent night.

The closer I get to the ocean, the louder the waves get.

They pound and crash against the pier, the tide rolling in with thunderous sounding claps in the pitch black. The moon is hanging over the ocean, the only sign of light; hope to be seen in its glimmer.

I drop down onto the sand and bury my feet in with my knees up toward my chest, so I can drape my arms around them.

"Are you ready to talk yet?" he asks, when he sits down beside me. "What the fuck is running through your head?"

"I can't let her get hurt, B. And I won't." I watch out toward the water, trying to focus on the sounds, hoping they'll ground me and ease the current of anger still surging through my body.

"We'll all do our best to protect her, man. But you have to be smart. You have to be careful. She isn't yours to protect. So your best bet is to show up in the morning, tell the social worker, tell the attorneys, the judge, whoever the fuck you need to tell exactly what Sky has told you. I know you have a bond with her. I know what it is and why. Use that; share her story. Protect her with the words you share with the people who can do something."

"I will," I agree.

What he doesn't know, what nobody knows, is I can do something.

*Not only can I do something, but I will do it.*

Sky will not suffer at any man's hand, but especially not at her father's.

# *Thirty-Four*

## Everleigh

I'm so sorry he isn't here yet," I say for what feels like the twentieth time in the last hour. "He's not answering his phone." I look at Teddy, Robin, the district attorney who wanted information for the criminal case, and the lawyer Robin got to take on Monica's custody hearing. They've all been incredibly patient waiting for Liam to show up this morning like he promised he would.

We've been sitting here for nearly two hours, now. I shared my notes, my files, everything I could, but they are all waiting for his statements. Only, he's not here.

He texted me early this morning to tell me he was home, he'd taken the morning off work to handle Sky's case, and he'd see me later. That was at around six thirty. It's nearing eleven now, and he's been radio silent. His phone is off, I think, because it keeps going straight to voicemail.

"You all have work to get back to," Teddy says, eyeing me momentarily before focusing in on everyone else, "we will get Firefighter Hayes in touch with you once we've heard from him."

"Yes, absolutely," I agree. "Liam must've been called in, or he couldn't get anyone to cover for him, and they might be on a call now," I offer as a half-assed, but still plausible reason. I don't believe it for a second, and I have a bad feeling, but I can't share anything with anyone else.

I've never regretted not having someone's number as much as I regret not having Brandon's right now, though. If anyone knows where Liam might be, it'll be him. I do have Jess' though. I could always text her. She may even know where Liam is, too.

"As soon as he can give his statement," Robin says, "we need it."

"I'll drive him to your office myself if I have to." I stand when everyone else does.

Just as everyone's ready to leave the room, the elevators across the office slide open, and Liam steps out, dressed to impress in his uniform.

"There he is," I say, pointing.

Everyone stops, and Liam looks up, finding my eyes then taking in the scene of everyone standing around. He crosses the office in a few quick, long strides. "I'm so sorry I'm late. I got held up with a work situation," he says, easily, casually. "Please forgive me for taking up so much of your time."

He seems cool and collected, but his eyes are as dark as last night still, and he seems off, at least to me.

"It's okay," Teddy answers, "we understand how important your work is. We appreciate you coming by at all."

"I wouldn't dream of not helping out Sky," he says, passing by me with a wink I think is meant to comfort me.

It doesn't though.

We all file back into the conference room, and I catch Rylee's eyes before I step back in too. She's been brought up to speed on everything going on, out of courtesy, and so I could get advice from her this morning before everyone else arrived.

I confided in her about Liam, too. I needed someone who understands the male urge to protect and given her history, I thought she might understand.

She gives me a reassuring smile, and then I take a deep breath and step into the conference room, closing the door behind me.

Liam sits down, taking command of the room with his words, his story about the day of the initial call, every conversation he and Sky have had about her dad. How she asked him for reassurance that her daddy couldn't hurt her.

It all breaks my heart, but it should go a long way in proving she's fearful of her father, and given his attack on her mom, it should make any judge decline visitation until his criminal case is over.

"Thank you, Mr. Hayes," Robin says, standing up. "If we have any other questions, we will contact you directly, but I think this will all be beyond helpful."

"It's my pleasure," he says, rising and reaching out to take her hand. "I'm happy to help in any way I can."

As he brings his hand back, something catches my eye, but he lowers it and tucks it into his pockets too fast for me to really see what's up.

Liam and Teddy, the attorney, everyone says their goodbyes and we all file back out into the main offices. Liam and I are the last two out, and we stop at the doorway.

"Hi, beautiful," he says then dips his head to kiss me quickly. "I would love to stay and talk, but I have to get back to the firehouse."

I take the opportunity to kiss him once more, then take him all in. His eyes are heavy, as though he didn't sleep last night. There's something there, something going on with him I can't put my finger on. I want to ask him, to see how last night went, but it all catches in my throat. "Please be careful. You look like you haven't slept a wink, and I don't want you getting hurt at work because you're exhausted."

He brings his left hand up and cradles my face. "Thank you for caring so much about me. I promise I'll be okay. Everything will be okay. Us, Sky, all of it."

"Liam…"

He leans in and brushes his lips over mine again. "I really do have to get going. I'll talk to you later, I promise."

"Okay," I sigh, giving up any hope I have of getting any answers from him. "I'll try to stop by after I leave here later so I can see you."

"That sounds perfect," he says, smiling against my lips. He kisses me once more then walks away, leaving me standing outside our conference room at work, watching him with confusion, concern, and a sinking feeling in my stomach.

**\*\*\*\***

# Liam

The second I got to the station this afternoon back-to-back calls came in. I haven't had a single second to stop and think about the events of the day. Not this morning, not what I did, not anything. We're pulling back into the station now, and my body aches from everything I have put it through today.

The last call was a complete bitch, and I'm spent. Fires during the dead of summer are miserable. The sweat pouring off me in buckets, the fatigue, the dehydration, it's all adding on to the exhaustion I already felt.

"Hey," Brandon says, as I'm walking toward the showers once we disembark the truck and take care of equipment and clean up, "where were you this morning?"

"I had that meeting at Corporate Cares," I remind him.

"No, I know that. But Everleigh texted Jess worried earlier. She said you were at least two hours late and everyone was ready to leave. Your phone was off when she called, hell, even when I called."

"I had a couple things to take care of on my way there." I shrug. "It was no biggie. I made it there before everyone left, gave them my statement, just like you and I talked about last night."

"Okay…" he agrees, with an edge of disbelief in his tone. "I'm glad you got there in time. I'm here if you need to talk, though, Brother. Anytime, day or night."

"I know, B. Thanks. I'm going to shower real fast. Everleigh should be stopping by after she leaves the office, too."

"I'll keep an eye out for her," he answers.

"I appreciate it." I turn my back on him and keep walking toward the bathroom, raising my hand to examine the damage there.

My knuckles are cut and bruised, and anyone who sees them will be able to guess why, but I'll do what I can to push it off on the fires and calls from today.

By the time I'm out of the shower, I can hear all the guys talking and laughing. Mixed in with their voices, I can hear her.

Everleigh...

I hurry up and dry off, then change into a fresh uniform, replacing my Class A's with my normal shirt and pants.

I do my hair quick then walk out into the living area. Everleigh is sitting on the couch, talking to Lieu, Terence, Brandon, Derek, and his partner, Adriana. I stand back out of anyone's line of sight for a few, taking in the room. She's so at ease with all of them, they're all laughing and sharing, and my fire family has welcomed her with open arms. It gives me solace, especially now that I'm waiting for the fall.

"There he is," Brandon says, interrupting Lieu when I walk into the room. "We were keeping your girl company for you."

"I appreciate it." I walk in and head straight for Everleigh. Hearing him call her my girl fills me with pride, possession, and protectiveness. She is my girl. "I hope you weren't filling her with bullshit stories from our past."

He smirks at me, and everyone laughs, but Everleigh's is the loudest, and the one I focus in on. "He may have told us a couple army stories," she answers, and stands to wrap her arms around me when I'm close enough.

"Great, just remember his goal is to make me look bad, and him look like the golden boy." I wrap my arms around her and kiss her head, then let her go and take her seat, pulling her down onto my lap. "He will always throw me under the bus if it means making himself look good."

"Not true," he says half-heartedly. "I'll let you look good sometimes, too."

Everyone laughs again, and I shake my head, about to raise my hand up to flip him off, but thinking better of it at the last second. I don't need to draw attention to anything.

"I have some work to get done in my office," Lieu says, standing. "It was great to see you again, Everleigh. You keep our guy here in line."

"Yes sir," she agrees, chuckling. "I'll do my best." Her words sound forced, but she laughs him off convincingly enough he doesn't catch it. Nobody does, really, except Brandon.

Everyone follows Lieu's lead and busies themselves in other parts of the station quickly after Lieu walks away, so Everleigh and I have some time alone.

Brandon stays back, though. "You two good?" he asks. "I'm sure you all have something to work out from this morning, but I want to make sure too, especially after last night."

Everleigh slides her arm around my neck and grazes her fingers over the back of my neck. "I don't know," she answers him, "are we?"

They both look to me, and I close my mouth, nodding my head. "I'm fine, I don't need either of you to babysit me today."

Brandon sighs and shakes his head. "You're an irritating fucker."

"I try," I say back, with a snark to my tone.

"We're just worried about you," Everleigh says, then kisses my temple.

"I know," I say in a far kinder tone to her, "but you don't need to be." I kiss her cheek and glance at him, expecting him to walk away.

He doesn't though; he sits back down and stares at me. "Something is off with you today, but I can't put my finger on it."

I shake my head, glaring him down, hoping he will take a fucking hint and just drop it. He doesn't, of course, but I keep my hard, determined eyes focused on him anyway.

We engage in a staring battle for a few before the ringing of Everleigh's phone breaks us out of it. She slides off my lap and answers it, walking away from us.

As she talks, I watch her, and I feel Brandon staring at me. "What did you do this morning, Liam? Don't try to bullshit me. I know you better than anyone. You don't shut your phone off. You've been wired all day."

"Just fucking drop it," I say to him beneath my breath. "It's nothing I can talk about, and nothing I'm willing to say in front of her. So just keep your mouth fucking shut."

He stands and shakes his head. "I hope you didn't do anything stupid, Brother. Truly."

"Oh my God," Everleigh says in the kitchen.

Her words stop Brandon in his tracks as he's walking out of the room, and her shocked gaze looks up, locking directly on me. "Will he be okay?"

She goes silent, staring at me, waiting for the answer to the question I'm sure she just asked. She never looks away from me. Never breaks our connection.

Not as she finishes the call.

Not as Licu walks into the room flanked by two cops, including Brandon's brother.

"Liam, what did you do?" she asks in horror, and fear.

Brandon looks between all of us then approaches Jarrett and his partner. Jarrett explains it all quietly to Brandon, looking at me with pity and remorse over having to come here to arrest me.

"Fucking hell, Liam," Brandon says, shaking his head and hanging it low. "I'll come bail you out as soon as I can…"

"Thanks, Brother." I look at him then focus back on Everleigh, watching her approach me; giving her the hand she's reaching for, knowing she'll find the evidence there.

"Oh, Liam, why?" She uses the lightest, most careful caress I've ever experienced as she grazes her lips over my bruised knuckles.

"I had to protect her," I say quietly. "I couldn't stand back and allow another child I love to be killed by their father."

# Thirty-Five

## Everleigh

He was arrested?" Addie asks, handing me another glass of wine then sitting down on my sofa.

"Yeah, Brandon's brother, Jarrett, and his partner showed up. When the warrant went out, their sergeant recognized the connection to the fire station and sent them. Figured it'd be better having someone close arrest a firefighter."

"Oh my God." She takes a sip of her own wine. "You know Mom's been calling me nonstop all afternoon. She said you sounded sad when she called you earlier. She's worried. What do you want me to tell her?"

"Shit…" I mutter into my glass. "I can't handle Mom right now. Tell her to go on her vacation, have fun, be responsible, and you'll look after me. Maybe it's trouble in paradise."

Addie lifts her brows, asking me silently if I'm sure.

"He beat the shit out of Sky's dad, Adds. He is in the hospital. I can't just ignore that, can I?" I set my glass down and tug a pillow into my lap.

"No, you can't. But you need to at least hear his excuse."

"He said he couldn't let another father take a child he loves... I think it's pretty evident why he did it. He probably experienced it with another kid sometime."

"Maybe. I don't know. He's been so off since Zac died; I've felt like he's been hiding things. Then missing our meeting today, well, showing up two hours late, because he was threatening her dad, beating him to a pulp. He's too volatile. What if he went off in front of a kid? One of my girls?"

"Just talk to him, Ev. Figure all this shit out before you make any decisions. You owe it—"

"Do not tell me I owe him anything," I snap.

"I wasn't going to," she says in her quiet, big sister voice that has never failed to hit me like a sledgehammer and get my attention. "I was going to tell you, you owe it to yourself. I know you have deep feelings for him. Deeper than anyone you've ever met. Don't write him off until you have a good reason and you know your heart and soul won't regret it for life."

I watch her, stunned and speechless.

"Yeah, I know, Little Sister. I can see it written all over your face. Even now, you are so angry, but more than that, you're scared for him. Your heart is his now. So you better be damn sure about any decisions you make from here on out, because they all have the potential to devastate you."

She's right. She's always right. She's my big sister, my sounding board, the one person I've turned to for every big, and small, thing in my life. She can read me like a book, even when the cover I'm displaying is an attempt to misrepresent what I'm really feeling inside.

"So you won't tell me what to do?" I ask, hopelessly.

"I'll tell you to follow your heart," she says, and glances toward the window, "and to hear him out first..."

"Why do you say that?"

"Because he's walking up to your door as I speak." She stands up and pulls me into her arms. "I love you, baby girl, call me if you need anything. Even if it's later on tonight. I'll leave my phone on. And I'll deal with Mom."

"Thank you. I love you, Adds."

"I love you too, Ever."

We walk to my front door and she opens it before he can knock.

"Oh, shit," he exhales. "I'm sorry, I didn't know you had company."

"I was just leaving," she says. "I'm Addison, by the way. Your auction bidder." She holds a hand out to him, and he takes it, offering her a glimpse of the swollen, bruised evidence marring his knuckles.

"It's nice to meet you," he says with a chuckle, and a smile that definitely doesn't reach his eyes. "Thank you for setting us up. You may be regretting it now, but it's the best setup and blind date of my life."

"I was happy to do it." She shrugs and steps out. "You fucked up royally today, Liam. I can't tell you what's going to happen, and I can't feel sorry for you right now, but for what it's worth, you seem like a good guy. I'm sure you have your reasons, they just may not be good enough to keep my baby sister."

"Thank you." Her words shock him, and his face pales, again. "I am so sorry for any hurt this brings to Everleigh, but I can't be sorry for my actions."

"At least you're honest. It was nice to finally meet you," Addison says, "I just hope it isn't the first and last time we get to do it."

"Me too."

"My phone will be on all night, Ever. If you need me, I'm here." She turns and walks down the driveway to her car in the street, and she doesn't say another word, or even look back, as she gets in and drives away.

"I didn't expect you here tonight," I say to him, stepping back into my house and holding the door open for him.

"Brandon bailed me out. Charges are pending, some witnesses stepped up in my defense..."

I nod. "Brandon is a good friend."

"You have no idea." He walks in and leans forward to kiss me, then thinks better of it and stops himself, passing me instead to go and sit on my couch.

"What do you have to say for yourself?" I ask, shutting my front door and turning to face him, with my arms across my chest.

****

# Liam

That's the million-dollar question.

I didn't want it to come to this, but I guess I brought it on myself when I acted without much thought this morning.

"Come sit with me, please. There's a lot to this, and all I can ask is you hear it all out before you pass judgment or make any decisions."

"I'll hear everything out, but you have to be honest, Liam. About it all."

I nod and take in a deep breath. "I'll be nothing but; I promise."

She comes and sits on the couch beside me, with a small distance between us that feels as large as the Grand Canyon.

"This all started probably twenty-four years ago," I begin, to her surprise. "My mom had passed away, it was a freak accident, or that's what we were told. She was killed coming home from work one day, and that left me and my little brother, Lance, in my dad's custody. Dad was pretty great to us when we were little, but he had always had a terrible temper. The man could rage like no other."

The look on her face isn't lost on me. I apparently have the rage gene from my dad, because my actions today don't lend themselves to being the poster boy for cool, calm, and collected.

"Anyway," I continue, "After my mom died, my dad started drinking. I must've been around eight the first time my dad hit me. It wasn't very often, then. Usually he'd pop off when he was drunk, and I talked back. But over time, occasionally popping off turned into wailing on me for just about anything. I was six years older than Lance, and I always made sure to put myself in our dad's path. I can't tell you how many countless black eyes, bruised ribs, gashes, and lacerations I had over the years. Dad was smart, though, he made sure during the school year he kept it low, easily covered up. Christ, I was so fucking afraid if I told on him, they'd take Lance away from me." I stop talking and think about one particular beating, when I was around twelve. It was the worst it had ever been, and he swore if I opened my mouth, I'd never see Lance again. The memory is as vivid, fresh as if it happened yesterday, and I can feel the sting of the tears forming behind my eyes.

"Oh, Liam…" she says, but closes her mouth after. Instead, she scoots closer to me and brings my hand into her lap, warm and secure between both of hers.

"It went on for years. The drinking got worse, and so did the beatings. I made sure he never touched Lance, though. I protected him, Everleigh. He was my baby brother, and my dad would only lay his hands on Lance over my dead body." I look down at my left hand in hers, and then my right, shaking and bruised in my own lap. "In hindsight, I probably should have let him kill me..."

"No, Liam, don't you ever say that. You were his son, his child, he was in the wrong, not you." She turns to face me on the couch, and lets go of my hand, reaching up to wipe away the tears streaming down my face. "He was the bad guy. Not you."

"If I'd have let him kill me, he never could have killed my baby brother," I whisper. I'm afraid she didn't hear me I said it so quietly, but when she leans forward and starts kissing along my tears, murmuring how it's not my fault, I didn't hurt Lance, it wasn't my responsibility to stop it, I know she did.

"It was my responsibility. I was six years older than him," I croak out. "When I was old enough, I started standing up to my dad. I would fight back. When I was sixteen, I put my dad on his ass. I was bigger, I was faster, I was stronger, mostly because alcohol and weight slowed him down over the years. After that, he had pretty much stopped beating me. I think he was a little afraid of me. One night, though..." I stop and look into her eyes, finding nothing but sympathy, caring, and something stronger in there. I lean into her touch and let her kiss more tears away.

"One night..." she encourages me to continue quietly.

"One night, I was out with some friends. It was a late night, and since Lance was only eleven, he couldn't come. My dad took a hand to him before he left for the bar. I could've killed him, Ev. I could've fucking killed him when I got home that night and found Lance, but I didn't. I didn't want to be another monster in Lance's life. So I took care of him. I got him to bed and I stood watch from his doorway, until our dad got home. Then I challenged him to try it with me." I stop talking as I feel the anger bubbling up inside me again, as though I were watching the scene play out in real time, not in my head. "My dad was so fucked up that night, he came in and passed out. I didn't get the chance to say anything to him. I didn't get to touch him. It would've been lost. He knew the next morning, though. He knew and he dropped down to his knees, groveled at my feet not to hurt him. He swore on his own life he would never touch Lance again."

Tears are streaming down her face now, but she doesn't try to wipe them away, she doesn't seem to even notice, because she's too busy trying to keep up with mine. Her thumbs are tender and thorough beneath my eyes. For every tear I cry, she wipes or kisses it away, or shushes softly, rhythmically.

"I was just starting my senior year of high school when that happened. Dad was good the whole year. He quit drinking as much, he was nice to my brother; he even took us to a few ball games. He was a wolf in sheep's clothing. It was halfway through the year when I decided I wanted out. I wanted to join the military, make something of myself so I could come home, be the man my little brother should've always had in his life…" I stop again, knowing the worst part of the story is coming, and I try to collect myself. I try to steady my breathing, let my heart settle from its frantic, throbbing pace.

"What happened next?" she asks.

"I enlisted as soon as I could. I made the old man sign the papers, with Lance's blessing. He thought I was such a badass. He wanted to be just like me when he grew up," I sob out, nearly choking the words. "Our dad hadn't… He was so fucking good. I still threatened to kill him though. I swore to him if he laid a single hand on

Lance after I left, I'd come back for him. I would kill him before he could do it again." The ache in my chest is so deep, it feels as though someone is shoving their hand into my chest and trying to pry my heart out through the bones, muscle, skin; everything that should be protecting it. "I made it through basic, came home, visited, was reassured by both of them nothing had been happening. Then I was deployed." I push up from the couch and start pacing back and forth; following the same cadence we would march to, trying to focus on each step in it. "What I didn't know," I finally continue, trying to see through the blur of my tears, "what Lance hid from me, was our dad had started drinking again. He was beating Lance regularly. I don't know why he didn't tell me, Ev. I have no fucking clue what he was doing keeping it to himself. I could have protected him. I should have. Instead, I was off playing soldier when my dad went on a complete bender, then returned home and beat my baby brother to death!"

# *Thirty-Six*

## Everleigh

His final words come out on a shouted sob. His whole body is shaking, his eyes are swollen and tears are pouring down his face at such a rapid pace, I'm not sure how he's able to see while he walks.

The final words break him, though, and he drops to his knees in the middle of the floor. "I killed him, Everleigh. I killed my baby brother. He counted on me to protect him. I should've been here. I should've stopped our dad. But I wasn't here. I was eight thousand miles away, fighting for someone else. Protecting a nation full of people I don't even know, and letting down the one person I should have fought to the death for."

I rise from my couch and rush to hold him, falling to my own knees, wrapping my arms around him. He folds into me, and this time, he is small enough, broken enough, I'm not cradling the man I love, I'm cradling the little boy who blames himself for the sins of his father.

I wrap my arms as tightly around his heaving body as I can and start rocking us back and forth, absorbing all of his sobs, his guilt, his blame with my own body as he releases them. "You didn't kill him, baby."

"I did, he was my brother. I should've saved him. I should have saved Zac. I won't lose another one. I can't. I can still save Sky…" his words are broken, hiccupped out in a frenzy of emotion.

It's hard to track at first. How they're all related.

Then it hits me.

This man, this beautiful, broken man is trying to atone for a past he was never to blame for to begin with.

"You couldn't have saved Lance, or Zac," I murmur into his soft, brown hair. "Their deaths aren't your fault, their lives were never yours to take responsibility for."

"They were," he cries out. "They were. When Zac died, I tried so hard. Chest compressions in the ambulance, helping do them in the hospital. But the bruises, the blood, the way he whispered for his mom… All I could imagine was Lance. His final moments. Losing Zac gave life to the photos I've seen of my brother."

"Shhh…" I rock more, rub his back, kiss his head, doing everything in my power to comfort him. "It's not your fault. It was never your fault."

He shakes his head against me; fighting my words each time I say them. I won't let him though. I will continue repeating them for as long as I have to until he really hears me.

I'm not sure how long it takes for his whimpers to soften into silent deep breaths, and his deep breaths to shift into slow, steady ones. The night has passed in a blur from the moment I got home and called Addie, to now, hours later where I'm holding my strong, brave, broken boyfriend as though letting him go might bring about his death.

There aren't words to be said. Nothing can change his past. Nothing can bring Lance back. Nothing can replace his final moments with Zac that reminded him of his baby brother. Nothing can change the responsibility he took on himself the day he walked into Sky Boughton's home and found her terrified and in shock because her father did to her mother what his father did to his baby brother. What he did to Liam, too.

I can't change any of it; I can't rewrite history. All I can do is live in the present and focus on our future, on trying to pick up the pieces his behavior today shook loose.

"Do you want to move to my bed?" I ask quietly. I don't want to startle him, or push him too far, but I think we'd both be more comfortable. I think he needs the sleep, too. Brandon told me earlier, when I was at their station, he slept maybe two hours last night, and he doubted Liam slept at all.

"Please," he rasps out, untucking himself from my embrace, "please just don't make me leave tonight. I can't. Not tonight."

His words are like a dagger to my heart. He's lost everyone, he's been failed by those who should have loved him, protected him; I won't be another on that list. Not when I've given him every piece of my heart I have to give.

"Baby, I promise, you don't have to leave. You don't have to go anywhere."

He nods subtly and rises from the floor, taking my proffered hand so he can follow me. While we walk, I make sure the door is locked, and turn off each of my lights.

In my room, he moves on autopilot, stripping out of his uniform until he's in only his boxer briefs. I follow his lead and undress, choosing to sleep in my boyshorts and a large tee.

We both slip into my bed, and beneath the dim light of my bedside lamp, he looks like a little boy seeking out his own safety, his own protection.

Without hesitation, I open my arms to him and he lies close, laying his head on my chest, letting me hold him.

Neither of us speaks for the longest time. I even wonder if he's fallen asleep, until I glance at the clock, the movement getting his attention, making him say, "I'm sorry. I'm so fucking sorry."

"I know you are," I say, trailing my finger up and down his spine lazily. I press my lips into the crown of his head and kiss him over and over. "Can I ask you some questions?"

He nods his head over my chest, but doesn't move.

"Did you tell Sky what happened to you and your brother?"

"I didn't tell her my dad killed Lance, but I told her my dad was a bad man like hers. I told her I would always understand her, and protect her." His openness is refreshing, given how long he's held so much of who he is back.

"I wish you would've told me sooner," I murmur, thinking a little before asking, "Brandon and Jess know your story?"

He nods, and his hair brushing against my chin feels like a light feather rubbing against my skin. "Brandon was with me in Afghanistan before I got the call, and when I returned to duty. He's been with me through everything."

"He's a good friend," I muse. "Did he know what happened today?"

"No," Liam sighs, and the warmth and pressure from his breath seeps through my flimsy shirt. "He's so mad at me, but he's worried too. My chances of promotion were shot after I went off on the dad and got suspended the first time. Now that I'm suspended, with termination pending based on my criminal case, he's furious."

I close my eyes tightly, biting my tongue to keep from expressing my disappointment in his lack of thinking things through. "I can imagine he is. You're his brother, his best friend, and you may have thrown your whole life away today."

"Sky's worth it," he says quietly. "Whether anyone else's blood is on my hands or not, I couldn't let hers be. I wouldn't be able to live with myself. I hope you understand, Everleigh. I hope you understand and that your feelings for me are stronger than your anger over my actions."

His words leave me speechless. I understand his reasons. I understand his logic. I understand everything he did, but how could he throw everything away so easily?

*Guilt, Ever.* He did it because his losing everything would be worth it to bring back the people he blames himself for letting down.

"I wish you would have told me sooner. I would've helped you. We could've worked to protect her together."

"I know. I'm sorry." He raises his head slightly and looks at me. "I love you too damn much already to bring you down with me."

"Y-you love me?" I ask, stunned into near silence. "It's been six weeks, Liam. There's no way, right? It would be stupid to love each other already…"

"Love each other?" His sad lips break into the smallest of smiles. "Does that mean you love me too?"

I nod my head slowly. "I gave the first piece of my heart to you the day I walked into Sky's hospital room; I've been praying you wouldn't break it ever since…"

"Never," he says. "I would never break your heart. I'll cherish it; I'll protect it, and you, always."

"I love you, too, Liam," I admit in a stuttered whisper.

He pushes up to his side and leans down to kiss my lips. I can taste the salt from our combined tears, dried and resting on his lips and mine. I slide my hand up to his heart; feel its steady rhythm beating beneath my fingers, growing in beat slowly with our kiss.

The deeper it gets, the needier we both become. Tonight is about healing. It's about each other, going slow, tender, finding comfort in the trust we now have in each other. We undress slowly; his underwear gets kicked to the floor before he starts working mine down my legs. I pull my shirt off then push him to his back, moving over his body, settling just above his waist.

"I love you, Everleigh," he whispers, looking up at me with bright blue, bloodshot eyes. "Thank you. Thank you for listening to me."

I lower my hand to his face and brush it over his five o'clock shadow, rubbing my fingers over his cheeks before I lower myself to kiss him, rotating my hips over his growing arousal, and rubbing myself against him slowly.

We kiss softly, a brush of my tongue over his, a swipe of his against mine. Our breathing becomes one, and when I'm ready, when he's ready, I lift up enough to reach between us and take him in my hand so I can line myself up over him. The second I sink down and accept him into my body, I sigh out, "I love you."

With my eyes locked on him, I lower myself until I've taken him in completely, then I lean forward, locking my fingers in his and using him to help me move.

Tonight there's no dirty talk, no urgency to race to the finish line. It's slow. It's powerful. It's two lives agreeing to connect and remain open and honest to each other.

With my chest to his, our fingers wrapped together, I move my body over him, building us up together, slowly, evenly.

He starts moving beneath me, the friction against me more than enough to wind my body tighter and tighter with each passing moment.

I slide up, then down, roll my hips, meeting his lips in a soul-searching kiss… I repeat the same things over, feeling him swelling further, getting harder inside me. My own body responds by starting to twitch and shake; the nerves are firing in every single part of my body, allowing me to feel every sensation—his body beneath mine, the cool air over my skin, my clit rubbing over his pubis is the sweetest friction imaginable—and I can hear everything as though it's being magnified. His breath is rough, deep, and ragged. Our bodies are slick and working together, playing a gentle rhythm with each thrust of our hips. I can see deep into his soul when I seek out his vivid, honest blue eyes.

Behind them I see love, I see fear, I see guilt, and hope. The magnitude of his honesty, his openness, is enough to send me over the edge. I come over his body with a silent moan as he takes my lips with his and swallows each cried out wave of pleasure I emit.

Then he follows me.

His release pulses inside of me as he groans from deep in his throat. "Oh God, Everrrr…" he rasps out in my car as he finishes.

I collapse down onto his body, spent and exhausted. His arms wrap around me and his fingers slowly trace my spine while our bodies and minds come back down to reality, to the weight of the night, and what we just did together.

\*\*\*\*

# Liam

I can't believe we're here right now. When Everleigh would've had every right to send me away, refuse to hear me out, she opened her mind and heart up. She was willing to hear everything I had to say.

Then she held me through the second hardest thing I've ever done in my life. Telling her about Lance, about my dad, my guilt, my failures was like reopening every wound, ever ounce of pain I've felt over the last ten years... and she loved me through it.

I feel raw now. I feel exposed and vulnerable, but I trust her, and she trusts me. Whatever comes of my actions today, I will always have the fact the most incredible woman in the world loves me in spite of my failures.

I can find a new job. I can handle time spent in prison if it means Sky will never have to endure what I did, what she used to, again.

Everything is beyond perfect in my fucked-up life right now, and I'm beyond grateful. Nothing could ruin this moment, not a single thing.

"Hot Stuff?" she asks quietly.

"Hmmm?" I keep rubbing her spine and playing with the loose hair down her back.

"Can I ask you one more question?" She turns her head into my chest and kisses over my heart, something I've come to learn she loves to do.

"Anything," I tell her, smiling.

"How did you find Sky's dad?"

*No. Please, gorgeous, no. Don't ask that. Any other question is fine, just not that one.*

I stay silent for a few moments, trying to figure out how I should answer. Right now, I'm the only one on the hook for my actions today. How I got there, what I had to do to get his location doesn't matter. It can't matter. What matters is I take responsibility for my actions after I got there.

She can't know the truth. I can't put her in that position.

"I saw him when I stopped for gas," the lie rolls off my tongue easily enough. "I recognized him from the day they took him away, and I followed him. After what you told me about him fighting for visitation, and custody, I had to. I was filled with a rage like I've never known."

"Wow," she yawns out. "I can't believe you just saw him…"

"I couldn't either," I continue to lie. "Get some sleep, babe. I know you have to be back in the office early tomorrow before you spend the night with the girls tomorrow night."

"I think I will." She wiggles against me, making me chuckle, then she makes herself comfortable lying on my chest. "I love you, Liam. Thank you for trusting me."

*Dagger. Meet. Heart.*

"I love you too, Everleigh."

# Thirty-Seven

## Everleigh

By the time I woke up this morning, Liam was already gone. In his place was a note, covered in his chicken scratch handwriting.

*Babe,*
*I have to be at the station this morning to talk to Lieu,*
*the Captain, and the Chief. It's time for me to pay for*
*my sins. Please be safe driving to work. I'll call you*
*later.*
*I love you.*
*Love,*
*Liam*

I reread his note and smile at how easily the words come to him, how easily they came to both of us last night, then I tuck it into my nightstand drawer and get up to get ready for my own trip to the office. I'm sure Teddy will have questions, and I'll tell him as much as I can about why and how without betraying Liam's trust in me.

He was so open, real with me last night, I will cherish his story and protect it with my whole being, even if it means I get a slap on the wrist, too.

I get ready in a euphoric haze of love and belief that everything will go the way it's meant to today.

My drive into work is easy, full of music and positive thoughts.

Even my first hour in the office is cake. I catch up on some paperwork I need to do, make a few calls, plan a few daytime activities for the girls, and then it comes...

Teddy's voice booms out from his office and I take in a deep breath as I rise from my desk. I cross the office with my head held high and knock on his door.

"You rang?" I ask, trying to stay upbeat.

"Close the door," he commands, in a tone I've never heard him use.

I do as he says and then sit down in the chair across from his at his desk. "What's going on, Teddy?" I ask. I was sure this was about Liam, but I can't for the life of me figure out why he would be so angry.

"Why'd you do it?" he asks, perching his hands on his desk and peering at me over them. "Why did you give Firefighter Hayes Mr. Boughton's work address?"

*What the hell is he talking about?*

I start shaking my head and respond, "I didn't, Teddy. I wouldn't ever do that."

"Explain to me, then," he says disbelievingly, "why the police report says he got the address from his girlfriend so he could seek out Sky Boughton's father and threaten him?"

"I didn't," I sputter, "that can't be right. I didn't give him the address. I wouldn't do that." My heart starts racing out of my chest the longer Teddy looks at me. His stare is unnerving, and I can tell by his unwavering posture he doesn't believe me. But why? Liam told me

315

last night what happened. How he found Sky's dad…
"May I… May I see the police report?"

Teddy slides it across his desk and I lift it, reading over the highlighted portion from Rich Boughton's statement they took in the hospital. He claims Liam told him it's amazing what information the counselors have access too.

This can't be right.

"Teddy," I say, looking up at him. "I swear to you, I didn't give him the address. I wouldn't do that."

"Witnesses heard Liam say it to Mr. Boughton," Teddy says, taking the report back. "I know how protective you are of Sky, I know what he did to her mother. I would even understand you giving it to him. Maybe just to have for protective reasons."

*Liam… What did you do?*

"No, Teddy, no. I didn't. I swear," I nearly cry out. "I wouldn't. There's no way."

"It's in the official report," Teddy says in a softer tone now, no doubt in response to my tears. "I have to follow the official paperwork on this, Kid. I can't just take your word when witnesses heard him."

"What does that mean?" I cross my fingers in my lap and bite my lip. I'm asking a question I already know the answer to, though.

"I'm sorry, Everleigh," he says quietly, "I have no choice but to suspend you and pull your promotion off the table. You will be put under review, and pending the outcome of said review, your position with Corporate Cares may be reevaluated."

\*\*\*\*

# Liam

"You're one lucky son of a bitch," our chief bellows out at me. I'm in a meeting at headquarters with my lieutenant, the captain, and the chief right now, reviewing my actions over the last twenty-four hours and going over the official police report they were given upon request.

"I'm sorry, sir?" I ask, shocked.

He tosses the police report at me and shakes his head. "Witnesses swear Mr. Boughton swung on you first. They admit you sought him out, they heard you say it, but they all swear he swung first. Personally, I think that's the biggest crock of shit I have ever heard. There's no way a hothead like you, who is coming off one suspension for his asinine behavior, went after a wife-beating son of a bitch and didn't swing first."

I press my lips shut and sit silently.

The chief barks out a loud, hardy laugh. "Smart man. You better keep that detail to yourself and carry it to your grave, because if anyone were to get word, it would be all of our asses. Do you hear me?"

Again, I sit silently; refusing to acknowledge any bit of the truth he's spewing. It's best I cover my own ass, as well as everyone else's in this room now.

"That's what I thought." He sits down at the head of the long table and lifts his pen up, tapping it on the table. "Given witnesses swear you acted in self-defense, and you were smart enough to not say a Goddamn word without an attorney, the DA won't be pressing charges. Based upon his recommendation, we will not be terminating your job. You're looking at a month's suspension, no pay, and mandated anger management and counseling for your imbecilic behavior, though."

*This can't actually be happening.*

"Your suspension starts immediately, and progress reports will be required from a department assigned shrink and anger management counselor. Are we clear?"

"Yes, sir," I answer without hesitation. "I can assure you I will take this seriously; I will go to every appointment and work through any and all steps to make sure nothing like this ever happens again. I recognize I have a problem, sir. The last thing I want is to shine a poor light on the department, or any of you. This job is my life, everyone I work with my family. I will make this right."

"Save your sucking up for someone who might believe the line of shit you're selling me right now."

"Yes, sir," I mutter, repositioning myself in my seat.

"Let me make this clear to you, Hayes. One more complaint, one more misstep, if I hear you were asked to scrub every fucking toilet in your house with your tongue and you refused, you will be out. I will not tolerate a cocky asshole like you ruining our reputation. Is *that* clear?"

"It is, sir." This time, I don't say anything else to him. I sit in my chair, heart racing with disbelief, and elation coursing through my veins.

"Good." He rises from his seat again after signing his papers then he slides them across the table to me, and my captain and lieutenant. "You two sign off on this, and make sure he doesn't step a Goddamn foot in any of my houses until next month."

"Yes, sir," they both answer in unison. The chief moves toward the door and we all rise from our seats until he's out.

Our captain signs off on the paperwork, then gives me a disgusted once-over before following the chief out.

"You better take this seriously," Lieu says. "Using your girlfriend to get his address, beating the man senseless, going off on parents on calls… I don't know what your problem is, but I will transfer you out of my house before you have another chance to fuck up if you don't take counseling seriously."

His threat, more than anything the chief says, has me swallowing hard. "I promise you, Lieu, I'm going to get help. I won't let this follow me back to work next month."

"It better not. Use this time off wisely. Make peace with whatever demons are chasing you, and get your head right. One chance is all you have left. I can't protect you if you fuck up, and I won't."

"I understand, Lieu." His disappointment is a rancid, bitter pill to swallow. He signs the papers and then gives me one last look, walking out the same door the other two just did and leaving me to sit by myself and think about just how lucky I am.

# Thirty-Eight

## Everleigh

I'm sitting on his front porch when he pulls up and gets out of his truck. His smile is in complete contradiction to what he should be feeling, and it's in utter opposition to how I'm feeling right now.

"Hey, babe," he says, swinging the keys on his fingers. He's too fucking happy right now, and it's just pissing me off, considering I may have just lost my job.

"You're in a good mood," I state obviously.

"I'm not being fired. Witnesses said Sky's dad swung on me first and the rest I did in self-defense." His smile falls when he realizes I'm not reacting.

"Did he swing first?" I ask carefully, evenly. I know the answer this time, and if he lies…

"No," he admits, "I swung first. But I think they all got an earful about him being a wife-beater before I started. Nobody wants to work with a piece of shit like him." Liam sits down beside me.

"What's going on?"

"Well, thanks to you, I'm currently suspended, my promotion is off the table, and my job is pending review of all the facts…" I glance his way, and the last of his smile falls, being replaced by indignant scowling.

"What the fuck? Why?"

"Because," I grit out, "you're a liar. After everything last night… I'm going to ask you one more time, Liam, how did you end up at Rick Boughton's work yesterday?"

"I told you—" he starts out, and I rise angrily.

I turn on him and point my finger into his chest. "You lied to me!" I shout. "You got his address from my computer. You admitted getting it from me when you were beating the shit out of him. Even witnesses spoke to that in their statements. I sure as fuck didn't give it to you, though!"

"Everleigh," he says evenly, trying to placate me with his tone, "I didn't… You weren't supposed to get in trouble. This never should've blown back on you. How can I make it right?"

My heart drops at his admission. A tiny part of me hoped he would deny it, he would swear up and down he was being honest last night.

But he wasn't.

Everything we shared, everything I forgave him for; everything I felt and believed was just wiped away with one admittance of true guilt.

"You can't make it right, Liam. Whether I would have given you the address willingly or not had you asked, it doesn't matter; you stole it from me. It came from my access to confidential files. You. Betrayed. Me."

He shakes his head and stands. "Babe, no, I was trying to protect you. I didn't want you to have to lie on my behalf if anyone asked you anything. I never meant for you to get in trouble. Please, please, Everleigh. You have to believe me."

His pleas rip the shredded pieces of my heart even further. I know he loves me. I know he would do anything to protect me from danger, but who is going to protect me from him? From the damage he can do?

"I can't, Liam. You lied to me. Had you been honest… We could've handled it together. But yet again, instead of trusting me, you hid more. You hid the most important thing yet from me. This didn't just affect your life, Liam. I'm losing everything. You have successfully derailed my life right alongside yours. The sad thing is, you're going to get back on track. I might never be able to again. I may lose every single thing I've ever worked for."

"Ever, no…" he whispers, defeated.

"You know something?" I say, letting anger fill me so the hurt in my heart doesn't persuade me to forgive the unforgivable.

"What?" he barely gets out.

"Not a single thing you told me last night was your fault. You weren't responsible for Lance losing his life, you weren't responsible for Zac losing his, either… The one life you are responsible for ruining, though, and you couldn't even give me warning." I shake my head and let the tears fall. "I don't know if I'll ever stop loving you, Liam. Not the man you can be, the protector you are… I also don't think I'll ever be able to forgive you for this."

\*\*\*\*

I left Liam sitting broken and stunned on his front porch six hours ago. In that time, I've managed to get to my perfect slice of heaven, and then shatter into a million pieces.

My heart hurts so bad I can hardly breathe.

My eyes feel so swollen and tender, I can barely see through them I've cried so much. I lost everything I loved all at once today, and it was all his fault.

He used me.

He snuck into my office, playing me like a fool and making me think I was supposed to meet him downstairs, so he could access Sky's file without my knowing. I stayed long enough for him to admit that earlier, and by the time he finished explaining, I wanted to be sick.

I thought meeting him was the best thing that had ever happened to me, in reality, meeting him may very well have been the start of my demise.

"Hey, you," Addie says from behind me as she walks up slowly. "I thought I might find you here still."

"Still?" I ask, wiping at my eyes.

"Still. One of your girls ratted you out. I stopped by The Castle to give you a gift from Mom, and they told me you were suspended."

"How did you know to come here?" I ask, sniffling back more tears.

"Brooke told Nichole about your special place, and Nichole told me when I went over that I should check here. She said she didn't know where here was, but I did."

I nod my head then lay it on her shoulder. "He broke me, Addie. I told him I loved him, we… I thought after last night things would find a way to work out, and he pulled the rug right out from under me."

She rests her head on mine and wraps her arm around me. "Tell me what happened, don't leave anything out."

So I do.

I tell her about last night, I give her the watered-down version of his story—one I'll still protect in great detail with my life—and I tell her about his lie, about my job, the suspension, everything.

By the time I'm done, she's furious. She's furious at him. She's furious at Teddy. She's furious at every other person who has ever fucked him over so badly in his life he felt like he had no choice but to fuck me over too. "Do you want to come stay with me?" she asks.

"Please. I don't think I can stand being there, not where we shared last night, not where his scent will still linger and small signs of his presence will remind me of him constantly."

"Okay." She takes my hand and holds it tightly in hers. "I'll drive you to my house first, then I'll go to your place and get you whatever you need for a few days at least. Okay? We can reevaluate then."

"Reevaluate... I hate that word. Teddy said they'd reevaluate my position, too. We both know what they'll find though... Corporate Cares, my girls, making a difference is over, Adds. He stripped me of everything, including my heart. And I'll never get any of it back."

# Thirty-Nine

## Liam

*Y**ou have successfully derailed my life right alongside yours.*

The words replay over and over in my mind like a broken record. I derailed her life. The purest, most amazing, selfless, kind woman in the world—a woman I fell hard for—has lost everything because of me. Add to that the fact she was right when she said of all the things I should feel guilty about, ripping everything from her is it. That's at the top of my list, because I willfully put her in the position to lose everything for my own sick twisted reasons.

"What time is your session today?" Jess asks, when she brings me a cup of coffee. I haven't been back to my house since she left three days ago. I can't be alone right now, my own thoughts, the guilt; the truth behind every single word she said would suffocate me. It would kill me.

"I have to be there at noon." I take the coffee and give her a fake smile. "Thanks for this, you don't have to wait on me, though."

"Don't worry, it won't be a habit," she responds, smirking. "You look like hell, Liam. You need to shower and shave, pick yourself up."

"How do I do that?"

Jess sits down on the couch beside me and stretches her short legs out so her feet are propped on the edge of the coffee table. "You just do it. Fight through the pain, the guilt, every sad fucking feeling you have and you move. You get up, you go through the motions; you work to make yourself better. Because, Liam, as much as I love you, you need to be better. You need to do better." She nudges her elbow against mine until I look at her. "You're a good man, but it's time you get help to rid yourself of the ghosts of your past."

"It's the demons of my present I'm most worried about today."

"What do you mean?"

"I'm no better than him, Jess. I stay away from alcohol, but I still fucking snap. I lose my mind and beat the shit out of people. Hell, maybe he's better than me; he usually acted in drunken rages. What's my excuse?"

"Your excuse?" She shakes her head. "You are a million times the man your so-called father could ever be. You are nothing like him, Liam. You're good and kind. You have the biggest heart on the planet. You love fiercely; you protect those you love with your whole being. You aren't him."

"Tell that to Everleigh."

"She doesn't think you're your father. Trust me. The children she has dedicated her life helping, loving... she knows the hell you went through, Liam. She probably even understood and was willing to forgive you for everything, until you lied to her. This lie hurt her; it didn't protect her from the monsters you thought she'd run from. You didn't lie to protect her, you lied to protect yourself and any blowback your actions would cost."

326

"Okay, how do I make it right then?" I set the piping hot mug down on the coaster and hunch forward, bracing my arms on my legs with my head hanging.

"I don't know if you can." Her words hurt, they fucking kill. I know she's right though. "Not right now at least. You need to work on you first, then try to fix your mistake."

My lie was inexcusable, my presence in her life cost her everything, I'm too much of a risk to give another chance, logically I know that, but I have to try. I can't just let her walk away. "What if she never forgives me?"

"Then you walk away knowing no matter what, she made you a better man. She made you want to be better, and maybe the next time you fall in love, you'll learn from these mistakes and you won't make them again." She stands from the couch and smiles sadly at me. "I need to get ready for work. I'll be home later tonight. You have the garage code?"

I nod my head. "Yeah, Brandon texted it to me when he got to work this morning. He told me you would be out all day."

"Good, our house is yours. Have a good day, Liam."

"Thanks, I'll try." I watch her walk away then drop back on the couch, letting my head fall against the soft cushion behind me. Jess can't be right. I have to get Everleigh back, and I'll do anything to make it happen.

I'll walk through the gates of hell, sell my soul to the devil, offer myself up as sacrifice if I can make things right and get her to see I need her.

I'll prove I'm worthy of her love.

Somehow.

\*\*\*\*

# Everleigh

The beach has become my home. If I'm not visiting my sister, or going for a run, I'm sitting in the sand, watching kids run and play, families laugh and smile together, and missing my girls.

*Missing Liam.*

Teddy has called and told me the heads of the company are worried what might happen with any civil actions from Mr. Boughton, due to Liam's beating him. Everyone knows Liam is cleared criminally, by some stroke of luck, but the financial blowback that could come to Corporate Cares is enough for them to weigh firing me to save them.

As far as the evidence and statements show, I was complicit in Liam's actions. It doesn't seem to matter I have sworn on everything I had no idea he even got the address; much less from me, but perception is reality.

"You planning on sitting out here all day?" Addie asks, walking up behind me and sitting down in the sand to my left.

"I have nothing else to do. I can't go to the office, I can't see my girls, I don't have Liam anymore…" I bury my hands into the cool, grainy sand and rest my chin on my bent knees.

"You need to fight for your job back. He did this, not you. Maybe one of your co-counselors can bring the girls to a park you may just happen to be at?"

I sigh out loud and shake my head. "I can't do that to any of the counselors, it would cost them their job."

"What about your girls, Ever? They need you. They love you. Just disappearing from their lives isn't going to help them a single bit."

She's right. I know she's right. But if I get caught, I may really lose them for good, and I won't be able to fight that because I will have been the one to break the rules this time.

"I have to do this by the book, Adds. I can't risk anything right now. If..." I swallow hard, choking down bile the mere thought of this brings up, and continue, "if I get fired, I'll find a way to visit the girls, be a part of their lives even distantly. For now, though I can't go there."

"Are the older girls staying in contact in any way?"

"Nichole, Haylie, and Erica are all sending me messages when they get on the tablets. I don't think they'll get in any trouble, nor will I, if we just have normal conversations. I won't ask anything about The Castle or what's going on there though."

"This really sucks," Addie says, then wiggles her now bare toes in the sand. "What are you going to do about Liam?"

"The only thing I can, stay away from him. He poses a risk to my work, my future... It doesn't matter how much I love him; I can't trust him." I release a heavy shrug and stare out over the water. "Why did he lie? Why did he use me like he did?"

"He's a stupid man," she says, trying to add levity to the situation. My lack of response makes her move on quickly, "Okay then... I don't think he was actually trying to use you. I think he let his emotions dictate his actions, consequences be damned."

"Therein lies the problem... My career, assuming I still have one, revolves around working with girls who will constantly come from those shitty situations. He'll get attached, it's nearly impossible not to. What happens next time a dad shows up? What happens when some boy wrongs one of the girls? What happens if he doesn't stop himself?"

That's another part of this story I'm having a hard time wrapping my mind around. He sought Sky's dad out with the sole purpose of hurting him, and he could have killed him. He stopped himself... this time. I understand his reasoning, my heart breaks for the broken man he is and the guilt he holds about his brother's death.

I can't risk him going off on someone and not stopping.

"What if he does?" she asks. "Was this a rare occurrence? Does he have a history of violence?"

"It's his second suspension in six weeks..." I admit, sadly. "The last was for getting pissed at a baseball coach who wasn't being sensitive to, or understanding the fact that, a young kid needed to be airlifted to a hospital."

"Was it the kid's coach?" She looks at me with a shocked expression. "Or the opponents'?"

"Neither. It was a coach from one of the teams scheduled to play on that field next..."

"Jesus, people are insane. Not to make light of anything, I don't think I could have kept my mouth shut or not gotten in that coach's face, either."

"I agree. I couldn't believe that, and I didn't see a problem with him stepping in, but he took it too far. He seems to take it too far a lot. Even on the Fourth of July, Brandon told me Liam is quick to snap, he reacts first and thinks it through later."

"That's not always a bad thing, he's passionate. Acting first can be good."

"Oh, I know." I laugh a little. "Sometimes it's really fucking great... But sometimes, it's really fucking bad. His going after Sky's dad wasn't a snap decision, though. He took the address days before he paid him a visit."

330

She nods in understanding. "Was him following through with visiting a snap decision as a result of something?"

I stop and think of the phone call, hearing about the custody issue, how mad he was—now I know it's because his dad beat and killed his brother—how out of control he got immediately. "It might have been."

"That's worth thinking about."

I bite the inside of my cheek and fight the tears that are threatening again. I hate I'm an all emotion crier. I will cry happy tears, sad tears, angry tears, confused tears, and anxious tears all the same. "It doesn't change the fact I can't trust him."

"I understand, but you can't change the fact you love him, either."

"No…" I close my eyes, unable to see anything but his tortured baby blues in my mind. "I can only stay away from him to save myself and my girls in the future."

# *Forty*

## Liam

I look up at the Corporate Cares building and take a deep breath, straightening out my suit jacket and buttoning it, then nervously smooth it out over my dark washed denim jeans.

The last time I was here, I did something that cost Everleigh her job, stole her away from her girls, and led to me going to jail for a few hours and nearly losing my job, too.

There is so much about my actions I don't regret. Rick Boughton deserved everything he got. He deserves to rot in prison for what he did to his wife, but what I did to Everleigh I will regret for the rest of my life.

She told me I never should've felt guilty about not being there for Lance, or Zac, because they weren't my responsibility, but what I did to her was, and she was correct. What I did to her is on me, and only me, and I have to make it right. I have to pay for my actions.

I miss her so damn much, I've checked my phone hundreds of times a day for the past ten days just to see if maybe she changed her mind.

She hasn't.

I can't blame her for that, though. She's losing everything because of me.

But I'm going to try to make it right today.

I step inside the building and glance toward the stairwell. That was my first mistake, last time. I knew she wouldn't take the stairs, so I did. I snuck in where I didn't think anyone would notice me.

Today, I want people to notice me.

I want them to hear me.

I press the call button and step back from the elevator doors, waiting with shaky hands and swaying feet for it to arrive.

The ding before the doors open is like the start of the round in this fight for her job.

I step on and press the button for her floor, riding the silent elevator with my shouting thoughts to keep me entertained.

I'm not surprised when I step off, the office isn't that full. Most of the employees work in one of the two houses here, or they put on events and activities for the kids that keep them away, but the assistant at the front desk is there.

"I would like to speak to Teddy, please," I say, clearing my throat. "Could you please tell him Liam Hayes is here with regard to Everleigh Marshal?"

Her eyes flash up in surprise and she nods. "Please take a seat, sir. I'll let him know you're here."

I give her a curt thanks and move to take a seat, listening as she lets Teddy know I'm here. She glances my way, shaking her head. "No, sir. He doesn't appear to be. He wants to speak about Everleigh."

She hangs up the phone and peers over her desk. "He will be out to get you in a few minutes."

I don't know what he asked on the phone, but I can only guess it had to do with my behavior and or my demeanor. Since the last time we spoke, I've been arrested, released, and accused of beating the shit out of one of the girls' dads. He probably fears I'm here to cause trouble.

"Firefighter Hayes," he says as he walks up, forcing me to crane my neck to see his face. He's a big man. A giant teddy bear, according to Everleigh, but a huge man who looks intimidating and like he can take care of himself, nonetheless.

"Please, it's Liam." I hold my hand out, hoping he'll shake it.

He looks at me, then my hand, and hesitates a moment before offering his in return. "Liam, what can I do for you?"

"There are a few things I need to explain to you, sir. I haven't spoken to Everleigh since the incident, but I know she's been suspended and her involvement in my behavior is being looked into and evaluated."

He leads me to his office and closes the door behind me. "You're correct," he admits then sits at his desk. "We know you got the information from her."

I shake my head and cross my foot over my leg. "That's not right. I'm ashamed to admit this, but I played Everleigh. She had no idea I had Mr. Boughton's work address. She wasn't complicit in any way."

"How did you get it, then?" Teddy asks.

"I was close to Sky from the beginning, as you know. After her dad made bail, I was worried he may try to contact her, so I concocted this plan. I had my crew drive me here one day while we were at work, and I told her I'd meet her down at my truck. It was the day Mr. Donavan was here, actually," I say for point of reference, before I think about what else we did that day in her office. "I told her to meet me downstairs, I had a gift for her. I told my guys I was meeting her in her office. While she took the elevator down, I took the stairs up…"

"You lied to her." The shame and disgust in his voice is thick, and warranted.

"I did."

"While she was downstairs, you got on her computer?"

I swallow past my own embarrassment and nod. "I knew what I was looking for, their last name, I figured she'd have a way for me to find him, because I knew he wasn't staying at their home as a condition of his bail, the house was still locked up, so I needed another address for him. I didn't think she'd ever get caught though. I never had any intention of seeking him out, not unless I had to."

"Yet you did, and you beat him badly."

"I did. I had a reason, but I know it still doesn't condone my behavior."

"Would you care to share why? Give me any reason to trust you won't use her again."

"I wouldn't," I say quietly then add sadly, "besides, she's made it clear she no longer trusts me to be in her life. We're over. I just don't want to be the cause of her losing everything."

"That's good to know," he muses, "it will help when I talk to the board. But I think I need to know your reasons, all of them, for acting the way you did…"

I take in a deep breath then start from the beginning, from my childhood and experiences. I tell him every fucked-up, sordid detail and pray it will at least result in Everleigh getting her life back, even if it rips another gaping hole in my own.

\*\*\*\*

# Everleigh

I walk into the Corporate Cares office with my head held high. Two weeks of suspension, then today I finally got a call from Teddy telling me a decision has been made about my future with the company, and my girls.

Rylee is sitting in the conference room talking to Teddy, so I venture into my office; grateful all of my belongings are still exactly as I left them before I was suspended.

Irrationally, I take it as a good sign. Rationally, I know if I get fired, I'll be asked to empty it out myself.

I don't have the nerve to sit down or start my computer up, so I look at the various pictures I have hanging on the walls and scattered over my desk.

There's one of Brooke and me, from her last day at The Castle.

There are a few from the time I spent training with Rylee at the boys' house. So many familiar faces I've never kept up with, but I know if I were to ask Rylee about them today, she'd tell me exactly where each boy is now and what's going on in their life.

There's a couple of Addison and me, on vacation as kids, out celebrating our birthdays, getting jobs. There's even one of me with both my parents when I graduated college. That was quite the feat; they don't do well when they're together, thanks to my mom's deep-running feelings and my dad's inability to keep it in his pants.

They played well together that day, though. It's a happy memory.

Every single picture in here is a happy memory, and I'm terrified that will all come to an end today. I'm afraid

I'll never get another picture with the girls I'll always remember and love. I'm afraid I'll be lost and without a career. I'm afraid of losing the friends I've made working here because of one stupid mistake… trusting Liam.

"Hey, you," Rylee says, sneaking up on me and perching against my office door. "Teddy is ready to talk to you."

"Thank you," I say, turning and smiling at her. "I wasn't working, I just didn't want to interrupt your talk."

"You have a stronger will than me, then. I don't know if I could step foot in my office and not work." She shrugs like it's no big deal, but I know she means it. "Unofficially, Everleigh, I think you should be back at work tomorrow."

"What about officially?" I ask hesitantly.

"Officially, that's not up to me to decide, and I'm glad. That's what Teddy is paid the big bucks for."

We both chuckle and I nod. "Thank you, that means a lot coming from you."

"Do you still want those tickets for the next race here?"

I had completely forgotten she talked about getting some for Liam and me. I must've blacked it out as a part of the day he decided to betray my trust in him. "I'm honestly not sure," I admit. "Liam and I broke up."

"I understand. I'll let you get to Teddy. Good luck in there." She goes to walk out then turns back, "If you change your mind about those tickets, they're yours. Just let me know."

"Thank you." I watch her walk out, then I take a deep breath and make my way to the conference room, pulling up my proverbial big girl panties for whatever happens next.

"Everleigh," Teddy booms out, grinning. "It's good to see you back here."

"I hope it's good enough to keep me around a while longer," I quip, chuckling nervously.

"We do need to discuss that, yes." He closes the conference room door, then takes a seat beside me, angling his chair toward mine so we can talk face-to-face. "Liam Hayes paid me a visit four days ago…"

He what?

No, no, this can't be good. What did he do this time?

"Oh?" I cross my ankles together and tuck them just beneath the chair, trying not to fidget like a restless child.

"He had many interesting things to say."

"Great," I mutter, to Teddy's amusement.

"They were great, actually. It's because of Liam Hayes you're keeping your job, and after a six-month probationary period, will be back up for your promotion."

I clearly must've hit my head somehow and I'm having some crazy delusions. I'm pretty sure he just said I'm keeping my job because of Liam, even though Liam is the reason I almost lost it. "I don't understand."

Teddy laughs and reaches out to pat my knee in that fatherly way he has about him. "Let me explain it all."

# Forty-One

## Liam

I hand Brandon a beer then sink down into the chair on my back deck. My body is sore, and I'm exhausted from my long, grueling workout this afternoon, but I don't miss the way he eyes me, looking confused. "What?"

He pops the top off his beer and shakes his head, answering my question with one of his own, "Did you start drinking sometime in the last two weeks and not tell me?"

I shake my head. "Nah, I've been doing some talking with that damn shrink... Thought maybe it was time I keep some beer on hand here for you."

"I'm lost. What does having beer for me have to do with all the shit you've got going on?"

"Well, apparently I act selfishly a lot, and in that, I refuse to keep beer in my house only because I don't drink it."

He snorts. "No shit, you can act selfish. But, you also don't in a lot of ways. In more ways than you do."

"Thanks. I know I can. I love hard, but I act for me first, others second. Apparently, a lot of my behaviors, suspensions, blowups are selfish acts as a result of my own issues. They may be something I can say I did for others, like Sky; really, though, I'm doing it because of my own feelings and to ease my own mind."

His eyes nearly pop out of his head and he looks at me like I've lost my mind. "Fuck, man. Are you really buying into all that shit?"

"It's true, isn't it?" I eye him seriously, then open my water and take a drink.

"In some cases, yes. You do act selfishly. But at the baseball fields? When you're protecting innocent children? No, I don't give a fuck what anyone says, you're acting to protect, not to make yourself feel good. You weren't being selfish, just dumb."

"Are you sure about that?" I don't believe him entirely. I know I've acted selfishly; lying to Everleigh was purely selfish. How wasn't anything else?

"Liam, I know you better than anyone else in this damn world. You have a short fuse, and you take abused children personally, Christ you were one, but you aren't selfish. Do you need to deal with that shit and get past it for your own good? Yes, for God's sake, get help for *you*. Don't change because some two-bit department shrink tells you you're selfish."

"What about Everleigh?"

He chuckles. "That was selfish. You were a dumbass with her, and you're paying for it."

How right he is. "I'm miserable," I admit. "She wasn't some random woman, man. She's special. She saw me, supported me…"

"And you loved her, but you also fucking lied to her. That's the shit you need to figure out. Why lie? You opened up about the single hardest circumstance of your life, but you fucking lied about something that would impact her. Dude… why the fuck would you sabotage yourself like that?"

"I wasn't thinking. Zac, Lance, Sky… I've been so fucking in my head, B. I couldn't see the forest through the trees, but now the forest is decimated and the trees are rotted."

"Beautiful imagery," he rags on me. "If you don't manage to get your job back, maybe you can be a poet?"

I laugh hard for the first time in I don't know how long. "Fuck you. I go back to work in two weeks, thank you very much."

"As long as you pull your head out of your ass and keep it out…"

No words would suffice from this ribbing, so I do what comes most naturally and set my water down, then flip both birds firmly at him.

"Real mature."

"Fuck off," I cough out, laughing even harder.

"There he is, the dipshit I met way back in basic. You want to know what to do about Everleigh?"

I nod. "Yes. I miss her, B. Christ, man. My heart is fucked; she is always on my mind… Six fucking weeks together, and I feel like I lost my lifelong best friend. No offense."

"None taken. Jess is my best friend; you're my brother. I know what you mean."

I stand from my chair and start to pace. "So what do I do? How do I get her back? I already pleaded her case to her boss, but I don't know what to do next."

"Whoa, you what?" He stands and steps down into the yard, looking over my grass. "When did you do that?"

"A few days ago. It was the least I could do."

"What did you say to him?" He sits down on the double step, leaving room beside him for me to pass by and pace in my yard.

"I told him everything."

"As in?" he asks, watching me walk back and forth in front of him.

"As in everything," I stop and emphasize, "*everything*."

He whistles out a stunned tune and smiles. "You have it so fucking bad."

"Now isn't the time," I groan out.

"Seems like it is to me, I like watching you wig the fuck out. Is he going to let her keep her job?"

I start moving back and forth in the yard again, taking ten steps one way before turning around and taking ten steps back in the opposite direction. "He wouldn't say. She should, she didn't do a damn thing wrong. I made that clear. He said he appreciated my honesty."

I watch Brandon raise his beer to his lips out the corner of my eye while I walk, and wait for him to speak again. "You already did all you can do then. If she doesn't get the job, or reach out, I'd say it's over."

I shake my head, silently rejecting his words.

*There has to be something I can do. I just have to figure out what it is.*

# Forty-Two

## Everleigh

How did it feel being back with the girls?" Addie asks over the phone while I make my dinner. "Were they excited to have you there again?"

I smile so wide it hurts. "There aren't words. The hugs I got were priceless; all the activities they've done over the past eighteen days they showed me were so special. They all made welcome back pictures for me, Adds. I cried. Literally cried."

Her laugh warms my heart through the phone. "You cry over everything," she reminds me. "I'm so happy for you. I'm glad Teddy believed Liam, too. I still can't believe Liam shared such personal information and Teddy gave you your job back, but also suggested Liam volunteer with the boys' house. Do you have any idea what he said?" she fishes, again.

I know exactly what he told Teddy, and I know why Teddy wants Liam to help out. It'll do him and all of the boys who experienced any form of abuse like Liam did good to hear his story, to see what he's become since then.

"I do," I sigh, "but for the bajillionth time, I can't tell you, Addie. I'm sorry."

"I don't see what it matters," she says in a condescending tone, "you're completely done with him, remember? You've sworn it so many times in the past almost three weeks I'm starting to dream the words at night."

"I don't say it that often." There's no way I do, I've made my peace with my choice. It's what's best.

"Who are you trying to convince, Little Sister?"

"Nobody!" I bark out then slap my lips together to shut my mouth, mumbling, "I'm sorry."

"When you finally believe you're done with him, then I will. But I don't think you do, Everleigh. I don't blame you, either. He's working hard to right things, isn't he?"

I start sautéing peppers while we talk and groan. "That's what I've heard. Rylee told me he's going to The House tomorrow to get a plan in place and meet the boys. Teddy couldn't quit raving about how strong he had to be to share such an awful story. Even Jess keeps laying it on thick every time we talk. It probably doesn't help I ask her how he's doing, either, though."

"No," Addie chuckles, "I'm sure you asking doesn't help anything. If you miss him that badly, why don't you text him or call him?"

"You know why," I whine out. "I can't risk it."

"Can't? Or won't?" she challenges in that big sister way that makes me want to claw her eyes out, because how dare she be right again?

"I have to go," I respond instead. "I don't want to burn my dinner."

"Whatever you say, Everleigh," she chirps. "I see no harm in giving the man a chance."

"Shit," I lie, "the peppers are burning. I'll talk to you later, I love you, bye." I rush to end the call and hang up as quickly as I can to the sound of her laughing hysterically on the other end, then drop my phone on the counter.

*Addie is right… She's always right.*

*Besides, what would it hurt, Everleigh? Just ask him to coffee. That's it*

*Better yet…*

I pull out my phone and start a text to Rylee Donavan.

We'll see if all the old adages about distance making the heart grow fonder, and if things are meant to be, they'll always find a way to be are true.

\*\*\*\*

# Liam

My phone vibrates in my hand, and for what feels like the millionth time now, I raise it up praying it's her name on my screen. Like every other time, though, it's not.

Unlike every other time, it is her sister's name tonight.

**Addison: You get one more chance. I like you, and in spite of the fact you fucked up royally and broke my sister's heart, I think she loves you.**

**Me: What are you talking about?**

**Addison: She works tomorrow night. Can you be at our favorite restaurant for lunch around noon tomorrow?**

**Me: So she got her job back?**

**Addison: Didn't I just say that? Will you meet her for lunch or not?**

*Is she really doing this, giving me an opportunity to talk to her sister?*

345

**Me: Does she know I'll be there?**

**Addison: Does it really matter? We both know if you want a second chance, you're going to show up. Don't be late.**

**Me: I won't be.**

**Me: Thank you, Addison. I swear I'll make this right.**

**Addison: I'm trusting you to. If you don't, or you hurt her again, I'll make sure your death looks like a complete accident. Are we clear?**

**Me: Crystal. Thank you.**

I wait to see if she's going to reply again, then fall back on my bunk at the station, grinning from ear to ear when she doesn't.

There is no way in hell I'll fuck up again.

# Forty-Three

## Liam

I haven't stopped thinking about how I would handle seeing Everleigh today since her sister texted me last night. At calls, after calls, between calls she was all that filled my mind.

I find the idea of surprising her unexpectedly unsettling. A blind date was one thing, but a surprise date after everything I've done is another.

As I walk into the restaurant, twenty minutes ahead of schedule, I approach the hostess with a smile.

"Good morning," she says kindly, "do you have a reservation?"

"I do. I'm not sure who the name is under, though."

She taps on her tablet screen then looks at me expectantly, "What name might it be under?"

I start with my name, and then Everleigh's, before giving her Addison's last. I should've known Addison would make sure there's no hint of me being here before Everleigh arrived.

The hostess takes me to my seat, and allows me to wait there. The table couldn't be in a better location, because I can see who's walking in before they reach the hostess stand, so I can follow through with my plan without her knowing.

As the minutes get closer, my palms get sweatier and my heart starts beating faster. I don't know if this will work, I don't know what she'll think, I don't even know if I'll ever get another chance to speak to her again, but that has to be her decision.

No matter how badly I want for this to work, I can't put her on the spot like Addison planned.

When I see her walking up the sidewalk, glancing at her phone, I make my move.

I signal for the waitress and wave her over, quickly telling her what my plan is, what I'm hoping to do, and seeing if she'll agree.

Thankfully, she's young, and still a romantic at heart, because she's eager to put my plan into action for me.

I watch as she hustles up toward the hostess and whispers the plan into her ear, just as Everleigh walks in the door.

As quickly and stealthily as I can, I dash over toward the kitchen.

My waitress friend walks away from the hostess stand just before Everleigh approaches it, and she holds two thumbs-up against her stomach.

When I know the hostess is in on the plan, I exhale and watch as everything unfolds.

Everleigh is dressed in a light blue top with white jean shorts, and a pair of brown sandals. Her hair is flowing down her back in waves, and I can see the moment the hostess tells her Addison isn't here yet.

Everleigh looks around the restaurant then glances at her watch. I know she likes to do things in a certain manner on workdays when she'll be spending the night with the kids, and Addison's tardiness is going to throw that off, but it'll be worth it.

The hostess points back into the dining area and Everleigh nods her head, then follows the hostess back to the table that should be both of ours, but will only be hers today.

She sits down, and pulls her phone out, scrolling for a few moments and flitting her fingers over the screen.

There's the first text.

She sets the phone down and asks for a water; then looks out toward the window when my phone vibrates in my pocket. I pull it out and smirk at the text…

**Addison: I told you, you only got one chance. Where are you?**

**Me: Standing in the kitchen at the restaurant, watching your sister. It's a change of plans, but I need you to play along.**

**Addison: Explain…**

I pull up the note I saved on my phone earlier and copy it into a text to her, explaining what I'm doing, how I'm doing it, and why.

**Addison: OMG!!!! If she doesn't give you a second chance, I will…**

**Me: Thanks, but I'm only interested in one beautiful Marshal woman.**

**Addison: Smooth. I'll help. She just texted me again. The call will undoubtedly be next…**

**Me: Yep, that's what I'm thinking. As soon as she raises the phone to her ear, I'll send the waitress over.**

**Addison: Good luck!**

I take a deep breath and get back to watching Everleigh. Addison's right to wish me luck, because I'm going to need it.

\*\*\*\*

# Everleigh

I glance down at my phone again, each of my last three texts to Addison are sitting unanswered, and she's fifteen minutes late now. I don't have time today, so I jab the call button and raise the phone to my ear, tapping the table impatiently.

While the phone rings, I see my waitress approaching me with a wide smile and a bouquet of roses. "Your lunch date couldn't be here today," she says, then holds the stunning flowers out for me, "but he asked me to give you this."

I pull my hands back and shake my head. "I'm sorry, there must be some mistake. I'm meeting my sister today, not a man." I end the call to Addison when it goes to voicemail then fold my hands in my lap.

"You're Everleigh, right?" she asks, looking down at the card pinned to the bouquet.

"I am," I nod.

"These are definitely for you, then." She hands them back to me and grins wide. "He's really pulling out all the stops to get you back. Liam said to tell you Addison tried to pull another auction date, but he couldn't do that to you this time. These are from him, though."

Liam? Auction date? Addison?

I'm trying to process everything she's saying, but it's all so confusing.

"The card," she suggests, turning the bouquet so I can grab the card inside.

I pull it free and open it up, finding the distinguishably awful penmanship inside I know immediately is Liam's.

Derailed

*Babe,*

***Nothing will ever make up for the shit I pulled. I wouldn't blame you for never forgiving me, or giving me a second chance, but I'm asking you for one anyway. I'm asking you to take me back. To talk me off the ledge when I'm about to spiral out of control again. To be the last person standing in my corner when I've lost everyone else in my life I love. I will do anything to earn your trust back. If you want me to stay away from Corporate Cares, I will. If you want me to quit my job, give up everything I almost took from you, I will. Please just let me show you everything I can be for you, because of you. Show me I'm worth saving and giving a second chance. Because I'm fucking drowning without you.***

*Liam*

I read his note a second time, then reach out for the bouquet. "Thank you," I say quietly, rendered otherwise speechless by what's going on here.

Addison isn't coming.

Liam was here.

He's willing to give up everything for me, to have me, to earn me back.

And he doesn't even know what I did last night…

"You should give him a second chance," the waitress says. "If my ex had done anything like this, I'd be his again in a heartbeat."

I nod my head and chuckle uncomfortably as tears well in the corners of my eyes. "I'll keep that in mind. I think," I say, clearing my throat, "I have a call to make really fast."

I should probably call and yell at my sister, but for now, she's not who I want to talk to. I pull up my contacts and scroll to his name; beyond grateful I never deleted it. I let my thumb hover over the little green phone momentarily, then close my eyes and press down.

It rings once, twice, and a third time on my end, but he doesn't answer.

With my phone pressed to my ear, I can hear the rings going through on the line, but behind me a ringtone of Nickelback's "Savin' Me" is playing.

When the call goes to voicemail, I hang up and try one more time, rereading his note while I wait. Again, the song comes on, and I start to match some of his words with the words ringing out.

They can't be…

I turn in my chair and look around, spotting him a few feet behind me, standing with his phone ringing in his hand and watching me.

"Liam?" I whisper.

"I had to make sure you wanted me here before I surprised you this time." He shrugs a shoulder and slips his phone into his pocket. The recording on his machine kicks in, and I glance down to disconnect the call then set my own phone down.

"Why that song?"

"Because you are saving me. Everything I do from here on out, I'll do for you, because of you." He steps closer, slowly, to the delight of our growing audience.

"You talked to Teddy," I say.

"I did. I'm talking to someone else, too. A person who is helping me work through some of my demons." He may look like the thirty-two-year-old man he is, but the care he's using coming toward me, the fear in his eyes, and the uncertainty in his expression are more akin to a lost, hopeful little boy.

"I'm really proud of you," I whisper, taking a step toward him. "Thank you for being honest."

"It was the least I could do. I should have been from the start, about everything."

We each step closer again, leaving us about a half a foot apart now.

"Even so, I appreciate you telling the truth about what happened. I had my first night back at The Castle two nights ago, and I'll be there again tonight."

"Addison told me," he smirks. "She's a co-conspirator in all this."

"I figured," I giggle. I'm itching to reach out for him, but I'm still afraid to take the leap.

"I'm so sorry, Everleigh. I would take it all back if I could. I'll leave the department today, find another job, do whatever it takes to prove to you how much I'm willing to do to earn you back."

"As it turns out," I mutter and take another step closer, "all it took was time, and getting me my job back."

His eyes flash brightly, but he contains himself, and asks, "What do you mean?"

"I had my own big gesture planned already. This just proves I was right to do it." I step even closer and carefully reach out to straighten his black button-down shirt.

"I don't understand."

"How would you feel about accompanying me to the Firestone Grand Prix next month as a guest of Rylee and Colton Donavan?" I whisper, grinning up at him.

His eyes widen. They're the brightest blue I've ever seen them, and he starts to grin from ear to ear. "Really?"

"Really, Hot Stuff." I let him pull me closer and lift my hands to his chest, whispering, "I forgive you, Liam. Three weeks apart gave me plenty of time to think, and no matter how hard I tried, I couldn't let you go just yet."

His arms wrap around my back and his forehead lowers to mine. "I was going to fight for you. I just didn't know how, not until your sister sprung this lunch on me last night."

"She's obnoxiously good at meddling."

"Older sibling's prerogative," he says, chuckling.

"So you've said before…" I rise up on my tiptoes at the same time he leans in, and our lips connect in a soft, perfect kiss.

The restaurant breaks into applause around us, and Liam pulls away chuckling. "We have an audience."

"We do," I agree.

"Would you like to have lunch with me, Everleigh Marshal?"

"Is conversation on the table?" I ask, grinning against his lips.

"It is, but that's it. Just lunch and conversation."

# *Epilogue*

## One Month Later

## Liam

This is really fucking cool," I shout over the sound of the cars racing past us. Today is the big day, a dream come true, and I get to experience it with the woman I love by my side.

"How many laps are left?" she asks, shading her eyes with her hands.

"Ten. Only ten." I don't say it, but I can't help but think about how awesome it would be to watch Colton Donavan claim the checkered flag while I'm here, as a guest of him and his wife.

"Ten more laps until he wins then," Everleigh muses then slips her arm around me. "Are you excited?"

"Is it that evident?"

She nods her head up and down, grinning wide as a Cheshire cat, "Just a little."

I lean in and press a kiss to her lips, her jaw, and then just beneath her ear, whispering after, "Nothing will ever beat the excitement I had when you gave me my second chance, though."

She pulls back and lifts her hand to my cheek, then kisses my lips. With only nine laps to go now, I should be focused on the race, on watching to see if Colton can continue to fend off attempts by others to pass him, but I can't bring myself to care.

Not when her lips are on mine, reminding me how lucky I am and to cherish every moment I have. I lost her once already. I won't let it happen again.

That starts with making sure she knows that no matter where we are, what we're doing, or who we're with, she will always come first. I'll never hide a thing from her again.

We kiss through another three laps before she pulls back. "Watch your race, baby. I want you to experience everything we came here for today. That includes watching him win."

"Will I get a victory kiss?" I ask, turning my attention back to the track.

She laughs and slips her hand into mine, shouting, "I think that's only for the driver... not his fans."

"Like hell it is," I rasp out. "When you're a fan, the team's victories are your victories, and their losses are yours, too."

"Is that so?" she asks, as they complete another lap. There are only two left now.

"Definitely," I insist, before I get distracted by the action unfolding in front of us.

Colton has been edged out of first by a hair as they go into their last lap, but he's so close, all he has to do is make his move, and victory will be his. "C'mon man, you've got this, let's go, let's go, let's go!" I shout just as he makes his move and pulls ahead again. They blow by us, and I get a glimpse of just how close it is. "Hold on tight, Colton. You've got it... Yes!"

Our whole section erupts in cheers, hoots, and hollers as the checkered flag is waved, and the announcer's voice booms over the roar of the crowd and all the engines that Colton Donavan won the race.

Pandemonium ensues as the stands start to empty as his crew chief, the rest of his crew, and Rylee all work their way down to greet him and head to victory lane.

I turn to Everleigh and pull her into my arms, laying a long, hard kiss on her lips.

She gave me all of this, today…

She gave me my life back; one I'm living for myself first, but also for Lance.

****

# Everleigh

"Let's head down so we don't miss the celebration," he says when we finally part, each of us breathing harder than when we started.

I nod and take his hand, letting him guide me down the steps while I think about today, and everything he just said to me without words. His kiss conveyed so much more than celebration over Colton's win. He poured every single emotion he has into it, just like he's made a habit of doing since we got back together, and I'm grateful.

He can't always tell me what he's thinking and feeling right away, but he can always show me. He's found a way even when words are too hard. He's grown, and no matter what it is, he is always honest with me about everything now, just like I am with him.

We've been through more in nearly three months than most people will experience in an entire lifetime with their best friend and partner. But we came out on top. We clawed and crawled our way through the flames until we broke free.

He still makes mistakes. He still has bad days where guilt consumes him and he lashes out. But he's learning to manage them.

It's something I love seeing and being a part of, just like I'm loving seeing his elation today. We join the crowd of people who are a part of Team Donavan, and wait.

Liam films it all, takes every single second in, from the time Colton lifts out of his car, to Rylee and all their boys congratulating him, all the way up to Colton Donavan approaching us with Rylee tucked into his side.

They stop in front of us, and Liam lowers his phone to his pocket, raising his hand to shake Colton's instead. "What a race, man. That was a great win."

Colton thanks Liam and shakes his hand, before his crew chief shouts for him over the noise of the crowd.

Rylee tells me she'll try to find me later; otherwise she'll see me in the office next week, but to enjoy the rest of our time.

I nod and give her a quick one-armed hug while our guys exchange a couple more words, and when they both walk away to take care of whatever business they need to that comes after a race, I look to Liam, seeing him grinning in astonishment.

"What's that look for?" I ask him.

"Colton Donavan just invited us to their house for a barbecue next weekend... Apparently Rylee wants to spend some time with you and show you the ropes to prepare you to take on her role for the girls' side of Corporate Cares when your six months are up..."

My jaw drops, and I whip my head around, seeing if I can spot her anywhere, and through the crowd of happy boys, family, friends, and an entire racing team, she locks eyes with me and winks, giving me a thumbs-up before Colton pulls her away laughing.

"Oh my God…" I grin wide. "They're going to promote me."

Liam pulls me into his arms. "They're going to promote you," he agrees. "And Rylee Donavan is going to make sure you're the best fucking director of girls programming there ever will be."

I squeal in delight and wrap my arms around his neck. "I can't believe it."

"I can," he says, staring deep into my eyes. "You're amazing, and you've earned it."

"Thank you, Hot Stuff."

"Don't thank me, I'm the man who nearly derailed your entire life."

"True, you're also the man who has given me everything I've ever wanted, and supported me like no other man was ever willing to."

"If we'd had someone like you, Rylee, Corporate Cares to turn to, my baby brother might still be alive today. I would never take that away from other children who need you as much as we did, as much as I do still."

His words lodge deep in my heart, and standing in the middle of a large crowd of elated race goers, a single happy tear rolls down my cheek. "I love you, Liam."

"I love you too, babe. So fucking much. I'm so damn proud of you." He kisses my tear away then smiles. "Who would've thought a blind date set up by your sister winning an auction would lead us here?"

"Not me, but I know one thing's for sure…"

"What's that?"

"You will not be auctioned off ever again. God only knows what might happen with the next winner."

He drops his head back laughing. "As long as you're the one bidding on me... I think the odds are in our favor."

# THE END

## Want to keep up with all of the other books in K. Bromberg's Driven World?

You can visit us anytime at www.kbworlds.com and the best way to stay up to date on all of our latest releases and sales, is to sign up for our official KB Worlds newsletter.

Are you interested in reading the bestselling books that inspired the Driven World? You can find them on Amazon!

If you liked this novel, please consider leaving a review on Amazon, Goodreads, or BookBub today! Or you can join Anjelica's group on Facebook to discuss all things Derailed. She would love to hear from you!

Want to find more from Anjelica Grace?
Check out her other books below!

Cowboys & Angels Series:

More than Winning (A Short Prequel)
Hold on Tight (Book 1)
Never Let Go (Book 2)
Fight to Win (Book 3) (Coming in 2021)

Cocky Hero Club:

Doctor Desirable

# Acknowledgements

First and foremost, I have to thank Kristy Bromberg for opening her world up to be written in. Driven was the first book I ever read by Kristy, and it most certainly was not the last. To be a part of the KB Worlds, and the Driven World specifically, is an honor I will carry with me for the rest of my life.

To the readers—especially my new readers and anyone from the VPPC who has gone on this journey with an open mind—thank you for reading Derailed. Thank you for taking, and continuing to take, a chance on me and my words. I truly hope you enjoyed.

To my parents, thank you. I love you. I could not do this without your support and encouragement.

To my Honey Bunny and Bestie, you two mean the world to me. Thank you for standing by me and supporting me through every book, melt down, random thought, and weird moment I have.

To my incredible editor and friend, Karen, thank you for being my editor. Thank you for being my friend, giving me great advice, even better conversation, and a friendship I will forever cherish.

To Joanne, Brandi, and Brooke, thank you for the early eyes and critique. I appreciate you all beyond words. You make me a better writer.

And thank you to my Lord and Savior, Jesus Christ, without whom I would not have the blessings of this life, or each and every person who has made living my dream possible along the way.

# About Anjelica Grace

Yes, that's Anjelica with a 'J' not a 'G'. You can thank her parents for the birth certificate spelling mix up, but it makes for a unique and fun story.

Anyway, Anjelica Grace is a Denver native living in the same suburb north of the Mile High City that she grew up in. She's an avid reader, and blogger, turned Contemporary Romance author that has an affinity for crazy socks, Minions, and candy. But not chocolate.

Family and friends are the most important things in Anjelica's life, but when she's not with them, you can find her with a book in hand, writing, working as a RBT with autistic children, or studying hard while she pursues her other career dream of becoming a Child Life Specialist.

Still new to the publishing side of things, Anjelica started her journey off in late 2018 by publishing a short story as a part of a Christmas anthology with a group of amazing authors that helped and encouraged her along the way. Once she dipped her toe into the writing waters, that was it, she knew she couldn't stop or look back again.

# Find Anjelica Online!

Facebook, Instagram, Amazon, Goodreads, and Bookbub!

Real. Raw. Romance

## ALSO WRITTEN BY K. BROMBERG

Made in the USA
Middletown, DE
03 June 2022